Monsieur Ouine

Monsieur Oui

ne

Georges Bernanos

Translated and with an introduction by William S. Bush

University of Nebraska Press   Lincoln and London

**NATIONAL
ENDOWMENT
FOR THE ARTS**

A great nation
deserves great art.

Publication of this book was
assisted by a grant from the
National Endowment for the Arts.

Original title: *Monsieur Ouine*
© Librarie Plon, 1946, 1993
Translation and introduction © 2000
by the University of Nebraska Press
All rights reserved
Manufactured in the United States
of America
⊗
Library of Congress
Cataloging-in-Publication Data

Bernanos, Georges, 1888–1944.
[Monsieur Ouine, English]
Monsieur Ouine / Georges Bernanos ;
translated by William S. Bush.
    p.   cm.
ISBN 0-8032-1304-2 (cl: alk. paper).–
ISBN 0-8032-6161-6 (pa: alk. paper)
I. Bush, William, 1929–   . II. Title.
pq2603.e5875m613   2000
843'.912–dc21   99-39572
                    CIP

Cet ouvrage, publié dans le cadre   .
d'un programme d'aide à la publication,
bénéficie du soutien du Ministère des
Affaires Etrangères et du Service Culturel
de l'Ambassade de France aux Etats-Unis.

This work, published as part of a program
of aid for publication, received support
from the French Ministry of Foreign Affairs
and the Cultural Services of the French
Embassy in the United States.

Contents

Translator's Introduction

If any title at all springs to mind when the name Georges Bernanos (1888–1948) is mentioned to an English-speaking reader, it is usually that of his *Journal d'un curé de campagne* (*The Diary of a Country Priest*), to which the French Academy awarded the Grand Prix du Roman in 1936. The probing depths of that prize-winning novel seem to have secured Bernanos's reputation among English-speaking readers as "the novelist of the priestly soul."

Nor has the success of Bernanos's one play, *Dialogues des carmélites* (*The Carmelites*), best known in English-speaking countries in its operatic adaptation by Francis Poulenc, contributed to dispelling the too facile dismissal of Bernanos as a mere "French Catholic novelist." Even when placed in that very restrictive category, there is often a certain hesitancy to view Bernanos as equal to his more frequently cited contemporary François Mauriac. Certainly it would be hard to find an English-language critic declaring that the author of *The Diary of a Country Priest* was "the greatest novelist of his time."

André Malraux, who thus spoke almost thirty years after Bernanos's death, had by that time distinguished himself as de Gaulle's minister of culture. Neither a believer, nor inclined to favor Catholic novelists, he was in his own right a novelist of no mean distinction. In his own time critics referred to his *La Condition humaine* as one of the ten great novels "of all time."

That Malraux's time was the time of Bernanos as well as of novelists such as Gide, Mauriac, Giraudoux, Green, Sartre, Camus, Céline, and Genêt only adds weight to the importance of his assessment. The usual Anglophone dismissal of Bernanos as "nothing more than a Catholic novelist" would seem seriously called into question when a novelist-critic such as Malraux evaluates Bernanos as "the greatest novelist of his time" after thirty years of mature reflection.

From the beginning there were indications that Bernanos was by no means just another Catholic novelist. In 1926, some fifty years before Malraux's remark, when Bernanos's first novel, *Sous le soleil de Satan*, burst on the French literary scene as a bestseller, Léon Daudet, the son of Alphonse Daudet and an acclaimed novelist himself, had compared Bernanos's genius to that of Proust.

Part of the reason the English-speaking world has not taken Bernanos's work more seriously may be that, to date, *Monsieur Ouine*, his greatest novel, has remained virtually unknown. Yet *Monsieur Ouine* is the only one of the author's eight novels that he himself ever dubbed his "GREAT NOVEL." Repeatedly he inscribed these two proud words in bold capital letters on the covers of the copybooks containing his first drafts for this singularly ambiguous, mysterious, and highly paradoxical masterpiece. Indeed, because of its rather startling narrative structure, certain critics have insisted on viewing Bernanos's GREAT NOVEL as a precursor of the "new novel."

The circumstances surrounding the publication of the first edition of *Monsieur Ouine* in Brazil in 1943 (Rio de Janeiro: Atlantica) contributed nothing to assuring the novel's success in English-speaking countries. That highly faulty text was the only one available when Geoffry Dunlop translated it in 1945 under the title of *The Open Mind* (John Lane / The Bodley Head, London). Revealed ten years later to be not only bristling with errors but also missing entire pages, that original French text, reprinted in Paris in 1946, was never proofread by the author, preoccupied as he was with the war, the future of France, and the fate of Christian civilization.

Moreover, Geoffry Dunlop's rather idiosyncratic English rendering of that faulty French text published in Brazil a half century ago, in addition to being long out of print, would seem to do little to make this difficult novel more accessible to today's vast, international English-speaking public or enhance Bernanos's stature among English readers.

It was Bernanos's literary executor, the eminent Swiss critic Albert Béguin, who spotted the problem with both the 1943 Brazilian edition and its Paris reissue in 1946. Working from Bernanos's final fair copy, he replaced those earlier texts in 1955 with a text published by the Club des Libraires de France, universally regarded today as the only valid one. Prior to the present translation, however, it has never been put into English.

As one of the century's more astute critics, Albert Béguin was fascinated by the extraordinary qualities of *Monsieur Ouine*. He consistently defended it as Bernanos's masterpiece, maintaining that in *Monsieur Ouine* Bernanos had gone the furthest yet in pursuing his creative vision, risking in this attempt at literary grandeur far more than in any of his other seven novels.

Begun in France in February 1931 and completed in May 1940, *Monsieur Ouine* was continually rewritten, revised, and rewritten as Bernanos worked on its composition over almost a decade. *Monsieur Ouine* should have appeared as the author's fourth novel, following *Sous le soleil de Satan* (1926) (*The Star of Satan*), *L'Imposture* (1927) (*The Impostor*), and *La Joie* (*Joy*) (Prix Femina for 1929) but was repeatedly set aside to be taken up again as the author completed four further novels. This accounts for its being completed only in May 1940, in Brazil, a whole ocean away from France and on the very day Hitler launched his forces against France, as Bernanos himself remarked. From Pirapora, deep in the Brazilian interior, the author wrote Charles Ofaire, his Swiss-German publisher in Rio de Janeiro, on 10 May 1940 that he had just completed the last page of his GREAT NOVEL.

Thus Bernanos finally concluded that singular work that he had stubbornly refused to bring to term before the end of its long, nine-year gestation, much to the despair of his publisher, family, and friends. He had asked only to be left in peace, all the way to the end, to "dream out" this, his oneiric masterpiece. Even though it meant financial disaster and almost a decade of largely hand-to-mouth, nomadic existence for his long-suffering wife and six children, he consistently refused to be hounded into finishing it. He thus produced his last four novels, as it were, on the side during those nine years of "dreaming out" *Monsieur Ouine*. These works consisted of a crime novel entitled *A Crime* (1935), dashed off in haste for quick and much needed funds; the justly celebrated *Diary of a Country Priest* (1936); the short stylistic jewel *Nouvelle Histoire de Mouchette* (1937; *Mouchette*); and a posthumously published work, also begun in 1931, then abandoned for *Monsieur Ouine*: *Un Mauvais Rêve* (1950; *Night Is Darkest*). But the long, imposing final chapter of *Monsieur Ouine*, describing the character's enigmatic, dreamlike death, was to come only after he had written all these. In its subtly ambiguous and hauntingly pregnant pages is cloaked Bernanos's definitive vision as a great novelist. *Monsieur Ouine*'s last great scene describes an adolescent boy magnetically drawn to his suspect master's deathbed like a fascinated frog fatally fixed by a snake.

The curious juxtaposition the author made of this final chapter with the fall of France in 1940 serves as a clue to the deeper significance Bernanos attached to *Monsieur Ouine*. Thus *Monsieur Ouine* may perhaps best be read as a disturbing allegory of the end of post-Renaissance European civilization. Bernanos describes, with searing accuracy, what he believed to be the cancer devouring Western civilization. And that civilization, he would undoubtedly still remind us today, is not totally unlike the body of a machine-quickened patient in the terminal ward of a modern hospital, kept alive by forces extraneous to itself. Many European countries, even while prospering materially, are unable today to maintain their population, just as, for centuries now, Europe, with its touted material progress and technological advances, has been unable to raise – let alone conceive – any pinnacle of spiritual beauty to rival the Cathedral of Chartres.

Such were the matters Bernanos was prone to dwell upon, explore, and seek to understand in his many volumes of essays. In *Monsieur Ouine*, however, certain of Bernanos's preoccupations are made flesh. They are incorporated into the novel's intricate fabric as characters conversing and interacting with one another.

The setting for this high allegory is the familiar and humble one the author chose for his best-known novels: a fictitious village in the Pas-de-Calais region of northern France. This was the part of France Bernanos knew best as a boy because his Parisian family had acquired a large country home at Fressin, hard by the battlefield of Agincourt. There the boy, freed from the restrictions of life in a Catholic boarding school, spent his summers and holidays, exploring the woods and lush countryside.

In *Monsieur Ouine* the fictitious village is called "Fenouille" and is mysteriously subject to the troubling presence of the character of Monsieur Ouine, a retired professor of modern languages, now a permanent guest at the neighboring chateau of Wambescourt. The eponymous hero's unusual name conveys to the reader the character's perverse penchant for saying "yes" and "no" (*oui* and *ne*) at the same time. Such indeed had become the raison d'être of this former professor of modern languages, author of a work on pedagogy.

Moreover, saying yes and no simultaneously was a characteristic Bernanos ascribed in particular to his celebrated contemporary André Gide. When he began his GREAT NOVEL he confided to his young disciple, Dr. Jean Bénier, that he was going to write "the strongest thing yet against Gide." Indeed, Bernanos was deeply concerned by his contemporaries' deep-seated inability to distinguish between yes and no, an inability, Bernanos maintained, encouraged by Gide's outlook on life.

Taken into the chateau of Wambescourt by the rather dull local squire, Anthelme de Néréis, Monsieur Ouine soon rules the life of both Anthelme and his eccentric, outlandish wife, Ginette, dubbed "Woolly-Leg" ("Jambe-de-Laine") by the villagers because of her woolen stockings. The subject of dark gossip, Madame de Néréis dashes about country roads at all hours of the day and night in an open carriage drawn by a gigantic, whinnying mare. The great mare seems a sort of elemental life force, displaying an imposing, ungovernable dynamism. Disaster seems to erupt almost inevitably whenever the carriage of the lady of Wambescourt bursts onto the scene.

As mistress of Wambescourt, Ginette de Néréis, no less than her husband, conveys Bernanos's biting, yet melancholy, image of the old aristocracy, ending its days in inglorious decay in forgotten pockets of the provinces. This decline is accentuated by the dilapidated state of the chateau. Rain pours in, cascading down the stairways like a waterfall. The chateau's disintegration is further underlined by the physical decline of both Anthelme and the dying Monsieur Ouine. A representative of European culture, the old professor is figuratively being clutched, one last time, to the paternalistic bosom of a decaying aristocracy.

Within this framework Bernanos situates his chief protagonist, a fourteen-year-old, fatherless boy, Philippe Dorval, born during the First World War and nicknamed "Steeny." Stifled by the hothouse atmosphere of his female-dominated home in Fenouille revolving around his hypersensitive, widowed mother, Michelle, and her enigmatic English friend, Miss, Steeny is in the midst of an adolescent crisis. In the novel's opening chapter we perceive his visceral revolt, first against Miss's attempts to play physical games with him, then against the secretive, cloying tenderness expressed between Miss and his mother. Ostensibly Steeny's tutor, Miss has brought with her to the secluded, peaceful house in Fenouille the dark, uneasy aura of her own bleak childhood in England. An orphan rescued by a Wesleyan pastor from a disabled, aging soldier-uncle who sexually abused her, she had been sent to good schools, qualifying her for her present post.

On impulse, Steeny follows Madame de Néréis to Wambescourt, where his crisis is only exacerbated. There the dying squire assures him that his father is alive and well and that his mother and Miss have been lying in telling him that his father died in the war. Cast into an irreparable solitude as he looks at life, the forsaken fourteen-year-old finds himself on that fatal night at the chateau yielding to desire's dark seduction. There, in the very shadow of death, Steeny, not totally unwillingly, succumbs to Monsieur Ouine's embrace after falling into a drunken sleep in the old professor's bed.

The events of that tempestuous night subsequently provide the motivation for the upheaval seizing the whole village early the next morning. At dawn the naked body of a young farm boy is found floating in the storm-swollen stream in the woods between the chateau and Fenouille. It is the little cowherd Monsieur Ouine had dispatched from Wambescourt to warn Steeny's mother in Fenouille that the boy was sleeping at the chateau. The nude body bears the marks of strangulation. A search for the assassin is launched.

As Bernanos's poetic prose becomes almost hallucinatory in its power of evocation, he weaves into his plot the obscure story of three members of the strange Devandomme family: the old grandfather, who dreams of descent from the old nobility; his orphaned and crippled visionary grandson, Guillaume, Steeny's one friend and confidant, whom he calls his "soul"; and, finally, the old man's headstrong daughter, Hélène, Guillaume's aunt, who has disgraced the family by her passionate union with an untamed outlaw, the poacher Eugène. It is upon this secretive and mysterious son-in-law of Devandomme that falls the accusation of the unexplained murder.

When the rumor begins to circulate that Eugène the poacher is to be arrested since he had been spotted with the victim that night in the woods, old Devandomme, intent upon avoiding public disgrace, precipitates the suicide of his hated son-in-law and thus, inadvertently, also brings about the death of his daughter. The love between Hélène and Eugène shown in the scene of their double suicide affords us a rare example of Bernanos's powerfully erotic prose, chaste though it may seem at a time when readers have grown used to far less noble, but more explicit, literary expression.

Other violent acts quickly follow the double suicide. Indeed, the whole village seems to seethe and ferment around the little farm hand's body, and the public funeral for the victim takes on epic proportions. Bernanos skillfully weaves many strands into his description of this event, producing a panoramic presentation of a whole social unit bent on a course of self-destruction. The priest's startling refusal to give his blessing at the funeral, the empty rhetoric of the French republic's representative in the person of the inspector of education, and, finally, the emotional collapse of the debauched mayor of Fenouille, kneeling in tears by the little coffin, all lead up to the lynching of Madame de Néréis, who, with her great mare, noisily intrudes into the charged atmosphere of the burial.

Bernanos's presentation of the friendless lady of Wambescourt striding across the cemetery, a predestined victim with whitened face soon to be reddened with her own blood, evokes a clownlike image worthy of a Georges Rouault. Instinctively the villagers sense in her not only an image of France's fading aristocracy but, with it, an image of their own destitution. The suspect lady of Wambescourt thus joins the humble cowherd as she too falls victim to the invisible evil devouring the decaying parish as it moves toward its demise. These elements of self-destruction are even more intensely analyzed in the two following chapters where sexual obsession is probed in the person of the mayor of Fenouille.

Though Bernanos's prose may be chaste, he was a reader of Freud and Jung and far from indifferent to the power of sexuality. In contrast to the almost adolescent concupiscence prominent in the novels of Mauriac and Green, Bernanos moves beyond mere empathy with his distraught characters, questioning, analyzing, and at times even elucidating certain subtle, hidden facets of one of mankind's most mysterious imperatives. One of the author's deepest and most fascinating preoccupations was to show how sins of the flesh can finally turn against the very flesh from which they seem to spring. For he understood that sexual obsession can bring about either physical destruction or else an impotence similar to that of a drug-induced state. The author himself seems to be speaking when he has the priest say to the doctor, regarding the source of the mayor's obsessions: "Rather than the obsession with impurity, you'd do better to fear the nostalgia for purity."

In these later chapters Bernanos uses the ineffectual and pathetic young priest to give us his own disturbing prophecies concerning the world's destitution. For the author understood the human race to be not only fallen, but also radically destitute and unable to save itself from death and disintegration. This conviction is evident throughout his drafts and manuscripts. Indeed, has the poverty of the human race ever been revealed as poorer or more threatening than at the end of the twentieth century when the possibility of annihilation has become generally conceivable, whether from man-made sources or from nature itself where lurk as yet unnamed, unimaginable forces of death?

The mysterious and rather startling resolution in the final panel of Bernanos's tapestry is classical in its stark simplicity: a last encounter between the boy and the dying old professor in a dialogue full of nuances, half-truths, and ambiguities, as well as an occasional deep truth. Steeny's last encounter with Monsieur Ouine may well be read as a sort of allegory of Bernanos himself receiving what he believed to be the last gasp of wisdom to be drawn from European civilization – the civilization that had made him what he was. Thus we find Steeny (Bernanos) nihilistically suggesting that perhaps there is nothing, "absolutely nothing." In response, Monsieur Ouine (civilization), for a brief second, seems to drop all usual ambiguity to reply: "Idiot! If there were nothing, then I would be something, good or evil. It is I who am nothing."

Although the author had at one point thought of calling this novel "The Dead Parish," his emphasis in the end was not religious, but sociological. Moreover, the social disintegration Bernanos emphasized sixty years ago – drug abuse, alcoholism, child abuse, homosexuality, murder, and suicide – seems startlingly contemporary.

The young priest of Fenouille may seem to be unfairly foreordained for failure, thrown as he is into such a "muck heap," as Monsieur Ouine terms it. Yet in this work, as in his vision of the real world, Bernanos did not hesitate to pit Christianity against two uncompromising realities of modern times: blind faith in science (represented by Malépine, the village doctor) and blind faith in human nature (represented by Arsène, the mayor).

Bernanos's highly lyrical construction of a sociological microcosm of rural French society around 1930 illustrates not only the pathetic surviving remnants of France's old pre-Revolutionary regime portrayed by the decaying aristocracy and impotent church (represented, respectively, by Anthelme and Ginette de Néréis and the floundering curé of Fenouille), but also the post-Revolutionary civil order. Civil society is vigorously represented by the inspector of education (a caricature of the republic's civil idealism, reminiscent of Homais in Flaubert's *Madame Bovary*); by the doctor, high priest of the new religion of scientific progress; and by the still potent but pathetically neurotic mayor, who would like to throw off all Christian restraints to return to a pagan religion that, he imagines, would allow sexual freedom. Against these conflicting social forces Bernanos, in a rare tour de force, patiently traces Steeny's searing personal drama of seeking his lost father as he is initiated into the dark mysteries of adulthood.

Particularly striking in this novel for the first-time reader are certain elements of a murder mystery, launched in chapter 3 when the little cowherd is first mentioned and continuing all the way to the end of chapter 17 where Steeny is still asking: "Who killed the little hired boy?" Bernanos himself refuses to give an answer to this irritating question. Originally he appears to have conceived that the assassin was Monsieur Ouine, since, in the first draft, the doctor discovers a tuft of gray hair in the little cadaver's gripped fist — hair that one would assume belonged to Monsieur' Ouine, or else to the mayor, Arsène, or even to Woolly-Leg. In any case, this suppressed clue certainly rules out the implied guilt of the virile, young poacher, Eugène.

Nothing was ever really clear-cut, even in the first draft. Early in the morning after the murder, shortly after the naked little body has been laid out in the village hall, the lady of Wambescourt drives her great mare into the village and, with her usual theatricality, officially accuses Monsieur Ouine of being the murderer. She even brings with her a package of clothing and shoes belonging to the victim, saying that she found them in a closet outside Monsieur Ouine's room. This evidence proves false, however. The dead child was wearing other shoes and other clothing the night before, and the clothes brought in by Woolly-Leg had been abandoned at the beginning of November while the boy was working at the chateau. Yet a haunting question remains: how had the lady of Wambescourt learned, so early in the morning, that the little boy had been murdered during the night?

For the reader who insists upon resolving the murder in Bernanos's novel, all these strange and highly contradictory clues are frustrating. A study of the author's drafts and manuscripts confirms that he consciously pushed the elements of the detective story back into a secondary place. His real goal was symbolic; the murder of an innocent child serves as a symbol of the slaughter of innocents in World War I where, Bernanos maintained, youth had been conscripted and sacrificed for the profit of their elders. Moreover, Bernanos associated the end of Western civilization with the defeat of France in 1940. He realized that his homeland, bled white just twenty years earlier by World War I, but still for him the noblest, most glorious, and most brilliant representative of Christian European culture, had shown herself impotent before the enemy and too anemic to resist another onslaught.

Disillusioned with the European situation, Bernanos and his family immigrated to South America in July 1938. It was in the backwoods of Brazil, where, after a year's search, he had just acquired a large cattle ranch beyond Pirapora, that his darkest suspicions were confirmed: the capitulation of France in 1940 and the signing of the armistice with Germany. Moreover, within months of acquiring his property and his herds, Bernanos suddenly found himself deprived of the needed personnel for running his ranch: his two older sons, his nephew, and his young disciple, Dr. Jean Bénier, had answered General de Gaulle's appeal to fight with the Free French and returned to Europe.

Forsaken and alone, the aging Bernanos, crippled since a motorcycle accident in 1933, was obliged to bury his dream of becoming a prosperous rancher. Unable to fight except with his pen, all he wrote in Brazil, apart from the last chapter of *Monsieur Ouine*, and particularly during those dark years of the occupation of France, were essays and articles devoted to sustaining French morale and trying to vindicate French Christian honor.

Underneath his voluminous writings on France there lurked a searing, prophetic insight into the future demise of Europe. Bernanos would probably say of what survives of European civilization today exactly what he has Monsieur Ouine say in describing Fenouille to the curé: "A bazaar, a fair, where everything, be it good or evil, is spread out pell-mell on display, in the most hideous disorder." Could a better description be given of what an ever increasing proportion of the world's inhabitants consumes nightly thanks to that great leveler of late-twentieth-century society, television, and, more recently, that much touted panacea, the Internet?

Already in the 1930s, in *Monsieur Ouine*, Bernanos seems to predict today's refugees and boat people, warning us that the footsteps of the starving and dispossessed would soon make the whole world tremble. In his posthumously published novel *Night Is Darkest*, written during the same period, he also foresaw the time when Christmas stockings would be filled with drugs and hypodermic needles. It is, however, in *Monsieur Ouine* that he makes his most striking prediction. Bernanos foresaw that modern medicine would be powerless to contend with the number of suicides caused by the survival of humanity's inner nostalgia for something for which it shall have forgotten both the concept and the word: purity. For long after the death of the concept, long after the disappearance of the word, the instinct, Bernanos insists, will secretly survive in the depths of the human heart. There, unexpressed and inexpressible, it will fester. "An epidemic of suicides" will result as people, violently driven by an inarticulate self-hatred, shall seek to destroy both themselves and others.

Monsieur Ouine is many things at once. It is a sociological study, yet it is also a highly poetic novel with the interplay of human attraction, as in life itself — be it asexual, heterosexual, or homosexual — potently at work. From its opening pages Bernanos relentlessly traces the impact of child abuse as it is perpetuated into adult life. Above all it may be seen as a novel of initiation, describing an adolescent's rite of passage into adulthood. As a novel of initiation, *Monsieur Ouine* achieves a nobility and diffused subtlety difficult to find in modern literature save in such rare examples as William Faulkner's vintage legacy, *The Reivers*.

Finally, to the extent that George Orwell's *Animal Farm* and *1984*, or even Aldous Huxley's *Brave New World*, may be viewed as prophetic novels, so too *Monsieur Ouine* may be looked upon as prophetic. Yet none of these elements, nor any imagined combination of them, can convey the poetic finesse or innovative delicacy with which Georges Bernanos wove the many dark strands of life into the rich, hallucinatory tapestry he called his GREAT NOVEL.

Bernanos once wrote in a dedication of a copy of *Monsieur Ouine* that he wanted hope to burst forth from this dark, chaotic book, just as light had burst from the chaos of precreation. It is the translator's hope that the presentation of the complete and corrected text of Bernanos's GREAT NOVEL, by elucidating the complexity and richness of the author's rare genius, may also give the English-language reader a better undertanding of André Malraux's startling assessment that Bernanos was "the greatest novelist of his time."

Monsieur Ouine

1

Between her two long hands — those long, gentle hands — she took his little face, gazing with calm boldness right into Steeny's eyes. How pale his eyes were! You'd say they were in retreat, disappearing bit by bit . . . growing paler still, turning bluish gray, barely animate, with a golden fleck dancing in them.

"No! No!" shrieked Steeny. "No!"

He suddenly jerked backward, his teeth clenched, his pretty face taut with anguish, as if about to vomit. Oh my!

From the other side of the closed shutters, a nearby voice called uneasily, "What's going on? What is it, Steeny? Is that you, Miss?"

But, in a fury, she had already violently pushed him away and stood in the doorway, completely indifferent.

"Why, Steeny! You bad boy!"

He shrugged his shoulders and cast a hard look in the direction of the door, the look of a man.

"Yes, Maman?"

"I thought I heard you cry out," the voice replied, already indifferent. "If you go out, look out for the sun, my darling. What heat!"

Indeed, what heat! The air vibrated between the wooden strips. With his nose pressed against the shutter, Steeny could smell it, breathe it in, feel it penetrate that magic place down at the bottom of his lungs where all the joys and terrors of the world are felt . . .

Again! Once again! It smelled of paint and putty, a smell stronger than alcohol, bizarrely mixed with the ever muggy breath of the great lindens along the driveway. But sleep had already treacherously caught him by the neck like an assassin, even before he closed his eyes. Slowly the narrow window shivered, moved, then stretched unduly lengthwise, as though blown from above. The whole room accompanied it; the four walls seemed caught by the wind and suddenly billowed like sails . . .

.   .   .   .

"Steeny!"

The shutters banged, light came pouring into the room.

"What madness to choose such a place to sleep! We could hear you from the other side of the lawn. Isn't that right, Miss?"

"It's just that Monsieur Steeny should not take midday naps; the doctor has forbidden it."

She placed her hand on his forehead, or rather, pressing her palm against his temples, she slipped her mysterious, ever fresh fingers into his tousled hair and moved them slowly, carefully.

"If madame will allow me . . ."

But madame nodded her head as if consenting to everything—what difference did it make!—so long as night came quickly. Night! She vainly tried to suppress the shiver of pleasure moving like a ripple across her pretty face.

"Steeny will come with me. I'm going to take the dog for a walk."

"No!"

Maman, in a gesture of defense, stepped back, propping her shoulder against the wall and folding an arm over her breast.

Though that "no" had been articulated in an rather low voice, it cut the air like a bullet. Had it really come from that little boy? But already she was facing the situation, holding her chin up, uncovering her chattering teeth. With all the strength and courage of her young life she confronted the familiar but invisible presence, the presence of him who had disappeared and been swallowed up, that eternally absent but ever present one whose voice she had just recognized.

"I don't like for people to say no, Steeny. And remember, never say no to a lady, ever. A gentleman doesn't do that."

Miss blushed with surprised emotion in a sort of delicious seizure. Her golden gaze enveloped her mistress.

"If madame will allow me, I'll go alone. Right, Steeny?"

From the outside she suddenly seized him by the waist, as treacherous and supple as an animal with her immense head of flaming hair, brutally jerking him back into the full sunlight, at the risk of hitting his chest against the ledge. For a long time now, he had known her calculated, tricky violence, these ferocious caresses, overwhelming him with curiosity, terror, and a sort of indescribable nausea. No, no! Let that secret be theirs alone. Desperately he avoided her gaze, clenching his teeth so as not to cry out. Maman smiled.

"Let him go, Miss."

She did let him go. He felt her cruel arms go limp around his shoulders. He felt her embrace relax as quickly as it had engulfed him under the distracted eyes of Maman who, somehow, seemed vaguely compliant. Then they went off together, turning their backs on him, closely pressed one against the other, keeping in the narrow strip of shade as much as possible. Softly he stammered after her, for himself alone, "You liar! You liar!" But why "liar?"

Maman was an unfathomable, sensitive woman, that is to say, admirably protected against the strong disappointments of life. She said that across the years, and as far back as she could remember, her memory only offered her a monotonous succession of futile happenings, similar to the crashing of the sea against a solid slope: the flow caressed it without using it up. To the former priest of Fenouille, courteously surprised to find her so resigned and docile before the will of a Providence that, be it understood, she feigned not to know (not out of malice, to be sure, but perhaps out of some sort of stubborn mistrust — very feminine, alas! — of a spiritualist philosophy that, one must admit, often proves exacting!) she had answered simply, "Gentleness always wins out." "Dear lady," the worthy man had cried, "you have just spoken like a saint!" And it was true that nothing had ever resisted that gentleness. Never. Ever. By always calling upon that irrefutable witness ("gentleness, my gentleness") she seemed to have got herself caught in her own game, like a child who has drawn an imaginary tiger on the wall. For so many poor devils gentleness is only a negative quality, a pure abstraction, nothing but an absence, an absence of malice or wickedness. But for her it had proven itself prudent in its aims, strong in its conquests, vigilant in its protection. How not think of it as some species of familiar animal? Between herself and life, this industrious rodent multiplied its dikes, digging, hollowing out, clearing up, watching the level of the treacherous water day and night. Gentleness, gentleness, gentleness! At the slightest suspect shadow on the tranquil mirror, the little beast raised its slender snout, left the shore, swam to the obstacle, using its tail and paws, and began to gnaw silently, assiduously, indefatigably. Imperceptibly the black spot would then diminish, disappearing even before the eye had perceived anything other than a thin silver ripple. Sometimes after dinner, in the lamplight, when a slight lassitude invited her to dreams and regrets, she would sigh, letting her chin drop between her hands. She thought about her strength and how too kind a fate had never allowed her to give her full measure — her profound experience of beings and their weaknesses, of their secret fragility — an experience scarcely controlled by the mind and hardly distinguishable from the obscure premonitions of instinct, which she was certainly incapable of passing on to anyone else. "I've never understood anything about life," she would say, "except that it has always carried me to the goal I wanted to achieve." And, for the edification of the priest of Fenouille, she added, not without coquetry, "When I was just a little thing, I had a terrible fear of men. Then, one day I understood that things that gesticulate aren't dangerous." But where did that supple genius come from, that insect's patience, that inexorable clairvoyance that allowed her, sure of her position, to await the adversary's lassitude, his first weak or forgetful movement? From her father, perhaps, who had died very young and whose pale face with its blue-circled eyes and nervous, restless mouth, made for lies and caresses, she also possessed, even as she possessed his gesture of imperceptibly drawing up her upper body at the slightest appearance of contradiction.

"Your grandfather," she said to Steeny, "was the most delicious man, seductive like a woman; your grandmother adored him."

Indeed, she had adored him to the point of flattering the only vice he was capable of having: laziness, which very quickly became monstrous and all-devouring. And once his modest job had been lost and his inheritance dissipated, the unfortunate woman tried, according to that terrible expression (one of the most admirable in bourgeois vocabulary), to "profit from her education" by going out to tutor. To her family's supplications she responded with the prodigious assurance of sacrificial beings, "Lucien is more ill than you think," terrible words to which the unfortunate man, devoured by boredom, offered only a powerless resistance. In fact, surrounded by helplessness and sarcasms from those nearest him, he finally died, after an interminable agony, from a death that dragged on for months and got on with it as slowly as his life had done. Michelle was then eight. She would always remember that black December, the smell of guaiacol and tea, the rain resounding against the windows, and those terrifying silences. All night long her exhausted mother trotted from bedroom to kitchen. The floor squeaked, the water whistled in the kettle, the glasses clinked; the little girl would fall into an uneasy sleep until the light was turned on again in the corridor, glaring through the cracks around the door. Should she call? . . . But she feared even more seeing that burning, unbearable gaze appear in the doorway, lost in a half sleep resembling a sort of hallucination, the gaze of her who had been, as it were, metamorphosed by awaiting misfortune, a gaze that almost made her feel an outsider. What could she do against those two threatening beings bound together by some unknown pact, partners in a sinister game? So she buried her head in the hollow of her pillow, gathered together her childish strength, and forced herself to smile awkwardly, in secret, for herself alone. Gentleness, gentleness, gentleness . . . A sure instinct warned her that any revolt she might make to achieve a bit of relief would only subject her more completely to those two companions engaged in a frightening adventure. It was just a question of closing her heart, of breaking contact — that rapid little tricky heart whose beat she listened to with her finger on her temple — her very life, her little life, her life to be protected, to be defended! "Look out for the heart!" the doctor repeated every evening, from the depths of the dark vestibule. "Take care of the heart; the heart can give out." Day after day she believed that her own fate was tied to that failing heart, and she was ready to detest that gray, taciturn man who thus pulled her into the dark, into death, but she finally understood that there was no connection and that even once the other heart was immobile, her own would go on with its task like a mouse nibbling away. It was just that the habit had been established of looking out for that too fragile little servant. Gentleness, gentleness . . . "Michelle is an angel!" Maman cried. "Poor darling, she seems to understand everything, she does understand everything!" And it was true that she vaguely understood that the end was approaching but, indeed — O wonder!— that dreaded day was just like other days, neither better nor worse: the half-closed curtains, the table laid, the white tablecloth, the whispering voices, a mellow silence . . . Toward evening her miserable mother, at the end of her strength, as proud and as red as when, at Candlemas, she tossed steaming pancakes in the pan, threw herself on her daughter, "Oh, my darling . . ." Fortunately, almost immediately, she put her back down: "Don't take so much on yourself, my love. You frighten me!" Or else, "You've been so strong, so patient. Three months now I've left you, my goodness! Ah, Mimi, we'll never be separated again."

. . . .

In fact, they never were separated again. Maman died much later, six months after the marriage of Michelle in Béthune at Philippe's home – one of those horrid brick cubes with a tiny porch. Under the windows, in a cloud of golden haze, the absurd crowd of a northern-French Sunday passed by. The papers that evening announced the mobilization of the Russian army. "Be careful with her," sighed the dying woman one last time in the ear of her son-in-law. "Ah, yes! Philippe, be careful with her, try to understand her!" Alas, alas, it was already too late. That big youth with the tough profile belonged to the enemy race, to the voracious race of those who never measure their impulses and throw themselves on the beloved woman as upon a prey. For a moment she had seen Michelle weaken. Between those powerful hands, that girl who was so solid and so good suddenly appeared another being, unrecognizable, with her face hollowed and sorrowful, with long pouts and sharp, strident laughs cutting through the thickness of the walls, causing the old lady to tremble in her chair: "You'd say it was the cry of a wild goose at night when the wind is down." For a few weeks the brick house resounded with furious scenes, then, by degrees, the echoes grew calmer and silence fell around the greedy man as ingenious gentleness began once more to spin its webs. "He's a poet," sighed Michelle, "a big child. He snatches you up but five minutes later doesn't know what to do with you and looks for a dark corner to put you down in." He disappeared during a counterattack on 28 December 1916. "In addition to the various pieces of information gathered, and notably from the very precise statement of Lieutenant Deboulov, it is unfortunately certain that in the territory between Saint-Jean-du-Loup and Hill 193 none of the wounded could have survived because of the thick layer of gas remaining in the hollows that made it impossible to hold our position the morning of the 29th."

.

Steeny was only a made-up name, a nickname borrowed by Michelle from her favorite English novel. Steeny's name was Philippe, like his father's — he who had disappeared, had been swallowed up. He didn't like that nickname too much, to be sure, but his real name frightened him. As a game, perhaps — or perhaps with some other motivation? — Miss sometimes called him by it. And it was she alone who dared pronounce the two funereal syllables of "Papa," usually on the spur of the moment, and Steeny would shiver in spite of himself . . . The portrait of the dead man was on his little worktable between the two old volumes of Quicherat; sure of finding it there every morning, he scarcely looked at it. For years that father he had never seen had remained for him a legendary character, just barely distinguishable from other heroes, from those stupid, sordid, and wordy war heroes whose stories were told in the *Young People's Journal*—until the day he had crawled on hands and knees into the depths of one of those immense wardrobes in the attic that Michelle called, for some reason, "purgatory," which served as a second linen room, where he had suddenly picked up a strange odor, a strangely alive odor; and almost immediately he recognized — but from where? from when? — tobacco, pepper, sandalwood, that sandalwood Michelle hated. Oh my! Snatched from his hiding place as though by an enraged hand, he found himself sitting on the floor, automatically crushing to his breast a stiff, cold, corduroy jacket he immediately threw back into the shadows. Since then the name of Philippe frightened him. Poor Philippe! Twenty times, a hundred times, he had made himself promise, he had sworn to himself to go back up there, on an afternoon like this one when everyone was asleep. Being caught by Michelle would be ridiculous. He would grab as many of those relics as he could by the armload, by the great armload, just as he would have carried the other's bleeding body under fire . . . And that funereal odor would float about for a long time until evening when Michelle, leaning her head and wiggling her nose, would say, "Ugh! How awful!" Fortunately the booty would already be in his wardrobe and he'd have the key in his pocket. "Steeny, you've been smoking! Yes! You've been smoking, I swear it! Your whole room reeks of tobacco, it's disgusting!"

. . . .

But today as yesterday, as always, it was only a dream: that enterprise to introduce a dead man into the heart of a life already so full. For ten years, except for brief holidays, Philippe had seen nothing of the world except the house surrounded by pines with its old-fashioned garden, its vegetable plot, and its little tree-covered promenade. Beyond lay the tiny village and the thin blond road twining around itself like a viper, going nowhere. Michelle had wanted this solitude. "I shall not make Steeny into one of those horrid grimacing little men, one of those little schoolboy monkeys." Besides, the only school to be considered was at Boulogne and run by priests of the diocese, former assistant priests without a parish who smelled of grime and ink. "I met the superior once – an old woman, a real old woman, soft and round-faced with enormous hips. 'Madame, you give us a child and we give you back a man.' 'A man, monsieur, I know what that is! He has lots of time to become that.'" And no doubt she loved her son passionately, yet she had put off for as long as she could that inevitable, fatal hour when she would behold before her that enemy of all rest, that tyrant: another Philippe . . . Another Philippe?

2

"Well, Steeny, all on your own?"

It was the lady of Wambescourt, Madame de Néréis. She tried to smile but only managed a complicated grimace while her poor crazy head went in all directions, as if seeking an invisible support somewhere in the air.

"Maman's here," Steeny replied in an insolent tone. "She's having her midday nap, I think. Do you want . . ."

"No, no, don't budge, my darling! Don't go . . ."

While energetically gathering the folds of her long black coat about her, she let her handbag slip from her grasp, but caught it again, then cast a frightened look in the direction of the closed shutters.

"No! Don't go! Let Michelle sleep. It's so good to sleep, Steeny . . . Oh, dear God!"

With a strange shiver she stretched in the sun. The light dug into her tortured face gloomily slashed by her painted mouth.

"Steeny, my angel, won't you walk me to my carriage? I left it at the entryway to the park because of the flies. Along the river they were awful. I thought the mare would take off."

"Take off? Really, madame . . ."

Philippe shrugged his shoulders with a knowing air. There was no horse anywhere he feared and these stories of runaway mares made him laugh.

"You're making fun of me, my angel . . ."

She walked ahead of him. Her step was large but uneven, proud but hesitant. With the high heels of her boots slipping on the pine needles, every bend of her knees caused the smell of ether and pine resin to rise around her.

"Yes, indeed! You're making fun of me. Don't say you aren't, Steeny! In this sort of silk sheath, am I not ridiculous with my long, spindly paws? I look like a black spider with a white head. That must make you laugh, right, Steeny?"

"Me? No," Philippe answered quietly. "It's just that for me you're like a character out of a novel."

She suddenly stopped with her head thrown back, her eyebrows raised and her mouth enraged. What was she going to say? But her gaze, confronted by Steeny with a sort of outrageous curiosity, moved away from him and escaped. Then she turned back, lunging herself forward as if to regain her equilibrium. Philippe thought of a gigantic wounded bird, walking along on its wings.

"Well, you mustn't, my angel. Characters in novels, pooh! pooh! And just what do you do with people like that, yes, you, Steeny?"

"Oh, nothing! And that's just why I like them. They're not good for anything. Neither am I."

Again she stopped. Her eyes, ressembling those of a hunted animal, turned first to the right, then to the left before she continued her dancelike walk. Steeny was out of breath trying to keep up. To bring it all to an end, all he would have to do would be to slip away quietly across the open woods, but he preferred telling himself that the die was cast and that this absurd creature would do what she wanted with him for the rest of the day. Perhaps he would be returning at sunset to confront Miss's smile and Michelle's gentle voice from behind the door: "Where's he been? Had dinner at Ginette's! Why, he's crazy!"

Indeed, except on rare occasions, Ginette was no longer seen in Fenouille, even though Michelle still took up her defense. This was from habit as well as perhaps because she hated those pious rivals who had put her too under an interdict, excluding her bit by bit from those happy strands on which respectable society plays its innocent games. The old Marquise Destrées, whose perenniel black skirt smelled of leather and who, with the edge of her hand, could break the neck of a hare in a single blow, had stated once and for all: "I don't formally close my door to Madame Dorsel, but Ginette has made it impossible to receive her." She had added, "My poor cousin Anthelme has gone mad." It was said, in fact, that the house was falling into ruins. The roof had caved in, the rain flowed from step to step in a waterfall, and the vestibule, soaked with black water forced up from between the joints of the tiles at every step, smelled stagnant. For forty years Anthelme had lived a quiet life, eaten well, drunk even better, and, peeing straight, had a fresh breath. Over a ten-year period he wouldn't even have worn out his corduroy trousers. But then there came that fatal autumn when, in a street in Vittel, he met Ginette de Passamont, the daughter of a nonaffluent pharmacist from Lyons — Ginette de Passamont, whom he brought back a few months later along with a whole cortege of friends recruited in railway stations and luxury hotels who disappeared when the first frost lay on the abandoned lawns, leaving the fat fellow alone in the arms of his sweetheart, his mouth agape, shivering in his thin, tobacco-colored suit, silk shirt, and fancy boots . . . Then they saw him as he used to be, out in the countryside, alone, herding his dogs before him, scarcely aged, yet unrecognizable, his face bathed in a bizarre, suspect glow. "Anthelme disgusts me!" was the unanimous cry of all the women. For some time afterward his former hunting companions, whom he met from time to time by chance, circulated exaggerated stories from one chateau to another while that supposedly high-living glutton, that pig Anthelme – damned old Anthelme! – spent his days in the backrooms of the Hudeville bookstore, worrying about the fate of artists, and spoke of using his money to support a poet, or a thinker, or a theosophist – any one of those formidable categories of beings condemned by society to die of hunger – letting it be understood that he himself had wasted his time running around at the rear end of woodcocks, like a moron. Nevertheless, he had always had a taste for music. He could carry a tune and play it on the piano with one finger. Moreover, he knew how to blow a hunting horn. So it was that he planned to take up music theory seriously and go twice a week to Boulogne for concerts to clean out his ears. "Because, cousin, taking up literature at my age is pure hell!" But as soon as anyone pronounced the name of his wife he was troubled and stammered, his lips trembling, "Yes! . . . Yes! . . . Quite happy alone . . . A few friends from Paris . . . We keep to ourselves, completely to ourselves . . ." He had however carried out his dearest project: he had taken in a former professor of modern languages, an eminent man, Monsieur Ouine, who, though unfortunately consumed by tuberculosis, had connections with the ministry of education and was the author of a new method of teaching. Moreover, respectable society had nothing but high regard for this respectable boarder who raised his hat to everyone and of whom the dean of Lescure declared: "He gives the impression of a rare self-confidence, of an incalculable psychic power. In the course of our too short conversations never have I managed to get him, in his courtesy, ever to say a word either for or against religion; he seems interested only in the moral problem."

One after the other the gossips, who quite readily started out attributing amorous designs to him and made a lot of noise about feeling sorry for poor Anthelme, were silenced, and more than one chatelaine deplored the choice that gentleman had made of a suspect household and the fact that it would thus be impossible to invite him. Michelle was still tolerated at receptions on New Year's Day when they, pretending indifference and detachment, would ask her, "It appears he's an exquisite conversationalist?" But, alas, Michelle hadn't set foot in the chateau of Néréis for two years now. Monsieur Anthelme was ill — perhaps mad — Monsieur Ouine was never seen, and Ginette went tearing around the roads behind her great Norman mare as if pursued by disembodied spirits. "One evening last winter she came into my house, fainted into an armchair, then left as she had arrived, without opening her mouth."

. . . .

Philippe untied the tether, then straightened the carriage on the edge of the slope. But Ginette had already got the reins together. He barely had time to get out from under the wheels and jump desperately into the body of varnished walnut bouncing ridiculously on its springs. "God! What an animal!" The long bay mare chomped down on the bit and dug her four shod hooves into the road with a powerful movement of her haunches. The squeak of the leather deliciously accompanied the wild smell of horsehair and of her beautiful, shiny, sweat-spotted coat. It was the first time Steeny had seen the famous animal up close, yet all he had eyes for was his strange companion who had just carried him off by surprise and now was carrying him away in the wild, accelerated rhythm of some probably mad dream about which he knew nothing. How was it possible that with no discussion whatsoever he had followed this Madame de Néréis whom the village wags insultingly called "Woolly-Leg?" Normally he avoided her or observed her with curiosity, but never answered her, much to the chagrin of Michelle who, nonetheless, willingly admitted that Ginette had a "disconcerting behavior." Nor had he followed her from boredom, or because he had nothing else to do as had already happened so many times with things he kept secret. The perfidious attack of Miss, the indifference of Michelle, the departure of the two women together, their caressing voices so tightly intertwined, one merging into the other, their scarcely caught, conspiring laughter had suddenly forced such an abyss of solitude between him and his familiar world – ah, that intimate, conspiring laughter! – and now the apparition of this outsider: all was but one and the same story in the dazzling starkness of this searing day. How was it that these humble juxtapositions, so little different from so many other incidents of daily existence after all, seemed to him to belong to an unknown system of sensations and images coming from another world? By what miracle, at what moment, had the closed, inflexible spiral been broken so that he had emerged from childhood, almost without knowing it? Who could say? But it was enough that the prodigy had been accomplished: tomorrow – the tomorrow that, until then, had been only a pale, still-below-the-horizon image of yesterday, the tomorrow he had been awaiting with tranquil heart and discovered anew each morning with no surprise – that tomorrow was no more. O wonder! Life had just slipped away from him all at once, like a stone from a slingshot.

"Lean over a little, my angel."

She was approaching the crossing at a fast trot. The slope rose gently toward the sky, then went down, then came at them full speed. The two wheels jumped across the road with a crack as sharp as pistol fire. The carriage seemed to hesitate for a moment, tilted, then the hedge, like an arrow, suddenly sailed by the side of the impassive animal, whose rump was only slightly blackened by foam-fringed sweat.

"Do you understand why? It was for taking the turn," she said, excusing herself with a hint of confiding in him. "You'll have to lean a little more still, dear angel."

Her poor face, smeared with red, did not come to life, and in the full light her eyes, circled with blue pockets, revealed her vulnerability. Yet her hands, crossed on the reins, had not gone soft.

Where had Philippe seen those hands before? Was it because the sleeves revealed her too thin wrists? How naked they were! Philippe noticed moreover that the wax from the reins had blackened them a bit, that they ressembled a schoolgirl's hands stained with ink. A broken nail was still bleeding. What strange hands they were, suspended in silent flight between heaven and earth, carried off behind the proud beast! Where had they come from? Where were they going? Toward what fatality? Suddenly Philippe pressed his lips to them.

. . . .

The carriage had been rolling across the grass for the past minute.

"We'll go in by the pastures, Steeny, we have to. It's absolutely necessary. Monsieur Ouine is at his window day and night, watching everything."

She jumped to the ground, caressing the mare's long, glistening neck.

"You see that mare, Steeny? Well, you'll find her right here, she'll not have moved a hoof except to chase flies. We never tie her up."

"Oh!" said Philippe, "I myself am not too interested in trained animals, you know. Those feats, trained horses, so what? Why not a circus horse? Can she dance?"

3

The pink paper covering the walls of Monsieur Ouine's room was a little faded but clean, and he himself had whitewashed the ceiling. Unfortunately age-old filth was still discernible under the white daubs, outlining there a whole mysterious geography of capes, and gulfs, and islands. Whatever paltry light came through the narrow window was further reduced by pines outside, three half dead trees with black tops and thick, ever creaking branches.

"Such good fortune . . . Such very good fortune . . . ," the old man repeated in his gentle voice. "Usually I doze off for a few minutes around seven o'clock. But I distinctly heard the door of the vestibule slam. My sleep is light . . . In any case, it's better to speak no more of this unfortunate misunderstanding."

Monsieur Ouine was seated on the edge of his bed, legs hanging over, a bowler hat resting on his knees, his sailor's jacket buttoned up to the collar, his big shoes carefully polished. He might have been taken for a sort of foreman had it not been for the extreme nobility of his face. Its lines were so simple and pure that neither age nor suffering, nor even the fleshiness of an unhealthy obesity, could ever alter its look of deep benevolence, of calm, lucid acceptance.

"Listen," he said after a silence. "Listen . . . Do you hear our friend going up and down the corridor? Poor creature! Ah, Philippe!—Steeny is an absurd name I find too painful to use—you must hope to learn what pity is before its source is contaminated by your experience of disgust!"

While one of his stubby hands gently stroked the rounded crown of the felt hat, the other came to rest on Steeny's shoulder.

"Don't be surprised at finding me here, Philippe. Don't pity me. I love this house. I've known unforgettable hours here. Ah, yes . . . For days on end this room you see here—so absurd with its maid's bed and its washbasin and chamber pot—has been for me a little bark on the storm-tossed sea. It is I who wished its austerity, this exaggerated poverty, so propitious to a certain half sleep steeped in dreams. How many times was I obliged to rub and wax and polish its red floor tiles to get rid of the smell of mustiness and stagnant moisture emanating from the walls and poisoning the air outside! Square by square I had to scrub the grout, soaking it with chlorine between each tile, as you would a tiny wound. Oh, you're not going to believe me, young man, but grime attacked that way by acid, muck awakened after a century or two of dryness kept emerging bit by bit between my fingers, bursting out in great gray bubbles. Exhausted, I would stretch out, drenched in sweat, the wet sound of those horrid bubble bursts still echoing in my ears. The past is devilishly tenacious, my boy."

"Nonsense!" said Steeny. "I'd not have gone to so much trouble, Monsieur Ouine. For me the past doesn't count. Neither does the present for that matter, or at best only as a kind of little shadowy fringe along the edge of the future. Ah, the future . . ."

Instinctively he turned his head toward the window and the light. But it proved a vain attempt. The sad gaze he felt bearing down on him drew him away from it bit by bit, back toward the bed with its pale sheet disappearing into the shadows.

"I am your friend, Philippe," Monsieur Ouine said simply, but with tremendous authority.

He raised his head and, in a flash – O impossible dream!– Steeny thought he had recognized the predestined companion of his life, the master who was to initiate him, the hero pursued in book after book. Now, having discovered him old and ailing, so different from what he had imagined, he thought he felt his own breast being gnawed at by that same subtle fire that, under the poor sailor's jacket, must now be devouring that other breast. Trying to stifle an unwanted sob, he too raised his head, confronting the unknown challenge offered by this house with all its secret powers, all of them faithful servants of the most secret power of all: death – death that even now was at work so nearby, there, right under their very feet . . . Monsieur Ouine had not ceased stroking his hat.

"You're a good little boy so you'll excuse me," said the professor after a silence. "I am ashamed of having spoken to you in such a stupid, paternal manner. Would to God I were your equal!"

.   .   .   .

His gaze dimmed slightly while, at the bottom of the neck, he discreetly pressed against the upper part of his chest with the five fingers of his free hand. Except perhaps for the gray tint perceptible on his sagging cheeks, there was nothing else however to indicate an attack, yet Philippe's instinct warned him, with an unheard-of strength, of the certainty of an imminent, hideous danger. Then it all disappeared again.

"Yes, forgive me," Monsieur Ouine repeated. "Upon seeing you in the company of that unhappy woman, my only thought was to spare you a sight that would be very cruel and demeaning for a boy of your age. But then no doubt you are more capable of suffering its degradation than I am."

"What degradation?" asked Philippe. "How could seeing

Monsieur Anthelme again be degrading for me, whether he's dead or alive? Besides, what proves to you that Madame de Néréis . . . She met me only by chance, understand . . . I was supposed to walk the dogs . . ."

"Walk the dogs!" cried the professor of languages, "Alas! there are more dogs here than you'll ever be able to walk, a whole pack of them . . ." Then, after a silence, he began again. "My child, I have done for that simple good man who is about to die what I would never have done for anyone else. And understand, it was not out of compassion. I am wary of pity, sir. It exalts rather vile feelings in me, a sort of itching in all the wounds of my soul – a horrid pleasure. Nonetheless it is true that the sight of a certain disintegration eventually becomes intolerable. I protected these people from themselves – I leave you to judge for yourself whether or not I knew everything there was to know about them. Why, there's not a single corner in these rooms that doesn't remind me of an effort or battle or some pitiful lie I crushed there by chance, as I might have crushed an insect. Now, alas! that task is all over. There is nothing left to kill. Their poor secrets lie about everywhere. Oh, you must understand, they don't care: they come and go as they always did, endlessly repeating the same tales; they forget that their hiding place is now empty. In the final stages of degradation a man loses his own truth forever. Those beings you find here have trampled on theirs without even recognizing it. Indeed, it is quite possible that our friend met you only by chance; she could have had the idea just when she saw you . . . My, my, how that mare must have trotted from Fenouille to Néréis!"

"Well, she really knows how to trot, that's for sure . . . But listen, Monsieur Ouine . . ."

"Just say 'monsieur,' Philippe."

"Oh no, no! Either you are Monsieur Ouine or you are nothing. So listen then, Monsieur Ouine. If you think it will do any good, I'll go to Monsieur Anthelme's room. Why not? I don't know how to explain it, but ever since this morning something extraordinary's been happening to me. The gardener filling his pipe or an empty cart passing by – everything seems to beckon and call to me ... How suddenly everything seems to have opened up around me! Life seems great and deep! Never have I been less afraid of death than I am this evening."

"I'll teach you to love it," Monsieur Ouine suddenly said, lowering his voice. "Death is so rich. A rational man discovers in death everything that fear and shame keep him from seeking elsewhere, even the beginnings of gratification. Remember this, Philippe, you will love death. I fear the day will come when it will be the only thing you love. My modest little room in all its austerity seems so sweet to you precisely because of death's presence here; you've already taken refuge in death's shadow without even knowing it."

He had just laid the absurd felt hat at his feet. His two pale hands, slightly swollen, now traced a mysterious tree with great, indefinable, palm-shaped leaves.

"Well?" said Steeny, as if to arouse him. "What are we going to do, Monsieur Ouine?"

But the old man's gaze immediately caused him to look down.

"I'm not going home tonight," the boy continued with sudden anger. "My heart's too full, too heavy. Besides, I hate that house: whether it is today or tomorrow, what difference does it make? Sooner or later I'll surely cross that ridiculous garden with its crumbling stairs, tree-covered little promenade, and two dried-up pastures for the last time. And I'll see for the last time the stupid white facade of that sugar-cube house that refuses to melt in rain or sun and pray to heaven I'll find in its place a pool of mortar and whitewash."

.   .   .   .

Standing in the doorway, Monsieur Ouine gave a friendly wave, then carefully closed the door as he went out. Vainly Philippe tried to catch some sound. But all that seemed to be stirring was the wondrous silence of the little room, softly turning on an unseen axis. He even thought that he could feel it slipping across his forehead, over his chest and along his palms, caressing him like water. How far down was he to sink, and to what peaceful depths? During the course of this capital day he had never felt farther from his childish world, from the now colorless world of childhood, nor from yesterday's joys and sorrows, from all joy, all pain. That world in which he dared not believe, the world hated by Michelle — "You're dreaming, Steeny! Ugh!" — the languid dream world that had once devoured his weak progenitor, with its fabulous horizon, its lakes of forgetfulness, its vast siren songs — had now suddenly opened up before him and, at last, he felt the strength to live there, amid the many specters, spied upon by their thousands of eyes, until the supreme faux pas was committed. "In our world there's no chance of winning: you have to fall; even Monsieur Ouine shall fall." Thus spoke those shadowy mouths, all of them. And as for himself, Philippe, he wondered what real difference it would make after all. He was only astonished at not being able to find a place for his new master within the ranks of his favorite heroes. What serenity reigned in the orbit encircling this heavyset man with the pallid brow . . . "Maybe he's what they call a saint?" Philippe reflected with theatrical terror.

One could not say that the silence was broken, but it did flow by him, little by little going on its way. A scarcely perceptible shudder seemed to seize him from behind. "Damn!" he exclaimed, "Ginette's crying."

Great concentration was needed however to make out her monotonous weeping sustained by a deep drone — Monsieur Ouine's voice, no doubt — which suddenly rose, then fell. Silence.

.   .   .   .

"Well, Monsieur Ouine . . ."

The professor of languages sadly shrugged his shoulders.

"Do you like smells, young man? I hate them."

"What smells?"

"Any smell. Although there are few sights that succeed in shaking my composure, I must say that a certain stench immediately terrifies me. Yes, young man, it is only little by little that terror penetrates me through my eyes."

His palms pressed together, he gingerly sniffed his fingernails one by one.

"Our friend doesn't smell good," he finally said, smiling slightly.

"What friend? Monsieur Anthelme? Why not?"

"Diabetic gangrene, I think," the old man replied, relaxing all of a sudden. "Fortunately such decomposition is painless, as you'll be able to judge for yourself. Six days ago our poor patient took to his bed. The negligence of these country people being what it is, alas! he kept his socks on, just as he always did. Well, yesterday we had to remove them in a pail of warm water to make it easier, since it was obvious that the skin would come off with them. And he just sat there puffing on his pipe, either laughing at our squeamishness or mimicking our grimaces like a monkey . . . My, my! And he used to be such a strapping fellow, so full of energy!"

He spoke calmly, deliberately, in a voice hardly lowered at all, yet Philippe, not without a vague sense of fear, thought he felt that they were enclosed within the same silence, a silence absorbing only the higher registers of sound and leaving the illusion of becoming itself some sort of audible purity. For Philippe was dreaming of the limpid magic of water, of its supple, caressing embrace, of its eternal miracle.

. . . .

"Well, even so, I find it rather discreet for Anthelme to leave the world this way, all alone and with no fanfare. As for the beastly neighbors, we can certainly do without them. He'd do better to die lying beside a ditch than to have that old Madame Destrées come running to his deathbed with her gun, her raincoat and boots, and her 'dear cousin' here and 'dear cousin' there . . . That horrid old lady even smells like a game bag, the old cutthroat! Still, dying without a priest or doctor or lawyer . . . brr! All right! Go ahead and laugh, Monsieur Ouine."

"Come, come now, Philippe, why ever would you think that neither doctor nor lawyer was called in? It's true of course that we'd not have much for the latter to do. But the doctor from Boulogne has already been here three times and we shall be seeing him again tomorrow, even though these visits are strictly a matter of form, in any case. For a long time now our friend has been nothing but a poor mass of fermenting flesh saturated with sugar and alcohol, just like a batch of must. He even has its honey smell. As for the priest, please realize that I risked the impossible in attempting to persuade Madame de Néréis not to forbid him entry. I begged, I threatened, I even tried deceitfulness, but nothing worked. How could anyone want to keep that sad wretch, that poor, broken creature, from taking advantage of the supreme chance left to him to enter death with some nobility? I would perhaps even have been willing to cause a scene if the priest, Monsieur Doucedame, hadn't thought he shouldn't run the risk . . . Do you honor God, my child?"

But immediately he reached out with his hand and pressed it hard against Philippe's mouth.

"No, no, that's all right, not a word. You were going to say something stupid," he continued, still smiling, though his lips trembled with impatience. "A boy of your age never willingly answers such a question."

Suddenly turning his back, he took a few steps toward the window. On the sheet, where the hat now lay on its side, its felt crown revealed a thin pink strip of its once garnet-colored lining. For all the world it resembled some animal's delicate pink mouth. "Does he go to bed with it?" Steeny thought. He burst out in an irresistible nervous laughter he had already held in far too long. The funny black globe rebounded from the hollow of the pillow, hesitated, disappeared, then finally rolled over and over along the side of the bed like a cork buoy on the swell of the sea. "Leave me alone! Leave me alone!" But, as if the force of laughter had broken them, Philippe's arms hung useless at his sides. Bent double and choking, he tried to get his breath.

"Don't move anymore now," Monsieur Ouine ordered severely. "Be still, here, this way, head up! You must learn that nerves can do very little to a man on his feet. And remember this too: little boys and women should never laugh: there's malice in laughter, a certain poison. With a little good sense you might have been spared the humiliation of that stupid attack here in my presence. Here, breathe in a bit more ether."

"What attack are you talking about!" shouted Philippe, pale with rage. "I just choked from laughing, that's all!"

"I fear you may be subject to such attacks," Monsieur Ouine continued impassively. "Alas! we have a double origin, and the first third of our life hardly suffices to kill the woman in us. But then perhaps I've overestimated your strength. I have become a very simple man, very, very simple, and I no longer make any calculations. After a certain number of useless experiences—which one of us hasn't gone out to look for the lost sheep and tried to bring it back on his shoulders?—I no longer go out after anything. Like those masses of living jelly at the bottom of the sea, I float and I absorb. We shall teach you that poor secret. Yes, you will learn from me how to let yourself be filled with the passing hour. How many times, along the edge of the Frescheville woods where I used to go to reread old letters from young men—such unfair, proud letters that I destroyed only with regret—yes, how many times have I seen you there crossing the road, going off toward Hagron, killing blackbirds! At first glance I recognized your uneven walk, sometimes imperious, sometimes slow, and all those little starts you made, as though there were some sort of call, those brusque, absurd halts in full sunlight... Ah yes, that was the memory I cherished for so many years: a life, a young human life, all ignorance and all daring, that one lone part of the universe that really is destructible, that one promise never to be kept, what a unique marvel! Don't let yourself be deceived, Philippe, true youth is as rare as true genius, or perhaps it is that true genius, that challenge to the world's order and to its laws, a sort of blasphemy. Yes, a blasphemy. Nature, like a hideous housewife, takes advantage of everything and broods over youth with a watchful hatred, amorously opening up mass graves for it. But youth jumps over them and keeps going. When all else changes and decays and returns to the mud from whence it came, only youth will still be capable of dying, for youth alone can ever truly know what death is. Ah, Philippe! Every step that you took forward in the burning stream of day, every step you took in the evening as your shadow followed you, stripped from me a fear, a scruple, or a lie I had unconsciously spared. Then, one day, those letters I held in my hands seemed sad, ugly, so I threw them down, discarded them, and sprinkled a handful of earth over them; I didn't even bury them. They were, however, the only memory I had retained of years such as I hope you will know. But all was blotted out by your presence."

. . . .

The voice became softer and softer, a barely perceptible murmur, wrapped within that same, seemingly eternal silence . . . The shadows seemed summoned there on purpose to enclose those incomparable, priceless words within soft gray folds. All the malice, irony, and cruelty left to Steeny from his childhood now surged from his heart to his lips. His prettily shaped mouth took on that brutal line that Miss hated so much and that she sometimes would wipe off absent-mindedly, using the end of her finger with its painted nail . . . Could you have fun with that old man? Where was the sensitive, vulnerable spot of that massive chest, of those short thighs resting so awkwardly on the edge of the bed, of that body that, like that of a mature woman, one imagined as fatty and fragile? Philippe would like to laugh as he had laughed a moment earlier, just as he always laughed whenever a certain, so familiar, regret suddenly risked becoming intolerable, that laugh Michelle called, "Your baby laugh, your crazy laugh." But now, forget that crazy laugh ... Too late! Already he was being carried away by another feeling surging up within from his most obscure depths, from that half dead, stagnating part of the soul where a deformed, basic pity, as all-devouring as hatred, keeps vigil. What easy triumph could possibly equal the lacerating joy and internal upheaval of a victory over disgust, of voluntary submission to a sort of humiliated greatness that, because it was repugnant, was unrecognizable? He seized the soft fat hand, pressed it gently against his breast, then to his lips, then burst into sobs.

"My child," Monsieur Ouine repeated twice, not raising his voice, but with a terrifying strength.

The former professor immediately pried away the friendly fingers, remained for a moment inclined toward the floor in the position of a man struck by some unforeseen blow and who only slowly takes in his surprise, terror, or joy. He nonetheless completed his story in the same tone.

"That's what you have been for me since then, Philippe. I've been expecting you, though. This unforeseen encounter and the madness of a lunatic were necessary for us to meet, face to face, right here, where I should never have hoped to see you, in this room that you will nevermore forget now — what's the difference! . . . Still, one more thing now, the last one: what do you think of me, yes, right this minute?"

"You frighten me," Steeny said. "I would follow you to the end of the world."

He shook his head, his gaze bursting with the irony and audacity of youthful pride.

"Tomorrow perhaps you'll make me laugh."

But already Monsieur Ouine was busy around the pine table, covering it with a cloth, putting out a simple place setting, and opening a jar of jam. The bread happened to be just the sort of sandwich loaf of which Steeny was particularly fond.

"You can drink some of this old Madeira. I left you a little while ago, my boy, with the intention of putting an end to this absurd misunderstanding. That is, I thought that I could easily win out over the unpredictability of my poor friend and that she would agree to drive you back home this evening. Well, we'll have to forget that. We're also unlucky in that the only neighbor able to help you out, Monsieur Malicorne, is away for the night in Boulogne. What can we do? My own state of health won't allow me to escort you, and I feel it is much too late to allow you to start out on a walk of a good ten miles."

"Bah!" said Philippe, his mouth full, "I'm not going to sleep tonight."

.   .   .   .

"We could of course keep you here, but we should first of all reassure your mother. The little hired boy from the Malicornes who brings our milk each evening used to have a bicycle. But he's sold it. Nonetheless I had him leave immediately for Fenouille, taking shortcuts. When do you usually have dinner?"

"Around eight or eight-thirty, Monsieur Ouine. But then I often hunt ringdoves along the edge of the woods, under those great oaks by the road. When I do that, I don't come in until ten o'clock. And then . . . well . . ."

He spread both hands in front of him as though tossing to oblivion his vision of a complaining Michelle with her distraught reproaches and long stares.

"And then what? What are you trying to say?" the old man asked in a tone close to anger. "Are you counting on me to abduct you from your family? Do I look like a kidnapper? Alas, you're all alike, all of you. There wasn't a single one of my old students who didn't plan to follow me to the end of the world, as you say. But you must realize, my dear boy, the world has no end."

Suddenly his voice softened, and Philippe thought he detected something like cloudy water in the old man's eyes, which a slight motion of the lids had just half-closed.

"But each one of us can reach the end of himself."

For a moment he remained immobile, his body leaning forward, his slightly twisted neck inclining his head toward his shoulder in an uncomfortable and almost frightening position, as if he had been nailed to the spot by the words he had just uttered.

"Well then, you'll sleep here," he finally said, "here in my room. Don't worry about me. I'll go stretch out on the sofa in the library, as I often do. I find it quite comfortable. Maybe I'll even go out to meet the little hired boy, for it's going to be a dark night. Don't worry about Anthelme: the final moment isn't as near as I had thought; the doctor's not expecting anything before next week. These kinds of death are very slow. As for Madame de Néréis, her insomnia is imaginary. To my knowledge, it's a fact that she only rarely undresses: a chair, the corner of a carpet, the corner of a room are all good enough for her. But the sleep carrying her off then is the sleep of a little child. I should add moreover that there is very little chance now that you'll see her leave her floor: I think she'd rather take a beating. You'll be able to rest without disturbance." "Monsieur Ouine . . . ," began Philippe.

He was almost ready to cry from nervousness and impatience, as well as from a sort of deep, hidden anger pushing him as near to laughter as to tears. "You don't really give a damn about me, Monsieur Ouine. Will I or won't I do as you say? One would think that you'd not even asked yourself that question; why, it's unheard of! What's worse is that your little scheme doesn't hold up to scrutiny at all, if you'll excuse my saying so. It's hard to imagine sending a little boy off to Fenouille when it would have been so easy and no trouble at all, just by warning me an hour earlier, to let me go myself. I know the way much better than he does. And, in any case, what a way to reassure my mother! 'Steeny at Ginette's? Can you imagine it? How horrible!' It's true though that in her mouth the word 'horrible' just means ridiculous or crazy. For nothing has ever really seemed horrible to Maman, nothing, ever . . ."

His breaking voice grated and had lost all control, all composure, and, in spite of himself, again took on the now abhorred accent of his childhood. He stared at his trembling hands in despair.

"What are you trying to say?" Monsieur Ouine interrupted. "Who said anything about keeping you here? You can stay or leave, you're free."

"No, I am not free! Philippe screamed. "I don't want to be free! I want to play a role – any role will do, but it must be a real role. And don't go thinking I'd not have accepted this role from anyone else but you, either! One would have to be very shrewd and very clever to know whether I really like you or detest you, Monsieur Ouine. I'm just following the slope of my path now, that's all. In a child's life there's never a slope to the path. With our little joys, sorrows, and rebellions, it's a velvet path; everything is as smooth and clean as a lawn. So if the ground seems to be missing under my feet now, it must be because I've emerged from the nursery! Ah, Monsieur Ouine! what good fortune!"

"Just be careful not to make yourself tipsy," remarked the old man without feeling. "You're already on your fifth or sixth glass of wine."

"A slip, a fall, so what? Lacking all else, couldn't we be happy with just a faux pas? Yes, I who am nothing if not pious – and Maman who, everyone knows, doesn't like priests . . ."

"Why is that?" Monsieur Ouine interrupted in a prickly tone.

"How should I know? Perhaps because she's afraid of them; maybe that's all."

"And you?"

"Well, I watch out for them. In a way, Monsieur Ouine, I watch out for God – that's my way of honoring Him."

Laughing, he wiped his palms over his burning face.

"Come, Philippe," said Monsieur Ouine, "it's high time you got to sleep."

"Fine, fine, so now you think I'm drunk . . . So why didn't you remove the bottle sooner, old schemer? Now, it's three-quarters empty. But then for what's wanted there's no need to be able to see straight, after all. And, anyway, I don't insist on seeing straight, I'm not frightened by shadowy masses. Miss says I have a synthetic mind . . . 'Like, those masses of living jelly at the bottom of the sea . . .' Ah, ah, Monsieur Ouine, there are days you're sure of not being disappointed with yourself, regardless of what happens, there are days visited by the gods!"

As he struck his fist down on the table he was surprised to feel only the bare board. Before him, in a poor brass holder, burned a candle. Some distance away Monsieur Ouine's body, immeasurably enlarged, bent over, was moving in all directions with a superhuman agility.

"Yes, that's it!" Steeny, now enraged, shouted at him. "Yes, monsieur! Talking about the last wishes of Anthelme makes me laugh! What did I have to do with that idiot? And if it's true that he insisted so much on seeing me before he died, then why did I have to be carried off like that? Maman herself would have driven me over. Besides, he and I would have been through a long time ago if you hadn't come and literally snatched me out of the arms of that lunatic . . . A lunatic . . . Poor Ginette! When I saw her pathetic little hand, all ink-stained, much too thin, much too long . . . It smelled of honeysuckle – or anise. I still remember a great immobile bee, just at the height of our brows, whisked away by the wind. As we turned, it whistled past my ear like a shot . . . Tell me now, Monsieur Ouine . . ."

The misshapen silhouette still danced about before his eyes with the same frenzy, but the answer came back at him from the opposite side of the room. He turned around in shock.

"You've just had a conversation with my shadow," the professor of languages said calmly. "It is very interesting."

He finished tucking the sheets in and fluffed up the bolster with little pats.

"Your observations are not altogether absurd. And I do regret, incidentally, that the state of . . . of Anthelme didn't allow us, a bit earlier . . . But, unfortunately, we didn't succeed in awakening him. Please understand, however, my friend, that I should quite heartily have desired never to see you here, in this house. But since so many circumstances have come together to bring you here . . ."

. . . .

The voice kept diminishing by degrees, becoming lower, ever lower, until it was nothing but a vague purr mysteriously scanned by the flickering of the candle, in a golden halo. "Steeny, naughty Steeny!" Was it Miss who now, once more, wrapped him in her cruel arms? He vainly strained to hear the great burst of triumphant, proud laughter: the pillow encasing his burning neck was carefully hollowed by an unknown, prudent hand. How cool the pillow felt! What's that? Come back tomorrow?

. . . .

. . . .

"Listen, Monsieur Ouine, have I been asleep?"

Without opening his eyes he softly continued to repeat this same question for a long time just to himself. But the old man was now far away, God only knew where — in what corner of that dead house? He preferred to imagine him farther away still, crossing the fields, or along his beloved road. The road! The road? Who spoke of the road? Not that one, not one of those pale, anemic roads, but his own, his very own Road, the one he had seen so many times in his dreams, that infinite road opening before him like a gaping mouth . . . The road! The road! So, confronting he knew not what huge, star-filled opening, he fell asleep, clenching his fists.

"I gave my word of honor!" Steeny repeated for the second time.

With no breeze, the heavy rain fell vertically on the steaming soil. Far in the east, as though on the edge of another world, the stormy dawn slowly formed its clouds behind watery mist.

"All right, all right!" said the crippled little Guillaume. "I understand, but don't speak too loud, Philippe. He came in this morning with a ripped ear, covered in mud, and had lost his gun. The police chased him from Dugny to Theroigne. You should have seen him empty the beer jug in a single draft, not touching it with his lips. What a thirst! From time to time, needing to breathe, he'd lower it a little and I'd hear him bite the stoneware as he groaned . . . My God! Oh, my God, Philippe! Will I ever be able to love him?"

"You'd just as well kill him," Steeny said seriously. He immediately burst out laughing and took his friend's hand.

"Don't laugh!" begged the cripple. "You really frighten me, Philippe. Yes, me, and I'm afraid of no one, not even of that horrid bastard. But there are days . . . yes, days, when it seems to me that you are pulling on me as hard as you can and that I'm going to fall — my heart's completely empty."

"Well, let go of me then, old man, I can easily fall all by myself."

"Never!" the boy said in a soft voice. "Never!"

From whom, from what ancestor, from what proud master had he inherited that little barbarian face with its Mongoloid cheekbones and deeply depressed eye cavities under the double arch of the forehead, its imperious, almost savage, mouth, and that stiff black hair? But even stranger or more frightening still, from where came the paradoxical mobility of those features, the perpetual trembling of weak muscles under the dull skin, the incessant plea of his stare like a flame beaten down by the wind?

Not even the old man himself, the progenitor with giant shoulders, that stranger who forty years before had come from the Flemish plains, had ever been able to meet the gaze of those eyes, so different from his own and of quite another species; he would turn his pink, clean-shaven face away, ever so slightly. How could he answer them? His son was dead, his daughter-in-law too, and, to top it off, he had ended up by allowing his daughter to marry that no-good drunkard. Added to that, the negligence of Fenouille's doctor had turned his grandson into a cripple. A cripple! God grant that the other one, that churl, not take it into his head to get his daughter pregnant! But he had to swallow his shame in silence, sitting erect at the table in the evening, secretly struggling against the hideousness of the aging he felt in his sides and neck and burning joints. Still, the old man did his proper part of the chores, ate his share at mealtime, drank his portion of brandy, and had put by enough to pay both the priest and the doctor, buy a coffin, and even reimburse his daughter for the two sheets she would lose to shroud him. No one knew better than he how to bleed a horse or relieve one bloated from fresh clover with the thrust of a trocar, or, thrusting his naked arm in up to the elbow, how to assist a heifer in her first labor. He had his own pew in the church and, in the old days, when the harvest was bad, he was paid with a simple, "We are much obliged, Monsieur Devandomme!" as they touched their high, black silk caps. For in spite of his marriage with Zeleda, few of them would have dared treat him as a cousin. But now he accepted payment, stacking up notes of ten or twenty francs he would smooth out one by one with his thumb, then tie together with an old shoelace. The first day of the month, without a word, he would set this packet out on the table and, pulling his huge hand full of change out of his pocket, say in a hoarse voice, "Here, little one, this is for your books." Then his daughter would fill a large glass with gin.

No more than her dead mother, Helen did not feel much love for that proud peasant father. She feared him, but with a nuance of deep and unavowed secret mockery. For her father's family was something unknown, as fabulous as an African tribe — the old man having neither brothers nor sisters and for forty years never having written to anyone . . . Well, then! It was to the local people that she belonged completely, to those drinkers of gin-laced coffee, those braggarts with their fine Sunday shirts fresh against their brown skin, their pale caps cocked over their ears, their pretty, rascally mouths, always moist, with that heavy way of talking picked up at dances in Etaples. Certainly her father would never have allowed her to accept a dance at the local fairs, and a furtive gaze into the windows of the tavern on Sundays, when you come out of mass, is very poor consolation for a girl! After which you had to go very properly and hem church linen over at the presbytery in that slightly bitter-smelling room. Consequently what a silent stab in her breast, what a tremor throbbed in her young blood just two months ago when she spotted Eugene, his short pipe in the corner of his lips, smiling with his eyes, Eugene Demenou who, six months earlier, had come with a team of woodcutters, horses, and wagons to chop down the Gardenne forest for the Jewish Federation of the Ardennes . . . Ah! ah! Already on the second day, with her head pressed into his homespun jacket smelling of moss and heather, she bit into his white neck!

To their double stupefaction the old man had replied, "All right, we'll have the wedding in August," just as he might have said, "It's apple time," as he glanced at the gilded frame where, under a layer of fly dirt, placid and imperturbable, the stout lady, dead for fifteen years now, still smiled her smile.

On the evening of the wedding, the little cripple was lying hidden in the grass up at the top of the pasture when he saw the old man coming toward him with his great heavy steps. The poplar scarcely trembled; an attentive cow showed the underside of her rose muzzle. In haste the child grabbed his crutches, raising himself up on his hands and knees. But the old man had already seized him and clasped him in his two hard arms, lifting him from the ground and pressing him against his old breast as knotty as the trunk of an apple tree. "Boy," he said, "boy, we've been disgraced."

. . . .

Four generations of them had lived there, but the Devandomme family had not come from Erighem. Nor had it come from any other village in the Flemish country. Perhaps it was from the Ardennes or from the Meuse region—what difference did it make? For more than a hundred years the burghers of Wormhoudt, Steinword, and Cassel had replied to the greetings of these good, quick-tempered giants, accommodating people known for training the best smugglers' dogs around, but honest in business and giving sons to the Church. Until that day . . .

As for that, it remained the secret of the mysterious little lieutenant in gold-braided orange trousers and apple green tunic who had just finished accompanying Charles X from Rambouillet to Cherbourg, then on to Scotland. A cutter had brought him from Dover to Dunkirk, and he was on his way back to Lorraine, riding a shaggy, short-legged horse, indifferent to the Orleanist police whom he defied with his Cross of St. Louis and an unbelievable uniform dating back to the time of the emigration. Whether because of the fatigue of the journey or, what was more likely, because of the smile and well-rounded arms of the pretty female ancestor he'd met near the fountain, he was detained for three days, during which time he went to bed late, rose early, and, whistling like a bird, was at the fountain at daybreak, brushing his horse. The local people laughed at the nasal Flemish he had learned from the members of the household cavalry of Cassel, but even more at his dainty size, his well-shaped calves, his prettily turned thighs, and dancing step. But as soon as he heard the name de Vandomme: "Vandomme? What's that? Vandomme . . . Good Lord, Vandomme! Didn't your honorable grandfather have the Christian name of Anthénor? Anthénor de Vandomme?" "Yes, monsieur." "My God! Did any of you know him?" "No, monsieur. We know that he was a big man with little respect for priests and, if the truth be told, he loved to carouse. In my youth the old men still remembered having seen him arrive one evening, just like you, on a hairy horse with his belongings in a valise . . . but at that time, who had time to worry about such things! The countryside was held by gangs from Hazebrouck to Gravelines; there was nothing but pillaging; villages were in flames for fifty miles around above the hillsides of Bamberque, all the way to Furnes. Finally he bought this land where we are and less than a year later married one of the Vanhouette girls at Herschell. Then he died, my father was still only a little fellow."

At the time Devandomme could say nothing more since the little man in green, beside himself, was already rubbing his tear- and tobacco-stained nose against his cheeks: "Marquis de Vandomme, I am your servant! Our grandfathers were like Nisus and Euryalus together, like Castor and Pollux, like Achilles and Patroclus. War and gambling and women and perhaps a bad slave deal in Africa broke up a friendship that had been so close: your grandfather disappeared, leaving mine in tears. Bless the divinity that brings us together! What need have I for other proofs! Who can brag of having met a Vandomme on this side of the Lys? And who moreover has ever had that Trojan name of Anthénor?" In addition he affirmed that something like that could lead to something and promised to do something with it and establish the line through authentic documents drawn from his own records. "You've been robbed, monsieur, they have divided up what was yours. And what is to be thought of a house as mediocre as the Crescent-Vandommes who took over your name, your coat of arms, and even the title of marquis! What a pretty litter of badgers! Dear friend, I can speak from experience: since 1780 we have been separated over a question of inheritance, and were it not for Robespierre and Bonaparte, I'd have stripped them as bare as St. John. But we are back in the game now, my friend, thanks to you!"

Outside the closed shutters the great wind of Flanders groaned like the sea. On dwarf hills from Rosendaël to Poperinghe overworked windmills called to one another with piercing cries. At intervals a cloud of frozen mist, coming from the depths of infinite ice fields, split the air like an axe, as ice particles fell whistling on the plain; on the other side of the road, frozen hard as an anvil, it sounded like the clacking of ten thousand wooden shoes, like an immense rout . . . Damned little man in green! He was still talking when they heard the angelus, and even Devandomme's father, his elbows on the table, had had the painful, childish shiver of a suddenly awakened sleeper . . . What an admirable story! The Vandommes, though rivals of the House of Lorraine and no less old, and nearly as powerful as it, had discouraged fortune bit by bit through strange excesses, lost their heritage, then got it back again twenty times, until that last lord, a slave trader in Africa . . . "Ah, my friends, I fear that neither time nor trials have cooled your warm blood's generosity. So be careful of it! Stay the good people you are when Providence, through what I'll do, gives you back the justly honored name of your ancestors, even though you cannot have their possessions! As for me, I swear to accomplish what I must do in memory of that best of grandfathers, who was such a faithful friend."

The former emigrant left one evening, having exchanged his short-legged horse for an excellent Boulogne mare on which they had to hoist him up, like a green monkey, for he had got gloriously drunk. Alas, no one at Erighem was ever to learn anything more about this marvelous little man: his body was found two days later in the midst of the Lambercke Forest, scalped by wolves, on the edge of a frozen pond.

.

"Tell me, tell me," the little cripple pleaded. "But first of all, are you really sure you understood him?"

"Yes and no . . . Not a single moment did he open his eyes or move his fingers I held tightly in my hand. But all the same his voice was loud and clear; it blared like a trumpet."

"A trumpet? Then how could you tell me just now that you had to hold your ear up to his mouth?"

"Well, I thought . . . But, yes, Guillaume, I assure you, it blared like a trumpet. It's true I was a bit drunk. Woolly-Leg had been scratching at the door for such a long time, poor crazy thing! She wasn't even sure that the other one had left; for she'd heard me moan in my sleep like Monsieur Ouine. Because he's always moaning in his sleep, can you imagine, and even when he's awake, his eyes wide open, all of a sudden — for ten seconds or twenty seconds perhaps — like this: uhhh . . . uhhh . . . It's horrible!"

"Well?"

"Well? Well, that's it! I think that the poor man's dead by now."

"And you have nothing more than that to say, Philippe? No? Oh, Steeny! I saw you the other night in a dream, nailed through the middle of your chest to a dry rock, a sort of flaming wall, a wall of salt, and, before I could articulate a single word, you yelled at me: 'No, no! Stay there! Don't move! Leave me alone!' exactly as if you'd been damned."

"Don't make me mad! That's the kind of story you read in textbooks. Besides, you know our rules: I always forge straight ahead. If life is nothing but a barrier to be got through, I'm going through it, and I'll come out on the other side, all bloody and in a sweat. And when it's time for you, we'll see you come out too, for you're following me, but at a distance, bearing the weight of my sins. After all, you are my soul, so don't go bothering me about it, our salvation is your affair . . . Now listen, Guillaume . . ."

With its tiny windows and pale, roughcast finish, the modest house, surrounded by a tarred surface, slowly emerged like a primitive ship's hull from night into day, its sides glistening with shadows. A passing cloud, pursuing its great course from hill to hill, enveloped it within its whirling outline before disappearing.

"Listen, Guillaume . . . I've not kept my word, I've not kept my word on the very day when I really understood what it means to keep your word, on the very first day of my life as a man. Can anything ever efface that?"

The little cripple's hand had come to rest on his own, and in his palm it felt as hard and cold as the hand of a dead man.

"It's my fault, Philippe. When you knocked, I immediately recognized you through the window. I should have given you time to catch your breath. Yes, you were speaking with the voice of a sleepwalker; your eyes were flickering like lamps."

His two crutches knocked lugubriously together, so he tried to cross them over his chest. But Philippe, flat on his stomach, didn't take his eyes off the resolute little face, level with the ground, slowly illuminated by the day. The insidious light emphasized its excessive, pathetic mobility. He observed the sad arch of the mouth, the pale dual hollows of his dimples, the anxious sweep of the gaze followed by an unexpected concentration, all the secret rites of a familiar drama he had known for so long.

"Too bad," he murmured under his breath as if for them alone, as if the old house could hear. "Don't worry about that, Philippe, never turn back, never think about anything but the day after tomorrow. But then let's hurry! Let's hurry and do great things together; I'm so afraid I'll not be able to follow you all the way to the end, that you'll have used me up before."

He slid both hands under his neck and, illuminated by the light, the whole of his face with its sweet, ageless smile again became unrecognizable. "Answer me, Steeny, don't be stubborn. Or else take me a little farther away, over toward the stables. They'll be up any minute now."

"It's not worth it," Philippe said. "I haven't got much left. Oh, Lord! Why did I tell you that story? It's true I hadn't slept much, and the downpour was pounding on my head, but I'd never so wanted to see you, to touch your hand, to hear you! Just think! From the top of the hill I'd been vainly trying to locate the station lights at Plantier, but there was no way, and the night pushed me on from behind . . . This morning they'll have found the bed empty, my hat still on the table, and when I opened the door, groping my way out, I must have broken something, a picture frame, a vase, I don't know what it was; it crunched under my boots . . . Then, after all, it was only a sentence that was so unclear, the imagination of a dying drunk, something he'd memorized perhaps? . . . Who could say? First of all, just think, he didn't even want to move his eyes. Ginette had pulled his thin arm out from under the covers and shaken him: 'Anthelme! Anthelme! Philippe's here . . . Philippe, little Philippe, you always wanted to tell him something. (Yes, my love, let's not push him too much, let's let him take his time; it's about your father, I think, my love!) Anthelme! Come on, Anthelme . . .' And he snorted, snuffling or moaning in little spasms, shaking his head in opposition – you'd have thought you were looking at a nanny with her little brat – ugh! Finally he did stop sniveling. Woolly-Leg immediately pushed me toward the bed with both hands, her head against my cheek: 'He's going to speak, my angel. Listen! Listen! Release his poor soul a little bit!' And it's then that he said that to me . . . that thing . . ."

"What exactly? Try to remember. Repeat it word for word."

"But do I remember it? He spoke to me of my uncle François, whom I've never seen, and who quarrelled with my mother, of my father who was his friend at the lycée of Etouy — his pal, his real pal! — each time adding on some more incomprehensible words. Ginette's long hands kept passing under my nose — I think she was pinching his sides; he was saying, 'Hee! hee!' and making a face. And don't forget that he stank of alcohol; everything reeked with the smell of alcohol . . . Finally he cried out — but I lied, it wasn't with the voice of a trumpet — he repeated twice, as loud as he could, 'Boy, Philippe is not dead. Your father is still alive, my boy!' After that he gravely shook his chin like some country bumpkin who's just pulled a fast one on someone — such as sell him a cow with a heart murmur or a no-good horse — and he began sniveling again all the harder while Wooly-Leg's tears flowed down my neck. 'Keep that to yourself, Steeny. He wanted it that way; we must respect his wishes, the wishes of a dying man, isn't that right, my angel?' Then she asked me for my word to wait and to say nothing to anyone without her permission. 'Not a word to our friend especially!' Our friend, that's Monsieur Ouine. I gave it, naturally I gave my word . . . Giving your word of honor to Woolly-Leg, I wonder what Monsieur Ouine would think of that!"

"You must bring Monsieur Ouine to me — yes! You must bring him to me, I want you to! Yes! I want it! Promise me that you'll bring him to me tomorrow? You'll bring him to me tomorrow."

"Tomorrow? Why not right now? Do I even know where he'll be tomorrow? Just imagine, old man, that he himself served me dinner on his little old wooden table — marmalade and soft white bread — a real nun's dinner, you might say! And then I drank as I've never drunk before, my friend. Then he must have put me to bed in his own bed. Maybe I saw him afterward, a little later, with a cap on, and in a funny leather overcoat and his ridiculous canvas leggings — you know, the kind they sell in bazaars. Maybe I saw him, maybe I didn't, maybe it was just a dream? When I woke up for good, he had left."

"Left? Left for where?"

"How would I know?"

"All the same, in the middle of the night with rain pouring down! Look! The pastures down there are flooded and the river has risen up to the Langle road."

"What can I say to you? He wasn't in the room anymore, that's all. After that you can easily imagine that he simply went to sleep somewhere else, on the floor above, for example. What's wonderful is that you can imagine him anywhere and in any situation, true or imagined, ordinary or unheard-of, tragic or comic, absurd — he fits into everything, he fits into all your dreams. As for me, on the other hand, I imagined him very easily out in the black night, 'with rain pouring down,' going toward some goal known to him alone, toward his own goal."

"I must see him," repeated the little cripple thoughtfully. "How dare you speak of him in such a way, when yesterday you scarcely knew him any better than I do! What kind of man is he? Ah, Steeny, I'm afraid for you."

"Idiot!"

"Oh no, Philippe, I see more than people think, here on my perch all day long, with that dirty village under my eyes. I had so hoped that you'd take me away from here, my friend! And now, it seems to me . . . Yes, it's no use your laughing! I know more about it than you now, more than any of them, I've suffered too much. You see, suffering is something that is learned. First of all, it's like a little murmur deep inside, day and night. Day and night, awake or asleep, it makes no difference! It even happens sometimes that you think you don't hear it anymore, but all you have to do is prick up your ears: it's always there and speaking in its own language, an unknown language. Weeks and weeks will pass, and then suddenly, all at once, you start to understand. Oh, no doubt there is understanding and understanding! Naturally there are no words or sentences that you can repeat as such, and yet a conversation is established, and you are no longer alone; you will never be alone again. Even when you feel yourself all hollow and all empty, suffering asks the question and gives the answer, thinking for you. All you can do is let it get on with its work. When I think of what I was just a year ago, why, Philippe, I'm ashamed! So awkward and so primitive! I couldn't have been of any use to you."

"And now?"

"Now I no longer try to understand, I don't need to; it seems to me that all your suffering passes through me."

He turned his eyes away. Steeny's handsome face had hardened and his lips trembled.

"Don't you dare . . . ," he said.

But his voice expressed not so much anger as a sort of fierce, irrational fear.

"Besides, it's not real suffering," he continued, shaking his head. "I forbid you to call that suffering. For a long time now I've no longer had a home — a brick cage with two pretty animals in it, that's not a home."

"Oh, Philippe!"

"Well, so what? If the word offends you, think about turtle-doves — or pigeons — I'm not going beyond the limits of poetic licence. Besides, the comparison is valid for only one of the two. You can't look at Maman without thinking immediately of a gilded cage. But the other one . . . I imagine her instead with a steel muzzle on her perfidious little snout, like my pet ferrets. What difference does it make? Don't you see, Guillaume, people are always talking about the father's house. It doesn't matter if it's a little stupid or a little romantic, but it's true that there's no such thing as a mother's house."

"Well, then?"

"Well, I've never felt myself so free, old man. Light as a bee. I'll make my honey everywhere."

"You're not thinking about what you're saying, Philippe. Why lie? You've said to me a hundred times: 'What I hate most in the world is for things to be too easy.' You're disgusted by things that are too easy."

"Well, then? When I add up the time we've spent looking for heroes in our books, it makes me want to give us both a kick, Guillaume. Every generation should have its own heroes, heroes according to its own heart. Perhaps we've not been judged worthy to have new ones, and they're just serving up those served up before. Served up since 1789 with a slight decrease around 1880, favoring the heroes of science, those other soldier-citizens, those other liberators of the people, those other champions of democracy, of rights, damn! Damn and damn! The most comical, old man, is that in 1914, forced to justify the definitions in the schoolbooks, the press, turning out their popular prints, could hardly keep up with the orders. Three . . . five . . . six million heroes all at once. As many heroes as there were coins to pay for them! It makes you digusted with those bronze statues. Long live heroes made out of almond paste!"

"Still, you're being hard, Philippe. Nothing can ever change all that."

"Hard? I'd say rather that I'm being eager. Ah yes, eager. Don't you find they all seem to be looking at life from afar, from the bottom to the top, their hat in their hand, as if it were a monument? Do you understand what I mean? A palace, a cathedral, a museum – or maybe just a police station or a savings bank – according to their own taste. For us, though, life should not be a goal, it's a prey. And not a single prey, but thousands and thousands of them. And what it's all about is not missing a single one of them before the last one, the last one of all, the one that always gets away from us – oops! It's a thing that moves and that you jump on top of. From that time on, provided you get hold of the beast, what difference does it make whether it's by trickery or by strength? You can chase it or wait for it, stalk it, make it break cover discreetly or with fanfare, or take it in its lair. Or you can swallow it as you go along, like a trout moving against the current and gobbling up spawn. He said to me, 'I shall teach you to fill yourself with the hour that passes!'"

"Who's that, he? Oh, no need to answer! Listen, Philippe, it's horrible; I'm sure you've just spoken exactly like him, I'd never have recognized your voice."

"True! But don't make fun of him, Guillaume. In full daylight, with his eyes half closed, his smooth, hairless cheeks, he looks like just anybody, a road engineer, a bad priest. You have to see him in his little room at Néréis — you'd say it was a maid's room — between those four bare walls. You know, in the midst of all those people who resemble one another and whose resemblance is so ridiculous, so odious and obscene — all just alike, how low can you get! — you'll suddenly meet certain ones and think: that one there is Rastignac, or Marsay, or Julien Sorel — but then you feel almost immediately that it's not true, that you're playing a game with yourself, with your dream, as a kitten might play with its tail. While Monsieur Ouine . . . Why, that word 'hero' — you couldn't even pronounce that word without laughing when he fixes his life-less gaze on you, that gaze that seems to float along on the surface of gray water. And yet . . . For our heroes, they too all resemble one another, you have to admit it! As for him, he is special, unique."

"Hush!" said Guillaume. "You don't love him."

"I don't need to."

"You're using him against yourself to avenge yourself. My God, Philippe! Nothing's going to stop you!"

"What are you complaining about? That was part of our rules, old brother. Straight ahead, always. And when the first step is taken, all you have left to do is keep your balance — the slope guides you by itself. That's why I'm wondering why I came to your house this morning. I've broken my word and I'm dying of cold in my soaked jacket. What a nice recompense!"

"Come closer," said the little cripple, gently. "Come closer so that I may hold your hand between mine . . . There . . . like that . . . My God, Philippe, you're going to leave me alone, I'll perhaps never see you again. How can I express in a minute what I've taken so many days to understand? And note that it would have been obvious to anybody. Philippe, in your house you've filled too long the place of someone dead."

"So?"

"Don't interrupt me. Otherwise I'll not be able to go on, I'll lose the thread. There is death and then there's death. Those who are worn out, those who are resigned, those who are ill and, because of fevers and sweats, have wound up disgusted with their bodies, hating them – I've known all that, Philippe – or else those who've been surprised by a catastrophe and entered the darkness with their eyes wide open, just as they were, with their poor little daily cares – a letter to write, a visit to make, a meeting, a drink somewhere, just anything – while . . ."

"How stupid you are! Whether the chimney gives way, the bus rolls over you, or the bullet's in the middle of your forehead, what difference does it make?"

"An enormous difference, Steeny! Death can take them unprepared, but it doesn't surprise them. Brought down in the midst of life, with all their strength and nearly always at the very minute when they were bringing their soul's last reserves of energy into play, do you understand? How could those dead be like the others? How can you expect them to accept it and be resigned to it? Yes, yes, just listen, listen to the end. Now this idea never leaves me, day or night. Especially at night. Toward two or three o'clock when the fever has dropped, there's a silence around me that is so deep – you can't understand! – so deep that I figure . . . My God, must we believe that nothing, nothing passes from one world into the other, nothing ever? A murmur, or a hum, anything? Have you never taken a walk on an October evening in the direction of Brinqueville, on the plain, when the wind is coming from the northwest? If you put your ear down to the ground and hold your breath, you'll finally hear a sort of muted rolling unlike any of the noises of the plain, it resounds in the hollow of your chest, squeezing your heart: it's the great tide of the equinox around Roulers or Briville over yonder . . . Perhaps you've put your ear just where you have to, to the place where it begins to be perceptible – it's no louder than the sound of a cartwheel – that immense breaking of waves that goes off repeating itself over thousands and thousands of miles of ocean, under skies other than our own – no louder than the sound of a cartwheel, do you realize? Well . . ."

"I see what you're getting at . . . But don't worry, old man, the dead are dead."

"Not those! Not the way you think!"

"How ridiculous! Quite to the contrary, people immediately forgot those dead you're talking about. There were too many of them."

"Forgot them . . . Forgot them . . . You mean they pretended to forget them, Philippe. They are still too near, much too near; they've not yet let go of the world, they're clinging to it. Come on now, Steeny, when a dead person is venerated, well, then he is really dead. Veneration makes a model of him, an example, a symbol – an abstraction. But these aren't yet at the point of being sustained by clouds of incense. People claim they've rejected them; that makes me laugh. As if those dead were conquered! And what if they were tyrants – that's it exactly – our masters, our real masters? 'They wouldn't have thought, they wouldn't have wanted . . .' Does one know what they think or what they want? What if they were the cause of this universal disorder? As for me, I see them clearly still, hovering at that threshold they crossed too quickly, trying to make themselves come back over it in spite of themselves – their attacks are shaking the world. One, two, three generations perhaps will have been ruined by them for lack of having been able to form another generation in their image – their true, authentic image, not those pictures for birthdays and anniversaries – but their true likeness, the likeness of their last gaze, of their last cry when all life abandoned them in a single blow and they clawed the earth they bit. But you'll see that they'll win, Philippe, they'll not always miss their aim. They'll finally have their own generation, and God knows what it will be. Their own generation belonging to them, body and soul. Surely nothing in common with that statue in the square before the city hall with its great big zinc moustache! Besides, it doesn't seem to me, old man, that we have long to wait for them, for their heirs—their legitimate heirs. They're already on their way. Take you, for example, Philippe . . ."

"Me!"

"Yes, you! Your eagerness, your hardness, your passion for revenge—that rage to contradict yourself, to go against yourself, as if you'd already accomplished great things, memorable things, and that they had disappointed you . . . Your admiration of Monsieur Ouine, for example, your idea of a reverse heroism . . . Alas, Philippe, it'll be too late when you get tired of these battles against yourself; I'll be dead."

In that minute his face, all luminous with intelligence and determination, confronted the bare landscape, so poor, so naked in the fog.

"I've often thought about that," Steeny said with a gloomy voice. "Do you think I'm so stupid as not to have understood a long time ago that it's not just me they're afraid of over there? But what difference does it make to me now? Yes! What difference does it make, especially to me, if my father is alive?"

"My God! Philippe, can you in believe such news and then speak of it as of something of no importance? You just don't believe it's possible!"

"Even if he's alive, he'll still be dead for me, as dead as he'll ever be, really, truly dead. I'll never forgive him, ever."

"You don't think it's possible?"

"Don't make me mad! Do you believe in those marquises of Vandomme? In all the history of the Ardennes and Lorraine there is no more sign of a Vandomme than there is on my hand; you've said to me twenty times: 'We've been had by the little man in green.' Well, then, you and I are now both in the same situation: no more ancestors, the world's beginning! That's the way I like it."

He had got to his feet, in his rain-soaked jacket, and just at the height of his shoulders Guillaume saw the immense line of hills disappear against the brine-colored, cloudy sky.

"Go on," said the cripple with gentleness, "go away! I mean, move away a little, turn your back to me. I'm sure you're going to cry."

. . . .

"Hup! Steeny . . . Over here, Steeny, my angel . . ."

From the hollow in which they had squeezed themselves the thorn hedge was a barrier they could not cross. Against the still dark sky, even when standing, Steeny could hardly distinguish last spring's growth along the tufted crest. But suddenly, in the silence, the shoe of an invisible horse struck a rock and almost immediately, two steps away, Ginette appeared at the fence.

"Come here, Steeny. Can you come over here, sweetheart?"

Between the gray slats of the fence that inexplicable, violent image of her painted face — made up from the collapsed point of her chin to her high chestnut eyebrows — seemed as lugubrious as a decapitated head at this hour, in this place, in the midst of such a peaceful setting. The great mare coughed in the fog.

"Would you like to do me a big favor, Steeny?" (Slipping her fingers between his shirt and his neck, she drew him gently toward herself.) "Run home and get your bicycle and run tell Monsieur Ouine that I didn't stop in Fenouille. I'm going much farther, much, much farther. All right? You'll do it for me, my love?"

"Maybe," Steeny said with malice. "But first I'm taking my bath."

"Oh, you'll do . . ." she began in her childish voice, turning her back.

But at that very second the mare's chest collided full with hers and, trying to grab the shafts, she rolled down the slope.

"Philippe!"

For a moment the surprised animal sought her bit, shaking the floating reins with rage, but now the boy's small hands were pulling on the bit's long steel protrusions, crushing the delicate mouth. What an admirable release of oneself, what a marvelous forgetfulness! He sensed that under his fingers and within his palms he was completely master of those enormous haunches, of that rump pushed back toward the earth, of those gigantic thighs trembling in pain and white with sweat between two mud splashes. Her resistance broken, she went backward, faster and faster, now retreating before him.

"Be careful!" cried the cripple from the other side of the hedge. "Be careful, Steeny!"

Careful of what? The great mare fell to her knees.

"Filthy beast!"

He let go the reins on purpose and wiped his face glistening with mud. What could he say? What was more depressing than a road washed out by a storm with its double flow of clay, the whole gutter of saturated earth spreading manure in oily puddles? No matter! He saw nothing but the vanquished animal, heard nothing but the squeaking of sweat-soaked leather and his own rough, quick breath coming at a horrid rhythm; with his mouth open he avidly breathed in a smell so hot and so living it seemed the smell of blood. Within him all that normally judged and reassured, accepted or rejected was silent. God knew how many times already, in the course of these last few weeks, he had believed that the daily restraints holding him back had become more fragile, that the monster would rise up . . . "What a rage he's in!" Miss would say with her ambiguous smile, "Look at him, madame! You'd think you were looking at a little bull." Precocious angers that, in spite of the tears, were three-quarters pretended, impotent shams of releasing the imprisoned god. Their lie never stopped poisoning his heart. Whereas today . . .

"Give me back that package, Philippe . . ."

Madame de Néréis's dress was split at the waist and revealed her poor jersey undergarment; a strip of silk had fallen into the yellow water. Was Ginette afraid? Her mouth traced a painful grimace, and the red of her lips had run all the way down to her chin.

"The one in your hand . . . there . . . Come on now, Philippe!"

Ah, a bump had indeed projected a formless thing out of the

carriage and he had caught it . . . "Philippe! Philippe . . ." How she was begging! And yet her gaze no longer begged. Without her knowing it, her two clay-gloved hands with ten painted claws traced some unidentifiable threat in the air, the awkward gesture of one of those childish terrors that will kill on the spot.

"Down with your paws!" Steeny cried, furious. "Couldn't you at least ask politely for this filthy thing of yours?"

He had sprung back and was twisting the package around on the end of its string. In order to keep her eyes on it, Ginette's crazed gaze moved back and forth like a weaver's shuttle. Damn! The rain-soaked newspaper burst open, scattering everything. Steeny leaned over to retrieve a little brown corduroy overcoat . . . "What's that?" he asked with mock laughter. But he had time neither to finish nor even to raise his head, and he let fly an ineffective kick. With a groan Ginette had thrown herself on top of him. When he got back up, his hands were empty and the great mare, now calmed, was moving off, first at a walk, then at a trot.

"You whore! You wretched, damned whore!"

"Come up to the house, Philippe," said the cripple in his grave voice. You can climb up there, just take my crutch. Hey, that's funny, your wrist is bleeding."

"That idiot bit me, I think," Philippe stated. "Yes, all her teeth marks are there on my skin. Oh, oh, Guillaume, she's now turning over there at Roches, you'd even think she's galloping! Yes, I'll say she's galloping! Where the hell can she be going so early in the morning! And don't go shrugging your shoulders like that, old man, you're annoying me . . ."

"I'm not shrugging my shoulders," said the cripple, "you just make me feel sorry for you, Philippe."

With a rapid glance his eyes took in his friend and then, with an extraordinary nobility of accent and a voice so grave and so pure that for a second it even seemed to efface the memory of that inexplicable, lugubrious apparition, he spoke again.

"You make me feel afraid and sorry for you . . ."

"Goodbye forever, Guillaume!" Philippe cried, then took off.

5

The little body had been brought into the assembly room of the town hall and laid out on the table, which had been hastily stripped of its green cover. To the right of it the rural gendarme had strangely placed the two shoes toe to toe, which, with their twisted soles, seemed to signal one another. That was all there was. A cart driver from Croules, a drunkard, had found it that morning by chance, naked, right on the edge of the pond, under the brambles. "It was the current that stripped him, for sure! What a current! The water foamed around him like beer." At first glance, however, he had recognized the Malicorne's little hired boy, a very good boy, not at all given to vice. Damn! His poor head was nothing but a ball of mud and pebbles. "I thought he'd been beheaded, the poor little thing!" he said.

The mayor had just slipped on his trousers. Already the blacksmith's anvil rang out at the end of the silent street, that immense, silent street, freshly washed, caught unprepared by dawn, still full of forms and noises of the day before. For a moment though it seemed clearer and of a lighter hue, and at the height of the great empty bay windows, throwing its reflection on the ceiling, so close, so fresh and limpid that a dying man would have rested his cheek against it . . . But already the shadow had attacked it sideways, speeding from one end of it to the other until it covered the last visible rise, mounting toward Trabloi where the last thin strip of golden light also yielded. With a roar the gray sky seemed to be thrown in all directions, then, just as suddenly, grew calm: a fine rain began falling and the angelus sounded.

"We're in for more rain," the mayor said. "Bad for evidence."

His great eyes distilled a suspect tear, caught and held by his eyelids, but now rolling downward. He'd have to crush it this evening before going to sleep, but night would form another one. Damned clown! His swollen nose, shiny with herpes, with its network of blue veins, its supple roundness and extreme mobility, frightened his wife. It exploded in the midst of that worn face with a frightening, mocking vitality. "It's my magic charm," he used to say to unmarried girls. And more than one of them had wanted to hold his monstrous nose in the palm of her hand, for the former brewer didn't bother hiding his taste for young girls. "Yes, my dear, can you imagine? I felt his heartbeat right at the end of it; it was like holding a live animal." He himself wasn't far from thinking as they thought, but for the moment he kept his secret to himself. Dr. Malépine, using the pretext of a secret boast that the mayor in his need to brag had confided in him, had pressed him, in the midst of the regional delegates' meeting, with certain preposterous questions, speaking of the hypersensitivity of the nervous centers of the tip, and finally treated him as a case of olfactory obsession. "Dear friend, Science calls things by their name: the nasal appendage is in your case one of your organs of pleasure. Please note, gentlemen, that this observation is not a new one:

Duriez cited the example of a patient excited enough by the slightest trace of iodoform to suffer a spasm. His nose would suddenly become colored, and, he even noted — something that seems unbelievable — it took on the phenomena of an erection." A poor wretch with a nose! At first he had laughed with the others, not understanding too much, and he wasn't the least bit ashamed to find himself compared to Monsieur Emile Zola. Moreover, for the slightest grain of doubt to be born, for that very first doubt, it had taken day after day of laziness, day after day of boredom, whole long days spent under the garden trellis, facing the thin brick chimney in the distance — the pink roofs of his old brewery, of his old, lost kingdom. And it was true that before the capricious market price for barley and hops had finally given meaning to his every hour, to every minute of his life, he had never been like the other boys . . . And, Lord, it was true that he had smelled and sniffed and taken in more scents than anyone, had lived his youth through his nostrils. But now old age was beginning and it also had its smell . . . His real memory lay there, between his two eyes, in the depths of the obscure caverns of his nostrils. In a gust of wind across the road; or in a passing car, warm under its raised top; or in a new handkerchief being unfolded; or in even less he found the flowing flash of memory, be it of a look, or a face, or of voluptuous signals such as the shadows of a bedroom, an iron bed, or the welcoming millstone dappled with sun at noon . . . Immediately his palms sweated an icy sweat! Unfortunately every one of his memories struck him at the same place in the neck, and his gaze had difficulty tearing those cobwebs spun across his eyeballs by the sudden gush of blood. O ye gods! Scandal of scandals and frightening damnation of idiots! Is it at past sixty that you have to discover that you're not like other people? He whom no woman had ever seen blanch now discovered he had a sort of comic modesty concerning that impure, inexplicably deformed nose. Useless defense! The sneaky idea had worked its way into the densest part of his brain and all the tweezers of the handsome, blond-bearded doctor could now never dislodge it. "Not like the others" — he, the municipal magistrate, the mayor . . . "Hey, Malvina," he said to his dumbstruck wife, "I'd just as soon be a priest!" What could be done? The imprudent Malépine, in speaking of neurasthenia, had only made it all worse. What! The imperceptible wound inherited from some unknown ancestor was there, somewhere inside his brain, that inflamed fold where horror had laid its egg, like a bluebottle fly! Fool that he was — poor fool! — to have drawn so much vanity in the past from his inadmissable talent! Just last week, out fox hunting over by the Goubaud hollows, his companions had stumbled on an old rusty trap at the end of a chain marked with fresh blood. "Hey, Arsène!" They all knew that in his youth he had been thought of being capable of sniffing out, at dawn, the still warm lair under the wet foliage . . . "Hey, Arsène!" But he very properly shrugged his shoulders, though with a grimace of distress. "Idiots! I really pulled one over on you in the past, you imbeciles!" And he'd laugh . . . Alas, the attention he drew henceforth to his bizarre mania, far from calming him, kept him unbelievably excited. A richer, denser air, heavy with smells slipping over each other and piercing one another without mixing, right up to midday when the force of the noon heat spread them out in a thick layer and made them bubble in the sun like fatty matter on water, had never, no, never been better savored and tasted by his accursed nostrils, filtered through invisible little threads, those trillions of nerve endings. Then, in the shelter of a wall, his hat pulled down over his eyes, he knew a sort of respite from having his five senses saturated: the black rest of drunkenness. No one doubted that the disgust, if not the remorse, stemming from pleasures that alas! would return no more, had become a sort of ridiculous delirium for the debauched man, totally besieged as he was by the fear of death. "Hey, Malvina," he shouted one evening, "I'm just a pig at heart!" And she invoked heaven as she raised her two thin arms covered with satiny down by her middle-age crisis: "This poor thing would like to be counselor General and he doesn't even respect himself!" No matter, that cry had soothed his heart all the same. Sometimes he would dream of pursuing his confessions on his pillow, in the middle of the night, of delivering himself once and for all, even if the old woman died of indignation or burst out laughing in his face. While waiting, he washed himself with lots of water every morning and evening, stark naked in front of the pail, rubbing himself with frenzy as if, as Malvina declared, he had a grudge against his old skin. Too bad for Malvina! The next hour was good, no dreams, almost pure. Answering the doctor who, in his language, congratulated him on seeking "through hydrotherapy, even though of the most primitive kind, the relief that certain naive persons expect to find in superstitious practices," he made this deep, heart-rending reply: "What's difficult, you see, is just being merciful to yourself."

. . . .

"Antoine! What the hell! A bit of respect! Respect for the dead!"

The old gendarme, with one arm on the table and with his head buried in the hollow between his elbows, was snoring. His right sleeve was just touching the bloodless little hand, open like a flower.

"And the inspectors still not here! In another hour anything can happen. I'm going to start the investigation myself. Where is the witness?"

"What witness?"

"The man who found the body."

"He's drunk," the gendarme said. "Dead drunk. He made them open up the tavern. It seems he's in there drinking all alone, his arse on two chairs set together, just like a captain."

The mayor did not flinch, but his full, slightly soft cheeks trembled, then reddened. Alas! For weeks now the frightening solicitude of doctor Malépine had woven its magic threads around him. To destroy the reputation of a municipal magistrate or to bring him down, what more was needed than a word one feigned to hold back too long, or a smile, or a silence, or the sudden slip of a look, or the way doctors have of looking into space as if following an invisible projectile, a destiny known to themselves alone. At the evening of his life as a successful business man, filled with the triumphant falling due of old debts to be paid, the former brewer, caught between his unhappy spouse, the confiding schoolmaster, and his gently ironic employees, found himself as disarmed as he used to be in the school courtyard, under the gas jet's single flame spitting and hissing in the wind, while he stuffed the pockets of the girls with crisp little biscuits — yes, even while wearing the tricolor mayor's scarf, he was still like a giant child, a fat boy, eager but fearful.

"We'll do without your commentary . . . no laughing matter . . . responsible for everything . . . You'd do better to show some respect . . ."

Through the half open door rose the smell of hot coffee from downstairs. In a trice the old stove on the ground floor had been emptied of its ashes and stuffed with dry wood, and Malvina, an apron knotted over her serge dress, had filled the coffeepot with little measures for the visiting gentlemen. Her dancing black eyes now darted from one corner of the immense room to the other, scrutinizing every inch of its bare walls. "It's our first crime," she thought. For she believed in crime. Moments before, while Arsène, beside himself, had been turning the window handle in the wrong direction and striking at the shutters with his fist, she had gone up to the little cadaver and turned it over with her silent, expert hands, for she had no fear of the dead . . . And then, well, that's all right! What she had seen was nobody's business.

"Listen, Arsène . . . Come on now, good, there, he's turned green: he thinks the body's moving about."

The rain pounded against the windows. At each hiccup of the drain a gutter answered, far away, with a sort of plaintiff cry, like the call of a toad. Was it really the gutter or maybe the weathervane, or even some thoughtful, bristling crow fallen from the sky? Outside the immense waves of the storm covered everything.

"Somebody's walking about, you big ox. Get up there!"

But he was so ugly, scaling the steps four at a time, his forgotten bottle of gin still in his hand, that she yelled, "Antoine must have left the door of the secretary's office open. It's the doctor, for sure. Put down your bottle."

"There's your bottle for you."

In a rage he threw it full force through a half open window.

"Well, doctor?"

But already in the doorway, once again, alas, his courage failed him. Doctor Malépine turned his beaming face toward the door and, as might a nursemaid to her charge, his mouth attempted a threatening smile.

"Aha! Still another hitch in the order of things! The citizen pays you homage, but the doctor is before you. Unfortunate contradiction!"

His rosy hand with its gold-circled wrist indifferently caressed the gray chest of the little dead boy. It was now as hard as stone.

"Impossible to come sooner—what weather! Tell me, dear friend, the whole thing is as simple as can be. There has been a crime."

"Are you sure?"

"Come, come now!"

With his index finger he moved the chin of the cadaver up and down to reveal, in the wrinkles of the neck, another deeper line, a thin fold the color of eggplant.

"Strangled . . . I'd say strangled by a very fine rope or perhaps a brass wire. You see, the cut is clean . . . No! What? What is it? This little spectacle moves you to that extent? Excuse me, I spoke as to a colleague, without precautions. Come, come now! All you have to do is just not look at him."

"Doctor," the poor man said suddenly with a dramatic seriousness, "they've got it in for me because of my mayor's scarf. They're after my scarf and they'll have it too. I've had some difficult hours. Seven years after having acquired our business—you're not going to believe me, Doctor—I still stuffed my banknotes in a pork bladder; the old lady bought me my first billfold in 1895. A filled billfold, completely round, filled till the stitching's bursting, that's what warms a man's heart. I wore it under my shirt day and night, summer and winter, it took on my warmth, it was like my skin to me. Good God! And now I'm losing their confidence, me the sort of man who owes no one anything, the sort of man who knows about life! Damned little tramp of a kid!"

He shrugged his shoulders in disgust.

"They call that a victim. In a way, Doctor, I find this here more repugnant to look at than the criminal. A criminal, he's like you and me, he comes, he goes, he breathes; he's something living. And you'd have to be mighty clever to read his face. For example, suppose you met him tomorrow in Montreuil or Boulogne, you could easily have a drink with him without knowing it. His crime! What's he still got left him of his crime! What are one or two poor minutes in the life of a man? While these stiffs have crime in their bellies, the pigs! Crime sweats from their pores. Naturally I don't blame them for their misfortune. Before their misfortune, I feel sorry for them, I respect them. But once it's done, once the law can no longer do anything for them, I find evil seems to come out of all their pores, they scatter dishonour all over the countryside, they compromise everybody and mock society. You'll tell me that murderers ought to be punished. Agreed! Only the affair should be taken care of by the police between themselves to avoid scandal, and according to who the victim is. For, between us, is there any sense in putting a whole administration under the command of a wretched little dead cowherd, as if he were a prince of science, for example, or a minister? That snot-nosed little kid is going to cost me my mayor's scarf, just as sure as I'm called Arsène; you can bury it with him in the ground. Look at him! He's lying there so peaceful and smiling, you'd take him for being from a good family, his own mother wouldn't recognize him. Oh, good God! When I saw him go by barefoot behind his herd, could I ever have suspected that one day . . . What wretched misfortune . . . All the more so since one never knows with these rascals, they don't do anything like other people, they have their tricks like savages. If you reprimand them a bit strongly or give one a good slap, there they go killing themselves just to annoy their boss, out of sheer viciousness. Or else the current dragged him along all night out of the riverbed into the bushes, and a poacher's collar snared him as he went by . . . Let's see . . . Yes, let's see . . . Isn't it better to settle this thing rather than risk getting people upset and turning the commune upside down? A peaceful commune like this one, the heart and soul of the canton! Damned wretched little cowherd!"

"Listen, my dear friend, you'll have to say all that to the coroner, who's my colleague. As for me . . ."

With the end of his fingers he distractedly patted the huge cheek of the former brewer, with the same familiar gesture with which he encouraged the confidence of a pregnant girl under the impassive gaze of the black marble Aesculapius presiding on his mantel.

"You're a child, my dear friend. Don't blush like that! All nervous people are children, real babies. Where the devil did you get the idea that so ordinary an affair could cost you your mayor's scarf? How could it? And why? What? What are you saying?"

"Pre . . . Premonition . . . ," stammered the mayor, blushing scarlet.

"Premonitions? Don't bother me with your premonitions. Just wait! One of these days perhaps I'll wind up sending you to confession — yes, I swear it! You have scruples, my dear friend, like so many old sinners when they turn sixty. In brief, there's something that isn't right, there, at the bottom of the epigastrium, right? Or maybe a bit lower still, if you wish, at the pit of the stomach, right, at the seat of the soul . . . There's a whole deposit of obscene images not too easily got rid of now, at least not the way they used to be, right? You old joker! Well, then, one dreams of innocence, of purity, of redemption — what have you — of stupidities. A man given to vice is always an idealist, remember that, my friend . . ."

He distractedly seized the stiffened fist of the dead child on the table, gently massaging it between his two hands, as if to open it.

"Note that you have a perfect right not to believe a word of what I'm telling you. When a big fellow's chased girls all his life, you're not easily going to convince him that he's reverting to his adolescent crisis again . . . Don't blush now, what the hell! Good God, there's nobody here but the two of us!"

"Nothing to reproach myself for . . . absolutely nothing . . . Stupidities just like everybody else . . . Walked with my head up, Doctor . . . Looked right into the faces of . . . of . . ."

"Good enough! That's just what I asked of you, to look people right in the face, calmly, right in the eyes. Even the best of them aren't worth much."

Having laid the still closed little hand on his knees, he delicately inserted the end of a ruler into the palm, unlocking the fingers one by one without forcing them.

"You see, Arsène," he continued — but this time in a low voice — "you'd be well advised to watch what you say. The duty of a magistrate is to help the law, not to hinder it . . . Besides, the hypothesis of suicide doesn't stand up."

"I'll find that noose, for God's sake!" the mayor cried suddenly with a thundering voice. "Yes, we'll go down to the riverbed with the inspector's gentlemen — there are mud slides along the banks, some idiot perhaps wanted to snare otters — people are so stupid! And who the hell would have killed that kid anyway? Let's imagine it was some marauder, some wanderer, the road's open to everybody, isn't it? And in that case one could say that the affair doesn't even concern the commune. While . . . while . . ."

Twice he slowly, solemnly turned his great purplish head from right to left with its vague, milky stare, so like that of very small children.

"I'd just as soon kill myself," he said.

"Wait and see what happens," the doctor replied, with an overly calm voice. "The end promises to be exciting, my dear friend . . ."

At floor level, the little empty hand, henceforth without a secret, oscillated imperceptibly, hiding and revealing in turn the blackened hollow of its palm. Brusquely the handsome doctor put it back up on the table.

"A carriage? Already? Ye gods! Those gentlemen from the prosecutor's got up early this morning."

"It's not the prosecutor's gentlemen," the mayor said from the window, "it's the madwoman of Néréis, Woolly-Leg, with her mare . . . Must be that Monsieur Anthèlme has passed on."

"Just a minute, Arsène, just a minute! Keep her downstairs, my boy. She is quite capable of having sniffed out our cadaver from her perch over there, just like a crow."

. . . .

Standing in the doorway the lady of Néréis said, "They've put him in here, poor angel."

The big man did not even turn around. With shoulders drooping, neck bent, and arms falling by his side in a sort of total abandonment, he exposed his sad face to the rain-streaked daylight. And for just a second the gaze of the handsome doctor, so lively behind his pince-nez, enveloped, as though with a touch of fire, that face, which suddenly became unfathomable — unified and as if blotted out by shame, by despairing self-pity, by remorse, a remorse with neither name nor cause.

"It would be advisable for you to leave as of now, madame," he remarked with surprising gentleness. "There's nothing you can do here."

But already she was approaching him with her magnificent gait. Her fall had plastered her thigh with a big patch of mud, and some of that mud was still on the back of her naked, bramble-scratched arm, as well as on her inflamed face where she had touched it no doubt with her hands. By a miracle she managed to stay erect in her ridiculous little water-soaked, velvet slippers; and as she walked, she was obliged to keep kicking aside a torn panel of her long skirt in a gesture of childish annoyance. She took a seat.

"So many difficulties, what a situation! The big mare sawed the reins into my hands — yes, Doctor, just look at them — what a mad creature! Up there, on the plain, can you imagine, that western squall hit us from the side; she started whinnying in terror, yes, monsieur, I thought I couldn't hold her and that she was running away with me . . ."

"What are you doing with that damned package there?" asked the doctor of Fenouille. "You've picked it up on the way, fished it out of the stream, no?"

She laughed.

"Isn't it awful? It's those dirty children, Steeny especially, the mean little devil! He had a fight with the big mare, tore my dress, and I saw him down on all fours in the mud, flaming with anger — a real cherub . . . But that's enough chattering, Doctor. I didn't come here for any reason except to fulfill my duty; I wish now to speak with the examining magistrate."

"Oh, really! If it's about carrying out a mission, no need to wait, we'll get on with it ourselves. But first, Arsène, open the window. Even if nature hasn't endowed me as generously as you in regard to smell, I can still tell good smells from bad ones. And you have a devilishly bad smell, lovely lady, no offense meant!"

"Really? Lord, but I'm sorry!" she said. "Don't you think that . . . that that might come . . ."

She touched the mayor's arm with her long hand, still so pure under the mud and axle grease.

"Rubbish!" the doctor answered grossly. "We know all about you, and I know your rat's nest. I say, there, Arsène, give me the tongs, will you? I'm not going to touch that package without a pair of tongs."

"It's not so dirty, I swear," she protested with a frightening smile. "It's just mud, a little bit of mud . . . In any case, monsieur, allow me, I'll untie it myself."

Her magnificent, humiliated gaze, the magic gaze that had devoured the whole life of a man, moved between her two executioners like an innocent animal.

"Not on the table," the doctor yelled. "On the floor, don't you understand? On the floor, for God's sake!"

"All right, all right," she said. "Don't get angry, what difference does it make! See, there is the little shirt, the trousers, the suspenders. But I only found one shoe. Perhaps the current carried off the other one?"

Using the toe of her cracked boot, she set out each piece in turn on the floor.

"What's all this great display? Where did you find all this, my dear?"

Malvina watched in silence from the doorway, both hands on her apron.

"Go away, madame!" the unfortunate creature implored, shuddering.

"I'm in my own house, madame," replied the mayor's wife, nodding her head with a mocking seriousness.

"Very well, madame. Then I shall speak, madame, only before the examining magistrate."

"Oh no you won't! You'll speak right now, my girl!" the doctor of Fenouille concluded nonchalantly. "Get some paper, Arsène. Take my fountain pen, dear friend. I'm listening to you, my dear."

"Don't write anything! No, monsieur! Don't write anything," she moaned. "All of this is between us, swear it. Yes, yes, Doctor! Say, 'I swear it.' Not a word before you've sworn, not a word. And don't ever let him know about it – never ever – do I have your word, Mr. Mayor? Never! He'd kill me like a mouse."

"Ah, Ah, now you're getting there very nicely," the doctor said, laughing till he was close to tears. "Do you see her coming around, Arsène? Obviously it's about your boarder. Listen," he continued, "get on with it quickly, let's get this little formality over with. For a year now – and we shan't speak of those anonymous letters the public prosecutor throws regularly into the wastebasket – you have accused him of I don't know how many kindnesses, everything from simple swindle to the attempted murder of your own precious person and that of your husband – ridiculous accusations melting away with the first witness heard. Damned chateau of Néréis! Damn its squire and lady! Fire, you understand, lovely lady, fire is what's needed to put an end to that spawning ground of lies and frogs. A nice fire, I tell you, what the hell! And for the lady of the chateau, a sulphur shirt, as in the time of the monks, yes, a pretty little sulphur shirt, very stiff, very rough, and you inside it, wearing a pointed hat."

"What a sense of humour!" she said, forcing herself to smile. "But how dare you speak that way before the dead . . . Oh, my God! How beautiful he is, how he's listening to us . . . Well, Doctor, I officially accuse . . ."

Again she cast a frightened look in the direction of the mayor's wife.

"Gentlemen," she began again in a low voice, "I found these clothes in the bedroom . . . No, not exactly in the bedroom, let's be exact. You know that the door of his bedroom opens out onto a sort of hallway . . ."

"All right, all right," the doctor of Fenouille said coldly, "spare us the details. In brief, you officially accuse your boarder Monsieur Ouine of the murder of this young man. Very good. Dear friend, ask your wife for a few old newspapers and for some string. I don't think we're going to leave these filthy things scattered out on the floor any longer, are we?"

Madame de Néréis gently shrugged her shoulders and began to pick up the old clothes, one by one, laying out each garment in the hollow of her poor skirt. A large tear fell on her hands.

"And what do you as the mayor think about that?" the gallant doctor shouted suddenly with feigned anger. "Do we or don't we have the criminal? For ten minutes I've watched you stare at this very interesting helper of the law as if you wanted to devour her. Damn it all! I too have a score to settle with madame, and I'm not unhappy to have an opportunity to do it, damn it all! Isn't that right, my lovely? For a long time now you've been running about the roads, though any administration a bit concerned about the morality of this commune would have locked you up the first day. Yes, locked you up, confined you! When you're over there, surrounded by your lawns or at the rear end of your devil of a mare, you are a lady. But here, in front of me, you are only a case, and a rather ordinary one at that — you're nothing. Do you understand,

Arsène? This interesting individual has probably destroyed one man and has undoubtedly got nicely started on the other one. Well, removed from a situation where she can do harm – under my supervision, I should think – off in some well-run clinic, I tell you I'd turn her into a harmless creature, as gentle as a little dog. Look, see for yourself . . . All you need is tact and staying calm and authority, especially authority . . . I was Duriez's collaborator, which says everything. A very modest collaborator, dear friend, a simple extern assistant, but one who had his eyes open and knew how to get on with things. I was a real medical student . . . The real medical spirit is disappearing, dear friend; we are being replaced by bespectacled fellows, hairsplitters, experts in physics, in chemistry . . . Indeed, indeed, the medical profession is above all others, but it demands real character . . ."

The mayor of Fenouille agreed, nodding his head, approving with his enormous face made for laughter, yet harboring an unspeakable, ghostly tenderness. The words rang in his ears with a sort of incessant murmuring, with neither beginning nor end, to which the speaker's gestures and expressions seemed to add a supernatural exaggeration. For the vulgar brutality of that little man now held sway over him, over his own weakness. Just like an animal, he sought in the mysterious face of his master the sacred signs from which his punishment or pleasure was born.

"I say, there!" the mayor's wife called from the doorway, "are you going to use up all my string? Lend her your knife, Arsène."

"Enough string!" the doctor said. "Set the package on the mantelpiece. Good! Excuse me for having spoken so frankly, lovely lady. You are ill and I am a doctor, so an ill person is of more interest to me than a dead one. Come now! If there's still some little secret in your head there, tell it to me rather than to the examining magistrate . . . In your own interest – I insist – in your very own interest, my dear . . ."

His voice had lost some of its burlesque assurance while his hands, placed flat on his knees, traced the gesture of a bird catcher, a sort of timid, enveloping caress. And it was toward those hands that she irresistibly lowered her proud gaze, with the immense, inexorable patience of a trapped animal. For a second, sheltered under her long, closed eyelashes, her eyes moved toward the open window, toward the horizon, toward the disappearing hills, the telescoped line of the Vernoul woods, the cloud riven by the wind, toward space.

"Well, then – did I understand correctly?–your boarder is supposed to be the author of this murder?"

"Yes, Doctor," she said. "I swear it."

"Keep your oaths for later. First of all, what proof have you got?"

"I . . . well, I saw him."

"Good! Mr. Mayor, write down that she was a witness to the murder."

"Wait! Not . . . not of the murder, you understand. My goodness! That is, I was up all night, we were up all last night, last night like all the rest. Monsieur de Néréis died at five in the morning."

"Oh! What's that? Anthelme is dead?"

"Yes, monsieur," she said with the same smile. "At five o'clock. He did suffer, monsieur."

"Madame should think about making a declaration of death," said the mayor. "Madame is not above the law."

"Our friend must have gone out around midnight. He came back two hours later. I found this, I swear, in the back of the closet, under a huge sack of potatoes, yes."

"That's all?"

"Yes, gentlemen, that's all."

"That's all," repeated the doctor, imitating her, with a flutlike voice as he leaned his head to the left. "You call that a testimony, do you? But there is still the anonymous letter, that's for sure. I bet that they'll find an anonymous letter in the mailbox of the public prosecutor, right, my lovely? No doubt the honorable Professor Ouine will tomorrow be just where you hope to put him, gracious Nemesis . . . And as for the filth that is wrapped here in this newspaper . . ."

He took out his watch.

"We're going to know in a moment what to believe. I've asked the Malicornes to come at nine o'clock. Madame! Madame!"

"They're just coming up," said the voice of the mayor's wife from the stairwell.

"Just a minute! Just a minute! You can't come in here as if it were a mill, damn it all! There's a dead body, what the hell!"

Turning his back to the table, he tried to hide the cadaver, casting looks of compliance and distress, looks overflowing with sympathy and professional unction in the direction of the still invisible visitors.

"Excuse us, Doctor," the new arrival stammered, more upset than reassured by this pantomime totally incomprehensible to him. "He was my employee, I have my rights . . . You can come in, Alida, don't worry, there's nothing to put you off . . . Besides, in the town hall we're all in our own home, isn't that right, Arsène?" he concluded on a tone of false cordiality, evading the mayor's eyes.

"Do what you've got to do," replied the old woman from behind the door. "I couldn't bear to look at him."

The old man shrugged his shoulders in scorn, went up to the table, and heavily laid his hand on the chest of the dead boy.

"He never gave anything but bother," he said, "a poor little boy without meanness, but really annoying all the same. You should see him, Alida, he looks alive, as if he were going to speak."

"Don't insist, my friend," the doctor of Fenouille intervened with a great gentleness. "The examining magistrate will decide whether or not it's necessary for madame to look at the victim. Believe me, such sights are not for everyone. But since the first magistrate of this commune has seen fit to receive your testimony first of all, let me ask you a question, just one. You may answer it or not answer it, as you wish."

"That depends . . . ," the other replied. "Come on in here, Alida, I tell you, for God's sake! You see, Doctor, she's able to weigh the pros and cons; she remembers everything."

The old woman made her entry, walking backward, facing the wall.

"Do you recognize these clothes?" the former nonresident assistant asked in a solemn tone. "There's no hurry, my good woman, think about it."

"It's already been thought about," she said. "My goodness, of course I recognize them!"

"Aha!"

All of them, in no special order, approached the window, bending over the poor garments. The sickly smell of mud and stagnant water caused them to blink.

"Weigh your words, madame. You state that the victim was wearing these garments the night of the murder?"

"Oh no! Oh no!" she said. "Cloth garments? Come on now! He stopped wearing these at the first cold spell. I should tell you that toward All Saints' Day Monsieur Anthelme engaged him to harvest his potatoes for ten days at five francs a day. He came back with a brand-new corduroy suit, right, Jules? But I'm still waiting for those fifty francs, no offense meant."

"Madame de Néréis," the doctor of Fenouille began in triumph . . .

But their eyes searched vainly for that extraordinary woman. The deserted street, sparkling with water, gaped in the sun, reflecting the light like a mirror. And far off in the direction of Saint-Vaast, when they held their breath, they thought they twice heard — then once more — the whinnying of the great mare in the west wind.

"What really bothers me about them is their nature," Philippe thought. "The only thing I've ever loved is the road. A road knows what it wants. And not tomorrow; today. This very day."

"Today . . . ," he repeated, hastening his step, as if intoxicated. "Yes, this very day!"

Magnificent road! Cherished road! How vast its promise, how inebriating its friendship! Man, who had made it inch by inch with his own hands, had dug it to its very heart, to its heart of stone, then finished it off and cherished it, had discovered he no longer recognized it and thus believed in it. For was life's great chance, that supreme, unique opportunity, not to be found on it, there under his eyes, there under his very feet, on that fabulous, endless, open stretch, on that miracle of solitude and escape, on that sublime arch launched toward the azure? For though man had fashioned it and given himself that magnificent plaything, as soon as he trod upon its amber-colored surface he forgot that his own calculations had already traced its inflexible itinerary in advance. Thus, at his first step upon that magic soil, though bare and sterile under its rounded armored surface that defended what he had snatched away from earth's overwhelming, hideous fertility, even the most forsaken man regained confidence and patience, dreaming that for his poor, wretched soul there might perhaps be some fate other than death . . . Hope is unknown to him who has never seen the road stretching ahead, between two rows of trees, fresh and alive at dawn.

"It's today," Philippe repeated again, "this very day . . ."

Why not tomorrow? Tomorrow would be too late. Once you've lost the chance, it's lost forever. In just about twenty-four hours, he told himself drunkenly, a whole life can be lost. And a certain caressing voice he had never heard before, as hideous on that bright morning as lust on the face of a child, kept sighing after him: "Lose it! Lose it!" Yet some phrase he had read somewhere — unfortunately he'd forgotten where — throbbed within his memory with the regularity of a clock's ticking: "He who would save his soul will lose it . . . He who would save his soul . . . He who would save . . ." Hell!

His intoxication of the night before, his lack of sleep, and the dampness of his still wet clothing sustained his slightly feverish feeling, a sort of edgy anguish from which he derived an illusion of absolute lucidity. How magic that hour when our first youth, like some great poisonous flower, rises bit by bit from depths to which it will never return and, thrusting upward toward the surface of our consciousness, reaches our brain like venom. Magic hour indeed when the little human animal is finally able to give an intelligible name to his strength and joy and grace that are no more. No matter! For a few weeks now, perhaps only for a few days, he told himself, I am my own master . . . The road was so fresh and so pure, streaked with shadow, so similar at that moment to the idea he had of himself, that, had it been possible, he would have bathed his face and hands in it, plunged into it as into pure water. For constantly coming back to him was the thought of a completely new life, all luminous, totally intact — indeed, intact and unstained — a life just as he wanted it, miraculously restored to his hands again, so intact that the slightest caress, the slightest touch even, would smudge it forever, yes, a life remaining intact forever until the radiant burst of death, of a death as different as possible from the image of death he had always dreamed of, finally crowned its joy.

. . . .

"Oh, oh," he said suddenly, "it's the great mare!"

In the distance four horseshoes rose and fell, striking the wet earth without a sound. At least he couldn't hear them. Nor could he see the bounding rump. The sort of hallucinatory state in which he had been plunged enclosed him in a mysteriously protective circle: he thought he even felt this mysterious protection moving about with him like a palpable light, like the silk cocoon where the larva is left to mature. For a brief flash even the whole countryside seemed nothing but a strangely colored fog, a palpitation of forms and hues from which was suddenly detached, with sharp incisiveness, solitary and bare, the trembling mare, her head held high. A blue shadow sailed under his feet.

"Ho! Ho!"

It was not fear, but rather a boundless curiosity that fixed him to the spot where he stood, or perhaps even a curiosity stronger than fear. "What? What's got into her?"

At thirty feet away the mare clearly veered to the left, heading straight for him like a thunderbolt. In almost the same second he tried, in an absurd gesture, to push back her enormous sweat-drenched chest. But already he was lying at the bottom of the ditch, the breath knocked out of him. Up above him, in solemn silence, a wheel of the overturned carriage still spun at full speed.

"Just missed me," he thought. "The carriage turned over just in time."

He was excited by the idea that what he had just escaped was not a mere accident, but an actual attempt at murder. No, he'd tell no one, not even . . . Monsieur Ouine, perhaps? Then, suddenly, a horrid doubt shot through him. "Will I be able to get up? Can I walk?"

Before he had even finished asking he was already on his feet, staggering, dazzled by the light, as if just rising from a good sleep. Twenty steps away, the mare fed peacefully on the grass of the slope, a broken shaft dragging behind her. There was nothing on the road for as far as he could see.

"Where the hell did she go? Ginette," he called, scarcely raising his voice, "don't go acting crazy now, come on out, you filthy beast!"

Looking like a giant insect, the carriage, completely turned over, revealed its underside of black varnish, iron fittings and grease. Beside the carriage whip, snapped cleanly in two, a strap trailed in the grass. He crawled up the slope on all fours to get a better view.

"Just look at it!"

And just at that moment he saw her.

The last swerve had projected her to the opposite side of road like a stone from a slingshot. Her dress, now in shreds, was strangely bundled up around her long legs, and she was slowly dragging herself toward the shade like a wounded animal, her arms gathered under her breast, her face against the ground. Struck dumb with terror and disgust as well as by a more ambiguous feeling rising up in him, he watched her twist along the ground for a long time. The uncoordinated movements of her shoulders and hips, the horrid rigidity of her neck, and the limp immobility of her legs reminded him of how his old spaniel, Kim, had died. He had found him at almost exactly the same spot with his back broken from a blow a tramp had given him. Advancing imperceptibly by quick starts, she did not move straight forward but at an angle, just as the wounded dog had done. Philippe couldn't take his eyes off the slightly bloody trail her invisible face left behind as it dragged along the earth. What should he do? What he saw there seemed less like a living creature than some monstrous broken toy.

"Nice work, my boy!" a voice said.

The man, in no hurry to come down to the bottom of the slope, turned his swarthy little cropped head in quick jerks from one direction to another.

"Don't touch a thing, boy! Be careful! The law says you have to make a report first. You can ask the first person who comes along; it's a busy road. Goddam! Her carriage went all the way toward the left, and that shaft there is rammed in the ground a foot deep — she was aiming at you, boy, sure as anything!"

"Just mind your own business, all right?" Philippe snorted. "Don't make trouble. Where did you come from anyway, you big know-it-all?"

"Where did I come from? Where did I come from? Well now, boy, I'm going to tell you. I came out of the hedge you see right there at the end of the Fontan property. From that big walnut tree, mister, you can get a view of the road all the way to Meursault. I saw everything that happened."

He was a woodcutter from Alsace who had arrived with a crew to work the Saint-Vaast forest. The old forest had been sold, resold, then sold again, passing from hand to hand in the depths of sordid law offices until, suddenly, its fate finally fixed, it had been laid low in twenty weeks, brought down and trampled underfoot, sold off day and night by the trainload, with the last triumphant load passing through the village with band and flags. Then silence had fallen once more upon the gutted young woods, naked and trembling in the winter wind . . . This swarthy character had stayed on because of a broken leg.

"She's still now," he said, "really still. She's stopped twisting around, boy. She'll pull through, sure as anything; lunatics are worse than drunks, man! No one's got their luck! And

just look at that mare running loose! She behaves so nicely now,
grazing with that damned sideways look of hers, just look at the
bitch! She deserved to get her legs messed up in all that . . . I'm
just going to try to catch her."

He carefully tightened his leather belt.

"Without giving you any orders, boy, you could perhaps give me
a hand . . ." "Oh, I see!" said Philippe. "So it's the mare, is it? I must
say, old man, you've really got your nerve, any way you look at it!"

"Nerve? I've really got my nerve?" the little man shot back,
making a horrid face. "And where is it you would want us to be
moving your girl friend, eh? Tell me that! She got herself into the
shade by moving on the sly and without even seeming to, if you
please – the sneak! – and you're not going to be able to get her to
budge a single paw now. She could show an insect a thing or two
about patience, I can tell you, because that's what she really is, an
insect. But the people around here are too stupid, the young ones
keep their traps shut, the older ones pretend not to see anything.
They are too much taken in by the prattle of the schoolteacher.
Why, the kids now don't even dare speak of Woolly-Leg around
him for fear of getting slapped. And what business is it of his, the
little runt! Does he even know what an insect is? There's nothing
worse, mister. No wild animal anywhere is its equal. No mess, nothing sordid, nothing that can be seen, nothing that will set off the
police, the detectives, or the investigators with all their big guns,
nothing. Nothing but a tiny sting as she goes by; you scratch it,
then think nothing more of it. Oh, oh, day and night they hear her
buzzing about from one end of the country to the other like a giant fly. Madame de Néréis here, Madame de Néréis there. And she
doesn't hide her plans, drags them right under their noses, sticks
them right under their chins, she does, completely undisturbed.
And as for those boys who brag of having got her to lie on her back
for them, I'll tell you something, mister, all you have to do is watch
them blush whenever she looks them straight in the eyes, all
painted up, and smiles at them like a corpse. Boy, I'm telling you!

Those fellows aren't so bold after all! And it's because she knows the strengths and weaknesses of everybody, the damned mongrel bitch! And that for years and years, can you believe that?"

Still speaking, he moved sideways toward the mare, which was busily cropping the smooth grass of the slope. He went past the animal for a few steps then suddenly sprang, leaping on the trailing rein. Hanging on, he scarcely had time to throw himself out of her way. The mare, brought to her knees for a moment by the violence of the shock, was now rearing and whinnying. One of her shoes whistled past the woodcutter's ears.

"Well, now, that's really something!" Steeny said. "What a lovely way to catch a horse, I must say. Why didn't you use a lasso?"

"She's too mean, the bitch!" his companion answered quietly. "Straighten up there now, you filthy animal! I'm going to tie her up high, because of her rearing. You've got to admit it, she really can paw, can't she?"

He now let himself slide down the slope all at once by leaning back against the bank and crossing his too short arms laboriously over his chest.

"Nobody around," he said, "not even a cat. Funny road!"

Then, winking at Steeny: "How about it?"

The boy failed in his attempt to be insolent in returning the gaze now fixed on him. Something like a cold, icy breath passed over his young face, painfully constricting its features. And he felt, first with anger, then with despair, that his mouth, drawing up for a sob, was once again taking on a childish wrinkle.

"I'm . . . I'm . . . I'm just afraid she's dead . . . ," he said. "I'd never dare touch her. Now go away! Yes, go away!" he repeated, stamping his foot. "Get the hell out of here! Don't you think I can stop the first car that comes along without your help? I forbid you to stay here, you sniggering freak, do you hear! What I do is none of your business!" he shrieked. "Put that in your pocket and get the hell out of here!"

"Well, sometimes . . ." the other muttered, mockingly.

His eyes moved from Philippe to the stretched-out body, then came to rest on the banknote Philippe crumpled now between his fingers. Suddenly his face took on a look of theatrical gravity.

"Be careful, mister," he said. "She's poisonous."

Regaining the top of the bank in a single bound, he disappeared in a few steps, but then his dark round head could suddenly be seen again appearing and disappearing in turn, as he followed the top of the slope.

"You idiot!" he yelled back, "You ass head! She tried to kill you, I tell you. She tried to kill you like a partridge."

The road under him began to move gently, ever so gently, like a gilded animal on a merry-go-round. He could see it between his knees, furtively escaping him, and as soon as he tried to raise his head with his eyes open, it seemed to move in waves, stretching out in every direction, rising and falling against the horizon. So he closed his eyes again. But he could feel it now, under his knees, under his palms — damned road! — it was gently heaving with a slow, regular movement like a delicate belly. Just a second sooner he had been thrown down on all fours by fear, and now it was all he could do just to keep his balance, indeed, to keep his head on his shoulders, to keep it from dropping off, it felt so empty . . . On all fours? Come on now! Get up! Get up! And he tried to detach first one hand, then the other from the earth, straining to pull his body back to an upright position. But it wouldn't work! The whole countryside seemed to be carried along now, slipping into the hollow of the wave. Intermittently, the green and gray of the stretching plain appeared before him, pulsating faster and faster like the throat of a toad.

"Philippe! Come on! Get up, Philippe!"

Such a deep voice, so firm, so serious. Whenever it was broken by too harsh a syllable, he thought he could hear it continue on in a sort of proud complaint, caressing, threatening, scarcely human, yet vibrating in his own breast, espousing every fiber of his being, arousing in him a sort of curiosity stronger than fear, like the sight of blood. Why hadn't he grasped it sooner? Wasn't that the voice he really loved? Besides, what difference did it make whether it was loved or hated? He felt its power as though it were an insult, for it savagely wounded his pride . . . Happy the youth who, brought to his feet in a gasp of anger and astonishment by the initial outrage of desire, stands ready to face it.

"Little Philippe! Get up!"

He regained consciousness. No doubt his head had rolled on the ground. She was holding it tightly between her long, hard fingers, trying awkwardly to bring it up to rest on her knees. But the face bending over his own was not that of Madame de Néréis. Or at least the expression he saw was one totally unfamiliar to him. For what burned in those black eyes — or rather in one of those black eyes, since the other was closed, held shut by coagulated blood and dust — did not resemble at all anything he had ever seen. No pain, no shame, no compassion could ever for a second diminish the great penetrating fire he saw there.

"Leave me alone!" he said.

"No, no, Philippe, get up, my angel! Get up quickly, get up immediately. I'm better now, I'm perfectly all right even, it's all over with. I'd only like for you to pull me back a little there, yes, right here, so my back can rest against the slope."

He got up with a groan. The road was empty.

"Don't pull that way on my arms, Philippe! Put your hand under my shoulders . . . That's it . . . Oh! Oh!"

She breathed cautiously in and out, but holding her head up. And what impatience was in her hands crossed on her bosom, visibly held that way only by force of effort.

"So I frightened you, did I? Funny boy! Do you really hate me, Steeny?"

"I'm just sorry you didn't break your neck, that's how much I love you."

"You're lying! I just saw your feet, on the road. When I opened my eyes, I saw your shadow, standing still, right beside me. Then you felt dizzy, I suppose? Well, just imagine, I thought I was dead too. It was like a great cry, a very great cry, only your ears couldn't hear it, do you understand? A single, great cry coming from one knows not where—from the soul, perhaps? Only in the case of death, of real death, that is, that same cry would rise and rise and rise until the last little particle of silence had been crushed by it—squeak! My idea, Philippe, is that there is no silence in the other world, right? God! I've never felt my body so fragile, like a sort of membrane, a membrane of skin that you can see through, a membrane that a pinprick could burst—splish! And then the cry took possession of me all over, roaring away, and I was sinking like a scuttled ship to the bottom of all that noise."

Her features remained extraordinarily immobile. Was she dreaming? Was she delirious? But the hands she kept joining and disjoining with ever increasing anxiety were, in their own way, speaking quite another language. Their suspect mobility exasperated Steeny.

"Oh yes, you were just playing dead," he said, "you heard everything. That character was right! It's remarkable how you look like an animal, a real one—a giant insect. And one of those nasty ones, too, with antennae, and shells and great chewing teeth and pincers. Yes, and if I got dizzy, it wasn't for the beauty of your eyes, my dear. Just five minutes before you'd tried to kill me, hadn't you, or at least something pretty close to it? Come on now! Don't deny it! I felt myself being aimed at by the great mare as though she were the bead on a gun. And you just missed me. I was supposed to be on the other side of the road now, run through with a shaft: 'Poor Steeny! Poor little angel!' Oh, don't wriggle around so much, stay still, I'm not angry with you. After all, you had your risk too."

"Goodness, how stupid he is!" she said. "If some day you happen to break your right axle, what's going to keep you from veering toward the left, you too? But let's speak seriously, my angel."

She had just turned over on her side, slowly drawing her knees up with a groan. For a minute she remained immobile, her eyelids tightly closed and her lips so pale they scarcely seemed more than a thin shadowy line in the midst of her pallid face. Then suddenly she was upright, standing in the middle of the dazzling road.

She slipped her arm under Steeny's, but gave scarcely any support. Each of her gestures had something inexpressibly vague about it, something useless and unfinished, like the motions of an exhausted swimmer allowing himself to drift along.

"We must save him," she repeated with a sudden seriousness. "Yes, we must save him. Without us, Philippe, he won't be saved. Nothing affects him any more. Oh, if you had seen him coming in at dawn, soaked by the rain, but still calm. Not a single mud stain on his trousers, with his sailor's jacket, and his beautiful hands so clean, those hands that do good and evil with the same indifference, like the hands of some god . . . Listen!"

A train whistled at the bottom of the valley.

She staggered, straightened herself up, then staggered again. In anger she let go Philippe's arm, and the boy looked at her now with a sort of horror. Certainly, whether she were wounded or not, the strange creature before him no longer needed any help: the idea taking possession of her soul little by little had now become that soul, inflaming her every nerve center, regulating even the flow of blood in her arteries, as might a second, unconquerable heart. Steeny thought of the great mare driven at full speed toward the bank . . . Nothing would ever stop that mare either, he said to himself. She was quite capable of running straight into a stone wall. But for whom? And why?

"Listen, Philippe! There's a car that's just taken the Bernoville turn! It will be here in a minute. If it goes by Les Aigues, it can drop us at only a hundred yards from Wambescourt and then rejoin the road to Boulogne at Plansier. Quick! Quick! We must hurry, my angel!"

A moment later they were rolling toward the dark chateau. How it all now seemed like a dream! It's a thread unwinding, Philippe thought. You think it's going to break, but it never breaks . . . Will it ever happen or will I go right on, right to the end of the roll? But does the roll have an end? Quickly glancing around, he caught Madame de Néréis gazing fixedly at him. Smiling, she immediately closed her eyes.

Anthelme's room was now empty, and Philippe could no longer recognize it. By lamplight it had appeared enormous, with its great polished floor tiles and bare walls so high that the cornices were invisible. He now saw that it actually was not much larger than his own room at Fenouille and perfectly ordinary, even banal. Just dirty. But the grime of so many years no longer seemed revolting. It had taken on the marks of something necessary, that living vigor of certain molds. Far from destroying it, water seemed only to have spread its extension deep into the underside of the stones. After the walls had fallen, this grime would still reign over the ruins for a long time until the life-giving juices were finally sucked out by grass and ivy.

.   .   .   .

Ginette had made her way down the deeply rutted, long drive all alone, without a stumble. All alone she had gone up the stairs with her great, untamed, supple steps, each one so frighteningly distinct that they recalled the steps of a war dance. But today that suppleness possessed something both violent and fragile, and her look betrayed the hidden, exhausted stubbornness of some trap-ensnared animal, which, Philippe knew, after the terrible efforts of a night, then of a day and a second night of dragging trap and chain behind it, always expired on its feet, facing the inevitably fatal second dawn.

Far away a clock sounded nine shrill strokes. Nine o'clock. What must Miss and Maman be thinking at home now, those two friends? On such a black night the little cowherd certainly could not have arrived at Fenouille until very late, even if he had run all the way. Miss would have come to the door, shrugging her shoulders, yawning, her great white cape thrown over her pyjamas. Maybe she hadn't even told Maman about it until morning. "He slept over there, at that lunatic's! Go get him immediately! I'll tell Ginette this very evening just what I think of that!"

But Michelle's angers never lasted. She even seemed somehow just to put up with them, as might an indifferent spectator. Undoubtedly it had all ended with her crying on Miss's shoulder, pressing close against that fresh, mysterious neck under the cloud of golden mane. He twice passed his palm over his eyes as if to efface such a vision.

From now on that house with its tree-covered walk would be so far from him! Yesterday still — even this morning, perhaps — he thought he still hated it. But now he would go back with no regret, he would live there like a passenger, ever ready to take off, master of his own secret, and reassured that he really was alone. For what he had been waiting for had now happened. By repeatedly tracing a circle around that soulless house, a circle with a perimeter enlarged each day, for weeks on end — and for him each of those weeks was far longer than a year was for a mature man — he had already been freed, even though he had not realized it. And to break that circle nothing more had been needed than a mere gesture from the hand of an outsider, and, quite probably, even less would have sufficed. But of what importance was either the hand or the gesture, since his own adventure, designed for him alone, awaited him somewhere out there, as well as his own master? For though he thought he had been crying out with all the strength of his soul for liberation, liberation was nothing but an idle word. The means of liberation could not be found in any life. No. It was a master he was seeking, not liberation.

Dear Monsieur Ouine! When that simple man looked at him the first time, rebellion was quelled in Philippe's untamed heart. Yes, from the very first look, since, out of so many words, the boy had retained little except a certain monotonous accent of poignant sweetness, though shaped by sovereign firmness and imperiousness. "If I were going to be hanged," he thought to himself, "he's the one I'd want to read me my death sentence." And it was true that that extraordinary gaze, far, far too kind, much, too much weighed down by knowledge and goodwill, had, as it were, pushed even the memory of those two female tyrants and their exasperating tenderness back into the night, annihilating it. A single moment had sufficed to reduce all of yesterday's memories to a single, hateful, despairing image: that bedroom with its fresh cretonne, that little boudoir with its leafy paper and pompons, its thin-columned fireplace and garish, crude tulip lamp in the dark corner. Those innocent mornings, those noons of perfect azure blue, then the evening stealing from door to door, pierced by the lamps, until it finally came to lie down under the table like a family pet. The never completed rumination of empty hours, of their vain, sweet words, of their nauseous, false playfulness, their rustling of skirts, the sharp glare of their rings, their knowing little laughs, and their perfumes. All of that made you think of a gilded cage — even of a cage tied with a great pink taffeta ribbon — yes, a gilded cage with its four corners turned up like a pagoda, but a cage with nothing in it, absolutely nothing. Whereas, on the other hand . . .

Certainly the thought of that paunchy half-god with his absurd bowler hat on his knees brought out all of Philippe's natural insolence. "Let's bet I give it a kick!" But he knew he would lose the bet. Everything had its place in this marvelous adventure, and even the setting was the one he himself would have chosen, that tiny little bedroom, so perfectly like a maid's room with its iron bed, its paltry light, and the shadow of the pine on the wall. It was in that room that he had felt his life break in two — or at least something he naively called by that name — for he was to understand from now on that the past, like an eggshell, had only been a temporary shelter wherein his joy had already been maturing. What was that joy? Without bothering to give it a name, he tasted it, he possessed it, he absorbed it and he used it up. "You never can stand any sort of constraint," Michelle had sadly observed to him, "and especially those constraints required for happiness." And it was true that for years the very word "happiness" — its three syllables so silly in their juxtaposition — had seemed stupid to him. The word "joy" however intoxicated him with its one syllable, in which he discovered something short, something flashing and irreparable. Whenever he pronounced it in a low voice, it seemed to him that his heartbeat was transformed into a deep reverberation, so deep that it destroyed his pleasure in a second, leaving him in a sort of proud stupor, in a state of devastation at having accepted so great a risk, intoxicatingly certain that he was now playing a dangerous game for himself alone, perhaps even a game he had lost before starting? For he didn't like the word "victory" any better either, it was so enormous, so full of rhythmic mirth, ending off with a ridiculously weak sound. And certainly nothing possibly resembling a victory was evoked by Monsieur Ouine's physical presence, in spite of his mysterious authority. In a flash Philippe grasped that Monsieur Ouine corresponded perfectly to the part of himself he least knew, to a part so secret he couldn't even say whether it was his strength or his weakness, his life principle or his death principle. He felt confusedly at least that it was the part that distinguished him from all other men, the part that was responsible for his loneliness. And, in fact, Monsieur Ouine had been the first to enter into that loneliness without violating it.

· · · · · · · · · · · · · · · · · · · ·

He stealthily crept from the room. The shadows of the rising spiral of the stairwell claimed him, and as he automatically steadied himself with his hand, it felt clammy as it glided up the cold wall . . . "Where was she?"

She was there before him, against the railing, standing quite erect. A dim light from the floor above fell on her neck and shoulders, but he could see neither her eyes nor her mouth. One of her hands, seemingly suspended in midair, was at the height of her breast. Suddenly he felt its warmth on his lips.

"Speak softly," she said. "I've had poor Anthelme brought up here to his old room, the room he used to have as a little boy. Would you like to see him? He looks very handsome."

"Heavens, no, to be quite honest. And what have you been doing up there for the last hour? Spying on me, I suppose?"

"Yes," she said. "With you one never knows what one wants. You're an unusual little boy."

She stared at him for a long time, with that same undefinable look, as she backed away toward the wall. For just an instant her face was caught in the very center of a halo of pale light and, before she could close her eyelids, Philippe saw that her gaze had lost all transparency. "Perhaps she's been hurt worse than I thought," he reflected cynically . . . But she was signalling for him to follow her up the stairs.

Monsieur Ouine's door was open. Caught in the draft, the little red and white curtains grated as they shifted on the rod. She sniggered into her two hands, cupped over her mouth.

"A very long time ago, darling, Anthelme had a key made. We come in here whenever we want to. One time we even watched him sleep."

She slipped down onto the bed, snuggling into it, her back against the wall, crossing her arms over her pulled-up knees. The continuing draft from the open door irritated Philippe. He violently kicked the door shut.

"Philippe! Listen! That's enough, Philippe!"

Squeezing hard, Steeny's hand had seized her above the elbow, and she vainly twisted her arm with all her strength.

"Come on now! Yes, right now!—You are going to tell me—who is this Monsieur Ouine, anyway? What the hell is he doing here?"

In tears, she pointed toward her pale, swollen shoulder, which had just been exposed, completely nude, from under her dressing gown. She explained that a wheel must have struck it when the carriage turned over.

"And why did you drive that great mare right at me, you wicked thing? You were more likely to kill yourself than me."

"Shush,"' she said. "You were so tiny, so thin . . . Does a fly inspire pity? But come on now, all that no longer has any importance, my angel."

Managing to release herself, she gently pushed Philippe back with her outstretched arm.

"And why would I ever have hurt you, sweetheart? But I do watch out for you; you are like him."

"Like whom?"

"Like our friend," she said laughing. "What? You mean he hasn't even told you? No? My goodness, how stupid he can seem, and how funny he is, such a love! Hold on, I'm just going to show you his photograph."

She sprang from the bed, bursting with delight. Could this be the same woman who only that morning had been dragging herself along the road, her face in the dust?

The picture was so worn and yellowed that one could scarcely make out an already too fat schoolboy in short sleeves and short trousers. What could Philippe possibly have in common with that ridiculous boy? The same gaze, of course . . . Then, suddenly, as though it were coming through the faded paper, a second little shadow moved, then retreated, and, retreating still, reduced itself to the size of the two almost imperceptible eyes that almost disappeared to become nothing but two pale dots staring out at Steeny with a sort of imperious sadness . . . "My eyes!" he thought, "they are just like my eyes!" The lady of Wambescourt raised her finger to her mouth.

"Give it back to me, sweetheart!"

But it was already too late; the pieces went flying across the room.

"What have you done?" she asked. "Monsieur Ouine takes such care of his little treasures. Oh my!"

She slipped down at Steeny's feet, snuggling against him, her head thrown back. Philippe noticed the precipitous beating of the artery in a fold of her powerful, thin neck.

"We've talked a lot about you—how he loves you! The first time he saw you, a very long time ago, years ago, perhaps . . . the years pass so quickly here . . . In any case, my goodness, yes, it was a mournful, muddy September evening. 'As a dead man might look at his past, I've just seen myself again,' he said. 'That little boy I used to be, well, I've seen him, I could have touched him, I could have heard him speak . . .' Oh, to be sure, Monsieur Ouine is not of a very lighthearted disposition, but would you believe it, my angel, since that day we've never seen him laugh again."

"Of all things! And why not?"

"How would we know?"

Her long hands enclosed Steeny's own.

"I hate him," she said, without ceasing to smile. "We hate him here like death. Alas, he needs so much protection, and he needs to be served: his naivete is so extraordinary, going beyond anything you could measure. He can't do a thing for himself, he's as unable to cope as a child. Served, yes, that's the word. Blindly served—honored and served like a god. His whims are our commands. As for his willpower, we won't even mention it: he has no more willpower than a child."

Philippe sighed disdainfully: "That's all just lies! If you hate him so much, why do you serve him? You love him in your own way, that's all."

"Love him!"

Stunned, she raised herself up on her knees.

"Love him! Why, he's huge and obese and sticky with clammy hands, ugh! And don't you realize he's very ill? His old voice resounds as if he were speaking into a drum. God! Love him! But, my angel, it's precisely that: whoever approaches him doesn't need to love any more, what peace it is, what silence! Love him? I'll tell you, sweetheart, just as others give off light and warmth, well, our friend absorbs both of them, yes, all light and all warmth, don't you see? But in that coldness the soul finds rest."

"That's all nonsense . . . the soul finds rest . . . the soul finds rest . . . Well, then, tell me what your resting soul has to do in order to hate? My idea is that hatred doesn't rest; it moves about, it even moves about a whole lot!"

She shrugged her shoulders in pity.

"Well, if you were a man and not just an argumentative little boy, you'd know quite definitely that hatred does not move about. A clear icy water, that's what hatred is. At least that's how I see it, sweetheart. But you, I bet you see it as an enraged animal — just like the devil — isn't that right, Steeny?"

"Let's not quibble over words. In your language love and hate are the same thing."

"What? What are you saying? Who is capable of seeing clearly into himself? And, for that matter, who likes evil? And yet, if he had the power, which of us would dare chase it from the world?"

She rested her chin against her hand, and Philippe now saw those admirable eyes where once again light lost all color as it paled, disappeared.

"Oh yes, there was a time when I too wanted to please . . . But what's the use of pleasing? What's the importance of finding your pleasure in somebody else's? What did it matter to me if I received what I had already paid for in advance? But then what . . . what no one ever surrenders willingly, what you only give up with regret, with groans, with tears, that, yes, that alone . . ."

Her sentence tapered off into a sort of murmur she stifled

between Philippe's knees. Through the material of his trousers he could feel her long, heavy breathing, as steady as that of a resting animal. Was she asleep? He gently pulled back into the shadows, scarcely daring to breathe, and held himself immobile, as he did when he was stalking wood pigeons along the edge of the Fenouille woods.

"They talk about paying respects . . . God! Haven't I squeezed out of one man more than anyone else could have got out of ten, or even perhaps out of a hundred, lovers? You see, my angel, there is enough substance in one single man to nourish your whole life — but where is the person alive who can flatter himself on having drunk another's substance right to the end, right to the bottom, yes, right to the dregs?"

She suddenly raised toward Steeny a look heavy with mistrust but that, as she smiled, at once became luminous.

"But what need is there for me to teach you things as simple as that, sweetheart? You know them already, you are one of us. All one has to do is see you, look into your eyes, touch your hands, hear you speak. And he knows it too, yes, he does. Nothing escapes him."

She burst out laughing.

"Oh yes! You asked if we love him. The fact is that we love him and hate him at the same time. As for me, I hate him just as I learned to hate what they once called my beauty in the old days. Yes, I detest him as much as I detest my own body, that's the real truth of it. Look at me: I cover my body with absurd old rags, I take no care of it at all, I delight in humiliating it. And what kind of desire is it if it hasn't had to overcome disgust, violate your nature, and, through shame and remorse, assure its hold over you?"

She tilted her head forward and, through her shadow-filled hair, a profile of incredible purity could be seen. Every feature of her face had relaxed and was in repose, and her little girl's mouth seemed to open up to some mysterious water.

"Listen," she said, after a silence, "we have to save our friend . . ."

"Save him? What do you mean, 'save him?'"

"He's such an imprudent man, don't you see, so full of audacity . . ."

"Full of audacity? Him? Monsieur Ouine?"

"Oh, just be quiet," she shot back in a severe tone. "Do you really think that audacity is limited to your idiots with their engines and fast turns? Our friend does just what he wants to, nothing ever stops him, and he does it when he wants to. It would be easier to try to control God's thunder."

She laughed again.

"He's afraid of me, did you know that? Because he too is full of mistrust. How very good he is at disguising his great heavy step! At night I hear him breathing through the wall. His breathing is unlike any other, betraying even the slightest movement of his soul, coming up with schemes to disguise completely useless things. I know just where he's going and where he's coming from . . . Yes, I know . . . But no one will know it but us," she suddenly cried out, growing pale. "But first of all you must swear to me, Steeny. Yes, you must swear. It is absolutely necessary. Do you believe in God?"

"That all depends . . . yes, perhaps. But then what do I need to believe in God for? Your word is your word. Besides, I never lie."

He got up so abruptly that Ginette had to steady herself on both hands in order not to fall. Now he was standing, his head empty. Whatever he had left of insolence and irony had just disappeared in that instant, and he now drew upon a reserve of blind stubbornness, his final resource in desperate cases. Certainly he feared nothing from Woolly-Leg; what he did fear was inside himself and scarcely to be felt, a sort of slowing down, as though he were being held back by the thrust of some mysterious brake. Just a few seconds more and the delicate mechanism would cease working, would become just a solid block, one single heavy mass, rolled along by its own weight like a stone. For a long time now experience had made him wary of what Miss politely called his caprice, that monster inside himself that his reason could oppose only with the most uselessly absurd traps and escapes none of which could ever, in any case, succeed in breaking its surge.

"I'll swear anything you want me to swear," he said. "Do you think I'd squeal on you?"

Ginette got up, leaning on his shoulder. He now found her ugly, almost hideous. And that was precisely why he no longer hesitated. At such moments he closed off every channel of escape, desperately going against his nature with a horrid clairvoyance. And he would spend his life that way, dreaming of wonderful, mad adventures to the point of satiety, even to the point of nausea, only to accept, once he was exhausted, through pure defiance, an inglorious risk the absurdity of which intoxicated him.

"Well, then," she said, "our friend went out last night . . ."

She put a finger to her mouth.

"Well, now! You must swear to me never to say anything about it to anyone, ever."

As usual, old Devandomme had eaten his soup in silence, but his daughter, not even daring fill his glass, sat in the shadows by the corner of the stove, ostensibly mending her Sunday blouse, her head lowered with the look of a sly animal about her, a bizarre expression on her lips, and that bitter wrinkle imprinted by Eugene's first kiss on her mouth – ah, would she had died that night!

Though the plate had just chinked against the cider jug and her heart leapt in her breast, she did not even raise her eyelids, her gaze slipping between her lashes. Under her skirt her poor knees trembled. Since the mayor's first visit and Eugene's mysterious trip to Montreuil a week ago, she no longer slept and scarcely ate, other than imbibing, at all hours of the day and night, great bowls of black coffee, a sugar cube held between her teeth, the way the locals did. Her head seemed light, light as a soap bubble. The simplest tasks she used to do mechanically now tired her out, her thoughts always moving faster than her limbs, and

93

she would suddenly find herself all red from uncompleted actions. Though put off by the simplest task, she was ready for the worst, for that's what it had come to: yes, she would face up to the worst. That sort of vice she felt constricting her chest — no earthly power could free her of it. That her love was lost, she accepted, but she would make sure that its loss cost dearly.

The old man had simply gone to sit down in the corner by the stove. Phew! What if he'd come straight up to her? He'd come sooner or later, she was waiting, she was sure of it. But what difference did it make? She would not lack the strength to listen to him, but he'd get nothing out of her. If her heart failed her, which was not likely, it would just be too bad, for she'd then do what she'd never done before in front of anybody: weep. Anything was better than speaking. She'd cry, she'd sob, even if she died of shame — God grant that she might thus redeem the imprudence of having spoken!

.   .   .   .

Cursed night! She had waited till dawn again that time, without getting bored, without getting tired, since for a long time now she hardly slept anymore. Then sleep caught up with her just at daybreak. She had awakened sadly with the noise of the rain on the windows and that vague sort of anguish under her tongue giving saliva a sweet, sickly taste. At the bottom of the stairway she had seen that the coffeepot was still full, and, on the other side of the courtyard, still steaming under the shock of the cold downpour, she saw the open door of the barn where he ordinarily slept for an hour or two, rolled up in his coat . . . Then, as if to shame back luck, unhappiness, and her own premonitions, she bravely and quickly began her chores, setting out great pails of clean water on the paving stones and tucking up her skirts . . . Around noon the rain had stopped and a pale sun rose in the sky, but soon disappeared. While she sewed near the stove until evening, the downpour redoubled in strength. He hadn't come back until after nightfall. Hidden by the door and completely invisible, he had whistled softly. He liked for her to join him secretly, the way they used to meet, up above the stable. In a corner of the loft where no one ever went, he had devised an ingenious nest in the straw for her. "As long as the old man scorns me," he said, "I'm not going to take you under his roof, its more than enough already just to eat his bread!" Sobbing, she would embrace him, and under her greedy mouth his handsome shoulder, shiny like a woman's, would make a sort of adorable reptilian undulation that drove her wild. And often too — too often, alas! — that precious skin with its smell of brush, dead leaves, and ponds might retain another odor, though never the same, the favorite perfume of one of those whores he met in Montreuil or Etaples and who stuffed his pockets with blond cigarettes and postcards, decorated with multi-colored paillettes. But she was not jealous of those whores, no more than of the pretty, blood-sated ferrets sleeping in the bottom of his leather bag . . . But on that evening, that accursed evening, it was he who had pushed her gently toward the door — gently, but with a severe face. His curly hair, wet and glistening, was also full of dirt, and his mouth — yes, it was seeing his mouth, all twisted with fatigue and trembling, that had hurt her the most . . . "The Floupe is high," he said, "bitch of a river! The current's now carrying off half my traps, God knows where! I've walked through it for four hours with water up to my belly. Then the marquis's game warden pursued me all along the Arbellot wood at daybreak. On top of that I lost my cap, a new cap, what damned luck!" How exhausted he must be to tell me everything! she had thought. And the next morning when that funny man with the little beard had come, the one her father had started out by receiving so badly, she had thought — poor girl! — that it was one of Eugene's pals, one of his buyers who paid him cash for his game, and she had answered him with full confidence, only taking care that the old man not hear . . . And that was all. Besides, Eugene hadn't even reproached her for it. He'd laughed. "You've spoken to a fellow from the police, you big dumb ox," he said.

. . . .

God, but she was alone! Alone with her wild love, wilder than any wood creature — with that desire that exasperated rather than calming her anguish. Even in the mortal suspense of this hour, even while fighting the urge to immediately go and throw herself into the silent old man's arms and bury her head in his shoulder as she used to do — for from the depths of everyone's agony it is sweet childhood that rises first — and even in this hour when all hope was lost, the images that kept flashing under her closed eyelids made her blush with shame and pleasure . . . Why, nothing but death was going to calm that fire in her bowels! What a gallant, what a gay companion that big bold boy was with his sudden scruples and unforeseeable regards for her who, every time, left her naively overwhelmed by surprise and tenderness. God grant that she die first!

Besides, she had no clear idea of the risk he was running. What could the police or gendarmes do against such a man? You'd just as well have a battle of wits with a hare outside his hole, or you might just as easily put a grain of salt on a kingfisher's tail. From her youth she had scorned the chattering of the other girls, but it was from Eugene alone that she had learned a certain proud male silence making her pity everyone else. Now, day and night, there was nothing left but that silence in which she took her rest, sinking into it like a gentle patient animal — that silence alone. Outside it, everything was pale and cowardly. No, those lawyers wouldn't get the best of him! Even the Marquis of Mirandol's game warden had had to make a retraction before the judges in Montreuil one day . . . No, there was nothing to be feared from those bigmouths . . . But there was still her father.

She bent her head a little lower over her needlework; her eyes burned, but what a coldness there was in her breast! With every sudden movement the old man made this evening, a cold constriction could be felt, going from the depths of one armpit to the other, a constriction so painful that she slipped her hand under her blouse from time to time, surprised to be caressing warm, smooth, living skin . . . For two years now the old man had spoken to her only rarely, though without anger, just as he spoke to strangers. But now his voice trembled a little sometimes, growing tender. Whenever she turned her head, she sometimes caught what seemed a gaze of pity fixed upon her. Dear God! It would have been easier to bear his scorn! No doubt the decision had been taken, the warrant already issued, and her destiny – the destiny of her poor love – was between those old hands . . . yes, her love, as for everything else – no matter! Besides there was no "everything else," there was nothing else. The clock struck twelve times.

. . . .

"Give me my cap, daughter," he said.

His voice had awakened her with a start, as from a deep, dreamless sleep. She rose. The floor moved about under her feet as she raised her hands, feeling about in the dark of the hallway, then took his cap off the hook. The lamplight struck her full in the face upon her return, and the effort she made to smile and not blink was one of those that leave something like an irreparable wound at the very source of life – something not to be repeated. Just for a minute now, just let her hold on for one minute more against that frantic dizziness and those bright flashes she was seeing – one tiny minute, and then let her get down and roll on the tiles on the floor and stay there – ah, how sweet death would be!

The old man went straight toward the pastures where the cattle were, those sad-eyed, long Flemish cows that sometimes came grunting with pleasure to eat oats out of the palm of your hand. Lost in dreams, not a single one of them even raised its head, no, not one. But their humble presence was just what he needed. Even though he scarcely even looked at them either, he listened to their tranquil breathing. Where their great bodies lay the grass was sweet and warm with a faint smell of milk all around.

．　．　．　．　．　．　．　．　．　‥　．　．　．　．　．　．　．　．　．　．

Damned little man in green! From lack of use the memory of him had almost faded. But there he was again, appearing when misfortune struck, more alive than ever; he thought he saw him laughing, singing, emptying his glass, and those words he had said on a memorable night a century earlier, inflaming hearts, now came surging up from the shadows, out of the silence . . . Yes, he truly thought he felt the mocking, insolent gaze of a century ago weighing down upon him . . . So he shook his huge shoulders as might a horse stung by horseflies. "As tricky as he may have been, I'd have grabbed him by the scruff of the neck . . . ," he thought, "but there's nothing you can do against the dead . . ."

The dead. He scarcely thought about them either, yet when fate gets a hold on us, they come running from every side, as close together as a flight of crows. Could the pain of the living perhaps be nourishment for the dead? Oh, he wasn't afraid of those whom he had known and loved; as long as he was alive, well, they were not yet completely dead in him. But there were the others. And certainly it was not natural to refuse to settle accounts, but who could ever brag of having settled up with those fabulous characters whose names one doesn't even know? Besides, they asked for nothing, or at least for nothing a respectable man could give. You could chase them away a hundred times but they still came back—worse than rats. Grandfather de Vandomme, for example, what a man he was! With his woolen cap he was always full of beer, right up to the top, even overflowing, but accommodating to everybody — there was no one like him to delight the boys from the battery with a little song, and he was quick with the girls, as old as he was... At the brothel in Etaples, at seventy-five or more, whenever he suddenly heaved his huge body up all at once, with his giant hands flat on the table, casting his besotted gray gaze from one man to another, not one young chap would have dared touch his glass as long as he hadn't yet dropped back down on his bench with an enormous laugh. Yet never had his sons ever heard him utter a foul word, never an oath, and on the day after his sprees he had a way of smiling while eating his soup that made their blood run cold. Damn! On those days they'd have died for him, God strike them dead! Illness had caught him on his feet, just as he was, behind his horses, in the midst of the winter wind, on the edge of the steaming furrow. They had put him on a cart on an armful of straw and then into bed, his great muddy boots right on the beautiful new eiderdown, and once, then twice, he had opened his eyes, his tranquil, slightly astonished eyes. But not a word out of him until supper, nothing: you could only hear his loud breathing. And then his pals arrived in groups, coming through the pastures, fellows that the old mother had never seen, coming right in, not removing their hats, not wiping their feet, their pipes still in their mouths, and going over to empty them out in the ashes. "Come on now, Thierry," they said, "what about it, Thierry?" And at that point he opened his eyes, still peaceful, with a strange smile rising toward his eyebrows, and he said in the voice he used to order his animals around, "Enough of that! Get out! All of you!" The last one to go out was Mannerville, an old regimental buddy from the Twelfth Cavalry. The old man signaled to him with his hand. Then he caught his breath unhurriedly. The other stood straight, rigid in his corduroy jacket, completely red. "I haven't got anything against them," the old man said, "but there's a time for everything, understand? There's a time for fun and another time for dying, isn't that right? And in regard to what I am, I who call myself de Vandomme, it's a matter of not offending the children."

And then he whispered something to him in his ear. Immediately Mannerville ran to the door, called the men back, and they came back in, rumble-tumble, holding their caps in their hands, not very proud of themselves. "Vandomme . . ." he began. But then they heard the voice of the old man as calm as his gaze, perhaps even calmer: "Come on now, Louis, can't you say 'Monsieur de Vandomme?'" Starting again, the former cavalryman said, "Monsieur de Vandomme doesn't want to die owing anything to anybody. Sometimes you didn't agree with him, so speak up!" They more or less snorted, not too happy, and the Mirouette boy wanted to answer tit for tat: "Oh la la, just words . . ." And then they heard the voice again, calmer than ever: "Get the hell out of here, Mirouette! Make him get the hell out of here, Louis! Does he think that because I've drunk with him he has the right to spit in my soup?" With that they all went out. And the old man said nothing more until suppertime. Every time the old mother stuck her nose in the door he waved for her to get out, that everything was fine, as if he were afraid of interrupting, even for a second, that great breath that didn't want to die. Then he dozed a bit, and the skin of his cheeks turned gray, and his sons came and sat in the shadows at his bedside. But the dying man watched them without seeming to, between half-closed eyelids. And it was just at that moment that he began the death rattle, very gently, in such a natural way that one would have said that he was going to give a good cough to clear his voice, as he used to, before singing his song. To his boys he said: "You're Vandommes, listen carefully. Maybe I've caroused too much, it makes no difference, don't go judging your father. And if I spoke a bit haughtily to my friends just now, it's not that I really scorn them, no, not that. But seeing the state I'm in now, everyone should mind his manners. I don't want to be unworthy of my father or of his fathers. After all, it seems that once upon a time we de Vandommes were lords." Then he kissed the mother on her old mouth, quite simply, and died in silence, much later, all alone, with the door wide open into the kitchen where the pink tongue of the purring fire danced about the ceiling.

．　．　．　．　．　．　．　．　．　．　．　．　．　．　．　．　．

Damned ghosts! Soon the old man would have been underground
forty years and it was his turn – for him, Martial – to be the old
man . . . There they were already, surrounding him in their black
flight, the damned crows! It was useless to hate them – had he ever
really believed in those stories of counts and barons? – he was
headed toward a rendezvous with them and, regardless of what it
cost, he had to find them again that night. He had no means of getting through the night without them. For now that he knew what
his misfortune was, his only fear was that he might make allow-
ances for it. No! For once let misfortune take over for good and all!
Let it dig in, hollow out, penetrate the very depths of his life, right
to the bottom! Anything would be preferable to that vague, unde-
termined, horrid weariness of the soul. What wouldn't he give to
feel again that sharp pain between his shoulders brought on by terror in that first minute when the mayor had first confided in him!
For the ever present idea of his son-in-law as an assassin aroused
neither revolt nor scorn in him – perhaps he even felt an obscure,
inadmissable sympathy for him as an accomplice. And yet the thing
had to be done, and it would be done. All that was left, it was clear,
was for the boy to destroy himself. All he had to do was to know
how to present it to him, find the right words. But would he find
them when the moment came? For those phrases naively repeated
so many times seemed to have lost their secret, mortal meaning –
their very strength – and he had found himself substituting ten
others, twenty others, in spite of himself, each one less to the point
than the last one, and then so complicated, so obscure that they
were like having your mouth full of ashes. Ah, it was not, as he had
believed, one of those things done with a burning heart, but no
doubt wearily and disgustedly, just as an executioner with reddened hands might finally come to the last person to be executed.

He pushed on farther, right up to the Desvres road, cutting
across the pastures. For a long moment, on the horizon, his suspicious eye followed the vaguely luminous fringe being covered

little by little by the night. It reappeared higher up, furtive, treacherous, enclosed on every side and pursued from peak to peak by whirling masses of shadows, never stopping or even slowing its oblique flight . . . The village was there somewhere, buried in the lindens and chestnuts, with its little houses of brick or mud, scattered in no particular order, so sad in the December rain. And behind each of those low doors carefully closed, there was one of those men that he scorned—those bastards descended from Spanish ancestors, black as flies and sweating coffee through all their pores. And if he had dared, he'd have gone and sat on the little deserted square in the darkest part of the night, near the fountain. But as he stepped over the hedge he no longer wanted to. What was the use? There was no enemy there for him to defy, nothing but readers of newspapers, men who knew how to talk big in the taverns, braggarts more vain than girls and innocently cruel like children. And besides he had plenty of time to defy them! For he would not yield his place, he would not turn his back upon his shame, and he would never again see that country where he had so longed to die. Whatever happened, these people would never brag of having made him lower his eyes, and, whether they liked it or not, they would bury him one day, their hats in their hands. He would even leave the necessary money for a large stone, a beautiful big piece of Ardennes granite with his name written on it in capital letters, his name with the "de"—the name of a lord, after all.

His feet stumbled against the stump of an apple tree, and he fell to his knees, got up, feeling in the shadows. A strange light still seemed to creep about the village, a sort of fog with a reddish tinge chased away by dawn each morning, but returning every evening, seemingly formed by the winter rain over there above the colorless ponds behind the Saint-Venand and de Lamare woods. But then even that was extinguished. It was now that hour of the night never perfectly known by any man, never completely possessed, that hour holding all the senses in suspense while an ever denser shadow fills heaven's expanse, and saturated earth seems to sweat a still blacker ink. The wind had sped away one knew not where, wandering in the depths of immense deserts or on solitary peaks where the echoes of its wild rushing died away, one after the other. A breeze, a breath, a murmur, a swarm of invisible things slipped along at thirty feet above the earth as though floating along on the thickness of the night. And the old man, listening closely, heard the gentle rustling of the tips of the poplars.

He walked for a long time still, with great, heavy steps, sometimes with an awkward gesture made by his arm extended before him. How cold he was! His hands groped in the scarcely formed fog, which, until dawn, would keep getting thicker, and every breath filled his lungs with a subtle vapor smelling of smoke. From the summits he climbed, the immense rump of the Merlimont forest vaguely appeared as a black different from that of the sky, a night within the night. His son-in-law, that creature of darkness, must be moving about in there somewhere with his soft fox step, no less agile, no less indefatigable, no less prudent in his crafty indifference than those animals he pursued. Unless . . .

Slowly he went back up the slope toward the house, careful not to make noise with his hobnailed shoes on the flint stones of the courtyard. The imperceptible reflection of the pond made a pale spot on the window, the bucket was at the corner of the doorway, as was the mop that his daughter ran over the floor tiles after supper each evening . . . He strained to listen one last time, then pushed the door open. The warm air hit him immediately with a familiar caress so sweet that it seemed another skin from his own body enveloping him. The embers in the fireplace were still glowing under the ashes, and the old man's fingers were suddenly surprised upon encountering not the wood of the table but a fresh napkin, one of those fine, brand-new damask napkins still stiff from never having been used before. It was certainly not for him that Helen had got out the flowered plate, the pitcher of cider, and that piece of smoked bacon the color of old oak, placing it on a pewter platter . . . And no doubt her handsome rogue with the pale, ever calm eyes wouldn't even come; no doubt tomorrow she would find, poor girl, everything still in its place, at pale dawn . . . Tomorrow.

He went toward the fireplace and trampled the embers with his muddy shoes, then, hungry and thirsty, took off again. But as soon as he had passed his own fence, age seized him as unexpectedly as a gust of north wind at the highest point of his Presles field where he would stop behind his horses, all in a sweat—yes, age seized him and he did not know what it was; he turned about on his heels, retreating, causing the muscles of his powerful shoulders to tense as if he were facing an adversary, raising his fists to the height of his forehead, those same fists that had brought so many young bulls to their knees. Then he let himself sink down on the sticky, wet grass, his gaze still fixed on that bit of shadow invisible for anyone else: the house, the house with its warmth.

8

"Are you through rubbing yourself, Arsène? What's the good in a man in your position currying himself like an ass! And out in the courtyard at that!"

For a moment the steaming torso of the mayor of Fenouille appeared in the doorway of the shadowy woodshed. Once, twice, he wrung out the soaked towel, carefully using both hands, then spread it in the sun over the low door before disappearing again into the shadows. Wherever on the packed earth floor he prudently moved, stepping with scrunched-up feet, great puddles reflected the light.

"Your secretary's been waiting all morning for you to sign something. The mail's not even been opened, you poor thing! And don't forget that the doctor . . ."

The complaining voice seemed to be coming out of the wall.

"The doctor . . . And is he going to start quibbling with me about personal hygiene now?"

He appeared in the doorway, clothed only in a pair of mauve-striped cotton underpants.

"At least you could finish getting dressed in the woodshed, you disgusting thing! People will say you're a wild man, and red as a tomato at that!"

"So what, Malvina? A man's a man. For almost two thousand years modesty's kept people from taking off their pants; religion's held the country down in the muck, asphyxiating it, you might say. For the skin breathes, my dear, it's a known fact, a fact known everywhere."

"At least go through the kitchen, you're going to mess up my linoleum with that dirt on your feet. I've put your dressing gown above the stove. Drink your coffee while it's hot, you big innocent!"

But gently pushing her ahead of him, he closed the door.

"Just a minute, Malvina," he said, "I've something to say to you, my girl."

"Here it comes again!" she cried, discouraged. "First of all, you listen to me, Arsène. For two months now you've been harping on your dirty stories; you haven't spared me a single one. What do you want me to do, what can I do with your stories? Can I take on the responsibility for them? Hardly! Well?"

"It's just that I need to admit them," said the big man, shamefully. "Just being able to admit them; that relieves me, it makes me comfortable."

"But I swear that I forgive you, you big innocent! And though we can't always do what we want, we do have our pleasurable moments . . . But then I'd have to be sure that you really did do those stupid things."

"I swear on my dead mother's head . . . ," the poor man began.

"All right, all right, you've always had too much imagination, Arsène, it's imagination that's caused your fall, that's what I think, you won't make me change my mind about that. In any case, true or not true, I forgive you; let's not mention it again."

"Not mention it again! Good God almighty! It's talking about it that does me good! You women, if you'll forgive my saying so, go through life like animals, without thinking any more or any less about it. But I was made for something other than what I am, do you understand? I don't know what . . . Wait! A trout in a mill-stream, something fresh and pure . . . But even water . . . that is . . . well, for me there is no pure water. It may look that way to your eyes of course. But just put your nose up to the edge . . ."

"He's crazy," groaned the mayor's wife, "completely crazy! He now lives only for his nose, worse than a dog, the wretch! Get dressed, Arsène, you're going to get a chill."

The kettle hummed, the floor tiles shone, and the pile of dinner plates shook as a truck passed by on the road; everything was in its place. All one could hear were the stifled sighs of the mayor of Fenouille, struggling to tie his shoe.

"Malvina," he said, coughing to clear his voice, "do you remember Célestine, the daughter of old man Dumouchet?"

"Oh, Lord!"

"The one that got a job for herself in Boulogne and killed herself with rat poison, that one? Do you remember her?"

"Do leave me alone," the mayor's wife begged, "one more word and I'm leaving."

Standing immobile behind him, she looked at the reddened neck of her strange mate with an ambiguous look in which maternal pity finally won out.

"If you set such store by your stories, why not tell them to your pillow? In any case, it's all the same whether it's me or your pillow. For weeks now you've been rehashing your stories to me every evening until midnight. Do you think I've been listening? My poor man, I've been sleeping, I've been getting my rest. And when you stop, well, that wakes me up for a moment, just in time to say yes or no, and then you start again. Besides, you know, between us, can't we admit that what you men get up to never changes . . ."

For the sake of decency she tried to laugh, but the face he turned toward her certainly inspired no laughter.

"Mal . . . Malvina . . . ," stammered the unhappy man.

And now she too was stuttering, losing her head. All she could ever see was the ridiculous side of all the mayor's incomprehensible confessions. For herself, she thought of them as stupidities, as silly childishness. Some day, perhaps, the idea of madness did cross her mind, but the word "madness," like that of "religion," was one of those her conscience rebelled against, leaving her ashamed and stunned, as though it were an obscene insult. The word "illness" on the other hand only evoked the precise and simple image of a natural trial with an end that one always reached, one way or another, whether by death, or healing, or forgetfulness. What suffering was there, other than that of the body, that would not finally yield to the slow, monotonous repetition of the daily joys—work, meals, going to bed, and those beautiful Sundays resonating with the sounds of squeaking pumps and overturned buckets and with their smell of polish and fresh clothes—those delights of childhood miraculously rediscovered each week, right up until that very last Sunday with its black and gold: the cart decked out as a funeral coach, glistening under the wreaths, the cemetery with its yews and boxwood and the great rumble of peasants at the funeral feast . . . How simple life was, after all! It seemed that the eye could take it all in from one end to the other, just like a well-known field. What then did this big man find in it, her old companion—what was the enemy, the invisible obstacle?

"Come on, come on now, Arsène."

The mayor of Fenouille had placed his hands on his naked knees and lowered his head. He seemed to be crying.

"Come on, come on, old dear."

"Hush," he said gently, "it's not your fault. You can't understand. The doctor can't understand either . . . Sometimes I tell myself that only a child could understand me, a little child . . . Listen, Malvina . . ." He got up and came near her. His miserable gaze still danced about, and the huge hands with which he gripped the back of her chair to support himself trembled.

"Listen, Malvina, we don't know what fun is. You start out having fun, fair enough! And then one day it's the fun that starts having fun with you. Instead of being the cat you've suddenly become the mouse, you understand?"

She shrugged her shoulders indifferently.

"My poor thing, while you chat away your coffee's getting cold."

"Listen, my dear . . . When you're young, you have certain ideas, no one can do anything about it, it's in the blood. But then you have the right to choose, and you take up an idea as you might choose a pipe, and when the pipe is finished, you spit and it's all over with. Only one day you find it's useless to put your pipe in the drawer. Damn, the tobacco's no longer in your pipe, it's in your nose, your throat, your belly, it's coming out of your skin day and night, you've fallen into the juice, you might say, like a fly . . ."

"Come on, Arsène . . . Ideas never hurt anybody."

Awkwardly he placed his hand on Malvina's arm and, although he gripped the chair with the other, his wife still felt his whole great body pulsating against her.

"An idea is ferocious, you see! You think you're dirty and you wash yourself and don't see it anymore. But the idea of being dirty—the idea, do you understand?—well, you can't do anything to get rid of the idea."

The poor woman certainly could not have repeated a single one of the very revealing words of this extraordinary speech, but she did make an effort to seize something in the gaze of the unhappy man in whom, though she never admitted it, she used to believe she had found her master.

Besides, for an instant his gaze seemed to grow clear and steady. Then he lowered it again.

"You aren't following me," he said with a terrible sadness. "Rub and rub and rub again, stark naked under the pump, it's true I look like a lunatic. Too bad! What can I say? Go try explaining light to a blind man. A pinprick will make you jump, but you understand nothing about bad smells. Modern man's sense of smell's been atrophied, it's the truth, you can ask the doctor. You can no more smell things than you can see the dead, and if you did see the dead swarming all about everywhere, you couldn't touch your bread anymore. Besides, everything stinks, men, women, animals, the earth, water, the air I breathe, everything — the whole of life stinks. And sometimes in the summer, when daylight drags on and becomes soft, stretching out like bread dough, you can even believe that time stinks too. And what about us? You'll answer that you can wash and rinse and scrape, damn! Granted that in my case there's a bit of deception. For the smell I'm talking about isn't really a smell, it comes from farther away, from deeper down in the memory, from the soul perhaps, what do we know? Water is powerless against it, something else is needed."

He pressed his big moustache against the cheek of his fascinated wife.

"At my age you should be able to clean out your memory, just as you clean out your well, it's all the same. When the mud has been dried in the sun there are no more secrets. As for my secrets, I don't want any more secrets, my girl! And as for their mayor's office, please note that in my state I don't give a damn about it. Suppose I went into the village square some Sunday and said to them: 'There's no more mayor, no more municipal magistrate, nothing but a man, a completely real, completely sincere, completely new man who is going to tell you his sorrows . . .'"

Her head in her hands, completely shamed, she now wept in little sobs.

"Don't cry, my lovely," he said, "we've got to finish this off. If all those nights you'd listened to me instead of snoring, it would at least hurt a little bit less now, and I'd feel less alone, do you understand? I could live . . ."

"But since I forgive you," she moaned. "Come now, Arsène, I don't need to know — a woman fifty-eight years old, do you realize that?"

"Have it your way," he replied furiously. "Damned if I'm not going off to find the villagers!"

"You shan't go," she cried in despair. "No, you shan't go, even if I have to tie you to the foot of my bed, you big, crazy innocent. Am I responsible for your stupidities? Do you want to have them pointing at us all the way from here to Boulogne? And if you're so ashamed and suffer so much from your adventures, why do you always start over again, you Nicodemus!"

With his head down, he sniffed at the boiling hot coffee. She heard his teeth chattering against the bowl.

"What a shame it is," she continued compassionately, "what a shame it is to see a man like you, a mayor, lose his head over an insignificant story of a snot-nosed little wretch of a farm boy . . . What's wrong? What did I say?"

The bowl had just slipped from Arsène's hands, breaking on the tiles.

"You should've warned me," he said, growing pale. "You mustn't speak of that without warning. Otherwise I can't help jumping; it's my nerves."

He tried to laugh, but with her little round black eyes she looked him right in the face.

"Arsène, you're hiding something from me," she said.

"Who, me?"

But his face had gone purple, and his hands trembled even more. For such a long time now he had forgotten the happy rhythm of life, its tranquil flow. His own was now nothing more than drowsiness punctuated by brusque awakenings, by fits of irrepressible terror followed by a short moment of relaxation, of remission that, he said, left him low, with no will, no thought and in a delicious nothingness. And exactly at that minute, exactly at the right minute, how she could dominate him with her stare, that bird's stare as sharp as a jet splinter . . .

"It's going to be finished off," he sighed, "what can I say? at least it's a finished affair . . . phew! They'll probably arrest Vandomme's son-in-law Wednesday or Thursday — there are just suppositions . . .

running about the woods the night of the crime ... they found his traces ... the boy's mistake, you see, was that he began by denying everything ... pretended he'd slept in Vandomme's barn ... But the Maloine boy saw him cut a switch about four o'clock in the Goubaud hollows, seven miles from here, you realize what that means?"

His large cheeks were starting to pale and Malvina would have sworn that, as they did, they were diminishing in proportion, pulling the corners of the mouth up toward the temples in a sorrowful grimace.

"Ah, well," she said simply, "old Vandomme won't get over this one."

Alas! No, she didn't understand, "couldn't understand . . ." Miss gestured with her blond hand as if to wave away a wisp of smoke, a shadow, some tiny nothing.

With her back turned to the window, she appeared tinier than he had ever seen her, with that impossible, frivolous something that kept her so dangerously outside life with its risks, well out of reach, in a sort of magic solitude, peculiar to dolls. Distractedly she pretended to gather her scarf on her bosom, but Philippe knew very well it was a gesture of defense, that every nerve and fiber in her delicate body had just been alerted by her diligent little brain and that henceforth she was totally on guard.

"It's frightening how you're like an animal, you too," he said simply. "All women are like animals, it seems. How have I not noticed it sooner?"

"Thank you . . . Wild animals, naturally?"

"Wild, to be sure . . ."

"Boys have always thought that from the beginning of the world."

Discouraged, she shrugged her shoulders. God knew the care she'd lavished on Philippe! But Philippe was still just a man like the others, wasn't he; eager, insolent, capricious, cynical, and tender, an animal, but not at all a wild one – oh no! – but more of a pet, that's it! A dog, Steeny was a big dog, that's exactly what a man is, my friend.

She looked at him with her attentive, pale eyes. No, this time she would not – as so many times before – see him clinch his fists and thrust his drunken, little, tear-swollen face toward his disdainful, invulnerable adversary.

"You'd better apologize to your mother," she continued. "After all, your mother is so indulgent, so gentle, Steeny . . . So unhappy, and so alone . . ."

"Not alone at all, Daisy!"

She pretended she hadn't heard, but it was too late. Never before had he dared call her by that Victorian name and, feeling her hands trembling in rage as she tried to cross them carelessly under her scarf, she saw his insolent, ferocious look following them.

"What can a boy like you know about loneliness?" she continued, staring at the ceiling.

"In this house, Miss, I'm the one who's alone and you know it."

What power! What sweetness! He had just mastered blind revolt's first surges, and, within that untamed little body he had always yielded to, all was suddenly stilled. The roar he thought he heard rising in his ears every time his will gushed up, so awkwardly, so ineptly, that noise like a crowd, or the sea, had now fallen silent, and, it seemed to him, would remain so forever. His soul was at rest.

"What are you thinking about?" she asked boldly.

Since she could not escape, she had just as well confront him, goodness me! Let him ask immediately then, let him ask on the spot for what she had resolved not to give, for what would never be wrested from her—never would she be wrested from this house!

"I think that both of you will be pretty happy when I'm gone."

What peace, what strange peace! The words, as usual, came forward in disorder, but he, rising above them, dominated their tamed ranks. He would say nothing but what he wanted to say, and at the right time too, carefully measuring the distance and calculating the blows, like a man whirling a sling . . . "I really am master of myself!" he thought with a naive emphasis. But he was already well beyond such simple mastery. Only that elementary passion, instinct alone, has such an instantaneous, precise, and diabolical sense of limit, both in pleasure and in assuaging hatred. In fact, the stress of these last days had broken him: he was inebriated, completely intoxicated from security, from pride, and from having vanquished suffering.

She turned her half-closed eyes toward him. Her thin face was formed so that its oblique features seemed drawn toward the mouth, making her little triangular head rather resemble a snake's head. Steeny imagined her about to hiss.

"I understand, Monsieur Philippe," she said.

Although she pretended to be stretching herself, she could be seen gathering her forces together, then dropping her arms and widely opening her wonderful eyes, those angel eyes.

"I shall not abandon your . . ." (she hesitated for a second perhaps, just long enough to catch Philippe staring into her pale eyes) "Michelle," she added so naturally, so simply that he, finding nothing to reply, shrugged his shoulders.

No, he would not humiliate her! She was already beyond his reach since she had faced up to it from the start. The secret fear she had of the child had just been dissipated forever. It was a man she now had before her, and no man in the world had ever obtained anything from her other than the sort of attention one gives any turbulent animal. She sighed, then continued on the same tone.

"You've been told some horrible things, Steeny, or else you've dreamed them up. Whether they were told to you or not, in any case you surely dreamed them up first. So much the worse for you, monsieur!"

She had let the first words fall one by one into the silence, but the last ones she spit out all at once with an unbelievable insolence.

"I've always detested you," he murmured in a subdued voice, rather stupidly.

The luminous smile of Miss unexpectedly enveloped him like a golden halo.

"I've not liked you very much either," she answered, dreamily. "And maybe I was even afraid of you? A lot of pride, a lot of vice, both of them multiplied by boredom. What woman doesn't feel vulnerable in front of a little man!"

She gently shook her head, but he had just caught her sounding the waters with her quick, anxious look. Steeny's insolent reserve made her uneasy. Had she made a mistake? Had she spoken too soon?

"My dear little Philippe, how long have you been the friend of that frightful woman?"

"Who, me?" he answered with assurance, "Woolly-Leg? My goodness, for months and months maybe . . ."

"And she's the one . . . who . . ."

Careful now! Her arm, already raised in a gesture of loathing, had fallen. She gave a simple smile of disgust.

"Who . . . what?" Philippe asked insolently.

Another look, another smile. Miss's whole pretty face was now shaped by fear, with great hollows of shadow. It was really more like the face of a humiliated young male, like the face of some brother of Steeny.

"I think you're lying," she said, "but what difference does it make! God knows there's enough spite just in you alone, dear boy."

Philippe vaguely shrugged his shoulders in approval. For he had launched his challenge by chance, and he now naively, proudly took pleasure in the pain he had just caused, almost without being aware of it, like a young cat passing from a ball of yarn to living prey, from playing to killing.

Both were silent. They really had nothing more to say to each other before the irreparable and decisive truth. And certainly she was prepared to pronounce it first. Sooner or later the moment had to come when she would fight for the one chance she had in her wretched life. For fourteen years she had seen her rival growing up beside her, thinking that he was becoming less dangerous from day to day as his wound, kept open with so much artifice, went deeper and deeper into him. When he understands, I'll be saved. And what indeed was there to fear from an open rebellion that had to end up by cutting the outraged child off from that tiny little universe where she had slowly formed her own happiness? What he was now trying to get out of her could now no longer have much value in his eyes, whereas she was getting ready to defend something that daily became more priceless and that didn't allow for sharing, something she must either save or lose in its totality. Just a minute of distraction or fatigue and she could find herself excluded from this sure, sweet haven, flung back into that horrid crowd of men. Men! She did not fear any of them in particular, but the idea of their number, of their power, and of their gross complicity horrified her. Fat faces, cynical looks, and, hated most of all with a raw, bleeding hatred, that pale crafty smile of desire with its humble grimace. When she closed her eyes, it all seemed to come back to her at once, the whole course of her hideous youth at Stirling, near Swansea. Her father, a poor pharmacist from Lancaster who died very young—her mother taking in washing, surrounded by piles of laundry, with bare arms, ironing day and night amidst steam, smelling of laundry starch and hemp—the first of her mother's lovers she had spied upon through the cracks in the door, then another, and still another; then those suspect visitors, those "good friends," those paunchy protectors who stuffed her pockets with sticky candies; then finally the long, untamed death throes of her mother, borne standing up until the last day in front of the burning stoves; then the orphan taken in by her uncle James, an old soldier of the queen who claimed he'd left a leg with the savage Afghans (it had actually been amputated in a hospital because of a syphilitic eruption on the knee)—those first, miraculous, enchanted weeks in the brick cottage, until that evening . . . Oh, those suffocating summer nights, so sticky and full of the smell of the old man!— the flight to London, the Wesleyan minister who fed her so badly, dressing her like a little girl—short skirts, bare legs, socks—but who saw to it that she went to one of the best schools in London; then her fall, the abyss, the black visions of cities, ports, brightly coloured docksides, and finally that harbor of grace, that sweet house in Fenouille with its fresh lawns, its secrets . . . One evening, in tears, she had told her mistress everything.

. . . .

"Philippe! Steeny!"

He had thrust his hands forward haphazardly, or rather he had risen, let himself go, and already he felt the blond neck bending. The supple stretching of her sides both attracted and repulsed him, just as an object turning at lightening speed might attract and repulse one's gaze. There was neither fear nor anger in her, scarcely even a brief flash of surprise, then suddenly her attention reached its peak, like that of a trapped animal. What did that mad boy want from her? What should she do? Skilfully she disengaged her right hip, preparing for the fall with her bent arm, and rolled on the carpet with her adversary.

"Philippe! That's enough, Philippe!"

Her voice hissed between her clinched teeth. The game she was playing was a terrible one in which she risked losing everything. No matter! The body that Steeny pressed was as supple and defenseless as a little child's, but her face remained tense and impenetrable. For a second Philippe's mouth brushed the warm fold of her neck at her golden hairline.

He raised himself on his knees with a demonic agility. Never had he felt calmer or more master of himself, of his nerves, never surer of his hatred, as though it were a marvelous weapon. A gesture, one simple gesture that, moreover, had not been calculated and was almost unconscious, had just delivered his abused, humiliated enemy into his hands. The laughter arising from his throat expressed neither joy nor any sense of revenge, and in any case he let it die almost immediately on his lips. His eyes even turned away from the vanquished prey, insolently looking above her.

For a long while Miss watched him from under her long eyelashes. She disdained getting up again, smoothed the folds of her skirt, and ran her fingertip carelessly over the flowers on the carpet, but Philippe, stealing a glance, was delighted to see there were pearls of sweat on her bent neck.

"I don't want you, I detest you!" he affirmed in a calm voice.

She raised her head, her eyes still lowered.

"You are a tricky boy," she said, "a real girl. No matter! You'll soon have forgotten this and many other things besides. Men forget everything. We women never forget anything."

"So much the better," he said. "But you can get up now. You've been down for the count, let's say no more about it."

"N...no," she said. "My goodness, no. I see you better this way. Seen from below, a little face like yours couldn't lie. Your turn will come, Philippe."

"Maybe!"

"Lord! You should never reply to a lady's challenge, don't you know that? But you think you're invulnerable since you're strutting there on your two legs, like a cockerel."

With one long leg bent in a childish position — both hands placed flat on the floor, her bust inclined slightly forward — but so supple, so bold that Philippe could not watch her shoulders tremble under the light silk blouse without uneasiness. He retreated imperceptibly as if to dodge a leap.

"I could have taught you lots of things," she said. "Too bad! And this first of all: a woman who has been subjected to the tyranny of a man and then delivered from it will never be enchained again except by another lover. But you're more interested in bragging, in nipping and running around like a pony. But the day will come – this very evening, perhaps – when you'll jump the fence and all will be said."

"And if I don't jump the fence?" he asked.

His voice trembled a little on the last syllable, a little more than was necessary. Miss sighed.

"That would be wise," she said indifferently. "But then, Philippe, let's bet you do jump. Ah yes! You'll jump, my boy, and even . . . Do you want me to tell you?"

Her pretty pale eyes suddenly grew dark, and she stole a sly, violet-colored look at Philippe.

"You'll jump when you no longer even want to jump. Remember! Not a single one of your stupidities was done except through sheer stubbornness and when you were sure that you'd no longer get anything out of it except boredom. The marvelous thing however is that we women get as tired of foreseeing these stupidities as you men do of dreaming about them, so we all react with equal boredom."

She turned her head away and seemed to be speaking to the high windows where all the garden's shadows moved back and forth with solemnity.

"You'll jump the fence. Jumping the fence is nothing. How many ponies like you have wound up in India right off! Taking off is nothing. It's the return that counts."

She then raised her hands and put them firmly back down in the same place.

"You won't understand," she said. "But the only thing we are really glad to find again is what we thought we left forever. But it seems you French boys always cling with the tip of your fingers to what your palm has just released. Who can know, for example, what you want or don't want from your mother, Philippe? She is an unhappy, kind woman. Nonetheless she'll not stand having a master. It would be easy to break her, but she can't be bent without out killing her. What do you expect her to do with a dark, shadowy love that, while asking for nothing, exacts everything? At your age a little English gentleman knows no more about these things than a big puppy, and his imagination is as pink and fresh as a slice of beef. Yours is precociously already that of an experienced man, and you use it for nothing but oppressing your mistresses and wives, for you French, my boy, are domestic tyrants, a species of sedentary conquerors. For you the whole universe has to exist between your table and your bed — yes, your whole universe, with all its risks. All those conquests you've never made, those dangers you've never run, those opportunities you've missed, all have to be taken out on some innocent creature. But all your mother wants is calm, rest, and being able to forget. Do you really hope for her to start over again with her son the same thing that wounded her life forever? If only she'd sent you away sooner, while there was still time! This house is no longer any good for you Philippe — neither this house nor those in it . . ."

She lowered her voice and murmured as if to herself, "None of those in it, whether living or dead."

Then she was silent. She had said what she wanted to say and crossed her arms over her bent knees, leaning her head enough to reveal the shadowy line falling from her neck to her sides. She thus seemed to be regaining her strength, and Philippe thought anew of how ferrets roll up in a ball and, even with their sides smashed in, hold that position to die in it. There was a long silence.

Nothing in the world could now get another word out of her before he had spoken, yes, spoken, or moaned, or even struck — no matter what! Whatever happened, she would answer if he asked her. But a single word too much could lose everything and throw a crushed child back into Michelle's arms, this time forever, perhaps. Of all those obscure, elemental forces that in her deep wisdom, she knew how to manipulate, adolescent pride was the most fragile, more fragile than a woman's modesty — inconstant and fragile. In this decisive minute she scarcely dared look up at the high window where a pale, tender face was reflected amongst blue shadows.

"You're lying," he said with gentleness. "He isn't dead."

Before his hand had even touched her shoulder, she thought she felt its weight and closed her eyes.

"Took off, huh? Don't worry about me. Got the hell out of here, no?"

"Yes," she said. "But not like that, not the way you think . . ."

"There's only one way to leave," he replied. "And where to?"

"Go ask . . ." she began. "Listen, Philippe, we knew that Anthelme had told you. Otherwise you'd not have gotten a word out of me. But you must now be careful with your mother. What woman in her place wouldn't have done the same thing? And when you know . . ."

"What?"

"How can I say it? He's not dead, no . . . Alas, Philippe, he's deader than the dead."

Slowly she had raised herself up on her knees, and her impenetrable, pale eyes moved from the door to Steeny.

"Don't go right now! Calm down!"

At the boy's first step she was confronting him on her feet in the doorway. The shadow accentuated his handsome forehead, joined tightly at the temples, and the hard line of his jaws and cheekbones. The threatening pinch of his mouth was that of any starving London urchin in December standing between piles of oranges along the banks of the Thames.

"No foolishness!" he said with a harsh voice, which tremendously astounded him, and he immediately felt the mad rush of blood to his neck. His eyes in their orbits felt like little balls of lead.

"Do you think you're going to scare me, you snivelling street urchin! Sissy! You crazy loon! You idiot child!"

He thought he would violently shake the doorknob but didn't even manage to join his stiffened fingers around it. The paralysis went up the length of his arm to the shoulder, and for nothing in the world could he have moved his neck.

"You mean little brute! Oh, God! He's strangling me!"

But the cry seemed to emerge from the thickness of the wall, arousing no echo, and the frightening silence only appeared all the heavier to him, reaching a supernatural density in just a few seconds.

.   .   .   .

.   .   .   .

"Darling! Dear heart! Open your eyes! I beg you, open your eyes, my darling!"

With profound attention Philippe looked at the blond head gently lolling between Michelle's knees. Was it really that? Was that really what he had held up against the wall at arm's length? That breakable, clear thing, that fragile receptacle containing an ever changing light, even in its strange sleep? With his left hand still clinching the doorknob, he pressed his right hand against his chest in shame as though it were a murder weapon. It was possible that that hand had acted in spite of himself and even without his being aware of it while he was caught in a fit of temper! But the atrocious thing now was that that black spot within still persisted and that the returning light encircled it without elucidating it . . . He remembered nothing. Behind those eyelids Michelle was awkwardly trying to open were eyes that held the secret of what they had seen, of that still mysterious act that no doubt could easily be reconstituted by reasoning but nonetheless would remain as foreign to him as if committed by another. A part of his life, as small as he might suppose it to be — no matter! — had just escaped him forever; a part of himself, of his living self, had been struck dead, abolished. By what mysterious wound, by what open breach of the soul had it slipped away into nothingness? It seemed that with it all security and all certainty had vanished and that his conscience, like a leaking cistern, no longer allowed anything but muddy water, heavy with anguish, to rise to the surface. Drop by drop, through his disgust a sort of calm horror filtered from that rotten black wound.

"It was nothing, darling, the boy was a bit rough, that was all, forgive him, dear love!"

Just at that minute Maman's gaze met his own, and, for just a second, he saw her standing, pressed against the wall, her little hands convulsively clinched under her chin in a gesture of childish supplication.

"Philippe! Philippe!"

Staggering, Miss was now coming toward him, taking in the scene with her pale eyes. A rebellious strand of hair of a darker blonde fell down her shoulder.

With a calm voice she said, "Don't be so childish, darling. It's only Steeny, after all. I regret it so much . . . I'm so sorry!"

"Go away, Philippe! I've had enough! Make him go away, get him out of here, I cannot take it any longer! Look at him, it's Philippe! Just like him!"

Even if he had changed his expression or his gaze, it still would have depended neither upon him nor upon anyone else in the world. He felt as if his features were sculpted out of a material as hard as stone and that that fixed mask bore the likeness of another.

Now Miss was weeping in little sobs, her head in her hands.[1] He could only see the forehead of her face and the delicate ears and the perfect fusion of the jawbones with the imperceptible hollow of shadow where he would have liked to press his lips. An unknown pity, mixed with, or rather veiled by, a bit of scorn, a sort of inexpressible, inexplicable carnal satiety swelled his heart, and he sought in vain those forgotten words always residing in the deepest and most secret depths of his memory — which memory? —

1. The translator's research on the genesis of *Monsieur Ouine* indicates that Bernanos most likely intended the name to read "Maman" instead of "Miss."

words he had said before — but where and when? — in another age perhaps, in another world, of a timeless memory without name.

"Explain it to him, my love. Tell him everything."

. . . .

Again they were alone, face to face, and when she ventured laying her hand on his, he understood that the evil spell was broken, his mask had fallen.

"There now," she said. "Now you can finish her off if you want to, she's at your mercy . . . But do understand what I'm saying," she continued after a silence, "she'll be more easily killed than subdued. Yes, Philippe, her poor life is in the hands of the person who wants to take it, for no one has ever won the struggle against a child's fear. And do you want me to tell you something else? You'll be no better at it than was your . . . than he who . . . that is, well, you know whom I'm talking about . . . Her gentleness never fails to win the day."

With her strange gaze she looked him up and down for one last time.

"I was wondering what the color of your eyes was," Philippe remarked thoughtfully, "or even if they have one; it's all smoke."

He made a gesture of waving that vapor away, of thinning it out. Though sad and tired, his look was much more brilliant than usual.

"Please, forgive me," he said again, "did I . . . did I really hit you? Really? Strangle you?"

He pushed her before him, gently, without any resistance from her.

"Yes, I did, didn't I? And I had your neck against the wall, huh? Once? Twice? Many times? Well, now, good!" — he smiled — "Excuse me, I should so much like for you to put yourself in exactly the same place — ex-act-ly — is that it? And this hand on the doorknob . . . What! You're not going to try to make me believe that with the other hand I could have . . . Yes? Oh, to hell with it! I'll never know anything anyway."

He shrugged his shoulders.

"Can one imagine such a stupidity! How many hours of my life have already sped by me, under my nose—whish!—hours and months and years perhaps? Certainly years if I count the nights. And for a few miserable seconds . . . How funny that is! The camera worked, the lens is intact, the light was good, and there's nothing but a black spot on the plate—everything's black! Do you think that's possible, Miss?"

"I know you," she said through clenched teeth. "I know your whole accursed race! A race of men harder than hell itself. Look at yourself in the mirror: you look like a cat that's just stuck its nose in the cream bowl. God! Whether it's milk or blood, I'm afraid nothing's ever going to satisfy you. As they say in France, my dear: you're going to be left with your thirst."

"What's got into you?" Philippe asked, astonished. "I'm no longer even capable of hurting a fly. And as for those revelations you were burning to make, excuse me, I know more about them than you do, so it's useless to go back over that again. I'd not clearly understood what that idiot Anthelme said, that's all. There's just one question: Did you or didn't you ever believe my father was dead?"

"For five years. It was by chance that he was found again by the trustees of your estate, somewhere in Silesia, I think, in a very tiny village—but I don't know where. He'd been hospitalized at Bremen, then in the asylum at Luckau. The Repatriation Commission had him on its list when he took off."

"Good," said Philippe.

10

What a strange hut that frost-cracked cube of mud was! Its thatched roof was being washed away, and the last rains had left an enormous mud pile beside the sagging door. Inside, however, holes had been carefully stopped with clay, the walls whitewashed, and, suspended from the lowest beam, were the gun, shiny with grease, the knife in its leather holder, and the game bags still stiff with blood.

He had immediately sprung to his feet. His jacket and shirt were drying on the straw, and his naked torso gleamed in the shadows.

"I've got something to say to you, Eugene," the old man said.

Dumbfounded, the other man looked at him with the expression that used to get him so many slaps from the schoolmaster, an expression not so much of insolence or cheekiness but of a secret, deep timidity, isolating him from other men, making of him a ferocious, cunning hunter of hares and whores. But the old man was also looking at him without scorn. Never had the rebel for so long faced that too clear, too blue, too pure gaze that awakened in him something of the terrors of childhood. This time he vainly looked for the usual nuance of inexorable indifference and, surprised by what he saw, forgot to lower his eyes.

"Boy . . . ," the old man thoughtfully repeated in a low voice.

Was it the wind under the thatch, a cry from the sky, or the steps of some unknown animal? In a familiar gesture the poacher leaned his head a bit forward so as to hear better . . . But no . . . it was anguish that had just leapt in his heart.

"What's the matter, father?" he said.

The sense of danger was present in all his fibers, but what danger?

"They know everything," the old man said. "The order was to have been signed by the judge last night. You'll be arrested tonight or tomorrow."

"Good," he said simply. "We'll have to see."

"No," replied the old man gently, "no, Eugene, we'll not have to see."

A branch rubbed back and forth against the thatch above them with a silky rustle. The patch of sun, dancing from beam to beam, was suddenly immobilized and opened up in the center of the door, like a round eye.

"Helen did what she wanted to, boy," the father began again, "and it doesn't matter that it was against my will. But I believe you're a man."

"Agreed," said the other.

His wild gaze expressed no precise fear, but the total, candid acceptance of the still uncertain risk gave him a sort of extraordinary nobility resembling purity.

"I've done what I could, boy. If it hadn't been for the mayor, the order would have been given already. They've got evidence, they'll not let you get away. Everything comes to an end, boy. We all have our end, today or tomorrow, what difference does it make? And now . . . now . . ."

Damned sentence! It stayed there in the back of his throat, completely useless. It was not that he doubted the bastard's guilt, but the very idea of the crime was attenuated and erased, sinking into the deserted silence – into that prodigious sylvan silence of leaves and rain-drenched earth separating them from the world, where the other man was in his own home, an animal among the animals and free as an animal . . . Vainly he tried to straighten his tall frame, but both his sides and hips hurt, and his arms felt heavy. All the chill of the previous night still coursed through his veins; he felt like vomiting.

With one hand Eugene took down his jacket from the wall.

"Excuse me," he said, "but it had to dry out."

It was with the accent of an obscure complicity that the father's last words had resounded in his ears. Certainly for a long time now the old man's scorn had affected him no more than hunger or thirst, than wind or sudden downpours, all those mysterious fatalities that try a man's patience and irritate only women and children. "The old man has his ideas," he said simply. But now, for the first time, the old man seemed to be talking to him as an equal, and he suddenly realized that it was the one thing in the world he most desired.

"Whatever is it you want?" he finally asked. "You can speak frankly. There's nothing to be afraid of."

My goodness! Vandomme no longer knew. His will had always kept him going, but his thoughts now turned around in circles, faster and faster, like a giant fly. What he had to say should have been said right off, now it was too late. Decidedly that prepared sentence so bitterly flattering his pride now no longer had either weight, volume, or warmth – totally hollow and empty. And hollow and empty also those forebears without history and almost without names, those companions of last night in whose existence he would soon be the only one to believe. What did those phantoms have to do with this wild child of nature who was now cynically, fearlessly staring at him? How young he was! And how strong! Ah, his envy of all that youth and strength went right to the bone!

"You'll do it your own way, boy," he said.

In order to hear better, the former woodcutter inclined his head. Words for him had never been anything but dangerously abstract symbols, much too difficult to interpret and much more treacherous than numbers. Prudently, he only employed a small number of them, but he was marvelously sensitive to accents, gestures, and those thousands of nuances an animal's attentive gaze takes in with an equal, infallible astuteness. And besides, this time as always, instinct warned him more surely than could any words: the father's presence in his cabin at this moment equaled a death sentence.

"No harm done in understanding each other," he said. "In one way you are more or less silent by nature, like me. But the past is the past. If I've put you all in a bad situation, then I must do my best to make it up; I'm not a man to haggle over what your right is, as you said yourself. I'm not going to make you change what you've said."

His hand reached toward his forehead for an imaginary cap he pretended to push toward his left ear, then his arm dropped back down awkwardly. That damned still wet jacket froze his sides!

"It's true that I ran head-on into the little boy where the woods have just been cut, which shows that by wanting to take the shorter route by way of Mauchaisne he'd missed the path to Fenouille. We went back up together toward the pond, and there was no way you could see farther than your nose. The rain beat on our faces like a drum, and I lost my cap. It's possible they picked up our trail. I know the spot: the water flows over it there the way it flows over oilskin, just like it. I swear the soil in there will hold the inprint of a boar's foot for you from one season to the next!"

He tightened his trouser buckle, shaking his shoulders with the flashy gesture with which he used to confront a rival at the tavern door. His brown cheeks had scarcely paled, and his too thin mouth kept that same impenetrable grin that used to defy the priest, the schoolmaster, the boss, and all those reasoning powers against whom he was believed to have rebelled when, in fact, he was quite happy just to flee them, exactly as the animals he tracked day and night fled him: naturally, as they ate and drank, without hatred, and almost without fear.

"The unfortunate thing is that the girl and I contradicted each other," he said with a thoughtful grimace. "But I don't regret anything; guilty or not, you always lie to the law. If you let them get hold of just one truth, even if it's no bigger than a grain of rice, everything else will come out, you've had it."

With quiet audacity, his gaze now sought the old man's.

"I'm just not up to discussing it," the latter said, simply.

By mutual consent they both turned away, looking through the narrow opening at the forest, which, in the warmth of the light, grew calm and immobile. A fine, scented rain, smelling of musk, lay suspended at the height of the leaves while the breeze cradled an iridescent vapour from one extremity to the other of the immense, tall stand of trees.

In a voice purposely exaggerating his guttural accent, the former woodcutter remarked, "There are cases where one ought to speak up, but I'm just not worth it perhaps, is that it?"

"I've not refused to listen to you, boy," the old man said.

"Maybe. I'm no lawyer," the handsome rascal answered with extraordinary dignity. "But to begin with, what would all of you do with my explanation? You've got to have an alibi, I know their gimmick. And where am I supposed to find an alibi – or even see one?"

"Eugene," began the old man . . .

"That's all right, I understand. Devandomme, there are things in you that I don't approve of, but I've always respected you as a man, I swear! And, if we go to the bottom of things, it's got to be admitted I've never given you anything but trouble. That you don't want me going to Boulogne to get photographed for the papers, sitting between two policemen and everything, fine, I agree. But now, I have a question for you: does it interest you to know whether I killed the little boy or not — yes or no?"

"That's the concern of the law first," said the old man with a muted voice.

"All right then, you'll not know!" replied the other man on the same tone, with a terrible smile. "In a way you don't worry any more about justice than I do, right? So far as you're concerned you're satisfied for the affair to be properly arranged; me too! Between the two of us, man to man, that's good enough for me; I've never refused anybody's challenge."

The old man moved his mouth to answer, but turned his back in silence. At the door he hesitated again, then went out slowly, as slowly as he could, his head down, listening. The open door let in a flood of light so bright that he lifted his head and straightened his great shoulders, as if better to confront the great radiant swell rushing toward him from heaven's depths.

The little cripple seemed to be waiting for him, standing against the fence, a crutch set down beside him, hanging on to the bars with his little gray hands. The old man tried for a moment to smile, then blushed and turned his eyes away. Every time chance brought them together so unexpectedly, face to face, he felt a strange, indefinable ache in his heart. And it was true that he was ashamed of his health and strength, of his vigorous old age, in the presence of this young, fragile life with no protection from anything anymore and, as it were, floating on the surface of something indefinable and invisible, marvelous in its instability. But he was also afraid of it.

His daughter appeared for a moment at the narrow stable window, then disappeared again.

"Leave them," said the old man timidly, "leave your crutches. I'm going to carry you over there into the sun."

He sat down against the already warm slope. But the little cripple let himself slip along the bank, stretching himself out gently, both hands crossed behind his neck. The opening of his shirt revealed his pathetic chest.

"Little fellow," he said, "I'm not going to take anything from them any more."

He took off his cap, passed a trembling hand across his forehead and cheeks, then spat on the ground with disgust. The little cripple watched him in silence. He never asked questions.

"Damned bastard!" the old man added.

He too, like the other one, had only a small number of words at his disposition, but even that number appeared to him always to be beyond of what he needed. And even now the depths of that great solitude where, day by day, he had enclosed himself bit by bit, could not be measured by his ignorance. Was it possible that he would be uncomfortable in sharing his suffering, even if it were for just a second, just the time to catch his breath? Just one word should perhaps be enough, just a gesture. What gesture? Naively he raised his enormous fists, then let them fall back down immediately.

The boy was still looking at him. So he withdrew a few steps, his hands behind his back, then came near again, his head down. All his anger had dissipated, and even his hatred was stilled. Inside him, shame, nothing but shame, made a little noise like a gnawing animal. Ah no, God is not just!

"Listen, little fellow," he said.

The other, closing his eyes, did not even turn around.

"Listen, boy," the old man began again with a trembling voice, "think hard about it before replying, my man."

He blushed to his ears, but it was not he who asked the question, it asked itself, it came out all by itself — fell like a ripe fruit.

"What do you think of the little man in green and those Ardennes people, all those stories of lords?"

This time the little cripple tilted his head, and his gaze penetrated the old man's gaze as a red-hot horseshoe plunges into water.

"There is no little man dressed in green, there are no Ardennes people, there are no stories of lords either, there is nothing . . ."

"Huh?" said the old man.

It was not that the answer surprised him very much, for he was almost expecting it, but it was too quickly given. Two days ago he had spoken to his son-in-law, and since then the police had searched vainly for the bastard. However, a woman had seen him the day before in the direction of Plantier, and they thought he had bought provisions at a tavern run by a friend of his. Worse yet, the old man had in his pocket a note giving Helen a rendezvous for Tuesday night on the Roye road, near the river Roudre. Tuesday night—that was today. It was true he had found the piece of paper in the back of the stable under the straw and that it could date from several weeks ago as well, for humidity had already made the ink run. Too bad! This evening he would go to bed even earlier than usual, and if he heard the door squeak around midnight, he'd not stick his nose out of the window, he'd not spy on his daughter, no. Since he hadn't dared do the job himself, the die was cast now: God would judge.

The boy's look was still fixed on the old man. It seemed he was reading his thoughts as they came.

"You saw him?" the little cripple asked. "You spoke to him?"

He had just enough strength to nod yes with his head. What wouldn't he give to be able to find the proper words!

"I didn't have the heart, boy," he finally said after a horrid silence. The eyes of the cripple still burned, but one would have thought the little face was losing its color. But no, it did not lose its color, rather, it was disappearing, really disappearing, as might an old, used-up, dulled image.

"Nothing more," he said, speaking again, "never anything anymore."

Then his eyes grew dim too and he added in his childlike voice, "Lift me up a little, Grandfather, please, I'm too low. I'm stifling."

The ever jerking little hands, never calmed even by sleep, clung for a second to the arm of his progenitor. It seemed to the old man that they were pulling him toward the earth with a marvelous force, that that body weighing so little was frightfully heavy against his side. But what succeeded in breaking his resistance was the groan escaping the purple lips, almost against his cheek, a groan his ear hardly caught but thought it perceived, suddenly swelling a little — less of a complaint than a sort of solemn sigh, a solemn farewell. In that moment the accumulated fatigue of so many hours burst in the old man's heart, and, for a minute perhaps, for one long minute, he awkwardly tried to blend his own complaint with that call from so far away, that call from another world.

He gently laid the little cripple a bit farther down in a hollow of shade. Had he dreamed what he had just heard? No pity was asked for by the somber double flame of the gaze that had seized his own, and he too would ask for no pity. Whatever happened henceforth, it would be enough just to stand erect as before, as he had stood at the foot of the grave when the coffin of his wife was lowered into the ground by scraping ropes. The good people who wept at every funeral spoke of it among themselves, their eyes moist. "Good heavens! How brave he is!" Yet he was not brave at all. He didn't suffer either. He simply endured his pain in his own way, in a prodigious silence. Then, as today, the little murmur in the brain had fallen silent. From head to foot he was henceforth nothing but silence, stubbornness, and hidden patience. All those images of misfortune, the number and diversity of which had maddened his nerves for a moment, had melted into a single, elementary image: that of an obstacle, of an inert mass against which he pressed his forehead.

But over there in the cemetery of Fenouille, under the gaze of those people, he had still hoped for something, he didn't know what — and it now arose effortlessly, from the deepest part of himself, from his life's greatest depths, or perhaps even from the greatest depths of life itself. At the limits of his loss, the prideful dream he had vainly nourished for so many years, almost without knowing it — so tightly intertwined with the thread of his wretched and monotonous work, of his sadness, of his daily humiliation — there it was now, disappearing, being effaced, and he no longer recognized it nor was ashamed of it. A new, miraculous youth swelled in his chest, in his throat, bursting suddenly from his eyes like a jet of warm blood. He had not cried since his childhood, and the certainty that he was now crying for the last time, that he would never ever cry again, that this minute of grace was unique and perfect caused him bitterness as well as unspeakable refreshment. All his fatigue seemed to flow through his limbs into the earth where his rough shoes were planted. For a long minute he received the air's caress on his face, he fixed his gaze very firmly before him, without thinking. What was the use of thinking? Evil came from the brain, which is always working, that monstrous animal, that indefatigable pumper, unformed and soft in its case like a pupa. Yes, what was the use of thinking? A night of discussion with himself, of useless rumination, had sufficed to make of him another man, as weak as a woman. Why hadn't he slaughtered right off the man who perhaps tomorrow was going to dishonor his name? Now it was too late. But his duty was to endure, endure and nothing more. To endure, to remain, to stay fixed in the midst of things moving around him, to endure like a tree, like a wall, to hold out.

With the back of his hand he wiped his old cheeks. The cripple closed his eyes. One would have said he was sleeping, but in the half sleep into which he had sunk the thin little face had that strange expression it took on every time its gaze no longer glowed, that secret hardness accentuated by the outline of the Mongoloid cheekbones, with its indefinable smile. And it was that smile that the old man feared.

In a hesitant voice he finally asked: "Are you comfortable there?"

"Oh no, Grandfather! Take me home."

He took him up in his arms and carried him to the house.

His daughter watched them coming from afar, her back to the wall, her hand shielding her eyes. As on other days, she served them their coffee, then went to sit down in a corner by the stove, her bowl between her knees.

"I admit that my purpose in coming may seem indiscreet," said Monsieur Ouine, "but perhaps it won't be completely useless . . ."

In protest the curé of Fenouille shrugged his shoulders, but then gave a frantic look in the direction of the window's closed shutters. Though hardly visible in the shadows, the ruddiness of his cheeks, forehead, and ears did exaggerate a bit the rather stupid expression of his face, emphasizing its childish roundness. More childish still was his dragging, overaccentuated, low voice, losing control and choking over final syllables.

"Having just arrived in this parish, I can only be grateful to you . . . Such a difficult ministry . . . Our revered predecessor . . ."

"Your revered predecessor," replied Monsieur Ouine calmly — "you'll excuse my speaking with a cynical candor that is, in fact, much closer to my habits and character than is supposed — your revered predecessor was a fool." He pulled out of his pocket a ridiculous, stiffly starched cotton handkerchief, buried his face in it for a minute, then put it away in his hat. "Our relationship was cordial, intimate even. I think he took me for a man of letters or something similar."

"But I myself, Monsieur Ouine... Until now... I had thought..."

Monsieur Ouine's smile was so gentle and full of pity that the young priest again felt his cheeks burning.

"Our friend," the former language professor continued, "belonged to that category of innocent people from whom all our evils flow abundantly. Innocence, sir . . . Innocence . . ."

He breathed in noisily, as if stifling.

"Inno . . . Innocence, sir, is a disease proper to the age of maturity. At least only then does it attain its full and perfect potential for doing evil."

"But our children, come now, Professor, our dear little children?"

"Uh . . . uh . . . ," quickly began Monsieur Ouine, but then hushed.

His own cheeks had reddened, and the thick folds of his neck around the top of the hard collar turned from vivid red to a sort of pale blue. His entire face seemed swollen with anger, while his lips, allowing a burst of impatient breath to escape, responded more quickly than his still placid stare. For a minute they remained face to face, speechless.

"Allow me," Monsieur Ouine finally began again (his eyes had filled with tears), "I was young and I myself believed in childhood, but it only caused me too much suffering."

He rubbed the lapel of his jacket with his palm, appearing absorbed in looking for some invisible spot.

"We do no doubt encounter innocent children," he said, "and these shall remain such until the end. For innocence stands up to everything, it's more durable than life itself. I myself have known, alas, some of these unfortunate beings . . ."

"Don't you think . . . ," the poor priest began, but the objection he was going to raise suddenly appeared so vain to him that he dared not complete it.

"Against such monsters society defends itself," the former professor continued imperturbably. "Bit by bit it casts them away from its bosom, isolating them. Look at the fate of naive old maids, excluded by their own families. Sir . . . Sir . . ."

Though his voice was beginning to rise, he held it down.

"I do not pretend to define innocence, sir, it is something very different both from what we imagine and from what the word 'innocence' suggests. But I do know — experience has taught me — that innocence is always at the center and the core of a certain fermentation. The fact is that the earth ferments around the innocent."

He hushed, completely out of breath, his large head leaning forward, his hands posed on his knees. Several times the absurd cry of a carved wooden cuckoo clock was heard. Visibly relieved, he gave a blissful smile.

"Professor," the curé of Fenouille began again, not without a certain dignity, "it is true that I have a lot yet to learn about people and their unhappiness."

"I was not speaking about you," said Monsieur Ouine, almost tenderly. "No, monsieur."

Though still smiling with his mouth, his bloated features suddenly took on an expression of profound and almost familiar pity.

"People's unhappiness . . . ," he said, "their unhappiness . . . I believed in that also. Alas, sir! Pity could no more work within the context of man's unhappiness than a surgeon in a layer of pus. At the very first scratch . . ."

He took the priest's hand delicately into his own.

"At the very first scratch on that compassionate hand, I greatly fear all that filthiness might go straight to your heart . . . Oh, oh, 'sympathy,' 'compassion,' 'sympathein'—'suffer with,' well, 'rot with'—would be more accurate. Besides, you'd not be the last."

"What scratch are you talking about?" asked the curé of Fenouille. "Because disappointment . . ."

"Oh, disappointment has nothing to do with it," Monsieur

Ouine protested in a dreamy voice. "What does it matter to you if you're disappointed? You're not going to be disappointed, you're going to be dissolved, devoured! My goodness, to think your masters went to so much trouble to warn you about pleasures while leaving you as it were defenseless against . . . against . . . what a preposterous absurdity."

"All I fear is sin," the poor priest stammered. "Excuse me, but I cannot translate that into everyday language."

"Exactly, exactly. That's exactly what I wanted to say," Monsieur Ouine remarked with a smile.

Discreetly removing the handkerchief from the crown of his hat, he wiped his forehead and eyes.

"Even when men are not unhappy, Father, boredom is still there. No one has ever shared man's boredom and still been able to hold on to his soul. Man's boredom wears down everything, Father, it will soften the earth itself." His fat fingers moved as if kneading imaginary clay.

"But I am getting off track," he began again after a moment's silence. "I had quite another purpose in coming to see you than this chatter. Because of my withdrawn existence, my state of health, and even my natural disposition I am afforded only a few ways of being of use to you. Nonetheless, I am going to try. First of all I shall try in a few words to express feelings that, I admit, are rather complex . . . I am attracted by your solitude."

"Yes, I am completely alone," said the curé of Fenouille.

"More alone than you think perhaps," Monsieur Ouine continued with a painful expression. "How could your superiors, with no remorse and as a simple administrative measure, take you straight out of the seminary and toss you into this muck heap? Even so some muck heaps are peaceful and seem dormant enough. Quite in contrast to this one where, for some time now, the muck seems devilishly active. You'd even think you could hear it boiling and sizzling, though I'd say that that's scarcely even an image, dear friend. Someday we shall know the mysterious laws governing both the acceleration and retardation of those sorts of fermentation. In any case, there is no chance here for any mistake concerning what the next cause for fermentation will be."

"I am referring to the death of the little cowherd," he added after a long silence.

"Well, Professor," the young priest said, "the newspapers are much to blame for troubling minds this way."

Monsieur Ouine shrugged his shoulders.

"In every house there is now a cadaver," he said softly. "I admit, sir, that in the time of my youth this whole affair would have been of overwhelming interest to me. Perhaps that extreme curiosity to which, much too often, I have sacrificed my peace of mind might even have caused me to commit some imprudent action. Alas, no doubt such gratuitous curiosity can only be a derangement of the mind. Of course, your own mind is inspired by supernatural motives, but allow an old man . . ."

"Oh!" the curé of Fenouille felt obliged to protest politely.

"Yes, allow me to warn you, not against any particular person or persons, but against the whole lot of them."

"Monsieur . . . Dear Sir . . . Professor, I do humbly acknowledge your capabilities and your talents. Nevertheless . . . and as ill-placed as this remark may seem coming from the mouth of a priest . . ."

His hand — pathetically cracked by the winter cold and black-spotted since he smeared the cracks with ink — made a gesture as though to erase the imprudent remark he was about to make.

"The love that I have for my . . . well, yes . . . for my children — for my parishioners are my children — well, I cannot allow myself to be warned against my parishioners, Professor."

"Of course!" said Monsieur Ouine. "But we have misunderstood one another. My tastes, my habits — to say nothing of my deepest and most intimate feelings — make me in this respect your natural ally, a sort of modest collaborator. To put it briefly, in this whole village you and I are the only ones interested in souls."

"Please forgive me," the curé of Fenouille murmured humbly. "I spoke like an idiot."

"Yes, in souls," Monsieur Ouine repeated, dreamily. "Perhaps given my situation and my character it would be more appropriate if instead of 'souls' I spoke of our being interested in the truth of individuals and their secret motives, but the vagueness of those sorts of paraphrases puts me off."

He wiped his forehead and waited a long time, his shoulders shaken by a nervous cough, his face buried in his handkerchief. When he at last uncovered it, the curé of Fenouille noticed a remarkable alteration in his features.

"Certainly," said Monsieur Ouine, "Fenouille was already completely demoralized. But to turn this demoralization into something unbearable it took only the most ordinary crime – and besides, is it really a crime? No one knows . . . Sir, my days are numbered. For me to die in such circumstances, in the midst of the cheapest and most mediocre sort of detective story, would be most unpleasant for me. Oh, I'm not a moralist! Evil is evil. I'd even prefer that it have something in it to turn the stomach of the squeamish; I'm not afraid of its stench. But this modest village has been turned into a bazaar, a fair, where everything, be it good or evil, is spread out pell-mell on display, in the most hideous disorder. I cannot stand that, sir."

"But I am obliged to stand everything," said the curé of Fenouille in a soft voice. "And that too I shall stand as all the rest, whether I'm alone or not."

"Why should we not resist it together?" proposed Monsieur Ouine. "Make use of me. I've lived here for years and I know this little village. It has its secrets. But neither curiosity nor love can ever quite take in the secret of the destitute. That secret yields itself only to him who is silent. So don't intervene too soon. Perhaps you've already received a great deal of confidential information . . . I mean, that sort of written thing that the law calls – ha! ha! – anonymous? Letters that might . . . that might be of a personal interest to me . . ."

The curé of Fenouille quickly reached for the interior pocket of his cassock, then brought his hand down on the table. Monsieur Ouine smiled.

"Give it to me," he said softly. "Or rather, give them to me, for you no doubt have received more than one, I think."

"Sir," the priest said, "perhaps I shouldn't even have read them. God is my witness, however . . . that . . . I'd never have shown them to anyone, not even to my superiors."

Monsieur Ouine made a gesture of polite indifference.

"Alas, sir, I've indeed received a lot of others," the curé of Fenouille stammered. "Should I burn them? Or should I not? It's like having an enemy presence in the house, monsieur, and I can only breathe easy when I'm in the church, and even there . . . Is it possible that a village so lost in the woods, so far from the city . . . What have I done to them, sir? I've even on occasion wondered if . . . if these horrid things . . . didn't all come from the same hand, but the idea seems somewhat far-fetched to me . . . someone wanting to drive a poor priest like me to despair and mess up his life, is such an idea something really worth entertaining? Excuse my asking you this question, sir, but is the purpose or your visit that of a friend . . ."

"I am not your friend," the professor replied in a serious voice. "And even should you immediately lose your confidence in me, I still shall hide none of my own wretchedness from you: sir, I have doubted your trustworthiness."

The curé of Fenouille opened his cassock and, with trembling hand, drew out a bundle of letters.

"Kindly give me an envelope," said Monsieur Ouine. On it he wrote, "To the Examining Magistrate," then placed it back on the table with a grunt of pleasure.

"With God as my witness . . . ," the poor priest began with ridiculous emphasis.

But he did not finish. His insignificant face, so little designed to express anguish, was suddenly deformed completely and would have seemed literally twisting under the blow of an almost theatrical despair had it not been for a heart-rending appeal in his eyes and the sort of proud innocence seen in the eyes of children and also in gentle animals tracked to the point of surrender.

"Take them, sir," he said, "take them, take everything away . . ." As he spoke he threw three other packets on the table, all incongruously tied with that pale blue string used in candy stores. "A priest should never complain, I know, Professor, for another's pity is of no use to us. But at the moment I am more afraid of my loneliness than of pity. Loneliness had already taken its toll from me before I was old enough to bear it. My father was a miner in the Lens country, dying at the bottom of the mine two months before I was born. My mother didn't survive very long afterward so I was reared by an aunt. She had a tavern at Noirentfontes. Ah, sir, even today the face of a drunkard still horrifies me! Yet I am not innocent; I know what evil is. But at an age when children are all caught up in games, in songs and laughter, I had already sensed that one can never come to terms with evil, that justice and injustice are two different worlds. The only real joy that God ever gave me was on a day in October when for the first time I entered the courtyard of the junior seminary — I thought I'd die from joy! I'd found a family, sir, do you understand that? A home! But, alas! Today my best friend from among those boys there is a notary's clerk in Marseille. Another one's a policeman, another one a coachman. So here I am, no less alone than before, even more alone . . . You may say to me, 'Well, you have your superiors, your fellow clergy . . .' Ah, sir, nothing differs more than one priest from another! Our loneliness is an absolute loneliness. When I've spoken of these things, they've felt sorry for me, they've smiled. But it's every fellow for himself, right? To each his own! And then, don't you see, there is still that extraordinary, that impenetrable and inflexible optimism of our superiors, those older priests: 'You must come to terms with it,' they all keep repeating. No doubt. Indeed, sir, I am coming to terms with man's proud stupidity. I do not rebel against evil. God Himself did not rebel against it, sir. He assumed it. I don't even curse the devil . . ."

· · · · · · · · · · · · · · · · · · · ·

With his arms he made the pathetic gesture of one who, having
uttered a torrent of words, realizes that he has only succeeded
in taking measure of his own unhappiness and despair at never
being able to share his secret, ineffable essence with anyone.
Monsieur Ouine tucked the tied-up packets under his arm.

"I wish you good day," he said.

"Don't leave just now," begged the curé of Fenouille, beside
himself. "You have before you a man who has been pushed too
far . . . that's exactly it . . .pushed too far. My goodness! Deep down
they all want only one thing, yes, one thing only that is only more
exasperated by aging, infirmities, and illnesses. And, to spare their
pride, they can call it any name they want to, but what they all really want is to be delivered from their sins, that's all . . ."

While he spoke, Monsieur Ouine, incessantly bowing in his direction, moved backward toward the door. At the last words of the
priest, he stopped brusquely.

"Man's last disgrace," he said, "is that evil itself bore him."

He rubbed his hat on the cuff of his sleeve and, with a deep
bow, went out.

   The road turned abruptly almost directly in front of the
presbytery, then disappeared down into the valley of the Louette.
The slope was so steep there that when the wind blew from the
plain at dawn on Wednesdays, the grinding and caterwauling of
brakes on the carts heading for the market at Fruges could be
heard from one end of the village to the other. As though heaven-
sent, that plaintive shriek now rose behind Monsieur Ouine. It
came through the fine, insidious mist falsifying all perspective,
through the cold vapor that Monsieur Ouine breathed with difficulty into his rotting lungs, sounding like the call from a thousand

feet above the hills of those black winter birds thrown off course and caught in the vise of a polar storm. "Dear me, dear me!" said the professor of languages.

. . . .

He had just reached the little bridge below and, spreading out his handkerchief on the stone step, sat down, his hands resting on his knees. The water, bluish like the weather, rolled past his feet. Along the bank, on the surface of the narrow grass-fringed inlets, a thin gray soap film remained from the strong soap used on washday. The water under the film was tinted rose as it moved. Sometimes a big bubble would make it past the stems of the reeds, then spin around before bursting with a sound imperceptible against the monotonous, fountainlike gurgling.

"Dear me, dear me!" repeated the professor of languages.

For years now—or had it always been so?—certainly since the first attacks of the illness that was now devouring him—he had dreaded dawn. Noon at least overcame him, throwing him on his bed with his shutters closed, even in the middle of December, for his attacks seemed to obey the mysterious rhythm of the clock rather than that of the season. But the anguish of daybreak curiously prolonged his insomnia and became as it were an unbearable expansion of it. The sharp coolness and limpidity, the murmur of invisible springs, this renewal of all things isolated him more painfully even than silence and darkness where his nerves could find a sort of calm, funereal security. But morning seemed to exclude him disdainfully from life, rejecting him along with the dead. He hated it.

. . . .

He laid the packet of letters beside him with indifference. Nothing was now left of that burst of curiosity that, almost in spite of himself, had pushed him toward the young priest. Had it been curiosity? The taste for risk? He couldn't say. He only knew that up there, behind the lindens and yews, he had had his last chance. Now it was no more. The magic circle, diminishing around him each day, would no longer allow itself to be broken.

The faith he had in himself, hard as a diamond, had never really been destroyed or even altered, and it must, until the end, replace all success, all hope, and all joy. The approach of death perhaps made it even tougher and more brilliant. As indifferent as he might be to his future fate — if, indeed, the dead have one — that faith no doubt was still what was most capable of enduring and surviving among those many goals to which wretched humanity aspired. Yet the idea that in dying he was supposed to regret anything whatsoever or deny any one of those hours that, one after the other, had marked his progress toward his deliverance and total freedom hadn't even occurred to him yet. And it seemed less and less likely that it ever would occur. Whenever he tried to return, quite apart from memory, to that confused mass of childhood impressions, to the first, moving, swarming part of life that is the last to return to the immobility of death and, no doubt, is what renders every death agony a private, unique, and incommunicable drama, he would recall never having really hated but one single restraint, whose principle was found within himself: the awareness of good and evil, that other being within his own being, that worm within.

. . . .

The mist rose little by little toward the expanse of pastures until the slow oscillation of the air pushed it aside about halfway up. The village was still completely visible, crowned by its tall slate belfry and its houses crouched like so many animals. But at that distance Monsieur Ouine's weak eyes could not distinguish one from the other: they formed nothing but a uniform pile, a single mass that his eyes passed over repeatedly with disgust.

For today as in times past, as when he was twenty years old, towns or villages – how should one say it? – even the most humble house from which smoke arose filled him with uneasiness, causing his heart to contract. And certainly the presence of his fellow man was neither helpful nor even friendly to him. Rather, every gathering of human beings tormented him with uneasiness and curiosity as well as an undefinable sickness whose secret he could confide to no one. How many times, upon returning from his long walks in the evening, had he got himself all muddy along uninhabited lanes for no reason other than to avoid the principal street of the village, abandoned at that hour, with the golden yellow halos of its lamps, where his gaze, plunging into a room, might have caught a family at home in the evening: the old man spitting into the ashes; the grandmother, still nimble; the horrid bundled-up brat tied with a towel to a straw-bottomed chair; the flushed cheeks of the daughter; sometimes a little angel-eyed boy dreaming, his pen stuck in his mouth ... How weary, how alone he always felt in front of those animals scarcely distinguishable one from the other, all of them exchanging glances and even the air they breathed from birth to death under that same grimy ceiling, between the table where they ate and the bed that would soak up their death sweat. The resistance and soft elasticity of that mixture could be conquered neither by will nor intelligence nor tyranny – nor indeed even by curiosity, that most powerful of means for breaking things up when it was pushed as far as hatred. In his imagination he could almost see – indeed, he thought his eyes did see – those lugubrious layers, those pools of mud, as though from another world or another planet ... And whosoever tried to touch these things – some miraculous being, a man born truly free – found his legs buckling under him and disappeared almost immediately with grimaces and gesticulations as all that human spawn, living and dead, sucked him in. In times past, however ...

With the numb fingers of his two puffy hands he painfully felt his chest. His lungs were no longer even irritated by the bite of the cold air, and, although the spasm following each breath was prolonged by a slight distress, he did not find it unpleasant. For as far back as he could remember, suffering and thinking were for him one and the same thing: the working of his brain had always to be accompanied by some voluntary or involuntary wound to his flesh. When he was twelve years old, he had hidden at school, under piles of red, purple, and green copybooks, a volume of Spinoza, stolen from the master's room, and no poetry could have matched in his eyes those dry pages, read word by word with dogged patience, though he succeeded in tying them together only by such an immense effort that he often fell forward, his face crushed against the wooden desk, with such a violent contraction in his chest that he thought he was dying. And, to be sure, it was not truth that he was hoping to reach at the end of those abstract formulas, which, in any case, were nearly always incomprehensible, for he had never felt any appetite whatsoever for truth, regardless of what kind of truth it might be. With his gaze seemingly lost behind his absurd steel-framed spectacles, and his fingers with nails bitten to the quick clenched against his fatigue-hardened face, he hadn't known what to say to that history professor who one day surprised him and was astonished by such unusual zeal for reading the Jew of Amsterdam. The professor, a sardonic, thickset peasant from the Auge valley, smelling of pipe tobacco and brandy, gently caressed his cheek and, signaling for him to follow, pushed him out of the study hall into the dark stairwell chilly as a cellar and on up to his room, where he paternally had him sit on his knees . . . Other than the pale illumination coming through the windowpanes from the gas jet burning day and night in the courtyard outside, there was no light in the room. Scattered books lay in great piles against the wall and behind a red serge curtain could be seen the unmade bed, the whitewood table, the washbasin full of dirty water. "Well, now, my little philosopher . . . ," the heavy Norman kept repeating in a monotonous voice, "well, now, my little philosopher . . ." And he, Ouine, for the first time in his life – and for the last time too, no doubt – tried to make it all clear, tried to explain himself, while the words seemed to gush up from some forgotten and suddenly rediscovered part of his soul, flowing forth from an unquenchable spring. His mouth scarcely had time to pronounce them before still others rose up from the depths of his throat, words he could not hold back, words ending in grating sobs. God, how sweet those tears were! Yes, yes, how liberating their hot shame! They flowed more abundantly and more easily than the gush of words, and he let them run down his cheeks, inundating his mouth with their warm, salty taste. His steel-framed glasses came loose, slipped off, and smashed at his feet on the tiles. And then he could no longer see anything but a halo. At first it was indistinct, but out of it there emerged, bit by bit, as from out of a pale mist, the face of the history professor while, at the same second, he felt the prickling of his red beard and perceived, almost touching his own eyebrows and looking back into his own gaze, an unknown stare, empty and frozen like that of a dead man . . .

12

She had not heard him, poor girl! Was she even still capable of seeing or hearing? And yet, long before the water-soaked dead leaves had made that horrid sucking sound under his steps, long before that tall fine figure appeared at the height of the path – ah, so young; you might take him for one of those youths who knocked down bird's nests, their faces smeared with blackberries, one of those friends of long-ago Sundays, those beautiful Sundays! – her heart was already miraculously light and free in her breast with she knew not what absurd, dazzling hope.

"Listen," she said, "I thought I'd made a mistake. I've been here in the dark for such a long time."

As usual, she stood away from him, very properly, without even a smile in her eyes. For that's how he liked her. But, to her great surprise, he suddenly pressed her violently to his breast in silence.

"Come over to our place," he said in a voice she recognized but had heard only once before, on the wedding night.

"It's just that it's not a very good night," she said, "and I still have on my shoes with holes in them. How can you expect me to go all the way to the hut? It's past ten and the mare's not even had her hay."

"I'll carry you whenever you get tired," he answered.

She had started immediately, walking behind him without a word. And, beginning then, she stopped anticipating or thinking. How stupid to think, since one always thinks alone, alas, whereas the lover's first word brings a forgetfulness more perfect than sleep, melting so deliciously in the veins, changing blood into wine!

It was indeed a dark night. Toward which of the huts were they going? The nearest one was in the Elan hollow, but he preferred the Relais, an old post house going back to the time of the lords, where he had made himself a comfortable little nest the game-wardens knew nothing of. The path they were taking was the one that should follow the road to Roye, and the edge of the woods was sometimes so close to the road that the wind from the plain hit them in the face with a heavy, saturated air that slowly, heav-ily rose above their heads. They found the beech-covered, hidden slopes of the Rouvre, almost bare under the high vaults of vege-tation, then, once again, their feet sank into the sticky decay of dead leaves that squished under each step, spitting out a rust-colored water. Her legs were frozen up to her belly, and her poor wollen scarf kept getting caught on the scaly bark of the trunks. Lord, she'd never have the strength to make it back before dawn! But already her heart was calm as though awaiting an event too prodigious for any feeling other than a solemn expectancy. What was to happen would happen. And what was to happen had no re-lationship with anything in the past, for this night was surely go-ing to open onto a new and dazzling day.

"Where are we going?"

"To the Relais," he said. "Are you cold?"

"A little," she answered timidly.

For she had seen him unbuttoning his corduroy jacket and was enchanted by the idea of feeling the sweet warmth of his young fraternal body on her neck and shoulders. Lord, had he ever before shown himself so considerate and tender? As he slipped it on her she quickly kissed the dew-drenched fabric.

"Here we are, my pet."

There was a completely new door with solid hinges, locked with a padlock. And the hide-out was no longer recognizable: the walls were covered with mats he himself had braided, and he had built himself a bed with very smooth planks painted a dark forest green. His best gun was there, thrown across it, its great squat figure "12" shining like a living creature. She suddenly wanted to touch it, to slip her small hand secretly along the barrel.

"Go ahead," he said in a strange voice, "it won't bite you!"

His eyes expressed nothing, neither anger nor tenderness, nothing at least that she was familiar with, unless it were perhaps a sort of deep attention. Then suddenly he picked her up, folding her against his breast, and his violent mouth was already seeking her own when, with gentle firmness, he set her back down.

"Better not," he said thoughtfully.

He blushed to the tips of his ears. She tried to smile.

"What's wrong?" she said. "Not ready?"

"Don't joke," he said, "don't joke before you know, for I want you as much as ever, dear girl, even more; no offense meant . . ."

And immediately he backed away a couple of steps, his shoulders shaken by a shiver.

"It's too bad there's no other way to make love," he continued in the same barely distinguishable voice. "Yes, another way, a real way—I don't know—a way that could be done only once, for example—one single time with one single woman. As for whores, I've had as many of them as I wanted, I swear, but you . . . you . . . No one knows what you are with your nice little body weighing no more than an armful of fresh rushes—and with a man's courage."

She blushed with pleasure without looking up.

After a long silence she finally said, "Eugene, don't try to tell me everything today . . ."

It was no doubt the boldest thing she had ever said to him, for he wouldn't allow her to interrogate him, and even now he could not repress a grimace of anger, but the double wrinkle at the corner of his curling lips vanished immediately.

"The old man came."

"Here?"

"He certainly didn't go to the pope's."

"But tell me!" she said with a voice that she tried to keep from trembling. "What did he want with you?"

But he shrugged his shoulders and moved off toward the door. It was no use; she came and placed her little hand on his sleeve.

"The police?"

"Leave me alone! Believe what you want to."

"Oh," she said, "I believe anything, I'm used to it."

She couldn't find the words, and the idea that she could no longer hold back and that she must for the first time break that interior silence where her love was kept hidden made her tremble like a leaf.

"Come on," he whispered between his teeth, "don't go getting upset."

The reproach made her blush again, but she didn't really have time to suffer from it for she was gathering her strength. All the life forces she could muster were turning around a few too simple poor words, like a flock of huge birds.

"If the old man has betrayed you," she said, "I . . . I . . ."

But she started trembling again from a great coldness invading her breast, and her heart pounded against her ribs with great silent thuds.

He looked at her with that same attentive gaze, and submissively, shaken by shivers, she turned her miserable little face toward him.

"No, he's not betrayed me," he said, "and I'm not going to betray him either."

He breathed calmly, deeply, swelling out his chest.

"Pass me the liter of rum, my pet; it's just behind you, on the plank. It's freezing cold in here, isn't it?"

But with her eyes half closed and her hand resting against the wall, she seemed not to hear him.

"What are you thinking about?"

"If you drink, I'll drink too," she said, "but I'd rather not."

She looked at her muddy shoes and her soaked stockings in distress. And her fingers with their worn-down nails made her ashamed too. She hid them under a fold of her skirt.

"My father hasn't . . . hasn't . . . ," she began.

"Hasn't what?"

"Nothing. I'm crazy."

"Hasn't what? It's not really the moment to play games, my girl."

"Hasn't spoken to . . . to the police?"

"No. It just seems that the order has been issued. I could be arrested tomorrow."

"That musn't be!"

She had said it just like the old man, with the same very low voice, with a proud accent. Then slowly, prudently, without lifting her head, she let a meaningful look slip toward her lover.

"All those times we could have taken off, gone far away—I don't know, across the seas, you know, gone to other countries, just us two . . ."

"No foolishness now," he said harshly.

"I was talking about it without believing in it," she said, excusing herself. "But I have dreamed all this time of a great, very tall forest with nothing but trunks, trunks like columns, very straight and very black, and I thought I saw the sea through it, very far away, just a blue fringe . . . At least I thought that it must be the sea, since I've never seen it."

The last words were stifled in the back of her throat as she retreated a little into the shadows to retie the string she used as a garter. She caught his stare and blushed to her ears.

"I was just going to clean the stables," she said, "and I came as I was, you see."

But her poor smile was finished. From her eyelids great tears rolled downward.

"If I'd been able to go back to the house I'd have put on my dress and stockings."

"You're not going back?"

"No, certainly not," she said, simply. "You think I'm that stupid?"

All at once her eyes were dry and burning in the thin face, and, full of an implacable, though inexorable, sweet will, she turned toward the door.

"They're all going to get caught," she said, "all of them . . ."

She turned her back toward him, and he could look at her as much as he wanted, with a naive surprise mixed with fear and a kind of hidden resentment. Certainly the image of death had not entered all that far into his brain, yet no force in the world would now dislodge it. Vainly he tightened his belt with the flashy movement of his hips used so many times to defy his rivals in the cafés of Meknès, but, alas, there was no enemy before him, no known, familiar force against which he could measure his own, but instead a simple and terrible feeling he had no name for, a bare wall, smooth as a glass, where even terror's fingernails could get no hold, a pride harder and more transparent than a diamond.

He was seeking, yet he sought vainly, the sentence that had to be said, the sentence he had always found every time he had put his life on the line and taken his chance, but his thought turned around itself, like a rat in a trap. And, besides, his life had been played, his chance had been taken. There was nothing more.

"Ah, well, that's fate!" he said finally, as if to himself.

She shrugged her shoulders in indifference. Perhaps she might have preferred that he refuse her sacrifice and beg her to live, to survive him, using those words one reads in books, yet it didn't displease her at all at that solemn moment of love to see his real face again, for she had known for a long time that he was both a greedy and a hard master; she had served him as such with a sort of fierce obstinacy and without vain self-pity. As for death, it didn't bother her. It seemed to her something out of childhood, a sort of fairytale. It was so unreal for her at that moment that it never occurred to her to throw herself into his arms, to clasp to her breast the threatened companion, whom she looked upon with an all-enveloping, peaceful gaze. She scarcely was aware of a vague and almost voluptuous fear, of a mysterious movement of tenderness for her own, now endangered, body as, under her loose blouse, she distraughtly caressed her young breasts.

"That's the way it is; what can you do?" she said. "We'll not even have had one good month, one peaceful month!"

She came close to him, pressing her lips gently to the hollow in his chin, with a shiver of pleasure. Never had she felt herself so soft, so supple, nothing but docility and caresses. It seemed to her that she was floating weightless in the depths of a calm water where no movement could reach her. Even the thought of the approaching end reached her only in a deadened, discolored state through that limpid depth. Ah, let what had to be done be done quickly so that they might slip from that peace into the other one . . .

Timidly she pulled back a little, still without daring to unlock her hands encircling his shoulder. What was he looking at now with that savage stare? The hour had come when all the hatred opposed to their humble destiny was going to be rendered impotent, and he looked as if he were confronting it, his head lowered, his muscles tensed. How much time had been lost for their love when they still had time! And now . . . now it was true that she didn't understand at all, but what difference did it make! She only desired his beloved will; for him she was ready to sacrifice even the consolation of a last farewell.

"Listen, Eugene," she said, "perhaps . . . perhaps it would be better . . ."

The voice of a mother could not have been more gentle, and she closed her arms on her breast in a cradling position, instinctively making this sacred female gesture her own.

He retreated imperceptibly, then stopped, his hands falling

down by his sides, his shoulders thrown back in the attitude of a man who has just been shot right in the chest and is immobilized for a second before falling face first to the ground. But only the body had that tragic resignation, that abandonment. The hollow of his pale cheeks, the painful pinching of his lips still showed stubbornness and craftiness beyond anything expected, even in the abandonment of hope and even beyond all fear and all thought; it was not the refusal of death but an inflexible love of life, the love a dying animal gives to life in its last bloody gasp.

"It's funny," he said, "you're like the old man, exactly the same. You don't seem to want to know whether I killed that little boy or not."

"What difference could that make to me, my love?"

This time she caught his rebellious stare full on: he no longer resisted her, and she saw his proud eyes light up by degrees. God, there he was just as he used to appear to her behind the hedge, his hair unkempt and his neck bare, with his bold, gentle smile. With her two weak hands she gently covered his beloved face, looking away, her cool palms offering it a first shroud.

"Don't touch it — don't touch your face, my beloved . . . promise me!"

At the same time she pulled his shirt aside and placed her mouth over his heart. Had he understood? Could she say more? No, how could she? Now they had to act quickly. Quickly! Quickly! She could feel his eyelids beating for an instant under her left hand, which still held them closed. With her other hand behind his back, she groped, then drew the black shotgun with its squat barrels toward her and her own chest. Skilfully slipping the butt between the planks and the mattress and fixing the double steel mouth under her breast, she leaned on it with her full weight, feeling for the trigger with her thumb . . . Impossible to know if the gun had fired or not, but the cabin was filled with scarlet red smoke darkening in a second to become a patch of silence and of night.

13

They decided to bury the little boy on Thursday, the weekly school holiday. Before dawn the old bell ringer woman had set up the trestles for the coffin and the large candlesticks and had unfolded the white hangings smelling of linen, incense, and some other sweetish substance. A little later the schoolmaster appeared in the schoolhouse door in black trousers, polished shoes, and a brand-new false shirtfront resounding like a drum when you tapped on it with your fingers. By nine o'clock groups were forming in tavern doors; with the sun arose a sort of Sunday joy, and the first, so grave, tolling of the bell filled the heavens.

As he stood in his doorway, it burst upon old Vandomme's ears, its thunderous rolling enveloping his poor empty house, shaking it. Then there was nothing more than a drone like a swarm of giant wasps, shot through with sonorous flashes, and, just above his head, the shattering of a crystal sphere in an explosion so clear and pure it seemed to be transmuted into brilliance, falling back down on the vast sunny landscape like a shower of light . . . Sometimes, when the wind changed, there was the heart-rending, almost human cry of its echo.

. . . .

Too bad! The old man's head trembled a little between his shoulders, but he went forward another step, bravely confronting the sort of mockery that would break over him from the enemy village. Nothing would keep him from being there at his post in a few minutes; before no one would he lower his eyes. When facing hatred or scorn, the only danger risked by a despairing man is to pity his own misfortune, and, as for him, well, he felt no pity whatsoever for himself. He'd die with dry eyes. He had had only one moment of weakness, which had really been quite slight — or, since he could not sleep since the death of his daughter and son-in-law, was it perhaps only a bit of dizziness caused by insomnia? — when, in the pallid reflection of the morning light, he put on his good shirt, broke his nails on the buttonholes, and tied the ridiculous little black tie that slipped out of his enormous fingers every time . . . It used to be his daughter who . . . No matter! His daughter and her lover were already buried, over there, in a back corner of the Poperinge cemetery — twin graves with neither names and nor crosses — and he had had to abandon the little cripple, in the middle of an attack, at the hospital of Merenghien. Now he must take his place again, reassume his rank, clinging to them both, impassively devouring his humiliation to the end, day after day, in front of all of them, without hope of reaching the end of that hideous provender, before dying in the midst of it like an ox on a litter of straw.

There was no pity for himself, no regret whatsoever. The pride that he had nurtured for so many years in the most secret part of his soul, that pride so perfectly incorporated into his life and into its very substance and to which he probably could not yet give its true name, that pride had just consumed even his remorse. The assurance of his absolute solitude and of the sort of damnation into which he had fallen shattered his nerves at that moment with such force that, for himself alone, he tried awkwardly to express, through some sort of image, a feeling that was almost inconceivable. He thus suddenly reflected that he was like an old tree filled with the dust of its own rot. Shrugging his shoulders, he marched bravely toward his fate.

The road where his path ended was empty. Carefully he wiped his mud-caked soles against the bank. His rolled-up trouser legs revealed his gray woolen socks, and the tails of his coat, with its ridiculous little, outdated collar, were whipped against his thighs. Good God! the windows of the tavern were solid black with the backs of the men. As he passed by, they turned around all at once, pale through the pipe smoke, pale like those faces seen in dreams. Get on with it boy! His big shoes dragged on the pebbles with a horrid grating in spite of himself. He vainly tried to throw his shoulders back and put his leg forward — it was as though he were not budging, as if he were dragging along . . . Get on with it, boy! Faster, still faster . . . "He's something to see, man, just look at him!" All together they came out to the entryway, pushing one another aside in order to see better, and, never really exploding, the great burst of threatening laughter diminished into a prolonged murmur. For, to their amazement, the old man had begun to run, his back bent and his head down, as though in spite of himself and even unaware of it. Still running, he took the path to the cemetery, not stopping before reaching the high oak church door and propping himself up against it with both hands.

The church had lost its sweetish smell of resin, moss, and wilted greenery and was now as dark and hot as a stable. From the apse the light of the candles crept over the paving stones of the nave, and, before getting lost up under the vaults, inched up the tall stone pillars with their eternal sweat of icy water, a dead water, slippery to the touch. The choir was full of men standing either immobile or else all coughing at the same time, like animals in a herd. Alone, absolutely alone, more isolated by the double row of candles than by an abyss, the tiny coffin stood draped in white among the shadows.

When it was all over, no one could say how it had happened, nor by what miracle. No, no one would have wanted to believe that that mud hole of a little village had a soul, yet it did, and one so resembling an animal's soul: slow, dreamy, and completely victim of an aimless, scarcely perceived, and unwinding curiosity, full of scarcely formed images, suddenly accelerating and going berserk, torturing the brain. It was true that all of them felt the same impulse to group themselves around the little cadaver as tightly as a herd of cattle surrounded by wolves . . . Ah, just let it take along with it underground all that had been stalking about among them day and night for a week! But reaching the end of the patience and wiliness of the dead is not that easy.

It had all begun by boredom. From the time of the offertory of the mass, boredom had descended upon them, melting and dripping down from the high vaults. Vainly they secretly nudged one another, exchanging conspiring looks or harsh, self-pleased coughs from pew to pew. It seemed that boredom had closed their eyes and stopped their ears. Noël Chevrette later said to the judge: "I was so bored, Your Honour, that everything seemed to have turned black around me, for God's sake!" Moreover not one of them could possibly have foreseen the surprising length of the funeral, which the mayor of Fenouille had declared official and which, rather inexplicably, lasted far beyond the normal time. When the priest, under the surprised gaze of Faublas, the sexton, took off his black chasuble and seemed headed for the pulpit (in fact, he only went to the altar rail), there rose from the depths of the church a muted groan that seemed less a murmur of impatience than a sort of moan from a sleeper caught up in his dream. "If one of us had walked out at that point," the same Noël was to say, "we'd all have followed. Only, don't you see, it was still too

early in the morning, no one had drunk, we were all sober . . ."
And when the judge remarked that the crime thus seemed all
the more inexplicable and, in the eyes of the law, took place with
no excuse whatsoever, he added, "It was those awful things the
priest said that put fire in our bellies. Alcohol from the day before
is sneakier, it doesn't flare up as quickly, but it's meaner and it
lasts longer . . ." And the blacksmith, Guy Trioulet, one of the
killers, said: "We'd had it up to here with that little dead body—
we couldn't take any more. So many reports, so many lies, and
those damned anonymous letters that people had begun to burn
in secret . . . To put it briefly, for days the village had been pad-
dling around in its crime, everyone for himself, everyone for his
own account, but that eventually could have come out all right.
What was unfortunate was that all had gone to mass together, all
at the same time. It was like some rising vapor suddenly going to
our heads all at once. Honestly, sir, we began to lack air after the
priest spoke, I swear it! The air got all hot and heavy, like our bake
house when I slaughter my pig."

.   .   .   .

But no one, alas, could have restrained the poor priest at that moment. As timid as he ordinarily was, the rumble coming toward
him from that crowd had stirred him, not so much with fear as
with a sort of unhealthy curiosity, and, from the moment when he
had dared look out at those hundreds of faces transfigured by an
expectancy equal to his own, words that, unbeknown to him, had
slowly been taking shape during the course of those past two
weeks slipped out of the most secret part of his being, like a sword
from its sheath.

He was however to retain no memory of them. Perhaps they
were only an unintelligible murmur in his ears, answering the
other murmur coming toward him that had to be faced, regardless
of the cost. In any case he remained incapable of repeating anything at all precisely—not a single one of those statements that

touched off the conflagration. And perhaps too it was only when put together that they formed awkward, artless sentences, though each one had nonetheless an irresistible appeal, a cry launched toward all those faces, the only thing visible in the half darkness of the shadows, those naked faces so closely pressed together that the whole cursed village seemed to form a single nude body twisting its disgusting nakedness next to the coffin.

"What . . . ," said the poor man with his sad voice, "what have you come looking for this morning? What are you asking your priest to do? Prayers for this dead child? But I'm helpless without you. I'm helpless without my parish, and I haven't got a parish. There's no more parish here, my brothers . . . just a commune and a priest, and that's not a parish. Certainly I should like to be your servant, I love you; I love you just as you are; I love you in your wretchedness; it seems to me sometimes that I even love your sins, your poor, joyless sins. And it is true that I suffer and pray for you with all my might. Many people, here or elsewhere, will perhaps say that that is enough, that I should just pray and suffer as long as you refuse to give me your souls. That at least is what my masters used to teach me in seminary. My goodness, perhaps I think like them. But I'm no longer completely possessed by that idea, that's all finished. What am I in your midst? A heart beating outside its body, have any of you ever seen that? Well, that's what I am, my friends, I am such a heart. But a heart, let us remember, is like a pump circulating the blood. Yet I pump as hard as I can, only the blood doesn't come any more; all this heart takes in and gives off is air. And you . . . Yes, you . . ."

He moved his thin head from right to left like a drunken man. A murmur rose from the back pews, then rumbled, swelling little by little until he lifted his head again. Then all was quiet.

"Oh, naturally you weren't expecting such words from a priest. And it's true that they are harsh and weigh heavily upon you. And that's exactly why I'm no longer keeping them in myself. Let them fall on your heads, my friends, and, if I'm doing evil in saying them, let God punish me with you! Whether I do good or evil others will judge . . . others whom . . . whom I shall obey without a murmur, but not before . . . not before . . ."

He lowered his head and immediately the muted rumble began to increase. The faces, immobilised by expectancy, all had the same convulsive movement. Again he thought he saw the white flanks of that great, living, naked body twisting before his eyes.

"Monsieur le curé," a voice whispered in his ear, "my dear friend . . . get hold of yourself . . . calm down . . ."

Monsieur Ouine had pushed his chair forward bit by bit and was now standing near him, in the shadow of the pillar, looking at him full of compassion. But already the sad voice rose again, but only slightly, so that the first rows believed they were the only ones able to hear him, although his voice carried all the way to the end of the large nave.

"I used to be really afraid of you, my friends, I have to admit it. Yes, indeed, before knowing you, I was afraid of you. You must grasp this, you must understand it . . . Young men studying in professional schools are preparing for a career, you know; they have a plan all mapped out, with everything regulated: first the path to follow, then, after that, a profession, a family, legitimate ambitions, in short, they are integrated into society a bit like—I don't want my comparison to offend you—like a worm in a piece of fruit. But we priests, my friends, there is no place for us, we belong to no one. We've forsaken our families, our homes, our villages, and when we've finished with our notebooks and textbooks, our Latin and our Greek, they send us out into your midst with one single task, that of "getting along," as they say, of acting for the best. And, my goodness, they could scarcely give us any other. But think of it, my friends. When you've done all the things that have to be done—the ploughing and sowing, the harrowing and caring for the animals—well, your day is finished then, and you lie down content. A successful day is a beautiful thing! Well, we priests, we too have our daily tasks, but when we've finished with them, everything still remains to be done. Yes, everything, save your souls! We're young, we feel filled with zeal and desire and strength and — and why shouldn't I use the right word, even if that word doesn't mean much to you anymore — yes, the word "love," my friends, we're filled with love, the very conception of which I fear you have lost, a love watching over you day and night, a love that hurts. And in that love, as is only right, there is something both of God and of man — something of the lonely man, of the man who comes and goes among you, always, always alone. For you can speak to me of your sorrows and joys as well as of that by which, alas, you measure them: your money, the money that is the hard, implacable law of your life, but I, what can I speak to you about? Yes, yes! I know that those are not things that one ordinarily says in such a place; so just listen to me all the more carefully, if you can, for you are not going to hear these things a second time. I have never seen you gathered together in so great a number before, and I shall undoubtedly never see you so again — all of my poor parish before me, face to face . . . Well, it is true that when I just now turned toward you to wish you the help and strength of the Lord — *Dominus vobiscum* — that the idea came to me — no, that's not quite right! — the idea shot through me like a lightning bolt that our parish no longer exists, that there is no longer any parish here. Oh, naturally the name of the commune still figures on the registry of the archbishop, but nonetheless there's no parish here anymore, it's all over with, and you are free. Yes, you are free, my friends. You are a hundred times freer than savages and pagans, you are completely free, free like animals. And, surely, that didn't come about in a day; it goes back a long way, for a parish is not quickly killed! This one would have held out to the end, only now it's dead. You'll answer that, whether living or dead, that doesn't stop the grain from ripening, that doesn't stop the apples from falling off the trees for your cider. Agreed. The threat doesn't come from those innocent things. What threatens you is within you, it's in your breast, my friends, it's under your skin. My goodness, how can I explain it to you, how can I make you understand! That there may be sinners — and great sinners — among you doesn't really matter, for every parish has its sinners. And as long as the parish is still a parish, the sinners and the others make up just one great body where, even if the grace of God doesn't circulate like sap in a tree, mercy still does circulate. For you will vainly say, my friends, that man is not made to live alone, or even in couples, like tigers and snakes. Alas! The most modest gathering of men is impossible without a lot of waste, and what can one say of the cities, of the great cities? But when night comes, the city awakens and gives off through all her pores the waste of the day just finished, she mixes it in her drains and sewers until it is nothing but a mucky silt flowing bit by bit toward the sea in the city's vast subterranean rivers."

Good God! What was he saying, what had he dared say only ten steps away from the tabernacle and before that strange crowd so full of stares, of a whole multitude of stares, of eyes opened wide: avid eyes, resembling black, immobile insects stalking their prey? He felt however neither shame nor fear; all he wanted to do was cry.

Monsieur Ouine's chair had been grating for the past minute as he worked it forward over the stone floor in regular little thrusts. But from where the priest was standing he unfortunately could not see any of the former language professor's features, although he did hear his uneasy breathing cut sometimes by a sort of incomprehensible whispering. Rather far removed from them and almost at the foot of the pulpit, the convulsed face of the mayor of Fenouille brutally emerged out of the shadows, fully lighted by a stained-glass window in the apse, which was covering his big face with little round spots of blue or mauve constantly dancing about. For a moment the priest thought he saw this face laughing, but immediately the sorrowful grimace of the mouth proved him wrong. It seemed to the curé of Fenouille that all murmuring had ceased and that the words he was about to say would fall, vainly and blackly, one after the other, into that gaping silence.

His humble stare paled in disgust as his arms, with solemn slowness, seemed to rise without his being aware of it, like those of an exhausted swimmer no longer struggling and sinking to the bottom. Far too simple-minded and far too little of a poet to measure the power and danger of the images he had used, what he had just evoked seized hold of him with an irresistible force. He was seeing, he was almost touching, those mountains of excrement, those lakes of muck.

"Alas, my friends, the supernatural life, the life of souls, of our poor souls, doesn't exist without a lot of waste . . . There is vice and there is sin. And if God allowed us to see the invisible world, which of us wouldn't fall dead — yes, dead — at the sight . . . yes, at nothing but the sight of those hideous . . . of those abominable proliferations of evil?"

This time there was no doubt, the mayor of Fenouille had laughed with his shoulders thrown forward and both hands flat against his thighs; he laughed again with the same laugh — a laugh resembling less a laugh than the convulsions of avid expectancy, an enormous aspiration coming out of his whole inflamed face. A huge tear rolled down each cheek.

"We'll scarcely succeed in coming to the end of it all together, my friends. God has allowed it to be that way. That's why he made his Church. And the parish is a little church in the great Church. There is no parish without the great Church. But if the last parish dies — which is impossible — there would be no more Church, whether great or small, there would be no more redemption, there would be nothing at all anymore — Satan would have visited his people."

His voice stopped on those last words with a long sigh, like that of a schoolboy who had arrived at the end of his lesson. His head inclined toward the right, his body already ready for flight; it seemed that the only thing holding him there in front of that murmuring congregation was the fact that his two thin hands were clinging to the altar rail. All the hobnailed shoes scraped in concert on the paved floor.

"There are still many parishes in the world. But this one is dead. Perhaps it has been dead for a long time? I didn't want to believe it. I said to myself, 'As long as I'm here . . .' Alas, one man alone does not make a parish. You let me come and go, and you think: 'We're no worse than the people of Noyelles, of d'Arcy, or of Saint Vaast; we can afford a priest like the others.' And you waited patiently for the chance to get your money's worth and thought, 'He doesn't cost much, he's always there waiting; some day perhaps he'll be good for something.' But when the crime was discovered, it was not me that you came looking for. A crime only concerns the law and the newspaper reporters, isn't that right? No matter! Just a grain too much yeast can turn the whole dough sour. For the evil was within you, but now it has begun to come out of the ground, out of the walls. And at the beginning that didn't displease you, did it, my friends? You felt good, you were warmed by it. The village was like a beehive in April. All because of the idea that the guilty person was undoubtedly in your midst, was one of you, your neighbor perhaps, right? Your blood itched in your veins. Every evening when I saw your windows gleaming all along our little valley, I thought that suspicion and hatred and envy and fear were at work and that the police would only have to come by the next day to do what had to be done. And then . . . And then . . ."

Old Devandomme was sitting only two steps away, the tails of his frock coat carefully arranged on his knees, with his fixed, grave eyes. His muddy shoes had made two great dark spots on the paving stones.

"And then," the curé of Fenouille stammered, "another blow . . . a double blow . . . a double death . . ."

He should have liked to have finished with those dangerous words as quickly as possible, but, to the contrary, he thought he heard them clearly and implacably detach themselves from the silence. And, with a no less singular fatality, his gaze could not detach itself from that of the old man.

"Death was soon to strike a double blow in your midst . . ."

Silence. Devandomme had slowly stood up, deliberately, unfolding his long legs one after the other, exactly as he used to do each evening at the table when he had eaten his last mouthful and closed up his knife. He looked like a man accomplishing a hard, urgent duty with no illusion, not so much in the hope of winning out over injustice, but simply in order not to turn his back on his misfortune.

"The boy was not guilty," he said with a muted voice, but articulating every word.

Then, with the same slowness, he turned to face the dark shadows of the nave, pushing back his chair.

"And now the evil no longer warms you," the curé of Fenouille continued. (It seemed that the words that he had just heard had broken the enchantment, gluing his tongue to his palate.) "You feel all numb and cold. They are always talking about the fire of hell, but no one has ever seen it, my friends. For hell is cold. It used to be that the nights weren't long enough to wear out your malice, and you got up each morning with your breasts still full of poison. But now the devil himself has withdrawn from you. Ah, how alone we are in evil, my brothers! The poor human race dreams from century to century of breaking that solitude — but it's no use! The devil, who can do so many things, will never succeed in founding a Church, a Church that will put in common both the merits of hell and the sin of all.[1] From now until the end of the world, the sinner will always have to sin alone, always alone — for just as we die alone, so also do we sin alone. The devil, you see, is that friend who never stays with us till the end . . . So it is that you've dreamed about your parish and your priest. You have suspected one another, you've maligned one another, you've denounced one another, you've hated one another, and now it's necessity that brings you together to fight against the cold, all together, to try to stay warm. Well, now! What do you want me to say? It's too late. You'll leave here this morning just as you came.

1. According to Catholic dogma, in God's Church the merits of the saints form a common depository of blessings for all servants of God, whereas the devil, the curé argues, has no Church in which the sins of his servants form a depository of damnation.

I can no longer do anything for you — I, yes, I — I am helpless without my parish. What good can it possibly do you today for me to bless this unfortunate little dead boy? He has been the innocent instrument of your loss and represents the sin of all of you. I will not bless your sin!"

His voice had dropped little by little, and the muted rumble accompanying it dropped with it and finally subsided. And that was all. No one would henceforth have been able to get another word out of the curé Fenouille. And those he had just uttered were already very far from him, outside him, while his stare, fixed until then, seemed suddenly to have escaped the control of his will, darting about from one extremity of the church to the other, like a frightened fly. For a moment he thought he would succeed in fixing it on the great black wooden cross suspended from one of the arches of the vault, but it slipped away again, moving about in all directions around the deep nave. The faces turned toward him through the light mist were floating above the heated bodies and still seemed to compose a single naked body, now immobile or else shaken by a feeble trembling, by a slow undulation similar to that of a dying man's body, following the last spasm of his agony. He stayed there, his mouth open, his arms dangling, his head tilted toward his shoulder, and looking so inane that the school children, crammed into the right side of the choir, nudged each other and laughed.

Whether he had the presence of mind to murmur a few words of blessing before returning to the altar or whether, as a certain number of witnesses stated, in the end he brusquely turned his back on them mattered little. For what was going to follow was to cause everything to be forgotten.

The absolution was completed without incident, though the voice of the officiant was sometimes obscured by the humming of private conversations. The first pews, reserved for the officials of Fenouille, had been vacated bit by bit but were almost immediately filled by those coming from the crowd at the back of the nave or from the overflow in the side chapels. A few girls, cunningly pushed from chair to chair by the boys, pressed tightly against each other on the steps of the pulpit with stifled little laughs, squeezing their skirts between their legs. The schoolmaster, gathering his herd together, had his pupils slip carefully along the wall to the small door opening out into the cemetery, then set about regrouping them a few steps away, not far from the gaping grave.

Behind him Monsieur Ouine said, "I was just going to advise you, or even . . ."

He patted his sweat-drenched forehead with his handkerchief.

" . . . or even (please excuse the indiscretion of an old colleague) I would gladly have proposed to you not to push this experiment any further . . ."

"This is not an experiment," the other replied dryly. "I am obeying orders from my superiors."

"Allow me," replied Monsieur Ouine, whose cheeks went purple, "I have some experience with the responsibilities of our profession. Here, as in school, your privilege is that of being a captain of a boat, you are master after God. Well, it is quite possible that in a minute or so we shall be witnesses to some very regrettable scenes, comic and tragic at the same time, I fear. The mixture of the comic and the tragic engenders the bizarre, and against the bizarre there is no answer save irony — a feeling unfortunately unknown to childhood."

"The painful duty which brings us together here . . ." began the schoolmaster of Fenouille.

"Just a minute!" Monsieur Ouine interrupted with a singular liveliness. "I deplore as much as you do the senseless remarks that we have just heard. But let's admit that, though there was perhaps not one chance in a thousand that they achieve their goal, the population of this wretched village affords us a curious example of an abolition of moral reflexes, leaving it defenseless against all sorts of infections. Anything at all could now be turned into poison, just as diabetics do with sugar . . . Yes, monsieur, there are such states where even the most human feelings, that of pity, for example, can become toxic. To the impure all things are impure, sir."

Under the stare of the stupefied schoolmaster, he shifted gently from one foot to another as if trying to ease an unbearable pain.

"I think I understand that you foresee . . . that you fear some scandalous happening, while actually this gathering seems, to the contrary, to be a comforting manifestation of a . . . of a sacred unity. In such a case . . . allow me . . . what kind of scandal are you speaking of?"

"I have always respected childhood . . . ," Monsieur Ouine said, accentuating his waddle, which, in contrast, made the fixity of his stare even more bizarre, "loved and respected childhood. Childhood is the salt of the earth. Let it collapse and the world will soon be nothing but decay and gangrene . . . Decay and gangrene," he repeated in a clear, loud voice.

At the height of his face, for a long moment, he held one of his hands, swollen no doubt by that same serous liquid flowing incessantly from his eyelids. Then he turned his back and, without a word, strode off between the graves.

The priest's last words were lost in the tumult, for the double doors of the front entry of the church had just swung open, and hobnailed shoes in the alley-way sent gravel flying in all directions. Almost immediately, the tavern next door emptied in a second, providing another somber flow of frock coats and felt hats, with all the quick questions being asked by the new arrivals increasing the rumbling. Had the curé of Fenouille waited a few minutes, this tumult would undoubtedly have died down; unfortunately, almost immediately he too appeared, preceded by his altar boy, and the crowd, closing in, bore him, rather than actually pushing him, right up to the edge of the grave where, slipping with both feet on the fresh clay, he fell down. A suppressed laughter, like the clacking of five hundred famished mandibles, tapered off into a sort of muted, prolonged moan, the kind that makes a hesitant, intimidated crowd aware of its own strength. The surplice of the priest of Fenouille was stiff with mud.

"Make way for His Honor the Mayor!" someone said. "In the name of the commune, make way for His Honor the Mayor!"

There was a great movement of expectancy, but it was the inspector of education who appeared first, clutching in his hand gloved in black silk in a piece of paper covered with handwriting so small he gave up deciphering it, but, in an almost unintelligible voice, began anyway.

"Ladies and gentlemen, the youthful memory before which I come . . . that I salute with respect is that of a humble child of the people whose life might have transpired in the obscurity . . . in the obscurity of labor . . . As obscu . . . as modest as may have been his prematurely interrupted destiny, the solicitude of the republic had already recognized . . . The republic, always filled with solicitude, had already recognized him as one of her own, and if the necessities of the obsc . . . of daily labor had not kept him too often away from the schoolhouse – the house you have in common, all of you – the republic would thus have dispensed to him, as to every citizen, the immense benefits of learning . . . Allow me to incline, to bow, to . . ."

Whatever he did, the same words, as if obeying some shadowy affinity, refused to be disjoined and seemed to stick together on his tongue. He wound up by spitting them all out at once, in a rage of confused spluttering. In any case, the listeners paid very little attention to this little baldheaded man, so similar to so many other little baldheaded men usually wearing beards, who speak in the name of the government at official ceremonies. The village could only stare at its humiliated priest.

Hatred of the priest is one of man's profoundest instincts, as well as one of the least known. That it is as old as the race itself no one doubts, yet our age has raised it to an almost prodigious degree of refinement and excellence. With the decline or disappearance of other powers, the priest, even though appearing so intimately integrated into the life of society, has become a more singular and unclassifiable being than any of those old magicians the ancient world used to keep locked up like sacred animals in the depths of its temples, existing in the intimacy of the gods alone. Priests moreover are all the more singular and unclassifiable in that they do not recognize themselves as such and are nearly always dupes of the most gross outward appearances – whether of the irony of some or the servile deference of others. But that contradiction, by nature more political than religious and used far too long to nurture clerical pride, does, through the growing feeling of their loneliness and to the extent that it is gradually transformed into hostile indifference, throw them unarmed into the heart of social conflicts they naively pride themselves on being able to resolve by using texts. But, then, what does it matter? The hour is coming when, on the ruins of the old Christian order, a new order will be born that will indeed be an order of the world, the order of the Prince of this World, of that prince whose kingdom is of this world. And the hard law of necessity, stronger than any illusions, will then remove the very object for clerical pride so long maintained simply by conventions outlasting any belief. And the footsteps of beggars shall cause the earth to tremble once again.

.   .   .   .

To be sure they saw him almost every day, a fold of his poor cassock tucked up at the waist, clipping his hedges or working his garden, and one night last winter someone had even picked him up at the bottom of the Sauves slope, next to his broken bicycle, glistening with rain and blood. But never before had they pressed so close upon him as he exercised his mysterious powers – indeed, the only one still inspiring them with a certain superstitious fear – his mysterious power over the dead. Whenever he passed their doors with a certain humble, hastening step that caused the housewives to say, "Look, the priest's taking the dear Lord to so-and-so . . . ," more than one of them would turn his head away and pack his pipe in silence . . . But now he was there, in the harsh bright light of day, with that vague perfume of incense mixed with the sickly odor of clay, his surplice caked with mud, and the little altar boy sniffling and holding the processional cross askew.

It seemed as if the words of the inoffensive priest had fused all the suspicions, resentments, and accumulated hatreds of the past few weeks — and even the horror of the crime — into a single sentiment that was so violent yet subtle, so unbearable for their souls that they could only be delivered from it by laughter. And so it was indeed laughter — but what laughter! — the laughter of a parish that had recovered its identity and was nonetheless unanimous, even though it was a parish that had disappeared, and this made their eyes and teeth glisten, bringing from the depths of their throats one knew not what rough sigh as they pressed against each other, confirming one another's presence with elbows, thighs, and glances in a sort of sinister cordiality.

"It's the mayor's turn!" the voice repeated.

The inspector of education, busy protecting his boots from the mud, still all red and shiny from wounded vanity, approved convulsively with his head and yielded his place in the midst of the immediately enlarging circle around the grave. It was noticed that the priest, still silent, did not even lift his head. Several people thought he was crying.

"My dear fellow citizens," the first magistrate of Fenouille began.

His speech — a text of twenty lines written in collaboration with the doctor and carefully traced by Malvina in capital letters on a sheet of white paper, a text he had repeated so many times in vain, had just seemed to explode in his memory like a dazzling firework. The words that just a while ago were scattered or seemed to hold together only by some miracle were now there, all gathered into a marvelous equilibrium, a tiny, henceforth immovable, constellation. "My dear fellow citizens" — he prolonged the silence for a longer time and far beyond its purpose in order to delight in its profound, unknown security — "My dear fellow citizens" — it seemed to him that all those looks turned on him expressed the same happy surprise, the same almost supernatural comfort, a sort of blessedness. The marvelous words still shone somewhere within him, though with a softer light ... With what fraternal sympathy did all those faces now lighten up and beam at him! He would say what he wanted to, he would speak almost without knowing it, with an ease, an ethereal lightness, he would speak as one flies ... God, had the hour of deliverance come? Were he and they, all together, going to know forgetfulness, the blessed forgetfulness of past mistakes, the blessedness of forgiveness? – "My dear fellow citizens" – yes, yes, no doubt about it, it was just a very simple text, but their eyes were already answering him, already giving signs of a sympathetic joy that absolved him. Heavens, his shameful secret was no more. It was going to gush forth in a second or two like a fountain of muddy water, and his old soul would finally be emptied out through his mouth, what bliss! While awaiting salvation, the certainty of achieving it made his knees tremble and his bones shake; his words flowed on and on without end, filling the silence. But now it was they who in turn spoke to him, crying out words he couldn't understand, words he didn't even try to understand. It was enough to confront them, offering, tossing them, the joy of his recovered innocence. Nothing more stands between us, my friends, no more lies – on every side the lie is giving way. And there fell from the heavens, no, there arose from the depths of the earth an unidentifiable, fresh, pure breath dissolving old poisons. In the tumult, which had become frightening, he explained that it was all over with that sickly, fetid thing sticking to his soul as it might have stuck to his skin, it was all over with that filth; he stamped his foot, pinched his nose and pulled at it, then suddenly looked with stupefaction at his hand wet with tears, before finally falling to his knees in the midst of laughter and mockery.

.   .   .   .

The schoolmaster had opened a path leading to the iron gate of the cemetery, but each time that he tried to get through the gate a flood of new arrivals pushed him back in with his pale little troop. The whole village was now there, and the noise it made ressembled no other except perhaps the sort of roaring made by water rushing through a just opened lock.

The deputy mayor, Merville, bellowed: "I order you to get on with the burial, Duponchel . . . Im-me-di-ate-ly!"

"Monsieur! Tell them to get back! Damn it! They're going to push me head first into the grave! How about giving me back my tools, you bunch of bastards!"

"Gentlemen, gentlemen . . ."

Suddenly it was as if the indistinct, muted rumbling of the tumult had been split into a multitude of different notes. Those trying to see had retreated from the central alleyway, leaving it empty, and all heads turned toward it, not in a single motion but rather in the way that heads of wheat in a field will be standing erect until a sudden change in the wind sweeps across them from one side to the other.

"Woolly-Leg! Woolly-Leg!"

From the other side of the hedge the great mare, pushed back by the crowd toward the slope, had reared to her full height on the bank and was trying to keep her balance. The carriage shafts had splintered, and with each of her pawings the traces whistled around her sides like the strings of a sling. One of them laid low one of the miller's sons, his cheek split open by the leather.

"Woolly-Leg! Woolly-Leg!"

In jumping out of her carriage she had twisted her ankle, and her feet, catching in the folds of her long skirt, caused her to move forward with jerking, awkward steps, which, however, inspired no laughter at all . . .

"Woolly-Leg! Woolly-Leg!"

She crossed the entire cemetery, going toward the grave. Sweat glistened on her cheeks, mixed with rouge, but her forehead, covered with a thick layer of face powder, remained as pale in the blazing light as that of a Pierrot . . . With each step she took forward voices were silenced one by one, and, when she had reached the edge of the grave, the silence from one end of the cemetery to the other and even out on the road was such that everyone could distinctly hear the rustling of her silk skirt on the mound of earth and the stiffled sobs of the altar boy.

No hand was raised against her, but they all stealthily pushed her toward the grave. What were they waiting for? None of them could have said. This abandoned creature whom they had so many times pretended to have pursued along empty paths only to come to an unexpected stop with a great laugh, this incomprehensible being whose degradation they had watched from year to year but whom no one would have dared insult to her face was still, for all of them, the lady of Néréis, who had always managed to cover her trails with the prudence and wisdom of an old she-wolf. And no doubt there wasn't a single one of the young regulars at all the country festivals who hadn't bragged about having one night possessed her in a ditch, on the edge of a slope, or in the hay of a barn, who hadn't proudly shown off the cigarettes with which she had supposedly stuffed his pockets, though no other proof of his good fortune could ever be produced. For even the most wily ones had long ago given up hope of catching her by surprise, having too often paid for their endless moonlight stalking with a case of bronchitis. "She's caught on to us," they said, exasperated upon hearing her answer the subtle suggestions of the boy they'd chosen for bait with a proper "Good evening!" Perhaps they hated her; probably without knowing it. Perhaps they saw in her, without recognizing it, the mysterious image of their own abject condition? Rejected by her own class, poor, degraded, suspect to everyone, she seemed the victim one class ceded to the other, a token sacrificed in advance. But they were still waiting for the slip that would make her theirs, for that ridiculous incident that would inspire derision and justify everything; while awaiting it, they sniffed her from a distance without attacking her. The modern world is full of these hidden hostages.

She appeared to be still free at that moment, but she was not. For an observer following this extraordinary scene from above, the unconscious movement of the crowd, starting at that moment, had the characteristics of the frightful solicitude that marks a famished carnivore's first approach to its prey. "We were just curious about what she was going to do," Clodiot, the woodseller, would later say. "We were really expecting to have some fun." Moreover, the conversations had started up again, and although looks were turned toward the lady of the manor, they were not discussing anything but the inexplicable speech of the mayor. "He's crazy!" they repeated to one another. "His eyes are inflamed; he should be committed! Damned Arsène! Damned clown!" At that very moment a voice that no one recognized at first thrice ordered, "Go home!" raising the tone each time. It seemed to come from every the corner of the cemetery to such an extent that the movement of the crowd found itself unexpectedly interrupted and deep swirls were visible in it as in the water of a millstream. They replied by an angry growl.

It was the deputy mayor, Merville, who, in despair at trying to make himself heard because of his short stature, had climbed up on top of a grave and, clinging with one hand to the cross, was gesticulating with his free arm. Private conversations melted into a single rumble, which swelled suddenly when Woolly-Leg reached the exact height of the little man who, however, had his back turned to her. Was she conscious of the danger? Did she want to face up to it in her own way, that is, by exaggerating to a ridiculous and absurd degree the falseness of her tone and attitude, the usual sign of a certain common type of nervous attack well known to psychiatrists? An opening in the crowd revealed her standing near the coffin, her long hands flat on its lid, her head thrown back. A lock of hair fell across her cheek.

"I shall avenge you!" she said in an unbearable, high-pitched voice.

A shove from the crowd almost pushed her into the grave, and her first cry of terror rose above the boos of the crowd like a clash of cymbals.

"Guards! Get her out of here!" the deputy mayor ordered. "For

God's sake get her the hell out of here! She's going to drive them crazy!"

Her arms stretched out in the form of a cross, the lady of Néréis cried out, "Vengeance!"

An enormous laughter came back at her, rolling first like thunder, then, when she wanted to place her hands on the coffin again to lean on it, Duponchel, the gravedigger, struck them with a light, sharp blow of his spade. The blood gushed, probably without her even being aware of it, so that, having pulled back the lock of hair falling down her cheek with the tips of her fingers, her white face appeared over their heads streaked with red, like the face of a clown. The laughter redoubled, then stopped again unexpectedly, and, for the first time, one heard the squealing mockery of the women massed against the iron gate. A clod of earth coming out of nowhere smashed against her breast, leaving a muddy splash on the front of her dress.

They thought they saw her stagger under the blow, but she had only adjusted her equilibrium, and with her eyes half closed and her long torso scarcely bent, she seemed to be offering herself to their fury while, warned by a sort of savage foresight, she sought a large enough opening in that thick human wall to allow her to hurl herself through it. That same instinct, imposing a flexible immobility upon her, gave her face an extraordinary expression of secret resignation that might have been taken for indifference or sadness. "She looked as if she were asleep standing up, like a real sleepwalker. For a moment we thought she was going to cry." But those nearest her noticed that "she made a strange noise with her mouth, like a sick person with the shivers," and the Belgian, Simonot, having pressed rather close to her, was stupefied at being unable "to move her an inch, no more and no less than a statue." "Her hips were as hard as brass," he said, "she seemed to be all tensed up."

That "strange noise", according to those who heard it, resembled a sort of sigh or a single trembling, very low note, a lament surely more animal than human. The memory of it came back to many of them only long afterward, for at the moment they did not think it could issue from lips so imperiously pinched shut. "To get out of the cemetery all she had to do was to leave quietly; we didn't want to do her any harm. Or she could even have talked to us. Usually her tongue was loose enough." They thought they saw her looking for someone in the crowd, and the Maigret woman even insisted that "she was waiting until the last minute for help that didn't come."

Naturally it all happened when one was no longer expecting it. As Simonot came near again, climbing on the mound, his Belgian face was just at the height of her own; into it she thrust her nails and, with arms upraised and stretched like an arc, she threw herself forward, plunging into a frightening silence. The cry that she had been holding back for such a long time gushed up from her throat and burst above their heads. Nearly at the same second she reached the cemetery wall and, while pressing her body against the fence, slid from bar to bar toward the gate with prodigious agility. Mad with rage, Simonot, slightly wounded in the forehead, displayed to everyone his bloodied face. One of the women shouted, "The bitch has put his eyes out!"

That cry was probably what decided Woolly-Leg's fate: the crowd answered it with an extraordinary murmur. For another few seconds it hesitated, seeming to turn in circles, with a cat's familiar movement of pretending to let its prey escape while pursuing its ferocious game.

Those who rushed to the fence swore they had not been able to stop her. "She slipped between our legs," they said. But she appeared suddenly before them, alone in the midst of the open road, and before they could even take a step, they saw an extraordinary sight.

At an easy trot, her reins dangling, the great mare came to her, biting her bit with a little whinny of pleasure. No one even knew where the strange animal had come from: her mistress had probably left her against the cemetery bank, out of the way, on the very narrow dead-end path that, a little farther down, opened onto the common pasture known as the Marsh Plain. The empty carriage scraped and danced along behind her at each bump. In a single bound Woolly-Leg jumped in, and, finding the road already barred on the right, let one wheel slip into the shallow ditch, turned around instantly on that fixed point, and, with a simple cluck of the tongue, caused the beast to jump fifteen feet without even touching the reins tied to the back of the seat.

"Look out below!" someone cried in a choking voice. But the warning came too late, blending into one of those horrid clamors resembling a chant and constituting a mob's true voice. When rearing on her haunches to jump, the mare in her thrust had thrown her right leg forward. The horeshoe lightly struck the chest of the little Denisane boy, who turned twice in a circle, then fell motionless, his nose in the dust. Then all one could hear was the treading of thick shoe soles rushing down the slope.

The first one to seize hold of the reins was a farmboy named Roblard, but he later denied having struck the mare on the nostrils. He was in any case so brutally thrown to the side that he dislocated his shoulder and took no further part in what followed. They say that the overturned carriage was dragged more than twenty meters; at least the next day the police found the deep mark left in the soil. But the weight of the clustered assailants clinging to the free carriage step was probably enough to right it again. Hearing the double crack of the whip above their heads, they let go and, in a stupor, perceived the black silhouette of the lady of the manor whom the frightening shock hadn't succeeded in dislodging from her seat. "We thought we'd missed her," they said, "but even so we ran along behind to see." From that moment they were sure that the carriage would go no further. "It jumped about like a frog because of the bent axle." At the turn the wheel came off and escaped toward the lower side of the road, zigzagging as it went.

They saw Woolly-Leg jump free of the debris and scamper up the other side of the slope; she appeared to them one last time against the gray sky, shreds of black silk falling to her knees in long fringes scarcely lifted by the wind. Some of them later bragged of having seen her weep, though with a face of stone. When they all reached the bank together and stumbled back, she raised her arms without saying a word. The skin of her left side, completely exposed, was white as snow. "We wanted to stop her, to take her to the police, to the mayor, but the women who believed the little Denisane boy dead were the most enraged." The first one to lay a hand on her was probably the Riquet boy, called "Pipo," a youth twenty years old. "He grabbed her by the throat; you can easily recognize his hand because of his missing finger." And the crowd, enraged, pressing against the hedge on the other side of the road then very distinctly heard the voice of the lady of Néréis. Twice she cried out: "Philippe." It was remarked upon that the real name of Pipo Riquet was indeed "Philippe," though it was impossible to affirm that it was to him that this extraordinary woman addressed her supreme appeal.

"Monsieur, things can't go on like this," the mayor's wife said. "Yesterday he smashed a window pane and cut the water pipe, claiming he was repairing it. Poor man! What's the use of keeping an eye on him day and night? His mind's going."

"I'll speak to him again," the priest replied in his gentle voice. "In any case, he's always good with me, very docile."

"Docile? You mean to say crazy — only not in the way you understand it, of course! Because he doesn't grit his teeth or foam at the mouth or try to climb walls — nothing like that. Because, don't you see, people think . . . But it's just that they don't know anything about animals. An animal that's getting rabies, at the start, couldn't be more affectionate, more gentle — it looks at you with eyes that are human, until the day . . . When I tell you that when I do manage to doze off at night and then wake up and see him still in the same place, in his dark corner with his poor buttocks right against the windowpane, well, then I can't help feeling sorry for him — I grow tenderhearted and I try to reason with him . . ."

187

"And then?"

"Well, there are times he doesn't answer; he'll sigh, sometimes he trembles. And then other times . . . Oh, ye gods!"

"Stay calm, madame. What's the use in going back over it? You're just making yourself suffer uselessly."

The miserable woman raised her flaming face toward him.

"Sir, I'm no longer young," she said with a comic seriousness that, nonetheless, inspired no amusement. "I know about life. And if you'll excuse my saying so, I suppose your own mother was rather like me — neither too good nor too bad, right? A woman is always a little just what a man has made of her, and as for a man, well, a man is very hard to define. We'll have to admit that he's still a boy, right, sir? Nice and affectionate at times but full of vices — girls disgusted by that only have to stay old maids. Nonetheless, this one we've got here . . ."

Her flat, gray face crowned by the ridiculous coils of her hair scarcely expressed any feeling other than a limitless astonishment. But the curé of Fenouille could not take his eyes off her strong, cracked hands moving convulsively back and forth across the table.

"Madame," he said, "we have a way of not taking evil into account, of not allowing for it. We must fight it according to our strength, and, for the rest, learn to suffer it in peace."

She looked at him, visibly making an effort to make sense of his incomprehensible words. Then, shrugging her shoulders, she suddenly lost control and buried her face in her hands.

"Last night he talked again for hours. He told all about his life, deliberately mixing up the true and the false, mixing them up so thoroughly that I got taken in every time, it's just like a dream. Of course he lies. He's always lied a lot, in any case. But he's got so refined and so subtle with it that I can never stop him now before it's too late and things are already too mixed up — my poor head gets lost in it all. And that's when he starts juggling around names and dates in a calm little voice — one would say that he's speaking to the judge — and I begin to tremble like a leaf. Yes, in those moments, you aren't going to believe me, I'm his, body and soul, I want everything he wants, I'd climb the scaffold with him. And yet God knows at my age it's no longer a question of what you'd suppose — please excuse my saying it to you — I don't even think about that any more. 'You're a good woman,' he says to me, 'you've got to share my shame with me.' The funniest thing, sir, is that I believe him. Oh, the shame of it all! A wife with nothing to reproach herself for, not that . . . though just between us . . . Arsène has never been what you'd call . . . well, I make myself clear."

"Madame," the blushing priest said, "from now on you must see the mayor only as a sick man, a very sick man, nothing more and nothing less."

"Well, then, you think like the doctor?" she said with a sigh. "You think that Arsène should be put into the asylum at Montreuil?"

"Forgive me," the curé answered gently, "I was only speaking of your own role, madame, not of mine. Alas, for me there's perhaps not going to be enough time. I admit that since the latest scandals my ministry has become difficult, and my superiors . . ."

He kept crossing and uncrossing his trembling hands.

"Oh, I had no pretention of curing him. But I just would have liked for him to understand . . ."

"Understand what?"

"What mercy is," he answered with a growing embarrassment. "I'd like to make him understand that he will have to be merciful with himself."

"Mercy?" she asked. "What mercy?"

Her gaze moved from the curé of Fenouille to the door without coming to rest on anything.

"You're talking a little like him," she finally said. "Mercy! Can you imagine any man so crazy that he'd not be merciful with himself? But then you surely know more about all that than I do . . ."

With a movement of her head she had once thought irresistible but now rendered even more grotesque by a last tear clinging to the edge of her chin, she stretched both arms across the table.

"I've never been particularly pious," she began in a confidential tone, "but I have let myself be persuaded that . . . the doctor himself . . . in desperate cases . . ."

"We priests are no sorcerers, and our doctor knows it very well," the poor priest stammered with a sickening smile.

"Who mentioned our doctor?" a jovial voice broke in.

Entering through the kitchen without a sound, the worthy doctor had come right up to the door and now extended a large open hand to the priest, who had gone white.

"Get hold of yourself, Monsieur le curé," he said, pivoting around on his heels. "My respects, madame. I hope I'm not being indiscreet."

He backed up to the fireplace and leaned against it, carefully positioning his elbows on the marble ledge. Then only did he pop out his pince-nez with a flick of his little gold-ringed finger in a familiar gesture that, to him, always seemed inimitable in its elegance.

"A sick man like this one," he said, a slight nasal tone still in his voice, "belongs no doubt as much to the priest as to the doctor. But first of all I have a duty to fulfill in regard to you, reverend sir. For me, a modest country doctor, the freedom of heart and mind is always the law, the only law, the supreme law. Moreover, since the opportunity is ripe, I want to assure you of my sympathetic feelings for you at a very difficult time. I am told that your attitude throughout the recent events has been judged severely — even too severely — by your superiors. Well, I esteem that you acted and spoke as is proper to a priest. Professional conscience is too rare a quality today for me not to bow very deeply before it, even if I find it . . . You were ir-re-proach-able," he concluded in a tone forbidding any reply.

He held the little chain of his pince-nez between his index and middle finger, his right hand seemingly frozen at the height of his forehead, while casting a glance of astonishment, rather than fury, at the mayor's wife. The priest did not seem to hear him and, still standing in the same place, his long body leaning forward, had almost turned his back on him. Malvina touched her finger to her lips.

"Doctor . . ."

The voice of the curé of Fenouille began with a tremble but little by little became firmer, though to the end a sort of proud and impenetrable sadness seemed to turn it into a simple murmur scarcely troubling the silence, as a thin little flame, battered by the wind, causes all the background shadows to slip slowly against each other without changing them.

"You see, Doctor, as I often say, you have to know, you have to understand. You mustn't judge us by our appearances. Our appearances are nothing. My goodness, which of us wouldn't like to appear differently? Only we have no choice. In seminary we all laughed about it. Yes, we were the first to make jokes about our poor, flowing cassocks and our gross shoes and woolen socks – to say nothing of the way we walk, which is ridiculous, since we try to put into it all that's left of our unwitting coquetry – of our youth. Oh, we tell ourselves that once we're outside those walls everything will be set straight by a month of freedom. Freedom! When we think that we've acquired it, it's already far behind us. Alas, our prison has no walls! We belong to everybody while supposedly belonging to nobody. There's nothing in all that to make us look like conquerors! And yet at the beginning of our ministry, as soon as we are left to our own devices, do you know what temptation we immediately have to fight against? No, don't bother to look, Doctor: it's pride. Our own special pride. For what you call pride – you in the world – would merit at the most the name of self-sufficiency, vanity, or conceit. But we are alone. And pride, like avarice, is a solitary vice. It slipped into us without our knowing it during those poor, laborious years that seemed so short to us because of a certain discipline whose incomparable wisdom we never questioned (And how could we have judged it? Our masters themselves applied it probably without understanding it much better than we did.), with every hour regulated, every minute. They were supposed to make apostles of us, beings whose kingdom is not of this world. Yet we still cling to this world, we hang on to it by hidden ties. Oh, it's no small matter to tear avarice out of the hearts of little peasants! After such an exercise our inner spring may be broken, but often it has just been stretched too much. So they think we have been rendered humble for good, and all that while actually we have considerable difficulty in not replying to society's indifference by scorn. Our experience of human beings and of their unhappiness is already both deep and naive, yet we don't know how to give you any proof of it since we don't speak the same language. Alas, while you are laughing at our naiveté, we have already weighed you on very precise scales, we've judged you!"

The mayor's wife kept her gaze on the corner of the table, with that look of protective solicitude and boredom assumed by housewives when confronting children's chatter and men's arguments. The handsome doctor, caught short by the sudden silence of the priest, answered off-hand, though his voice trembled in anger.

"You quite surprise me with that . . . allow me . . . with that attack that nothing in what I said . . ."

"It can't be helped," the curé of Fenouille continued. "I'll soon leave this parish. In a few days you'll see a young priest as simple as I was get off the train from Boulogne and climb the same hill I myself climbed, his pathetic little bag in his hand. Well, then perhaps what I've just said and what I'm going to say won't appear completely useless to you. If only it could warn you of the error you're going to commit! Oh, nothing will be easier for you than to reduce the one who's coming to a helpless state. He'll come to you, his ears still full of advice about moderation and prudence . . . I can hear his superiors now: 'Above all, no indiscreet zeal! Your predecessor's left you with a very heavy inheritance; a new scandal could ruin everything.' I presume that in this parish God is going to make Himself smaller than ever! Well . . ."

The doctor held his pince-nez clasped between his thumb and index finger at some distance from his eyes, as if studying some fabulous animal.

"You are saying some very astonishing things for a ... for a man in your position," he said, "and I doubt that your superiors ..."

"I expect nothing more from my superiors," the curé of Fenouille replied with a strange smile. "I no longer expect anything from anybody, at least in this world. Yes, this little village has got the best of me, and it will get the best of many others. It will get the best of you too ..."

"I must say that ..."

"This village and many villages just like it," the curé continued, still calm. "All those villages that used to be Christian, whenever they start going up in flames – ah yes! – you'll see all sorts of creatures coming out of them, creatures whose very names men have forgotten long ago, if, indeed, they've ever given them a name."

"What's that? What creatures? Come now! We've already got a pretty collection here, all identified, all classified."

"Oh, I've thought a lot about it," the priest continued without raising his voice. "I've even thought that the moment will come when the supernatural will express itself outside its proper channels. May I ask for a bit of your time?"

"Of course," the handsome doctor replied politely. "These are new ideas for me."

"I'm afraid that they may indeed appear so to lots of people. But to take up the expression that surprised you a moment ago, one cannot deny that God has made Himself smaller for a long time now – very small. Therefore one concludes that tomorrow He'll make Himself as small as yesterday, then smaller and smaller and smaller. Nothing however obliges us to believe this."

The same smile again appeared on his lips, and the village doctor answered with an uneasy grimace.

"For science itself after all recognizes certain of man's religious needs ..."

"Allow me! As a former extern to Dr. Bouvillon, I can say that modern psychiatry even attributes considerable importance to ..."

"It makes no difference," the priest interrupted in his monotonous voice. "I had just wanted to explain that the poor no longer have words to describe what they're lacking, and if those words are missing, it's because they've been robbed of them by you."

"You speak like a demagogue, sir! You could even be a dangerous man."

"Indeed," the curé of Fenouille replied coldly.

He took a step forward and, in a movement no one could possibly have expected from such a man, placed his hands on the doctor's shoulders and looked him right in the eye.

"You've sealed up the name of God in the heart of the poor."

"It's a beautiful image," the doctor observed, while behind him the mayor's wife stifled her yawn, "but it's just an image and nothing more. It would hardly have meant anything even in that long past time of Emile Combes."

"I fear your way of thinking may be false," the priest continued with a hard look. "That absurd confrontation would have been more valuable for all of us. That one did manage to aim all those ancient, and sometimes quite justified, resentments at the priest alone. It did keep the idea of the divinity alive, and, although we didn't know it, it was something like a cry to God for the injustice and hypocrisy and mediocrity of the best of us. For although blasphemy may bring the soul into play in a dangerous manner, sir, it does bring it into play. And experience itself proves that man's rebellion remains a mysterious act and that the demon does not know the whole secret of it. While this silent indifference . . . Yes, the hour is coming (perhaps it's already come?), sir, when the desire that one believes sealed away in the depths of man's conscience and that has even lost its name will suddenly break out of its sepulcher. And if all other outlets are denied it, it will find one in man's own flesh and blood — yes, sir, you'll see it escaping in unexpected forms and, if I dare say it, in hideous, horrid manifestations. Minds will be poisoned by it, instincts perverted, and . . . who knows? Why shouldn't the body, our miserable defenseless body, not once again pay the ransom of the sou . . . for the other? A new ransom?"

"Why, that's madness!" the village doctor remarked. "Pure madness! The three theological virtues passing from the invisible world into the visible one transformed into malignant tumors, I suppose? Well, sir, one is allowed to wonder just what those in high places would think of these extraordinary ravings."

"I am afraid that you will soon observe things that are even more astonishing," said the priest of Fenouille, still without emotion. "Certainly we are still held to great precautions in dealing with what is called the social," he began again on a note of confidence, "but what can we do henceforth in its favour, I ask you? We are not policemen, and our only role is that of justifying man's destitution as long as it exists. No destitution frightens us and we have remedies for all kinds, except for one, your own, or rather the one you have invented. Yes, monsieur, you may be free to inaugurate an order from which God is excluded, but you've thereby broken the pact. Oh, no doubt the ancient alliance won't be broken in just a day, for even when it's finished, the Church is bound to society by so many ties! But in a world organized for despair the hour will come when preaching hope will be the exact equivalent of tossing a live coal into a powder barrel. Then . . ."

"All we'd need, in fact, would be a small number of fanatics like you . . ."

The face of the curé of Fenouille suddenly lost its color and he swallowed several times before replying. Through the large gap of his clerical collar the mayor's wife saw, with curiosity, that his thin pale neck palpitated like a chicken's.

"We've left the destitute in your hands long enough," he said.

His lips still trembled for an instant, then his gaze, growing little by little more luminous, moved from one witness of that strange scene to the other, as though he were emerging from a dream.

"We'll take up this conversation again," the doctor said as his white hand gently came to rest on the shoulder of the priest after tracing an elegant curve in the air.

"These latest events are enough to upset heads more solid than ours, and though I may surprise you by saying it, I don't at all mind admitting that the passions suddenly released in this village do have a singular character to them. The expression 'collective madness . . .'"

"Good day," the priest said in his normal voice.

He turned one more time toward the doctor and, backing out of the room, even forgot to close the door, which the mayor's wife, shrugging her shoulders, went to push closed with her foot.

"What a character!"

"Everybody's going crazy," she said with a deep sigh. "There must be, as they say, something in the air, some poison, I don't know what it is. You know, doctor, in my time—I'm speaking about my youth, of course—old people didn't have half the vices they've got these days. As far as I'm concerned, the evil comes from that. Society's rotting away because of today's old people."

"Come now!"

"I know what I'm saying," the mayor's wife continued, her face burning. "My idea is that they are worried about dying and they just don't want it all to end. All that's needed is for their imagination to go to work, and they become as silly as they were when they were twenty, only now they have experience. Why, when I remember my grandfather Artaud, or my mother's brother, a Gentil—the Gentils of Mannerville—they were vigorous men, never sick, men who at eighty or more would cross our courtyard with a basket of apples on each shoulder; they couldn't see anything beyond work; work was their god. Didn't laugh too much except for a day of merrymaking, but calm. As for death, it meant rest—what else? and that fresh earth they'd opened up so many times, that they'd squeezed in their hands and sniffed as they might sniff a glass of gin—that earth didn't scare them. There's nothing to fear about the earth. Besides, the idea of death, what's the use? It's an idea that doesn't come naturally, it's a bad idea—and if we followed our ideas, where would it lead us? The idea of death, it's like a dead man, it's something not to be touched. But those old beggars today, their mouth is full of it. And the sadder they get the more vicious they become. And then, Doctor, that's precisely the word, sadness . . ."

"We call it anguish," the doctor of Fenouille remarked.

"I'm talking about sadness," the mayor's wife continued stubbornly. "In the old days a good worker had things that didn't go right, granted, he had his bad days. But that never lasted for long. Depr . . . Depress . . ."

"Depression."

"Depression was for the rich. There are all sorts of ways to show your nerves are bad, isn't that right? The rich have their own ways — the troubles of the rich are laughable since they collect them from their books and theater and music — and God knows where else! While the silly idiots of our kind are obliged to take their troubles out on themselves — they gnaw away at themselves, they devour themselves. Honestly, I'll swear it makes you ashamed even to look at them with their filthy, sneaky faces and their eyes all aglow. I can't help comparing them to animals, to dumb, speechless animals. That's it, exactly: they're sad, just like animals."

She let her chin drop down on her chest, yawning.

"Is Woolly-Leg dead?" she said after a long silence.

"Last night."

"I haven't mentioned it to Arsène. He doesn't know anything."

The village doctor made an indifferent gesture.

"I repeat, we can't do anything for him except get him out of here, out of this village, out of this house, and isolate him. You don't seem to want to understand. Did he have a good night?"

"Better. Rather calm. Only this morning he went out to see the beehives. And still . . ."

Without answering, the handsome doctor turned his back and disappeared. With her head lowered and her two hands crossed over her stomach, she listened a moment to the sound of his steps above through the thin ceiling; then all was quiet. In vain she tried to catch the sound of a door slamming or the noise of voices. She was about to go up herself when the doctor reappeared.

"Our patient's vanished," he said. "What a damned thing to happen!"

"Vanished? But his clothes are locked up, his shoes, everything. Why, he's in his pajamas, with bare feet, Oh, God!"

She explored the attic as well as the barn to no avail. At the entry to the stable she pointed toward an empty plank.

"That's where he usually puts his galoshes. I bet he's got them on . . . The mayor of Fenouille out in his pajamas and galoshes. Now isn't that really just too pitiful . . ."

16

Though he slowed his steps at the top of the hill, the curé of Fenouille came to a stop only after he had entered the garden gate and passed under the silly little arched trellis with its pompom roses resembling paper flowers, planted by his zealous predecessor in conformity to seminary aesthetics.

Sweat rolled off his forehead and cheeks and, astonished at the rapid beating of his heart, he rested both hands on the gate. "Have I really walked that fast?" he asked himself. He saw the empty road twisting down behind him toward the valley, and he vainly questioned it, as though it might give him its secret. Along it the trees cast great shadows.

He took a step toward the sad brick house, so dismal in its starkness amidst dwarfed trees, stunted yews, and raspberry bushes. A half open shutter revealed the gray wallpaper of the living room, where it was always damp, even at the height of summer. The acrid smell of saltpeter penetrated the overheated air filled with the droning of bees. Quickly turning away, he took the narrow sandy path leading to the enclosure and, reaching the hedge, stepped over it, then continued along the pastures toward the church.

All he hoped to find there in that moment was rest, dimness, and the kind of security that so many times these last few weeks, had moved him to prayer, as if in spite of himself. Prayer? The idea was suddenly before him: "How long has it been since I prayed, really prayed, prayed as I used to pray?" He did not know what to answer. Certainly he had not missed any of his daily devotions, even those that were sweet to him, much too sweet, of a sort of treacherous sweetness where he dissipated little by little his exalted feeling of solitude almost to the point of dizziness, backed by nothing but the silence, fixity, and terror of that dead village.

Did they merit the name of prayer? Or hadn't they rather broken the last ties attaching him to his hard work, to his parish? Never before had he had the temptation to feel sorry for himself or be moved by his own situation. But in that state of feeling sorry for himself he thought he now recognized the seed of revolt that, from day to day, had been poisoning his heart.

Toward the church, his church, he heavily raised his eyes. He felt pulled back by fear, or at least by an inexplicable mistrust. But fear of what? Of what danger? With little steps, he prudently approached the door, then opened it. With its shiny pews, its great floor tiles cracked and worn by time and giving off a lugubrious smell, its high bare walls with their thick crust of whitewash, and its bosses from which swallows' nests were suspended, the immense vessel seemed empty . . . Soon another priest . . . No matter! He had never been anything here but a passerby, and the old church pushed him away without anger, just as he was rejected by the village whose roofs he could see, for the church and village were one. As long as the old citadel raised its tower here, as long as the belfry launched its call into space, this church would remain a part of the parish, a part of the people out there. They might well profane her, attack her, but she would remain theirs until the end, she would never renounce them, right up to the last stone. Yes, all overgrown with grass, she would still offer the traitors and apostates her gutted flanks: their young offspring would come and play in her ruins. If nothing else, the old Mother would protect them from the rain and sun. Oh, no doubt about it, she had received him with gentleness, but it was as if he were but a temporary guest. Whatever happened, she wouldn't protect him from them, yes, from them, her sons. And as soon as he had left Fenouille, she — the parish — yes, she would know him no more.

Dropping his hand, the door closed behind him with a light scraping. No, this was one evening when he would not take refuge in his favorite place, in that darkest corner of the choir!

As he went back up the stony path outside, step by step, he once more cast a jealous look behind him, as if on the sly. Goodness, the evening was going to seem long! As usual he now had to prepare his strange supper: a pot of hot water into which, along with a piece of bacon, he threw pell-mell the vegetables he had picked up in the cellar with no regard for their identity. For he had never had a maid: Elisa, the bell ringer, came once a week to do the cleaning and his laundry. Too bad! He'd do without his soup this evening. That extreme poverty into which he was born and had grown up in had become so familiar to him that he no longer hoped, nor even desired, for it to stop. He now suddenly began to feel the humiliation with a sort of somber, prideful joy. When his courage failed him, the only image that now brought him any peace and calmed his nerves was that of a beggar on the road, a real beggar, a pack on his back, pursued by dogs.

The kitchen was just as he had left it four hours earlier, and yet his heart jumped in his breast . . . It was nothing but a half-filled glass of water, but he did not remember having left it there. His eyes moved systematically around the room. The closed shutters admitted only a gray, sad light, already growing dim.

For a long minute he stood there, immobile, prey to an inexplicable terror. The garden door was always open day and night: nothing was more likely than that the sacristan, for instance, had come by, or perhaps Denis, the gardener, who had sold him some seeds and was supposed to bring the bill this week. Shrugging his shoulders, he went out and found himself already in total darkness at the bottom of the narrow stairway.

For how many minutes did he stay that way, his two hands resting on the railing, his knees half bent in a position so uncomfortable that, in order to straighten up again, he had to make a painful, conscious effort, causing him to cry out? For sleep had overtaken him by surprise, even as he was standing, as though he were a child. Then he opened his eyes; it first seemed to him that it was already night, yet the light filtering in through the cracks of the door denied this. He moved toward the living room, then stopped again.

. . . .

"Monsieur . . ."

The face the mayor lifted up to him could be described as peaceful, or even happy, for the puffiness of the entire countenance further emphasized its stupid expression. The curé of Fenouille was taken in by it.

"What are you doing here?" he began with a smile. "They are looking for you everywhere."

The former brewer moved to get up but only managed to work himself a bit farther into the angle of the wall where he squatted, his knees on a level with his chin. He cast a glance at his galoshes and tattered pajamas and said with surprising calmness:

"They locked up my clothes; it's crazy. And they talk and they talk . . . Tomorrow the men from the asylum are going to come and take me away, but what difference does it make? Only I'm no more crazy than they are, Monsieur le curé. It's just that madame has her ideas about me . . ."

"What do you want with me?"

The mayor of Fenouille did not seem to hear and continued to caress his pink scalp with both hands, but the look he sometimes turned toward the door nonetheless remained strangely attentive and lucid.

"You've got to admit that I really did make them see something with my nose . . . ," he said. "But that's all stupid. And then, all the same, I was wrong the other day at the cemetery. What's the use? You have to stay what you are, isn't that right? Accept your fate. And by the way, in regard to that . . ."

He fluttered his eyelids with a sly little laugh.

"Madame" – for that's what he unfailingly called his wife in the old days when the brewery prospered, in those golden days of his life – "madame isn't completely convinced about putting me away because of the scandal. I know her, I know her nature. The more the doctor insists, the more she'll get stubborn; she's as suspicious as a mouse. That way, you see, all this could go on for months and months. But if you . . ."

He stopped abruptly, and his chubby face, cocked on his shoulder, had an unexpected and so gentle expression that the curé of Fenouille wondered for a second if they hadn't all been duped by this fat man and his complicated imaginings.

"You know my opinion," he said, "and I've not hidden it from your wife any more than from the doctor. But no doubt it's true that a stay of a few months . . . the peace . . . the quiet . . . Alas, our human methods are what they are!"

The mayor did not take his eyes off him, and at first he thought he detected irony there, then pity.

"What are you looking at my hands for? You're thinking that they're all scratched? Right. But haven't I got the right to trim my hedge? Only I keep that to myself; let them wonder! Let them get on as best they can! I wish you could have heard the doctor . . . He squinted with his pince-nez over my scratches, he almost sniffed them. 'Ah! Ah! How curious! How very, very curious!' he said. For no good reason he'd have suspected me of having killed the little cowherd. But what can you do? It's my own fault. It was my words at the cemetery that got them all upset. Idiots! Because I had . . . What! Can't a man just once – just one single time in his whole life – hope to find salvation?"

His voice broke, while his gaze, as if opening onto another soul, a deeper, more unknown part of his own soul, continued to smile. For a moment the priest fought against the absurd temptation to leave the wretched man there and take off, but then tears came to his eyes. He understood that it had been given him to see the supreme and still burning light of a sanity already withdrawn into the shadows. He thought of the last lighted porthole on a sinking vessel, in the rain, on a black night.

"What salvation?" he finally stammered.

"Salvation?"

The madman seemed to have forgotten the word he had just pronounced; he repeated it several times, winking his eye.

"I don't suspect you of any crime," the curé of Fenouille continued. "And you are wrong to believe that the doctor . . . Alas! Are you always going to be your own worst enemy? We're not allowed to hate ourselves. Even if you had committed a murder, in my eyes at least you'd only be all the more deserving of pity and compassion."

"In the asylum, you see, I'll have certain comforts," the unhappy man continued in a confiding tone. "That idea came to me these last few days. And whether I'm disgusted with myself or not, sir, there's nothing to be done about it, it can't be explained . . ."

"If you'll allow me to speak frankly to you . . ."

". . . can't be explained. I'm telling you no one knows what disgust is, but it's inside a man. It can sleep there like a seed underground. What they say about it is all wrong. As for me, I think it's like death—just like it. They don't imagine what death is like. What would a dead man think of himself, a real dead man—I'm not talking about a dying man—a real dead man in his coffin, when everybody around him has taken up living again, eating and drinking and sleeping just as before, yes, a dead man underground, all finished off, all rotten?"

"Come, come now, Monsieur Arsène, all of us have had moments . . ."

"Moments . . . Moments . . . What I'm talking about isn't a moment."

He seemed to be making a great effort to draw the resisting word out of himself; then, letting his arms fall:

"That's life," he concluded, discouraged. "That must be the way life is. But then you don't know any more about that than the others, isn't that right? Nobody knows anything. Mind you, I don't speak ill of priests, they have their secrets, their own special secrets, going way back to the time of the Pharaohs — how about the mummies? Those were their saints, the saints of that time. All said and done, priests are all right for a lot of people, only what can you do? I'm not superstitious myself, superstition isn't part of my makeup."

"Monsieur Arsène," the tortured priest said, "I've always thought that your . . . that your troubles . . . could only seem foreign . . . or strange . . . to people too superficial to share them with you or else too . . . too cowardly to dare look for them in themselves, for they are to be found inside each of us."

"Maybe so," the mayor of Fenouille murmured in a somber voice. "My idea though is that I'm not like the others," he continued with a sort of poignant melancholy. "It's bothered me more than once. Now the idea doesn't make me unhappy. But even so! A mayor at the priest's house, dressed in pajamas and galoshes, talking the way we're talking, how many times have you seen that?"

"But that's just it: to be properly dressed would only have depended upon your own good will. I take the liberty of speaking that way because it's my duty, Monsieur Arsène. And if you really want the truth . . ."

Frightened by the groan provoked by the words he had just spoken, he stopped as the unfortunate man retreated bit by bit, pressing himself into the corner as if he'd sighted some hideous specter seen by himself alone.

"Truth? If I want it? If I hadn't wanted it why do you think I spoke the day of the funeral, eh? That worthless trash who, instead of helping me, doesn't give a damn about me. I said to myself, I'll tell them everything — everything, just what I am — they are my friends, my brothers. For a moment there I thought I was free. Just a bit more effort, I thought. And just at that moment I opened my eyes and saw them all with their mouths gaping to their ears, holding their bellies from laughing so hard."

"They didn't mean any harm, Monsieur Arsène. They just didn't understand, what can you expect?"

"Not understand! Come on now! I understood myself very well, so far as I was concerned. I heard every word, I spoke as no one else has ever spoken, I'd have melted a dog's heart, even stones . . . Yes, and how about you, reverend sir, how about you? Answer me yes or no. Just between us, man to man?"

"I'll not lie to you," the curé of Fenouille said. "It is true that I wasn't well situated to . . ."

He stopped. The mayor had painfully stood up and was trying to cover his naked chest by closing his pajama top. His huge fingers were trembling, and he could not manage the buttons.

"Good day, sir," he said with condescension.

"If I had heard your words, I'd have understood them," the priest continued, "but what miracle can you expect from men who give themselves up to the basest passions and who, a few minutes later, were going to stain their hands with blood?"

"Blood?" the mayor cried out, pivoting around with surprising speed. "Blood! I learned from the doctor that blood was considered by ancient peoples to be like . . . like . . . They'd cut a bull's throat and . . ."

"Those are old stories. Neither blood nor water alone can give man back his purity of heart once he's lost it."

"Could be!" the mayor said in a slow bass voice.

"And which of us has never, ever lost his purity of heart? Which of us believes himself without blemish? But the grace of God makes a little child out of the hardest man."

"A little child?" the former brewer repeated softly on the same tone.

"If you have . . . in your past . . . certain . . . certain things that trouble your conscience . . . things that don't seem . . . to warrant forgiveness . . . things that seem to be irreparable, I can —yes! you should know it —I can . . . I have the power . . . the power has been given to me to absolve you of them."

"Absolve . . . ," repeated the wretched man, and immediately, for just a second, his face took on that mistrustful, shrewd look it used to have when meeting the cart drivers delivering barley and hops. "All right, suppose I tell you my secrets. So two of us know about them, then what? You'd have to take them out of there first of all," he said, striking his forehead. "A man is a man. Can you tear him down like an old, rotten, rat-filled barn and rebuild him with new material? No! Well, then, how can you talk about absolution? What I am is what I'll stay."

Making a disgusted face, he passed his trembling hands over his flanks and loins.

"Absolution would be to be reborn," he finally said in his strange voice and headed for the door.

"I swear to you . . . ," the priest began. His intention of touching that madman's heart seemed absurd, yet he couldn't just say nothing. "Just a minute!" he cried. "What had you wanted to see me about?"

"I had an idea," the mayor of Fenouille replied mysteriously. "In one way or another they're going to succeed in locking me up in the asylum, that's for sure. I haven't got a lot to say against it; it will be with my own consent. Only . . ." (he uneasily squinted toward the window), "you have to know the right word . . . There's something like a damnable urge inside me that causes me to break out of my own nature, do you understand? To be something that is not according to my own nature. Sometimes I only imagine that I am no longer the same and that I really do get out of my own skin, but sometimes not. And then sometimes, I still doubt, that's the hardest . . . I play the game for myself alone, all alone. Nothing else to do. I get urges to finish it all off all at once, I don't know how. Go on off to the asylum on your own, my boy, I say to myself. In the asylum everybody plays his own game, neither seen nor heard; here I'm causing you problems, I say, but there you'll be well off . . . In my opinion a madman is man who has come out of his house, locked the door behind him, and thrown the key into the cistern, splash! Isn't that true?"

"You don't get away from your soul as easily as you get away from your house, Monsieur Arsène."

"That depends on how you put it. Let's say, if you prefer, that it's a man who has cursed himself, who's denied himself . . . who's spit on himself, as you'd say."

"That would be a crime then, Monsieur Arsène. The crime of crimes, a suicide."

"Maybe," the major of Fenouille answered. "But what can you do? I'm not too brave by nature, and I don't imagine getting rid of myself any other way. Otherwise!"

"Get rid of yourself! First of all you'd have to have the right. Then you'd have to have the ability. For with God as my witness I tell you, you won't get rid of anything. There's no hatred that can ever be satisfied either in this world or the next, and the hatred that one has for oneself is probably the one for which there is no forgiveness'"

"I don't want to forgive myself," the former brewer said in his slow voice. "No forgiveness!"

"It's God who gives it to you. And I who am talking to you now, Monsieur Arsène — don't close your heart to the words that I'm going to say — I who am talking to you, I can give it to you in His name."

"I've not got anything against God," the mayor of Fenouille said after a silence. "Nor against you. When I was young I never set foot in a catechism class, as was to be expected; my father didn't like priests. 'Look out for hell,' the priest used to say to me whenever he met me along the road. He was a great big devil who could roll out a barrel of beer for you as easily as a kid rolls a hoop. As for hell, you see, it rather made me laugh. But today I don't find the idea so stupid. Fire puts an end to everything. There's no muck that can withstand fire, no smell. Water as pure as fire is unknown, and even in the purest water fire would find something to eat, right? In Boulogne I saw the boys there taking an old cargo ship apart, great steel sheets that had been repainted time after time, with scales as big as my hand on them — real garbage! Well, now, this fellow brought his blowtorch, and that whole filthy sheet started sizzling and spitting fire like a dragon. For a second you'd have thought it was the sun — that sheet of steel was giving off sunrays. I should have understood that day that water can never do anything for my sufferings, that there is nothing that measures up to fire. Fire is God, I told myself."

He raised his hand toward the ceiling, and the light sleeve of his pajama top slipped back to the shoulder, revealing his fat, hairless arm.

"You're not going to go out dressed like that," the curé of Fenouille cried. "I'm going to lend you a cloak. If you take the way through the pastures, you won't meet anybody."

The madman allowed himself to be dressed. But his face had taken on the tricky, stubborn expression of a rebellious child. The almost mischievous smile on that tormented face seemed to be a sort of sinister forewarning to the priest.

"Let me come with you," he said. "Or better still, let me go look for some clothing that would be more . . . more appropriate."

"Go to my house?" the madman asked uneasily. "I'm not against it. But they've hidden my clothes. It remains to be seen if they'll give them to you. Madame is stubborner than a she-ass."

He came back and sat down on the corner of the hearth. For an instant the poor priest hesitated about what to do, then, closing the door behind him, quietly turned the key in the door and fled.

. . . .

There seemed to be no one at the mayor's house. After a long time the doctor finally appeared at the door.

"Excuse my delay," he said. "Those fears I expressed a little while ago have unfortunately just been confirmed by something most annoying. Our patient has escaped."

"He's at the presbytery."

To the great surprise of the priest the doctor lost nothing of his funereal gravity.

"Is he all alone?"

"For more security I thought I should lock the door behind me."

"Is he calm?"

"Very calm. And if you'll allow me to express an opinion, from our conversation—which, I admit, was a bit extraordinary—I formed the impression that... well, that our poor patient is less..."

"Less mad than he wants to appear," the doctor completed in a sarcastic voice. "What an admirable discovery! What singular understanding! The first of my colleagues to come along will tell you that a mad person is almost never sincere, that the crazy image he carries there"—he struck his forehead—"does not convince him and that it just exercises a sort of fascination on him. But that's enough joking around! We should have taken steps several weeks ago. Even if his function here is nothing but honorary, it is a scandal to allow our community to be headed by a madman who could suddenly become a danger for us all. The poor devil has finally found some fortuitous, moving, and rather picturesque means of expressing himself that will arouse a professional reaction in you, if you'll allow me that expression. Today's priests fortunately leave the care of certain states to us, states that would have been taken for mystic states in times past. The symptoms of these states, like those supposed cases of possession, hardly interest anyone but us anymore... In the twelfth century, I suppose, our mayor of Fenouille would have seemed the prey of some lustful spirit with an exceptional stench, if we are to judge by his obsession—which is really after all made up of genuine hallucinations born from his sense of smell. But let's speak seriously"—he put his mouth to the priest's ear—"I've just found in his drawer a document of the highest interest, a sort of confession. It's important since it could legitimize a certain fear... To put it briefly, a suicide doesn't seem to me to be completely impossible."

"My goodness! Don't you think then that I should . . . He's all alone."

"Not so quickly, my friend. Just hold on. I said 'a certain fear,' but the word 'scruple' would have expressed my thought better. The reading of that document has made me think, that's all. Because in the midst of so many lies and fabrications I think I've encountered a fact — oh! quite probably, almost surely, imaginary — but that appears to me to be as it were the core of this bizarre tumor of the mind or, if you prefer, the bit of shell around which oysters, they say, secrete their pearl. Ah, ah, But this pearl seems to me to be completely black . . . I can in fact let you see this curious piece of literature right now. I'll even admit that I'd be offended . . ."

"Sir," the curé of Fenouille replied coldly, "I thank you for your confidence, but as small as may be that little bit of hope I have of being able to gain this unfortunate man's confidence some day, it would be very painful for me to owe the knowledge of a secret so important in his own eyes to anyone other than himself."

"I'm astonished," the doctor answered on the same tone, "that such considerations can stop you from doing your duty. The good of the patient is my only law; I know no other."

The sudden blush covering the cheeks of his rival no doubt appeared to him an appropriate reward, for he now took on an air of good humour, pulling from his pocket a sheaf of papers spotted with large drops of candle wax.

"Like Jean-Jacques Rousseau, our mayor must have written his 'Confessions' by candlelight. It's in an unusual style. But even more unusual are the notes in the margins filled with drawings whose character of monotonous obscenity you'd hardly approve of, I suppose, for at the very moment our patient lets himself go with his disgusting obsessions, he is still visibly haunted by the phantom of his lost innocence . . ."

"Please," murmured the curé of Fenouille. "These sorts of sufferings really deserve compassion. My experience, no doubt, is very different from yours, but as young as I am, I've often seen the underside of certain lives the world pretends to believe are irreproachable, and I . . ."

"If I understand you correctly, you are proposing that a certain lack . . . of religious feelings . . . could be translated by . . . certain pathological phenomena . . . that would go so far as causing even . . . a deep transformation of . . . of the human race? Have you thought that a thesis . . . as extravagant as that . . . would justify, or at least would tend to justify, certain revolts against society? Come on now! Men are men! You may in the exercise of your ministry perhaps find yourself more often facing true moral distresses than I do. But those that I see are totally indistinguishable from physical trials of which they are only the transposition into a nobler language. Let's admit rather that the conversation you just had with our patient caught you in a state of . . . nervous exhaustion, which is quite excusable. Believe me, that poor devil is nothing but a very ordinary case of sexual obsession, and the unusual form that obsession takes interests no one but psychiatrists."

"It doesn't matter!" the priest said. "You'll one day have the proof that you're not allowing for the supernatural. Yes," he continued after a silence, in a voice contrasting so strangely with his usual tone that each time he spoke it seemed to belong to another, "when you have succeeded in drying up not only man's language to express purity, but even his feeling for purity — indeed, even his ability to distinguish between the pure and the impure — well, the instinct will still be there. And that instinct will be stronger than all your laws and patterns of behavior. And if even the instinct is destroyed, the suffering will still be there, a suffering that no one will be able to name, a poisoned thorn in the heart of man. Just let's suppose that some day the sort of revolution engineers and biologists hope for is accomplished, let's suppose that all hierarchy of needs is abolished and that lust appears no different from hunger in the digestive tract, a hunger to be satisfied like all others by the strict rules of hygiene alone. Well, you'll see — yes, you'll see — mayors of Fenouille coming from all over, turning against themselves and against their own flesh with a hatred that by then will be completely blind, for the causes for it will remain buried in the deepest and most profound depths of man's hereditary memory. And then, just when you have flattered yourselves on having resolved the fundamental contradiction and guaranteed inner peace to your miserable slaves, on having reconciled our human race with what today causes both its torment and its shame, well, then I tell you that you'll have an epidemic of suicides you'll be able to do nothing about. Rather than the obsession with impurity, you'd do better to fear the nostalgia for purity. In the silent revolt against desire you like to see a kind of fear nurtured for so many centuries by religions that you view as the surreptitious aids of the lawmaker and judge. But the love of purity—there is the mystery! The love of it found in noble souls and, in the others, the sadness and regret, that indefinable and poignant bitterness dearer to the debauched man than debauchery itself. Those who are prey to anguish when facing suffering or death and who come to beg for grace from their doctor may pass for cowards, but I have seen—yes! I have seen—other looks raised up to me! And besides, there's no longer enough time to convince you, and the near future will take care of settling it for us. For the way society is going, we'll soon know if man can be reconciled with himself to the extent of being able to forget forever what we call by its true name, the old Paradise on earth, the Joy that was lost, the lost Kingdom of Joy. Even if Mercy were only an illusion, thousands of centuries old . . ."

He stopped as if frightened by the accent of his voice and blushed even to the whites of his eyes. His face had suddenly regained its sorrowful, resigned expression, making him look stupid.

"Let's not get carried away," said the doctor. "There will always be time to take up this engrossing controversy again. The most useful thing for the moment is to lay hands on our patient's clothes, or at least those he took off last evening before going to bed. I think that his wife, fearing he'd get away this morning, hid them in the oats bin, where we'll find them, no doubt. If you'll allow me, I'll accompany you back to the presbytery."

The path that the curé of Fenouille had taken so shortly before they now took slowly and in silence, side by side. The elegant doctor, intent upon not spoiling his new suit while cutting through dew-drenched hedges, led his companion over one barrier after another when crossing the pastures, which were narrowly divided up with one extending into the other like the pieces of a jigsaw puzzle: they constantly had to stop and get their bearings and thus lost a great deal of time. The door of the little enclosure was open. The priest's heart sank for he thought he remembered having left it shut. Up on the tiny porch his hand trembled as he put the key into the lock.

"Come on! Come on now! Even if our man has taken off, no great harm is done — we'll quickly catch up with him."

They found the room empty. A pitcher full of water sat on the table near an overturned glass whose contents were still dripping down onto the tiles.

"I don't understand," the priest said. "The shutters are closed, even upstairs."

Vainly they checked each window, climbing even up onto the roof. As they explored the dim vestibule one last time, the curé of Fenouille rushed suddenly back toward the kitchen. A trap door there allowed access to a cellar encumbered with bottles and old, unused barrels cut up into pieces by the sexton and used by the previous incumbent to fill his stove. By a door long since condemned, the cellar itself opened out onto the road down below. The poor priest had even forgotten it existed.

"Here's where he got away," he cried in a despairing voice. "What have I done!"

"Your forgetfulness isn't irreparable," the doctor said, still calm. "I'm just going to give a discreet warning to the local gendarme. We must try to avoid scandal."

On the thick brown panels covered with a deep layer of dust, the hand of the mayor of Fenouille had written in capital letters in a childish scrawl: "ADIEU."

"Turn down the lamp, my child," said Monsieur Ouine, "we'll once more savor this end of day."

The room was already full of the sickening smell of coal oil, and the little flame, lowered to the bottom of the glass chimney and ready to go out, gently flickered.

The iron bed was so narrow that the covers were raised by the slightest movement of Monsieur Ouine's thick thighs, revealing the roundness of his hairless, pale calf encircled by a varicose vein. But for a moment now the professor had been making an effort not to move, his hands crossed on his stomach. His clothing, folded with meticulous care as always, adorned the back of the room's one armchair. Under it he had arranged his black shoes with the gray woolen stockings he wore all winter, held up by ecclesiastical garters, plus his felt hat, its garnet lining shining in the shadows.

"I've never been able to stand the biting air of dawn; I don't know how to protect myself against its malignancy," he continued after a long silence. "Even in months like these, the heat of the day doesn't always manage to prevail, for it has a thousand subterfuges and escapes, gliding to the bottom of empty paths, turning off into the thickest part of the woods. Right at noon I've suddenly run into it and felt its bite, like one of those icy currents they say move in the midst of tropical oceans . . . But at this hour of twilight, when the evening starts to fall, the worn-out earth gives off a warm, rich vapor, a sort of sweat that it takes the whole night to destroy. And what is left of dawn in the air is caught in it, like a fly in glue."

Philippe dared not reply. The great black pine still rose in front of the window, and the tip of one of its branches scraped imperceptibly against the pane. Yet the sun weighed down with full force on the countryside, a lifeless, dull sun, drowned in mist, though Monsieur Ouine did not seem to see it.

"Open the window, please," he said.

Steeny pretended to obey, twice moving the window latch. He knew that even more than the cool air of morning his master didn't like the smell of overheated resin, which irritated his sore throat, throwing him into frightening spasms of coughing. In any case, Monsieur Ouine did not even turn his head. His swollen face, where wrinkles had disappeared and which, with the approach of death, took on a youthful look, a look of sinister childishness, expressed an unspeakable relief. His mouth opened, then closed again, several times, slowly, gluttonously. What was that mysterious evening, known to him alone, with which he, at that moment, was filling his lungs?

"Night is coming," he said. "You can turn up the lamp." (The thing definitely stank; Philippe blew it out.)

"Li . . . ght," the sick man articulated.

His voice, even when he emerged from his crises, barely resonated, like a cello with loose strings, and certain syllables were missing, rolling to the back of the throat, strangely absorbed into his large chest where his collapsing lungs had almost completely decayed. ("He can last twelve hours, or six months," the doctor from Montreuil had said. "A really robust man would have been buried a long time ago, but this one is of a soft, watery make-up. It's as if you struck an eiderdown with a saber.")

Philippe remained standing in the corner. He was hungry and sleepy, and he was bored. The idea of taking off, however, did not cross his mind. Devouring his lunch in haste, he would arrive every afternoon, hot from his run and exhausted by the sun, to find himself, from the entryway of the solitary house, enclosed in shadow and silence like a cool shroud. He had now given up trying to understand what power kept him there, what charm, what secret god, more secret than any of those others who used to speak to him in time past whenever he would escape the insipid white house, full of perfume, steps, and whispering between the two too sensitive women with their intolerable caresses. Sometimes Miss would call him across the park, then return, long afterward, her cheeks flushed, pine needles in her blond hair: "He's taken off, heaven knows where!" And Maman would answer in her gentle voice, "He's going to kill me yet. Oh, dearest, dearest, can it be?" Neither one nor the other would ever have looked for him, ensconced at the back of the dovecote and pressed against the grating, his chin resting on his two boyish hands joined together, so close to them that just by raising their eyes they could have spotted him. The roughcast walls, the worm-eaten planks, and the heavily peck-scarred feeding troughs were all impregnated with the wild smell of the birds. Sometimes Miss would say, "You should tear it down! It's not been used at all for fifteen years." Fifteen years! He imagined the departure of the birds and their distress. For hours, or days, or perhaps even months they must have encircled the old closed tower with their flight and cries and shadows . . . Then, one morning, they had all taken off for some fabulous country or other.

"Be so kind as to call Madame Marchal," said Monsieur Ouine. "I want to drink a little broth."

The timbre of his voice was stronger—the strings of the cello were taut again. It was in fact the hour for his morning injection to take effect. Sometimes it even dangerously stimulated his nerves for, as his life was being snuffed out, it had sudden bursts of catching fire again. And now Steeny foresaw the crisis. Monsieur Ouine's cheeks were flushed, and his dilated pupils gave him that anxious, fascinating look.

Madame Marchal was a midwife by profession. But, for a long time now, the people of Fenouille, favorably impressed by the rubber gloves of Mademoiselle Solange, a young lady with a diploma, a headband, and immaculate blouses, had ignored the older woman. Madame Marchal's huge peasant hands, though so very skilled, were thus unemployed. Fortunately she had some income and an attractive brick house near the local police station. There, with her expansive waist enclosed in her blue apron and spilling over the low chair used to wash many a newborn, she would sit and enjoy her coffee generously laced with gin, while she crushed a lump of sugar between her old gums . . . That she had accepted to stay with Monsieur Ouine to the end had been out of pure goodness of the soul, for she admitted that the patient frightened her. In times past the professor had come more than once to look at the Russian rabbits she raised with such pride. Monsieur Ouine had in fact taken an interest in those animals.

The dying man indicated with his hand that he himself would carry the steaming bowl to his lips. He drank in little sips, slowly, deliberately, forcing himself by a discreet cough to mask as much as possible the horrid noise of swallowing the liquid. His throat, swollen with pus, contracted with the passage of the liquid, and the uvula, at the end of each spasm, made a sound resembling the one Woolly-Leg used to make with her tongue to urge her mare on.

"Madame Marchal," he said, "take this young man with you and give him something to eat. I shouldn't mind dozing off."

His gaze emerged with difficulty from under his sagging eyelids, and Philippe noted surprise and confusion in it. It seemed that Monsieur Ouine had just recognized that the mysterious evening pouring out its coolness on him had only been a dream, like so many others, one of those thousands of dreams that, more and more numerous, kept surging up from the depths of his memory. Just a few more days and, according to the idea that he had formed of his future life (for his pride had never accepted the gross hypothesis of annihilation), that whirlwind of maddened, floating images would all at once be fixed in place, and the symphony's thousand notes would break forth in a single harmony. But had he spoken? Had he betrayed himself? The sight of the extinguished lamp reassured him, as did the completely innocent appearance of Steeny. Then, after a furtive glance at the window, his puffy hand started playing with a sunbeam coming through a crack in the shutter, which had just hit the bed like a flame.

. . . .

The empty house filled Madame Marchal with as much terror as disgust. She hardly left the kitchen and had made up a bed for herself in the pantry. Up until now, the patient hadn't allowed anyone to sit up with him at night. In case he needed anything, he insisted, he could quite well use the bell cord hanging at his bedside, which sounded like a school bell when it rang out in the stairwell. Sometimes, when the heat of the day had penetrated the stones and the old walls felt warm under your palm, the midwife, after a last shot of gin, would even risk going all the way up to the first floor, the only one, she said, that gave any idea of the house being inhabited by Christians, since it was there that Woolly-Leg had amassed her most recently acquired furniture. The horrid disorder of the wardrobes, as large as rooms, was so old that it inspired the simple, housewifely soul of Madame Marchal with respect. The unfortunate thing was that they were all as full of holes as a slotted spoon, gnawed by rats and mice, whose droppings covered the shelves like a soft carpet, giving off the sour smell of ripe apples.

The midwife, as usual, set before Philippe a lump of butter "fresh from the cellar," brown bread, and the porcelain jam pot filled with jam. A fly swam on the surface of the caramel-colored beer filling the pitcher.

"It's a pleasure to see you eat, Monsieur Philippe," she said.

"Really?" Steeny answered with his mouth full.

Outside Monsieur Ouine's presence he immediately took on again that insolent tone that exasperated the two friends in his home.

"As far as I'm concerned," she said, "I lose all taste for food in a situation like this one. If it weren't for coffee, I couldn't hold up."

She topped off her cup with gin, slipped another sugar cube between her gums, and drank in little sips.

"I really wonder what attracts a young man to such a sad house as this one," she said after a long silence. "Probably the old gentleman does have some affection for you, but at your age the affection of old people isn't worth much. And sick as he is now, does he even make sense when he talks? His great talent in times past was knowing how to talk. All he had to do was talk to people to influence them. Just a bit at a time and without seeming to, with his smile of a monseigneur and those fat hands he employed with such gentleness. What he could have done if he'd wanted! Only, you see, these last few years he no longer left the house; it's here he had his fun."

"What fun?"

"Ah, well! Woolly-Leg, of course!"

Before the midwife could open her mouth to answer, Philippe felt anger rising in him. It was no use for him to find his anger ridiculous, for the shame it inspired excited him even more instead of calming him. Then, all of a sudden and to his great surprise, his fury broke out into a nervous, uncontrollable laugh.

"Monsieur Ouine couldn't care less about women," he cried, "any woman! And as for men, Madame Marchal, he doesn't care about them either. But then how can you judge him, you can't even understand him!"

"Well! Well! Just look at the little cockerel! 'Any woman,' you say? Well, just let me tell you, my boy, that I happen to know a bit more than you do about what goes on in families. The cleverest man isn't exempt from making a fool of himself over a woman, and not always for a beautiful woman either, quite to the contrary."

"Women . . . ," Philippe began.

"Women . . . Women . . . One would say that the very word sears your tongue. Just wait until you know about them . . ."

"Know what? Boys run after women because they don't know what they're like. They just make fools of themselves and get all worked up. While I . . ."

"Ah yes! A proper, pampered, little gentleman, sweet as sugar . . ."

But Philippe's anger had already passed. Every time he escaped the uneasiness caused by Monsieur Ouine's voice and stare, an obscure feeling of freedom, of deliverance, provoked a silly nervousness in him that he attempted to dissipate by talking.

"Young men are quite different today from what they used to be, Madame Marchal. We're not much interested in women. Yes, yes, you can laugh, but I'm not alone, all my friends are like me."

"Your friends? And just where are your friends? You should be ashamed to talk that way when you've not yet even cut loose from the apron strings of your mother and that pretty schoolteacher."

"So what do you think of Miss?"

His eyelids had suddenly dropped so that they were almost closed.

"I don't have any opinion," the old woman said without concern. "Can't say I really know her. I'd say she's never talked with me more than ten times since she came to Fenouille, though I see her every evening. She passes as close to my door as this! But if you really want me to speak frankly: what you need is a master, Monsieur Philippe, a real master, a man!"

"Monsieur Ouine is my master," said Steeny. "I'll never have another."

"Too bad you're going to lose him so soon. Goodness! A boy like you isn't made to live in Fenouille, and when you've seen the world a bit . . . Why, when I was twenty years old with my diploma,

I too thought I was very clever . . . Mind you, I'm not questioning your friendship. But that doesn't alter the fact that even in Montreuil you'd find men far superior to this one. Monsieur Valéry, for example, the former head of taxation. In times past he and your master were friends . . ."

"And now?"

The midwife once again cast a furtive look in the direction of the door.

"He said . . ."

"What did he say?"

"I want you to promise me to keep this to yourself and not repeat it. But he said that Monsieur Ouine was the most dangerous man he'd ever met."

"Why dangerous?"

"Lord! You should know that better than me! Since Woolly-Leg's death you've not left the house. Everybody's gossiping about it. Maybe you have your own ideas, too? No doubt you find something to talk about other than the weather?"

"That's just where you're wrong," Philippe said solemnly.

His face took on an expression of theatrical seriousness, without appearing comical. His cheeks were marked by two shadowy hollows.

"Monsieur Ouine can talk of anything, of the simplest things (sometimes you'd even believe him completely naive or stupid, and he doesn't do it deliberately). Yes, the simplest thing, in his mouth, becomes unrecognizable. Thus, for example, he never speaks ill of anyone, and he is very good, very indulgent. Yet in the depths of his eyes you still see something making you understand how ridiculous people are. And if you take away that ridiculousness, you lose interest in them, they seem empty. And life itself seems empty; it's a great empty house where everybody enters, one after the other. Through the walls you hear the steps of those who are about to enter and those who are going out. But they never meet. Your steps resound in the corridors, and if you speak you think you hear an answer. But it's nothing more than the echo of your own voice. And when, all of a sudden, you turn around to face someone else, all you have to do is look a little more closely in the depths of those used, greenish mirrors, just like the ones here, and you'll recognize your own image under the grime and dust . . ."

The shadowy hollowness of his cheeks gradually enlarged, and the old woman, to her great surprise, saw an uneasy light, like that of autumn mornings, rise in the face of the boy, a light of inexpressible sadness.

"It's a shame," she finally said, "to hear a boy of your age who shouldn't be thinking about anything but having fun compare . . . uh . . . life to a . . . an empty house."

She had set her cup down on the hearth, and, with her body leaning forward, her huge breasts held in place by her arms crossed over her knees, she looked at Philippe with the cynical attention of women of her class, strangely pursing her lips.

"Don't trust him in any case. Don't trust him as long as he's alive. And he can live a long time yet. When a person's dying of tuberculosis, do you usually see him keep all his fat? The doctor can't get over it."

"Don't trust him?"

"Well, extraordinary things have taken place here. Yes, right here in this house. I knew Monsieur Anthelme. Before his marriage to Woolly-Leg he was a man like other gentlemen of his time, not too clever, mind you, but quiet, taking care of what he had, running around the fields hunting with his friends from daybreak to dusk, his gun slung across his shoulder. Good enough. Then one morning he took off. 'I'll be back Sunday,' he said. No hope of that! He came back six months later, and not alone either . . . Oh, at first Woolly-Leg — you wouldn't believe it! — everyone smiled politely at her, even the ladies. You'd have laughed to see the lords of the little chateaus hovering around her with their monocles, tan jackets, tight trousers and their damned pointed-toe boots. Monsieur Anthelme didn't seem to notice anything. They all slapped him on the back. Damned Anthelme! Marriages like that — I guess there are thousands and thousands of them, aren't there? Then, one day . . ."

She bent over painfully to retrieve her cup.

"One evening Monsieur Ouine arrived out of nowhere. Old Anselme carried his bag for him. Monsieur Ouine had on his frock coat, his bowler hat, and his huge shoes, and he was sweating great drops of sweat since heat has always been hard on him. 'I've never seen a man sweat like that,' old Anselme used to say. They received him in the pantry, for they seemed not to take him too seriously. But six weeks later he was king of the household. At that time I knew Florent, who was the gardener and had worked for Monsieur Anthelme's late father. His daughter worked here as a daily, quite a pretty girl. 'They scarcely see him,' Florent told me, 'and they never hear him: he trots from one floor to the other on his velvet paws, just like a real old tomcat, fat and shiny. And the way he talks! You'd think he was a priest! I don't like his looks. He even has a funny smell; he smells like a savage. Yet he's a man who takes care of his body, even too much so. He's very interested in flowers, only he never picks them himself: I choose the fullest ones for him, and he crushes them in the hollow of his two joined palms, bending his fat round face over them a long time, his eyes rolled back with pleasure."

"'Well, Uncle Florent,' I said to him, 'there's nothing bad in that.' I can still hear him answering me: 'Nothing bad, no. But there's a sort of bad atmosphere he carries around with him without even knowing it.' Bad atmosphere or not, six weeks later that old man was dead."

"From what?"

"From what? From flu, they thought. Or at least some sort of malignant fever? Oh, you can laugh!"

"I'm not laughing, Madame Marchal," Philippe said (and stared without blinking at the immense, reddened sky over the old woman's shoulder). "Perhaps he also might have died from . . . I often think that one can't resist Monsieur Ouine."

"Resist him? Old Florent was too stupid to resist anybody. At the end of the first week he'd have walked through fire for your Monsieur Ouine! Monsieur Ouine used to sit down near him while he was digging in the vegetable garden. He'd explain the stars and the sky and the order of the world to him. And since Florent's death, people say that the professor even sometimes goes to his grave in the old cemetery and stays there an hour or two, that wretched hat of his in his hand, standing the whole time with a fistful of wild flowers he ends up walking away with, just as they came, as if he hadn't thought any more about them. You see, all things considered, they did really get on rather well together."

"Exactly. One just doesn't conceive of an old fool being able to breathe the same air as Monsieur Ouine. It might be possible if Monsieur Ouine were capable of getting angry or of making fun of others. But he never makes fun of anyone. He's good. You see, it's not easy to stand the goodness of such a man."

The midwife listened seriously.

"My goodness," she finally said. "you've got to admit that it's hardly any easier for you to stand it either. I find you looking rather poorly, Monsieur Philippe. Without wishing your master any ill, since there's nothing that can be done for him, wouldn't it be better for him to pass on? Fortunately you're younger than Monsieur Anthelme. Otherwise . . ."

"Bah! Monsieur Anthelme died old."

"Old? At forty-six?"

"It surprises me that he lasted that long. Miss always said he had no more brains than his hounds and ferrets. But then what can you do? Monsieur Ouine would make even stones think!"

"Monsieur Anthelme didn't think. He was tired of everything. He was a man who'd let himself go. And his projects! I met him one day at his niece's, Madame Dorsenne, she was one of my patients. He told her that until then he'd lived like an animal and that he was only just beginning to understand. Understand what? He also said, 'I should have been a great musician.' And he'd never played anything but a hunting horn. He even sold his farm at Bloqueville to buy himself an organ, but his creditors got wind of it, and the organ was finally never delivered. For weeks it sat in its case at the Ouchy station."

"Well, what do you expect, Madame Marchal? An idiot should never dream of becoming a musician or a poet. Monsieur Ouine says that you always die from a dream."

He pronounced those last words in a tone of ridiculous seriousness, but his tight face, the strange expression of his mouth, and the evasive cast of his eyes inspired the old woman with a sort of embarrassment resembling fear, although she would not admit it to herself.

"Die from a dream? What are you talking about, Monsieur Philippe? Those are words that you are repeating without even knowing what they mean."

Philippe shrugged his shoulders.

"If men didn't dream," he said in the same tone of ridiculous assurance, "I suppose that they'd live to be old, very much older — forever perhaps."

"And the animals, Monsieur Philippe? You forget that they die!"

"Animals dream in their own way. If one could read their brain, one could no doubt see that they too desire what they haven't got, and they don't know what it is exactly. That's what dreaming means."

"Well then, Monsieur Ouine — doesn't he dream?"

"Oh yes, he does," the boy said. "But he resisted it for a long time. 'I don't hope for anything,' he said, 'neither good nor evil.' Today he claims he's opening himself up to his dream like a rotting old boat opening up to the sea."

"Well, you're in a bad way," the midwife answered after a long silence. "And you're not alone, either. You'd think this whole miserable village had been put under a spell. Since the murder of the little cowherd it's not recognizable any more, I'll swear!"

Her gray eyes surreptitiously watched Philippe as she continued in a muted, scarcely perceptible voice, without inflexions, as if she were reciting a lesson.

"The investigators, the police, all the law thinks that Monsieur Devandomme's son-in-law did it. He killed himself, therefore he's the guilty one, they think. A poacher! Come on now . . . The Devandommes are a proud lot in any case; they have their enemies. In brief, I thought that when the investigation stopped, things would settle down. But no! The village has never been more turned inside out than it is now. It's like a gigantic top spun out of control: it turns, it sings, and it will knock the walls down. Peaceful people who never read a local newspaper before are now the most worked up. It seems that the investigators are receiving whole bags of accusations every day. But even the authorities have lost their heads! Is there any sense, I ask you, in wanting to bury a little cowherd like an official, with flowers and delegations and speeches? And since they knew Woolly-Leg was capable of anything, couldn't they at least have kept an eye on her? I tell you, when I saw your Monsieur Ouine slip outside the church and go along the walls, taking his time, I said to myself, 'It's going to end badly, sure as anything, for the old fox is out sniffing around.' I myself was in such a state, the priest's words had got me all upset. And not so much what he said, but rather his voice and the way he said it. My skin felt as if a hundred needles were pricking it. People were listening with their mouths gaping open and didn't interrupt him, but their looks spelled trouble. It just drove them crazy not being able to understand. And then that fool of a mayor. Of course, everybody's known about him for a long time. He's a man who's seen too much of life, a regular old lecher. He's scared of death and he's scared of hell. They say that before his marriage he got one of his maids in trouble and she hanged herself, out in the stable. As for what he was supposed to be saying at the cemetery, there isn't anyone who knows anything about what it might have been. Just the nonsense of a madman, I guess, nothing more. Anywhere else he would have made them all laugh. But then, there by the grave—he even nearly fell in—it was a strange sight for men who had been drinking gin all morning at the cabaret! And then, Woolly-Leg . . ."

The midwife's voice had softened. With his chin resting on his hands, Philippe stared straight ahead with an almost frightening fixity.

"It's too bad she died," Madame Marchal began again. "They didn't mean to kill her. They just threw themselves on her the way magpies and crows throw themselves on a barn owl in full daylight. You should never play around with the imagination of the people in these parts. I don't want to say anything against Woolly-Leg. I've seen women far more depraved than she was, and all the men tipped their caps to her. And the boys around here aren't normally bad, but you've got to respect their customs. Well, she didn't respect them. A lady of the manor who takes to running around the roads from four or five o'clock in the morning behind a great devil of a mare so tall that no one can remember ever having seen anything like her, as well as being a lady of the manor who's rejected by the other ladies—well, that's enough to make them feel humiliated. But the worst, don't you see, Monsieur Philippe, is that she wanted to be laughed at, she made them laugh. A woman who wants to go in for debauchery shouldn't try to be amusing. It's sure that young men are no longer what they used to be in my youth. Nonetheless their appearance is often deceiving. It doesn't matter that they may do things to their hair and put on shoes of all colors and dance like fancy city boys—a woman with no morals who wants to have her fun with them ought to treat them like so many kids. Otherwise, they start playing rough, and when they play rough, you'll see their white teeth, real wolf's teeth, ready to bite. Just think! Those fellows' grandmothers didn't joke around about such things: they had modesty in their veins. A loose woman scares them a little bit at first, and then, when they're no longer afraid, they'll use her for their amusement just as if she were a stray cat—look out for the stones! And once stones get involved, you can bet something awful's going to happen. Besides, Woolly-Leg's wounds weren't as bad as they say, but she was just too rebellious by nature, she just couldn't get used to the hospital; she asked them two or three times to bring her back here — two or three times, no more — then she didn't open her mouth again. She just let herself die. The doctors couldn't get over it. If they'd foreseen it, they'd have let her come back, even if the house isn't known for being very healthy. Between you and me, I think that they exaggerate a little. For years now Woolly-Leg had got the idea of leaving the shutters closed in winter as well as in summer. So the humidity just crept all over along the walls . . ."

But Philippe was no longer listening. One by one the logs disappeared into the ashes. Madame Marchal, tired out by her endless monologue, closed her eyes as her head nodded slowly. Her empty cup, set too close to the glowing coals, suddenly cracked with a dry noise.

"Who killed the little hired boy?" the boy suddenly asked.

18

Cracking the door open, Philippe stopped dumbfounded in the doorway for a moment. Monsieur Ouine was out of bed! Monsieur Ouine was up! He had even more or less comfortably settled himself in the armchair, his bare feet in his slippers, but his shirt collar gaped open, disclosing his powerful neck, paler and smoother than ever. His lips were rather blue, and over them, at regular intervals, he kept passing his thick thumb with its broad, flat, ivory-colored nail in a strangely precise, mechanical rhythm.

He turned slowly toward Philippe without interrupting this activity, revealing a face the boy did not initially recognize. What! Had an hour been enough to . . . What a strange face! Its bone structure seemed destroyed, as if the skin no longer covered anything but a sort of soft fat. The collapsed muscles caused the enormous skull to stand out. The cheeks, no longer supported by the cheekbones, hung down toward the neck, at the level of the jaws, creating two pockets enlarging the bottom of the face to such an extent that the neck, when examined with more attention, seemed to be immeasurably elongated: one would have said that it bent under the weight like a stem bearing a monstrous flower. His sweat-drenched hair stood up in tufts. "He looks like Louis-Philippe," thought Steeny.

At the same time, he moved back toward the door to call Madame Marchal. But would the two of them have enough strength between them to get the old man back in his bed? Taking her time, the midwife came upstairs, puffing at each step. When she finally entered the room, she sized up the situation at a glance. Monsieur Ouine, with an imperceptible movement, had just ensconced himself a bit more into the armchair, though his hand was still raised, with his thumb at the level of his chin. Finally he lowered it gently to his knee.

In a colorless voice the woman finally said, "You must help us get you back in bed. You must behave yourself."

There was no reply.

She shrugged her shoulders, measured the distance from the bed to the chair, then turned to look at Steeny.

"What do you expect me to do? You're not even able to handle him; your arms are trembling right now. He's not the devil, however, even so! One could always try to drag the chair nearer the bed."

Philippe bent his back as he pushed against the back of the chair with all his strength, while she took the two lifeless legs of Monsieur Ouine between her crossed arms, slowly moving backward. With difficulty they advanced a few yards. But Monsieur Ouine's upper body dangerously moved back and forth, and, in order to keep it from slipping, Steeny pressed with his shoulder against the dying man's back.

"Phew!" said the midwife. "Let's rest!"

Caught now between the bed and the chair, she had to crawl between the patient's knees covered by the twisted folds of his loose cloth trousers.

"The grocer will be coming," she said, "it's the day he makes his rounds. He'll give me a hand to get the poor old gentleman into his bed. While we're waiting we'll prop him up with pillows. Lord! I'd rather deliver a baby. Sick men are worse than stuffed dolls, they don't help you at all. Come on now, Monsieur Philippe. One would say you were asleep standing up."

She stole a glance at Steeny's hands, while he vainly tried to dissimulate their trembling. He finally put them behind his back. With an expression of satisfaction the midwife's eyes moved back to the sick man.

"Well, if it comes to that," she said, "he could die just like that, and just as peacefully as between the sheets, can't he? When he's like that, Monsieur Philippe, he almost seems to hear us, but don't be scared: nobody ever comes back from where he is now."

"Oh, do be quiet!" stammered Steeny, completely pale.

"But I tell you he can neither see nor hear anything! He's nothing now but a real dead man. But then! You men are all alike. You don't worry about the living, but as soon as one of you starts dying, there you all are around him as if he were God! Women on the other hand understand things, they rarely lose their heads. Of course, Monsieur Steeny, I've seen a lot of my clients die, I've been the one who, as the papers put it, 'received their last breath.' 'Receive their last breath'—I ask you! Yes, clients of all kinds now! Rich and poor, old and young, good ones and bad ones. Well, Monsieur Steeny, I've not got a whole lot to say about the way they die!"

One last time she patted down the pillows, then pushed the table between the chair and the wall. Solidly secured in this way, Monsieur Ouine could peacefully complete his destiny.

"I find you extraordinarily heartless, Madame Marchal," said Philippe. "You're like someone taking care of a horse or a calf."

"That's just where you're wrong," the midwife replied without anger. "Given the temper you know he's got, you'd certainly have to believe that if he were still conscious of anything at all, he'd already have told me off. For in spite of his great good smile, making him look like a big round loaf of blessed bread, he still had a sharp tongue. But now he's there just as he was when he came out of his mother's womb – if you'll excuse my saying so in front of you. And what would you expect me to do for a newborn babe, my poor Monsieur Philippe? Just keep it clean and warm and not expect any thanks."

She gave Monsieur Ouine an undefinable look where prideful satisfaction born from secret resentment became almost tender and caressing.

"The doctor was quite right when he said that he would weaken all of a sudden and just when we were least expecting it. When I think that only an hour ago he was in bed, saying, 'Madame Marchal, take the young man with you . . . I wouldn't mind dozing off.' What I think is that the effort of getting up must have tired him out all at once. He must have wanted to go down to the next floor to Woolly-Leg's old room. Just between you and me, I think he slipped down there the other night on the sly. Probably looking for papers. I found the key to one of the cupboards in his trousers pocket."

She approached the dying man, laid her hand on his hip, and said:

"Look, Monsieur Philippe, just feel, it's still there . . ."

"Oh, leave me alone!" Steeny muttered. "You disgust me, madame!"

"Nonetheless, if I revealed the hiding place, I'd probably be doing a favor to more than one person."

"To whom?"

"To the police, of course! A man like him knew an awful lot about a whole lot of things. And he'd not be taking all that trouble just to hide bills or letters from his girlfriend. But you can rest easy, Monsieur Philippe, I'm not a policeman, and they can just get on with it the best they can!"

She moved calmly toward the door, opened it, then turned back in the doorway. The boy remained standing in the corner, his eyes downcast.

"It's hardly proper for you to remain here alone," she said.

"What's the use? It'll soon be six o'clock and the grocer will be here any minute now; I even think I heard his truck up at the Gastebled house at the top of the hill. And you can see yourself that your friend isn't suffering. And, besides, what do you expect? There's nothing more I could do by being here. With my varicose veins, I'd risk dropping him on the tiles, and you can just imagine, can't you, the doctor's reaction at finding his patient undressed and on the floor? Besides, it won't be the first time I've seen someone die in an armchair. In a way, it's even rather beneficial for a patient in a coma; I know what I'm talking about. Lying flat, the lungs fill up much more quickly; why, you'd already be hearing the death rattle. And then you can believe me, Monsieur Philippe, when I say that with you here he'll struggle more."

"Struggle? Does that mean then that he knows what's happening?"

"Oh, not at all! A coma is just like being asleep. When you're asleep you dream or you don't dream, depending upon something we don't know about — probably the stomach. Nonetheless the slightest thing — a door closing, furniture creaking — is enough to set your imagination off without your knowing anything about it. For example, last year I was taking care of old Monsieur Guiraud, the former notary, a fine old man, ninety-seven years old and still strong. And just at the end he started saying things — and I do mean he was saying things, too! The little nun who was nursing him almost lost her mind listening to the things he said to her! Finally he reached the last stages, good enough. For two days he quietly had the death rattle; you'd have thought he was snoring. Then, toward the middle of the third night — Lord help us! He started thrashing about so hard that even three of us couldn't hold him still any longer, just think of it! The little nun, weeping away, kept saying, 'It's the devil who's got hold of him for sure!' and she soaked him in holy water. Well, do you know how I finally calmed him down? I give it as one example out of a thousand, Monsieur Philippe. Well, while the gardener was busy tying a sheet around his shoulders (the way they tie up violent lunatics), I had the idea of singing him a sort of lullaby, a song from our own region, for Monsieur Guiraud was from the Ardennes, like me. You can imagine that the gardener was angry at first! He found that such things should certainly not be sung to a man nearly a hundred years old—it was all stupidity. No matter! I guess my notary finally started listening. Well, he stopped kicking and stretched out quite happily with a sort of smile. I felt a bit ill at ease, though. To be born or to die—I think it must all be the same thing. But then those are ideas that you can't understand. So I quite happily accept being taken for a hard woman just because I'm used to sick people and am not afraid of the way they look. Though if I told you . . . Well, are you going to come down with me or not?"

"No," Philippe said, forcing himself to speak up.

"Well, then, at least open the window," the old woman concluded. "There's a funny smell in here."

It was true. Funny perhaps, but certainly not disagreeable. It was the smell of apples from the last harvest as they begin to dry up on the shelves. And that smell had been haunting Philippe for several days now, even out in the sun-drenched countryside and under the great pines in the old park. Each morning he rediscovered it as he started to take his jacket off its hook. It slipped slyly across the strong wafts of cologne he doused himself with after his bath. Yet even by plunging his face right into the folds of the jacket's material, he could still smell nothing. One would have thought that the smell slept in the woolen folds and awoke only at the proper time.

Philippe nonetheless opened the window and looked out into the garden that used to be so dear to the master of the house—the garden that had grown wild. The scorched grass of the driveways had taken on a yellowish hue, and the heat waves could be seen rising from the earth in almost imperceptible layers. The boy pricked up his ears, anticipating to hear the sound of the delivery truck, and followed the circular flight of a bird of prey dancing like a fly in the depths of the sky's immense, vertiginous blue cupola. What difference did it make? Monsieur Ouine's breathing did not disturb the silence of the little room but just gave it a sort of funereal, almost religious, dignity. It seemed to Philippe that his own breath was being gently regulated by that so appropriate, so discreet death rattle. And perhaps their two hearts too? His hand seemed to come to rest on his chest of itself and stopped there, trembling. How was he to know that a little girl, thirty years earlier, in the depths of a pink and blue bed, had made the same gesture as light filtered through the cracks around the door, illuminating the brass knob and corner of the door frame, while her old mother, tired out with sleepless nights, caused the floorboards to creak in a sinister way?

19

"Madame Marchal," said Monsieur Ouine, "you can leave me alone. I'm feeling better."

Perhaps it was surprise that at the first moment rooted Madame Marchal to the spot, but her little black eyes immediately lighted up, all of a sudden taking on a cruel look — a look of cruel solicitude — silently staring at the sick man for a long while. "You'd say she was the cook feeling a hen before killing it," thought Steeny.

She approached the bed with a sigh and ran her hands distractedly over the sheet. Monsieur Ouine watched their movement with an intense stare. Little by little the death rattle of his false agony had changed into a profound, but natural, cough, and Steeny again wondered if the old master, incapable of ordinary pretenses, hadn't been staging a death scene just for himself.

"Good enough," said Madame Marchal.

With her torso tilted at an angle favoring her bad hip, she seemed to mime with her entire body both a last grimace and an ironic farewell to the dying man.

"His chest is clearing, he's surely going to talk some more, for he's still as full of air as a bladder." In a gentler voice she asked: "What's the use of all this? Hasn't everything that's to be said already been written down in books? Won't you ever finish teaching your classes?"

"I . . . am . . . a . . . professor, Madame Marchal," Monsieur Ouine managed to articulate between two whooping gasps.

With great difficulty he raised himself up, leaning his head over the edge of the bed. With a ritual gesture the midwife held the spittoon for him.

"Professor . . . of . . . languages," continued Monsieur Ouine with unspeakable relief.

He now caught his breath again.

"Of . . . living . . . languages, Madame Marchal."

"That's what I thought," the old woman muttered as she made her way to the door, but in such a low voice that the sick man must not have heard it. "Living languages! Ha! Ha! Living!"

At the door she turned around and, before disappearing, already in the shadows of the corridor, she shrieked in a strident, exasperated voice: "Living languages!"

. . . .

. . . .

"Come nearer, my child," Monsieur Ouine said. "Give me your hand."

He took the boy's hand between the soft puffiness of his own palms.

"Let go of my hand!" said Steeny brutally, then immediately regretted the inappropriateness of his response.

But Monsieur Ouine did not seem at all disturbed by it.

"Well, then, oblige me by helping me put my arms down to rest on the mattress. They are now too heavy for me to manage. I think they've always been so, but I only half suspected it, for nature is prudent and full of goodwill. Little by little she has imposed on the child I used to be, on the child I still am, these huge limbs, this obscene, big, pumpkin belly, this hairy, pale skin so covered with pockets and wrinkles. How have I ever managed to move all this about for so long?"

"You talk a lot to say nothing, on purpose," Steeny remarked cruelly.

"Indeed, I have many other things to say," Monsieur Ouine answered with deliberation. "Vainly have I tried to put them in order tonight, but they got away from me all at once, I am no longer in a state to hold on to them; such is undoubtedly decay's first symptom. And others are going to follow them. How long are you going to hold out against your disgust?"

Steeny gritted his teeth to keep from replying. He didn't know anymore whether he resented Monsieur Ouine because he was dying or because he wasn't already dead.

"You don't frighten me," he finally muttered with an indefinable, and so naive, expression of regret.

"It's probably because I'm talking," Monsieur Ouine observed humbly. "Whenever I stop talking, I myself experience something close to the feeling you just named in regard to my own person. Thus indeed have I held forth for the length of my solitary life; not that I've ever been one to talk to myself, in the proper sense of the expression, but I rather spoke in order to avoid hearing myself. I said just anything; it had become as natural for me as for a ruminant to regurgitate its cud. Perhaps I have two souls, just as those animals have two stomachs? Or perhaps two consciences? Which one will disappear first? It would be interesting to watch it happen. What are you muttering about now?"

"Nothing. I just think you're feeling better. I'm going to call Madame Marchal."

"No. Not that. There is no hurry. My boy, you've already sacrificed many whole days for me. Now just give me tonight, and tomorrow I'll return you to your family. After that I'll bother you no more, at least while I'm alive, for, quite naturally, I'll have no power at all over the image you'll keep of me, whether it be real or not. May that new creature prove as favorable to you as was the other one, such is my wish."

"I'm not afraid of ghosts," Steeny grunted.

"I hope I'm not yet a ghost," replied Monsieur Ouine with a smile. "But it is difficult for me to affirm anything regarding that matter. Good people say about a man who dies calmly that the unfortunate creature didn't see himself die. For me those words have a hidden meaning. Perhaps I'm no longer even capable of seeing myself die? At least not with that inner gaze I got too much pleasure from but that now, like a delicate little machine gone berserk, is turning around on itself at the approach of the only thing that merits being seen but that it will never see. If only I could see it with your eyes! And I do mean your eyes, your real eyes, not the inner eye that at your tender age is, I hope, still closed. Yes, your eyes, your real eyes, your eyes that are so new, so fresh."

As he spoke these last words, Monsieur Ouine's voice grew weak, but the silence that followed them brought no relaxation. It was a silence full of other words, unpronounced words, which Steeny thought he heard hissing and twisting in the shadows like a tangle of snakes.

"Who's keeping you here with me now?" Monsieur Ouine asked suddenly.

"Keeping me? Why 'keeping me?' Like a frog fascinated by a snake? Listen, Monsieur Ouine, I do what I please, everything that I please, and when I please; that's the way it is!"

"I have never had any intention of fascinating you," Monsieur Ouine said in a plaintive tone impossible to answer. "But the word 'snake' has given me precisely the image I was looking for. I'm wearing myself out, not in an effort to rediscover myself but to join myself together. Yes, to join myself together like a snake cut in two by a spade. But, alas, it's too late. The pieces of my life, of my being, will never be joined together again."

This time the silence was a true silence, which Steeny dared not be the first to break. Quite visibly Monsieur Ouine was bathing in it too; his face was calm.

"I think that I've come through that crisis," he declared. "We have come through it together, even though you weren't aware of it. I'd quite happily get up were I not afraid of another syncope. Or was it really a syncope? It seems to me that at no moment did I lose either my sight or my hearing. I just deliberately slowed them both down as if I were before a keyboard where I amused myself by brushing my fingers over the keys . . . No, no! Don't call, I'm definitely not going to get up, it's not worth it . . . It's better that you begin my last bottle of port alone . . . Just push the table a bit closer . . . Good! Whenever you bring the glass to your mouth, the paleness of your eyes will take on the exact color of old, tarnished vermeil. Now don't go knitting your brows! I remember that first evening when . . ."

"I didn't know how to drink then," said Steeny, red with embarrassment.

Twice he emptied his glass, one after the other. Monsieur Ouine's stare had a mysterious expression in it.

"Don't push this bravura too far," he said gently. "This is neither the time nor the place. Excuse me for speaking to you in this ridiculous tone. Whatever you in your malice may think of my lessons, I am a professor before all else. Yes, I am truly a professor, this language has become natural for me. Why are you laughing?"

"Because I don't believe you, Monsieur Ouine."

"As you wish. I know you attribute poetic gifts to me. What difference does it make! For days and days now, my dear child, I've taken advantage of your generosity, of your politeness, and what is even more perhaps — yes, let's say the word — of your curiosity. Now the moment has come for me to reward you: I owe you a secret."

Monsieur Ouine sighed, closing his eyes and stretching his legs clad in black serge out on the bed. He had undoubtedly been preparing that sentence for a long time, but it seemed as if it had just escaped him, as some precious object might slip out of a too attentive, too affectionate hand. His closed eyes and thin mouth with its pinched lips all seemed to trace the same ironic expression on his austere face, where the shadow of the temples now seemed sinister and purplish.

Steeny emptied his glass, then refilled it. Monsieur Ouine remained impassive.

"I don't give a damn about your secrets," the boy shouted in a rage. "And I know that you don't give a damn about me either! There's still as much life in you as in a litter of kittens; it's all a big joke! Six months from now we'll still be here, face to face, just as this evening, with that bottle between us, yes, with an empty bottle and a secret that's empty too, for all secrets are empty!"

He walked back and forth across the narrow room until his head started spinning. Monsieur Ouine's bed drew him and repulsed him in turn, as he kept bumping into it. Was that bed empty too?

"Secrets!" he began again. "Bah! They're all jokes, I tell you. Listen, Monsieur Ouine, I recently read a very curious story" (in fact he hadn't read it at all: he was making it up as he went along), "and it was screamingly funny. Some sailors — not real sailors, of course, but characters like us — saw a bottle floating in the wake of the boat and decided immediately to go pick it up, can you imagine that? Their captain threatened and begged and wept in vain, for a storm was raging, but it was nothing to them! So all of them go setting out in a lifeboat, leaving the captain alone on the bridge, swearing after them like a man possessed. 'We'll be back soon,' they cried. 'No use making such a fuss over such a little thing, Captain!' And right until nightfall they kept maneuvering their boat toward that wretched bottle amidst enormous waves. When night finally fell, it still didn't deter them at all; at every flash of moonlight between two dark clouds they'd spot the shining object, sometimes on the right, sometimes on the left, it was just a paddle-length away. 'There's a message inside, I swear it,' the cabin boy cried. At daybreak a wave higher than the others threw the bottle into their boat. Well . . . Aha! I know you're thinking that it was empty, aren't you! Well, it was broken, Monsieur Ouine, it had burst into pieces upon impact, and no one ever knew if it had anything in it or not . . . And the big boat? Their lifeboat had taken off with the wind behind it, and they never saw either their captain nor his boat again, so they died. That story's killing, its terrific! And that's what secrets are, Monsieur Ouine. There are no secrets, the bottle's always empty, ah! ah!"

Steeny pronounced those last words with emphasis like weary actor at the end of a long soliloquy. And he certainly expected no reaction to that stupid story; he had been talking just to be talking, talking for himself alone, to distract himself by the sound of his own voice, as mechanically as he was pacing the room, quickly passing from convulsive gesticulations to the immobility of an animal frightened by its own shadow. Yet the answer came back to him.

"I too am empty," said Monsieur Ouine.

These words surprised Steeny less than did the enormous sigh that followed them. It seemed that the massive chest of the professor of languages emptied itself not only of all the breath it contained, but also of all cares, of all foresight, of all human worries, and so profoundly and so completely that Steeny thought he himself was being exhaled by that monstrous sigh of relief, holding his own breath as though he were holding on to life itself. Monsieur Ouine's hand felt for his in the shadows.

"Young man," he said, "is it possible? I can now see to the bottom of my own depths, there is nothing stopping my gaze, no obstacle is in the way. And there is nothing there. Remember that word: nothing!"

Steeny scarcely recognized that voice, and had it not been for the bloated hand weighing on his palm and for its soft grip, he no doubt would have thought he was dreaming. For the voice of Monsieur Ouine didn't seem at all made to express a feeling as simple and as naive as surprise — surprise, one might say, in its purest state, surprise caught at its source with no additives of curiosity or irony. For Steeny himself had had little experience with such intense movements of the soul that man calls by ordinary names, as he always does the gods he fears. Of surprise as of anguish most men know only the scintillating, streaked surface, like that of watery abysses. For man's double secret remains buried in the memory of his first childhood, a childhood as gorged on milk as a sick person on bromides and morphine, speechless, almost sightless, and unknown by all — completely inviolable — for the cradle is shallower than the grave.

"Let me go, come on now, don't hold on to me that way, I hate being held . . . I'm not going to run off, it's crazy."

"I'm hungry," said Monsieur Ouine, but this time with a sort of mindless astonishment.

"That's still no reason to squeeze so hard," replied Steeny, forcing himself to laugh. "Come on now, Monsieur Ouine, it's not me you're going to eat after all."

Trembling with frustration and anger, he pulled away the puffy fingers interlaced in his own with his free hand. A single step carried him to the other side of the room, but the dying man's head immediately followed his movement as he leaned against the corner, repeatedly passing his tongue, saturated with the sweetish wine, over his lips. Ugh!

"I'm hungry," Monsieur Ouine repeated. "I'm raging with hunger, I'm dying of hunger."

"Nothing to make such a fuss about, Monsieur Ouine. We'll stuff you with bread and butter, that's what we'll do, bread, butter, and jam, ah yes, you old hypocrite."

He scarcely even lowered his voice for this last insult, for Monsieur Ouine certainly could not hear it: Monsieur Ouine was delirious. In any case his delirium had nothing frightening about it yet, nothing that would make one think of a death agony.

"Never again shall I be filled," remarked the professor with gravity. "To fill me would have been a great task and that task hasn't even been undertaken. Vainly did I open myself up; I was all dilated, I was nothing but an orifice, breathing in, swallowing up, with both body and soul, gaping all over. Offered so many pastures and buried in fodder like an ox, how much care I lavished on discovering the juiciest morsels, the richest ones, poor in appearance only, though sometimes repugnant and disdained generally by stupid people. I never hurried, I flattered myself on knowing how to wait, I carefully calculated both the pleasure and the good I'd draw out of them, calculated the exact moment to catch them at their most perfect succulence, at their ultimate limit of maturity, just slightly removed from the beginning of decay — and I always did it alone so as not to have to share either my trouble or my pleasure with another. Alas, what would I have been able to share? I was all desire, instead or satisfying my appetite I bloated myself with desire, I took nothing substantial into myself, neither good nor evil, and my soul has become just an air-filled bladder. And now it's my turn, young man, for my soul to suck me in, I feel myself softening and disappearing into that voracious gullet, it's softening up my very bones."

"Bah! When you speak of your soul, you're like a frog speaking of a snake."

"It does fascinate me, I must say," Monsieur Ouine continued, quite unruffled. "Is it its hunger that I feel, or is it my own? In fact I've been much concerned with my hunger; I took pleasure in my appetite, but today it's my appetite that's taking pleasure in me. Oh, oh, my boy, if this is nothing but a dream, it's certainly a very strange one. But are you still in a state to be of any use to me? Aren't you drunk?"

"If you keep going I certainly shall be. What pleasure can you get out of talking about such things? Of course, you don't frighten me, but you do annoy me, that's what it is, you set my nerves on edge, as they say."

"That's enough!" Monsieur Ouine cried suddenly in a sharp voice.

Almost lightly he jumped out of bed. Against the murky light of the window his heavy figure, outlined in black, was so indistinct that Steeny first thought the old man had turned his back to him.

The puffy face with its closed eyelids moreover had taken on the same pale gray as the sweat-drenched strands of his hair.

Whining, the strange dying man said, "I don't want to frighten you, just stay still for a moment, just for a little moment . . . er . . . er . . . it's a favor I'm asking of you. Right now everything that moves is escaping me, as if it were suddenly jumping out of my world into your own. Whether it's from failure of my eyes or of my brain, I don't know. Perhaps also I may have finally found my point of equilibrium — my exact point of balance — my center?"

"You'd certainly lost your point of balance a little while ago. But come on now! You can jump out of your bed onto the floor well enough."

"I still have the use of my legs," Monsieur Ouine protested. "I even feel full of vigor still."

He twisted about heavily on his heels, then went back to the window, hopping along.

"Night is falling," he said after a long silence. "Well, is it or isn't it falling? Get out of here, you little fool! Every time your services are needed you're drunk. And what can I do with a drunkard at this point?"

"I'm . . . less . . . drunk than you!" Steeny cried as he took a step forward.

"Take care not to lay a hand on me," Monsieur Ouine said severely. "I don't wish you any ill, but you have no need for my secrets."

"I didn't ask for your secrets. Tell them or don't tell them — that's your business. They don't frighten me either."

"Frighten you? They couldn't frighten anyone. As far as I'm concerned, henceforth their intricacies shall seem as vain as those of dreams. But are they even secrets? Perhaps they used to make me ashamed. But now I'd like to hate them, only I can neither love nor hate them for, without my knowing it, they have been slowly weakened by malice. They are like wines that have been kept too long and lose their flavor, turn pale pink, and, as they die, devour the cork and even eat into the sides of the bottle.

I committed evil in thought, young man, believing I could thereby distill its essence — yes, I nourished my soul from the condensations of that still, only now, when I can no longer do anything for it, my soul is in a rage, I don't even have any remorse I can toss it to appease its hunger, I'm lacking time. Where I am now, nothing less than a whole lifetime would be necessary to succeed in coming up with some remorse. The word itself has lost its meaning for me, and for years now I've pronounced it just out of habit. I can no longer conceive of that doubling back on myself, of that disavowal, of that bizarre decomposition . . . A whole life, a whole long life, a whole childhood . . . a new childhood."

"Pooh!" said Steeny. "Childhood for a man like you, aren't you ashamed? I don't attach any more importance to a child's existence than I do to a suckling pig's."

"A new childhood, a whole childhood," Monsieur Ouine murmured in a low voice accented by vast, covetous longing.

He was seated on the edge of the bed, his feet resting on his heels, his long legs lost in the folds of his trousers. His head was bent so far forward that it caused his flat, formless neck, marked by a purplish red, to stand out. Thus he continued grunting and groaning, bent over in an uncomfortable position that probably made his suffocation even more painful.

"A . . . whole . . . childhood," he repeated between gasps, "A . . . complete . . . childhood," and, with his heavy, hesitant hands, he seemed to be caressing and kneading. This time, rather than the sort of almost ferocious curiosity that, more than any other feeling, had attached him to this master sent by chance, it was compassion that won out in Steeny's heart. Slowly he went up to him and placed his cool hand on Monsieur Ouine's neck. This was the only sign of affection he had ever shown him, or had even been tempted to give, since their first encounter.

Under his fingers that neck was as hard and smooth as a marble of well-polished oak, but Steeny had no time to be astonished by this. He suddenly found himself sitting on the floor, his legs stretched out, his head at the height of the old man's knees, with Monsieur Ouine's face nearly touching his own. He felt neither its heat nor its breathing.

"I have no secrets," said Monsieur Ouine. "Perhaps in the old days I did have a great number of secrets at my disposition, perhaps then I'd only have had to choose between them. But now I've got no more secrets, if indeed I ever did have any. God has played that trick on me, young man."

Steeny was covered with the shadow of the big shoulders. They had the form of a lowered arch, a powerful vault, exactly calculated and unshakable. They gave the boy the almost crushing impression of eternity, of eternal balance, of unchanging, unending endurance. However he felt no fear whatsoever, but rather a vague, undefined pity, a sort of sorrowful serenity like that following great crises in illnesses when the awaited dawn of convalescence is still below the horizon.

"I need a secret," Monsieur Ouine said again. "I have the most pressing need of a secret, even if it were as frivolous as you can imagine or more repugnant and hideous than all the devils of hell. Yes, even it if were no larger than a tiny lead shot, I feel that I could gather myself together around it and take on weight and solidity again . . . A secret, you must understand me, my child, I mean something hidden and worth the trouble of being admitted — yes, worth an admission, an exchange, a burden to be passed on to someone else."

"How the devil could that possibly do you any good? What for?"

In spite of the question's ironic tone, it did not seem to mortify Monsieur Ouine. He reflected a long time before answering. His hand weighed heavily on the boy's shoulder, but less heavily than his gaze, so close that had Steeny wished to look into the old man's pupils, he would only have had to push himself backward a little. All he saw was the light of the gaze, its reflection, its indefinable and contradictory expression of dream and trickery.

"That would save me," said Monsieur Ouine in a voice that was almost indifferent and, in fact, expressed no desire whatsoever to be saved but rather a resentful detachment from his own fate, a sort of frozen conviction. "That would break the balance if there were still time. For I now have nothing more to give anyone, I know it, I can probably no longer receive anything either. But still! Something can fall away from me, like fruit off a tree, or, at least — for it's no longer a question of flowers or fruit — like a chip from a stone block. All that would be needed would be a push, a flick. The tiniest little pebble . . ."

Above Steeny the shadow of Monsieur Ouine's shoulders still formed a thickset, solid arch, and that image gave a sinister meaning to his last words.

"All right, then! Try, I find it so simple. Just any secret . . . Well . . . Are you speaking seriously, Monsieur Ouine? Everybody has his little hiding place, his little cabinet of poisons, something you lock up with a key."

"Exactly . . . precisely . . . ," Monsieur Ouine stammered (and his other hand, which had remained free, now also slowly came to rest on Steeny's shoulder), "but that key could be of no further use to me, the door is wide open, the bottles are empty, the poisons scattered in the air, diluted to the extreme, inoffensive. It would take centuries to obtain from them enough to kill a mouse."

"Are you really thinking about poisons? As for poisons, really! Everything's a poison whether it's nectar or pure water, it all depends on who consumes it, on their sadness or their joy, on the day, the hour or — who knows? — perhaps on the label on the bottle."

"Water . . . pure water . . . ," Monsieur Ouine repeated in a voice that could scarcely be heard. "No, not pure — insipid, colorless, neither cool nor warm . . . No cold could affect it, no fire could be put out by it. Who would like to drink that water with me? Steel is less hard, lead less dense, no metal could ever affect it. It is not pure in the exact sense of the word, but intact, unchangeable, polished like a diamond mirror. And my thirst resembles it; my thirst and that water are one."

"That's because you yourself are intact and unchangeable," said Steeny without paying much attention to his mechanical answer.

"Indeed, I am." (And the last word was lost in a sort of unintelligible grunting.) "Oh, God! And I thought it was I who was using a file and a chisel when actually I was only passing a pencil over that matter so gently that it wouldn't even have erased a flower's pollen."

Monsieur Ouine's voice — at least whenever it managed to be distinct — appeared to have lost nothing of its professional gravity, and yet its timbre seemed strangely broken, giving Steeny that uneasiness caused by a little child wearing the mask of a mature man. And in spite of himself, little by little, he felt his own voice blending with that of his master, so closely that the two seemed but one. They talked thus, in the shadows, equal to equal, like two old tramps at the turn of a deserted road, in the most perfect solitude.

"One doesn't engrave anything on one's life; that's all foolishness," said Steeny. "Perhaps you only write on the lives of others — perhaps — and still we don't know what we've written on them, how could we?"

"Have I written nothing on yours?" Monsieur Ouine asked. "Uh . . . Uh . . . Don't hurry in giving your answer. Or rather don't answer at all; your answer would have no value in my eyes. To have written, of what importance is it? It is enough that I might have erased even one word, one single syllable, of that unknown language that was already written there. Oh, young man, if I had only cracked that mirror, I could have succeeded in making myself small enough to slip completely into that crack in the metal."

"To hide from whom? From what? What are you so afraid of, Monsieur Ouine? Is it death?"

"I don't know what you mean by that word," said the language professor with solemnity. "I am not a chemist, and my attention has never been much attracted by that sort of resolution of the humors normally indicated by that word. That is, death for me has always been the denouement of a moral drama. And that drama, I'm afraid, I've now missed. In me there's been neither good nor evil, no contradiction whatsoever, justice can no longer reach me — I'm out of reach — that is probably the true meaning of the word 'lost.' Please note, neither absolved nor condemned, but lost — yes, lost, gone astray, beyond reach, not even worth considering."

"But justice is not the only thing; there is mercy, pardon. Or perhaps just nothing, absolutely nothing. Why not?"

"Idiot!" groaned Monsieur Ouine (but his voice expressed neither anger nor indignation). "If there were nothing, then I would be something, good or evil. It is I who am nothing."

The words fell quite literally from Monsieur Ouine's lips on to the young face lifted up to receive them, and, indeed, that face did receive them. More than hearing them with his ears, Steeny received them with his face, his forehead, his eyes — the words bathed his temples, instantly filling his breast, like a block of ice.

"That's enough!" he thought he was moaning, but pride still stopped his mouth, for the mercy for which he begged came only from himself.

"Curiosity is devouring me," Monsieur Ouine continued. "At this minute it hollows and gnaws out what little is left of me. Such is my hunger. If only I had been curious about things! But no, I was hungry only for souls. Hungry? What am I saying: I coveted them with a different kind of longing not meriting the name of hunger. Otherwise a single one of them would have sufficed, the most wretched one: I alone would have possessed it in the most profound solitude. But I didn't want to turn them into my prey. I watched them take their pleasures and suffer as He who created them might have seen them Himself; I myself provided neither their pleasures nor their sufferings; I flattered myself on giving only that imperceptible impulse, as one might slant a painting toward the light or the shade; I felt myself to be their providence, a providence almost as inviolable in its designs and as unsuspected as the other Providence. I congratulated myself on being old and ugly and suffering from gout; I'd open up to the sound of my own voice; I'd quite scrupulously exaggerate the timbre of its nasal bassoon made for reassuring little brats. And with what jubilation would I penetrate those modest consciences so little different from one another, so common – little brick row houses blackened by habit and prejudices and stupidity, just as other kinds of houses are blackened by a city's soot – souls so like the company houses of mining towns. I moved in with dignity, I filled them with my goodwill, with my discreet solicitude, and all at once they'd give me their secret, but I wouldn't hasten to accept it. Looking at them like a hen at her brood, I'd gather under my wings everything that those kinds of houses innocently offer the outsider or the passerby – houses without souls, souls without names – their silly comforts, the embroidered table mats, the photographs hung on the walls, the stand with its plaster statue of a girl, the mirrors darkened by fly specks more mysterious than the edge of the woods, the lone carpet shiny with dirt, the canary in the cage – ah yes, my gaze penetrated all those humble defenses giving shelter to that mediocrity quietly devouring itself. In appearance I in no way interrupted that sort of reabsorption but, unbeknownst to them, I little by little just made it impossible. In my hands lay the security of those souls, but they did not know it. I hid it from them or revealed it to each of them in turn. And as one might play a delicate musical instrument, I manipulated my gross security to make music, drawing a very special harmony from them, one with a superhuman quality: I gave myself that pastime of God, for such is the recreation of a god, such his endless leisure . . . So that's the way those souls were. I would not allow myself to change them, I revealed them to themselves, as cautiously as the entomologist unfolds the wings of an immature insect. Their Creator knew them no better than I did; no amorous possession can compare with that infallible possession – completely inoffensive to the patient, leaving him intact yet completely at our mercy, a prisoner while still guarding the most delicate nuances, all the iridescence, all the variegations of life. That's what those souls were to me.

That is what I did with that poor, unlucky fellow de Néréis. That's what I did with Woolly-Leg here, in this old house destined to retain my memory, where every stone has been impregnated with my pleasure. From a common bit of dough I made an air-filled sphere – lighter and more intangible than a soap bubble – these bloated fingers that you see here have worked this miracle."

"Well, then? You won't have lived in vain then?"

"But have I really done what I just said?" Monsieur Ouine moaned. "Did I even want to? Did I just dream it all? Wasn't I just an open, fixed eye, a gaze, an impotent covetousness?"

"Woolly-Leg is dead," Steeny said.

"She has escaped, that's the word; she has escaped beyond all reach – escaped is perhaps not the proper word – she has launched herself upward like a flame, like a cry."

"Did you love her?" Steeny asked.

Once more he uttered the words before completely grasping their implications. Monsieur Ouine did not appear to hear it however. He continued to moan and gasp, though the moaning had nothing in it of a complaint. Rather did it express the same, deep, ever increasing surprise of a man whose last steps have brought him to a peak that had long seemed immobile, but where he discovers immense spaces and horizons stretching beyond at such a pace that his gaze cannot even follow the vertiginous spiral of its repetitious unfurling. Steeny thought also of the grumbling of the gluttonous idiot he had seen one day at the door of the canton asylum, whose tears and saliva flowed down, mingling together in his steaming tin bowl.

"You were wanting secrets just a little while ago," he said, still tossing out words as they came. "Well, there are some secrets for you!"

"Secrets? Bah! If they were real secrets I would not get rid of them so easily. I don't even rid myself of them; instead, they fall off me, detaching themselves, as if they never even belonged to me. They neither add nor subtract anything to my weight, and besides I no longer have any weight. My child," he said, taking on once again his old tone of insistence, "during my university career, as well as afterward, I never dreamed of denying the existence of the soul, and even today I couldn't put it in doubt, yet I have lost all sense of my own, even though just an hour ago I experienced it as an emptiness, as a waiting, as an interior breathing. No doubt it has succeeded in swallowing me up. I've fallen into it, young man, just the way the elect fall into God. No one cares about asking me to account for it, it no longer even knows my name. I could have escaped from nearly any other jail, if only by desire. But I have fallen precisely there where no judgement can reach me. My child, I am going back into myself forever."

To Steeny's astonishment, Monsieur Ouine's precipitated puffing finished off with a laugh that was at first stifled, then frank and clear, such as one would never have expected from that austere mouth. At the same time the shadow of his large shoulders no longer bore down on him from above: he found himself on his feet, free.

Monsieur Ouine continued to laugh in little hiccups, his head slightly leaning to the right, one eye open, the other closed, giving his face a rather common expression. In the fold of his cheek glistened a single large tear.

"What I'm going through is a cursed moment in time," he said with an enormous sigh. "To go back into yourself is not a game, my boy. To go back into the womb where I was formed would have cost me no more; I've turned myself inside out, literally, I've made my wrong side my right side, turning myself inside out like a glove."

The soft sound of his laugh scarcely even rose above the silence; it now resembled the movement of water flowing along a clay rut, or the sound of a downpour on pebbles, or some other unintelligible murmur of things; it no longer had any human meaning. That it issued from that heavy body, now collapsed under its old clothes in the pale whiteness of the unmade bed, in no way even surprised Steeny. And besides, it did not rise but flowed through the shadows like a thin, muddy trickle, never to be grasped or stopped, having neither beginning nor end.

"Well, now, Monsieur Steeny, without giving any orders, you could lend me a hand, I'm not strong enough to move him."

(Whence came that sound of water flowing? It was the doctor washing his hands in the basin sitting on the floor between his knees.)

"If the moment of death goes back for two hours, the old gentleman died just after I went downstairs. But, really, doctor, that surprises me. I expected to find him bright as a button."

"The death of an old person is often deceiving," remarked the doctor, who, lacking a towel, shook his hands above his head to dry them. "Generally speaking, children die better, Madame Marchal. Oh, I say there, young man, there's no use feeling for his heart, and in any case you're looking far too far to the left. On that question, as on so many others, physiology doesn't agree with literature."

"I swear to you, Doctor, that at the very minute you opened the door he and I were still chatting."

"That reminds me of the title of a novel I read a long time ago called *The Talking Dead* or something close to that. And as far as you're concerned, young man, I tend to believe that the explanation of the enigma is to be found at the bottom of that bottle of port."

"Come on! Come on! If you stay there glued to the bed I'll never be able to pull the sheet up," Madame Marchal grumbled furiously. "I'm not saying that this is any place for a boy like you, but since you were here, couldn't you really have found something more useful to do than drink port? At my age a woman has the right to say what she thinks."

It was a marvel watching her carry out her task of shrouding the dead man, passing again and again between him and the light of the lamp placed on the floor; she seemed almost sprightly under the expanse of her woolen skirts. One would have said she was measuring the weight of her burden as might a great, patient insect; then she suddenly extended her short arms with an infallible precision, and the docile cadaver rolled from one edge to the other, like a canoe rocked by the current. In a second and before Steeny's astonished eyes Monsieur Ouine was stripped of his familiar coverings and, as it were, slipped himself into an old-fashioned, long nightshirt embroidered with little red flowers on the collar. Then Madame Marchal folded back the sheet, exactly as one might seal an envelope, and the face of the professor of languages seemed gently, ever so gently, to sink not so much into the hollow of the pillow as into an invisible matter where, like a seal in hot wax, its shape was suddenly caught and hardened, resembling miraculously its old image without missing a single wrinkle or the tiniest mole, with its exact number of hairs, yet totally different from the old face—the face that spoke and laughed and trembled even in dreams with the movement of thought, which never stops, day or night—yes, trembling with thought, the way the leaves of silver birches shimmer in the breeze. Little by little that mass took on the color of clay and appeared to harden in the air, to the extent that the lamplight refused to be joined to its contours. Only the nose remained alive, appearing disproportionately lengthened by the collapse of the facial muscles around the two eye sockets, like some vicious little creature endowed with a life having henceforth neither cause nor purpose.

CPSIA information can be obtained at www.ICGtesting.com
Printed in the USA
LVOW071247070412

276421LV00017B/3/A